"SAY IT, ABBY. TELL ME YOU WANT ME."

His voice carried the urgency she felt, but the words jumbled and knotted inside her. Only her hands seemed to work properly. She laced them around Cam's neck and pulled him to her. His kisses trailed down her neck and met his fingers at her breasts. Fire raced to a secret spot deep in her belly and exploded into a blazing furnace, and she fought to keep from melting to the floor.

"Tell me you want me, Abby," he urged again. . . .

DIAMOND WILDFLOWER ROMANCE

A breathtaking line of searing romance novels . . . where destiny meets desire in the untamed fury of the American West.

HOSTAGE HEART

LISA HENDRIX

DIAMOND BOOKS, NEW YORK

This book is a Diamond original edition,
and has never been previously published.

HOSTAGE HEART

A Diamond Book/published by arrangement with
the author

PRINTING HISTORY
Diamond edition/January 1994

For information address: The Berkley Publishing Group,
200 Madison Avenue, New York, NY 10016.

ISBN: 1–55773–972–2

Diamond Books are published by The Berkley Publishing Group,
200 Madison Avenue, New York, NY 10016.
DIAMOND and the "D" design
are trademarks belonging to Charter Communications, Inc.

PRINTED IN THE UNITED STATES OF AMERICA

10 9 8 7 6 5 4 3 2 1

To my husband and my son,
who made this easier
than I had any right to expect

HOSTAGE HEART

Chapter 1

Denver, July 1886

"Are you certain, dear?" Mrs. Goodman squinted through the dusk at the man and woman standing a few yards down the wooden platform. "They do not appear to be suitable escorts for a young lady of quality."

Abigail took another good look at the couple. The man, probably fifty years old or more, tugged at a celluloid collar that rubbed an angry red mark beneath his recently shaved jaw. His suit bagged both in the pants and across his chest. The woman looked much too young to be his wife. She wore a ruffled dress of blue gingham that appeared a bit tawdry combined with her vibrant red hair and rather abundant curves.

"You would think a merchant might have better clothes, but things are so different here in the West." Abigail pushed her doubts aside and touched Mrs. Goodman's arm to reassure her. "Franklin mentioned in his letter to Father that the Nagles would be our chaperons, and they do have his letter of introduction."

"You're positive the letter's from your fiancé, Miss Morgan?" Harold Goodman asked.

"Oh, yes, sir. I know his hand well enough. This is from Franklin." Abigail held out the letter, its upper corner carrying the insignia of the Fidelity Cattle Company. Mr. Goodman held the letter under the glow of a gaslight to peruse it.

"I can't imagine a man in Tanner's position sending someone untrustworthy, Portia, particularly not to escort his fiancée." Mr. Goodman pocketed his monocle and handed the letter back. "Then I suppose we take our leave here. Your train leaves within the hour, and I have a late appointment with the *News* editor in town. I must get Mrs. Goodman safely back to the Windsor before then."

Mrs. Goodman turned her critical eye toward Abigail. "I do wish you had chosen something more stylish, dear. All those lovely clothes, and you're not even wearing a bustle. It doesn't seem quite proper to let you go off dressed that way."

Heavens, Abigail wondered, what would Mrs. Goodman say if she knew about the shocking lack of a corset beneath her peacock blue traveling suit?

Whether it was excitement or simply the fact of being a mile high, Abigail had found herself short of breath all day. She'd never been one to wear a corset when she didn't have to, and fighting a pound of whalebone for every breath just didn't make any sense. Best to keep her mouth shut and pray Mrs. Goodman didn't notice.

"You know how uncomfortable bustles are when traveling, Mrs. Goodman."

"But first impressions are so important, dear, and you *will* be a community leader."

"My wedding gown has a bustle so large I won't be able to sit down at all. The people of Saguache will be thoroughly impressed."

"I do hope so." Abigail suddenly found herself trapped against Mrs. Goodman's ample bosom and smothered with teary kisses. "Oh, my dear, do be careful. I have come to think of you as my own daughter. I could not bear it if those people should let anything happen to you."

"I'll be fine. This is such a short trip, compared to how far I've come already. We'll arrive in Henry in the morning and be in Saguache well before evening tomorrow." Abigail extracted herself carefully from the embrace and took the older woman's puffy hands in hers. "Franklin will meet me there, and he's made arrangements for me to stay with the schoolmistress until the wedding. You've both been so wonderful. Father felt much better about letting me travel when he learned you were coming. Thank you so much."

It took another five minutes to get the Goodmans on their way. When they finally stepped into the hired carriage, Abigail sighed with relief. Lifting a hand to tuck in a stray brown lock of hair, she already regretted the ornate arrangement of curls she'd let Mrs. Goodman talk her into.

Eighteen hundred miles of cinders, smoke, and clattering wheels would have been trying enough without Portia Goodman flapping her hankie and reading the most gruesome and outlandish passages from her collection of dime novels. By St. Louis, Abigail had been ready to jump ship—or train, that is—and find another way to Colorado. The only thing that stopped her was the promise her father had extracted from her in New York. She was to stay right by Mrs. Goodman's side all the way to Denver. Annoying as it was, she'd kept her word.

Mrs. Goodman turned one last time to wave, her lace hankie fluttering. Abigail forced a smile and waved back.

"Fussy old biddy," she murmured under her breath.

"Ain't she at that." The man had ventured up behind her, wife in tow. "I'll see to your trunk, miss."

"Thank you, Mr. . . ." Abigail glanced down at the letter, searching for the name again.

"Nagle. Orris Nagle. This is my wife, Ellie." He flicked a hand in the right direction and then motioned a pair of brawny porters over to load her baggage onto the train.

Ellie Nagle stepped forward and bobbed her head politely. Abigail acknowledged the pretty redhead with a distracted smile as the men lifted her beloved cherry-wood chest and struggled toward the baggage car. The heavy quilting strapped around the chest would do little good if they dropped it.

"Don't worry none, honey, those boys look strong as bulls."

Abigail glanced back at Ellie, frowning; the overfamiliar "honey" reminded her of Mrs. Goodman's cloying manner. "I'm sure they are."

If Ellie noticed the frown, she ignored it. "Got us a big basket of eats—sausages, bread, beer, apple pie. Shouldn't be hungry on the way."

"Thank you, but I'm afraid I don't drink beer, Mrs. Nagle."

"Just Ellie. You one of those Temperance ladies? We're getting a passel of them these days, with that school full of Presbyterians in Del Norte."

"No. I just never developed a taste for beer."

"You will when you get thirsty enough, honey."

"Mrs. Nagle, I'm certainly grateful to you and your husband for coming all this way to meet me, but please do not call me honey. I have been 'honeyed' and 'deared' half to death since New York. If I hear it one more time, I cannot be responsible for my actions." Abigail smiled to ease her words a bit.

Still the words came out harsher than intended. Ellie looked as though she'd been slapped. "Now, listen here, you . . ."

"Ellie calls everyone honey, that's just her way." Orris stepped up quickly to take Ellie's arm, pointedly staring his wife down.

"That may be, but I would prefer not to be called that. Now, Mr. Nagle, where might I purchase some cider before we board?"

* * *

Despite the rough start, the Nagles turned out to be satisfactory traveling companions. Neither was especially talkative, and they left Abigail to her own devices for much of the overnight trip, which was what she wanted most after the company of Mrs. Goodman.

The rocking Pullman, as usual, put her right to sleep. She barely noticed the midnight stop in Pueblo, when the Durango-bound coaches were split off the main Leadville Express to continue southward. After the transfer in Alamosa, Abigail spent most of the short ride to Henry on the rear platform with the conductor as the Nagles enjoyed their sausages inside the car.

After they'd left the town of Henry, however, Abigail began to wish she'd established better rapport with her escorts. Sitting wedged between the stolid Nagles for miles on a buckboard tried her as none of the rest of the trip had.

Not that she wasn't grateful. She was certain she'd have landed in the dust a dozen times if Orris hadn't seated her in the middle. The man drove as if they were racing to a fire. Every bump and ditch in the road tossed her against his bony hips and shoulders and threatened the straw shade hat perched on her rapidly disintegrating curls. She should have taken Ellie's lead and twisted her hair into a bun and hid it under a serviceable sunbonnet, away from the dust.

With little hope for conversation, Abigail spent her time staring out at the land. At first the rolling hills seemed desolate in their gray-green sameness, but as her eyes adjusted to the strange landscape, she began to notice a certain vibrancy to her surroundings. Along the occasional streams, cottonwoods and willow trees sheltered black and white magpies that chattered enthusiastically at the crossing wagon. She caught the flash of a jackrabbit bounding into the brush as a hawk swooped from the clouds. There were flowers among the bitterbrush and chico. One was especially brilliant, a red flower that Mr. Nagle told her was called Indian paintbrush.

All around them towered mountains, nearly encircling the broad, arid valley with white-glazed peaks. The sight of them alone could make it worthwhile to live in this place, Abigail decided.

The wagon took a rut particularly badly, and Abigail grabbed for a handhold.

"Not much farther, miss," Orris said.

Ellie straightened on the other side to peer ahead, anticipation lighting her eyes. "Not far at all."

Abigail stared down the road but could see nothing worthy of Ellie's excitement. There were certainly no signs of either a town or ranch nearby, only what looked like cattle moving amid the brush.

As the buckboard rolled along, she saw that there were not only cattle in the distance, but also a handful of men on horseback.

Mrs. Goodman's outlaw tales rushed into Abigail's thoughts. "Is it an ambush?" she asked Orris, her heart thumping. "Can we outrun them?"

"We don't need to outrun them." Orris waved his hat, and the men raced forward. "As to whether it's an ambush, now that depends on your point of view."

"Oh, of course, they must be Fidelity men."

Ellie snorted back a laugh, but Abigail ignored her, intent on searching for Franklin. The men were close enough now that she could make out their faces. "Franklin doesn't seem to be among them. How disappointing. But we must be fairly close to town if his men are meeting us."

"These ain't Tanner's hands." Orris slowed the buckboard to a stop as the first of the men pulled up. "Hey, fellas. This is the lady that's come to marry Franklin Tanner. All the way from New York City." He reached for a proffered canteen and took a healthy swig. Abigail wrinkled her nose at the smell of whiskey. "Where's the boss?"

"That livestock we rounded up was givin' us some trouble, so he's got 'em snubbed up to a bush over yonder." The rider gestured with his thumb to an area beyond his shoulder. Ellie giggled again and tucked a strand of red hair back underneath her bonnet.

"Then I guess we ought to join him." Orris snapped the reins and the wagon jolted forward. "Got some folks you'll be wanting to meet, miss. Just take a few minutes."

He turned the buckboard off of what had been passing for a road onto a barely discernible track through the brush and high grass. She grabbed at the seat for balance as the left rear wheel bounced over a rock.

"Where are we going Mr. Nagle? Franklin will be waiting for us in Saguache."

"He'll wait."

Beside Abigail, Ellie could barely contain herself. The wagon followed the track down into a ravine, and Abigail suddenly understood why Ellie laughed.

There by a muddy trickle of water, trussed up like a piglet at market, lay a portly man of some fifty years or more. Beside him sat his long-faced wife, bound more genteelly but no less securely. When they saw the buckboard, they both began squawking against their gags with some urgency. Abigail knew these were the "livestock" mentioned earlier.

She also had a sick feeling she knew their names.

"Perhaps I should make some introductions." The low, polished voice came from a man standing off to the side of the group. Abigail peered down at him, trying to make out his features hidden in the shadow of the wide-brimmed plainsman hat he wore. Without looking up, he gestured toward his captives. "Miss Abigail Morgan, I'd like to present . . ."

"The real Orris Nagle?" Abigail guessed, struggling to remain calm.

"And his charming wife, Eleanor. I'm afraid they had to postpone their trip to Denver by a few days. At my request."

The woman posing as Ellie hooted in laughter, and jabbed a finger into Abigail's side. "Didn't suspect a thing, did you?

I swear, I could get me a job on the stage. If there's one thing I've learned since I came out West, it's how to *act*."

"Better not tell your regulars," said one of the riders.

At this, several of the men broke down in laughter, whooping along with the woman.

The man in the plainsman hat lifted his hand, and the laughter stopped. "Miss Morgan cannot appreciate the joke." He addressed an explanation to Abigail. "Our friend here is a member of the *demi-monde*. A very popular one."

Abigail still didn't understand completely. "I'm glad you all find this so funny," she snapped. "Now, set these poor people loose and take us into Saguache immediately, Mr. . . ." She groped for a name to call the grizzled man on the buckboard beside her, now that the old name belonged elsewhere.

"Not me, miss." The former Orris jumped down and started peeling away the ill-fitting suit, beneath which he seemed to have a full set of clothes of even more dubious quality.

Approaching the wagon, the lanky man tilted his hat back slightly and said, "I'm sorry, introductions of my companions will have to wait." For the first time Abigail got a fair look at his face. Not that it did much good: a thick, untrimmed beard obscured most of it. Then Abigail noticed the rich brown of his eyes, surrounded by a fringe of lashes so thick as to be almost feminine. They made a dark contrast to the sun-bleached blond of his untrimmed hair and beard. She nearly missed his next words. "As for myself, Cameron Garrett, at your service."

"The Garrett who stole Franklin's payroll last spring?"

"You've heard of me. Glad Tanner thinks enough of me to bring me up in conversation." He walked to the side of the wagon, drew a long knife from a sheath on his gunbelt, and slit the straps on the chest. The padding fell away, and he tried the lid. "The key, please."

"I'll thank you to keep your thieving hands out of my things."

"Okay, but a bullet may muss your dresses." Garrett shrugged and pulled out a revolver, taking precise aim at the lock.

"Don't! There are nearly a thousand dollars' worth of clothes in there." Abigail scrambled frantically for her handbag. "Besides, it was my mother's. Here's the key."

"Very wise." Garrett holstered his gun and accepted the thin brass skeleton key that Abigail produced. "If it's any consolation, we're not after your frillies, or even your jewelry. I happen to know that Tanner's attorney visited you at the Windsor yesterday morning. I assume the packets he had with him are now in your trunk?"

Abigail nodded, watching helplessly as Garrett leapt onto the bed of the wagon and began rifling through her carefully packed trousseau. She could see dust drifting off his clothes onto the tissue paper wrapping her best velvet gown. She could only imagine what his grimy hands might be doing to the Brussels lace of her wedding dress as he groped around.

He found one packet quickly. A check of the contents seemed to satisfy him, and he tossed it aside. "Legal papers," he explained to his men as he reached back into the chest.

Abigail fidgeted as Garrett dived back into her things. It wasn't long before he came up with the other envelope the banker had left. A smile spread across his face as he flipped through the bills inside. "About five thousand dollars. Looks like we're collecting the reward on my head."

He tossed that envelope aside with the first, then lifted the top gowns out of the chest and set them on the open lid.

"Now, that's enough Mr. Garrett. You have all of Franklin's property."

"Not quite." Looking perplexed, Garrett lifted out a few more items, then beckoned to the redhead. "Get back here and bundle up a couple of changes of clothes. Something to ride in and whatever goes under it all, plus a warm coat. See if there are some decent boots in there, too."

The woman happily scrambled over the seat to take Garrett's place, after he'd picked up the envelopes and leapt to the ground. A tall bay gelding tied by the stream nickered when Garrett approached and untied the flap on a saddlebag.

The redhead rooted through Abigail's belongings even more thoroughly than Garrett had. "You still buying me those silk drawers you promised?"

"You know it," he answered.

"I want real pretty ones with lots of lace. Like these." She held up a pair of Abigail's drawers for inspection.

One of the riders guffawed, and Abigail felt color rise to her cheeks.

"Lace it is." Garrett patted his horse on the rump, then spoke over his shoulder to Abigail. "Time for you to get down, Miss Morgan."

"I will do no such thing. I insist you take me to Saguache right now."

"Orris, does Tanner realize what a stubborn creature he's marrying? Frankly, it surprises me. He's always gone for the defenseless kind." Grimly Garrett took a folded piece of paper out of his shirt pocket, then leaned over the hapless Orris Nagle to tuck it in his jacket. "The next time you see that mongrel, you give him my regards and that note."

Mrs. Nagle grunted once again against the kerchief between her teeth, the intent behind her words clear as could be.

"Don't fret, madam. I promised you'd both be returned unharmed, and so you shall be. Just do as you're told."

"Got everything, Cam." The redhead plopped a neat stack of Abigail's new clothes on the seat and started repacking the chest.

"I thought you weren't after my things, Mr. Garrett," Abigail said. "Now you're letting this . . . female steal my clothes."

"Since she's accusing me anyway, can I pick some pretties for myself?"

"Absolutely not. Those clothes are for you, Miss Morgan. You said I had all of Tanner's property. Well, I intend to, at least for a time. You'll be coming with us."

"I am no man's property, Mr. Garrett." Abigail gripped the seat beneath her until fine splinters pierced her lace gloves, but she met his gaze evenly. "I'll see you horsewhipped if you so much as touch me."

"I've gone to great trouble to arrange your stay with us so that you were not put in danger by a train robbery or a shoot-out with Tanner's thugs." Cam Garrett's voice remained calm, but it carried a strand of steel Abigail hadn't heard before. "I would hate to have to risk all that now just because you're reluctant to join us. However, if you do not obey me instantly and in every particular, I cannot continue to guarantee your safety."

"You wouldn't dare hurt me."

"Try me. Now get down."

Abigail reached for his helping hand as though she might cooperate. As he leaned forward, she planted her foot square against his chest and pushed hard. "Go to Hades, Mr. Garrett."

He staggered backward a few inches with the shove but recovered quickly. "That's it."

To the laughter of his men, Cam Garrett's hand shot out, and he grabbed Abigail's wrist. Before she could so much as blink, he yanked her off the wagon. Air whooshed from her lungs as she landed awkwardly across his rocklike shoulder. She hung there like an empty flour sack, sucking at the thin, dry air, looking at the shiny seat of his blue denim pants.

"Bundle up her things and let's get going." Garrett walked over to his horse, bouncing altogether too much for Abigail's stomach.

"Let me go this instant, you heathen!" She cracked him across the back with her handbag. "I'll pickle your miserable heart and feed it to swine, if they'll have it."

For all her noise, Garrett totally ignored her. "See that the Nagles can get free in a reasonable time, and make sure they know which way's home."

"I will unhitch the horses to slow them down a little," said an accented voice.

"Fine. Have we come to an understanding, Miss Morgan?" Garrett let Abigail's head slide precipitously groundward. She grabbed for his shirt.

"I'm to do what I'm told," Abigail answered quickly. "Set me down."

He did so without further comment. Abigail rubbed at what must be a bruised spot, where her ribs had met his square shoulder, and watched him prepare to mount up.

Reins firmly in hand, Garrett bent and locked his fingers together and offered her a leg up. "You'll be riding with me, for now."

"I'm not dressed to ride astride."

"Make do. There's way too much traffic on the Saguache road for my taste. I'll give you a chance to change into your riding gear when we've put a few miles between us and Tanner."

"This is unconscionable," Abigail protested, but she swung astride the saddle and poked at her skirts and petticoats to arrange them in some semblance of modesty and comfort. She glared at the redhead. "I don't even know if she chose the proper riding clothes."

"That funny prune-colored rig?" the woman asked.

Abigail nodded.

"Then I got it. Too bad you're not outfitted like me." The redhead was up on a horse of her own, also riding astride but with her skirts spread haphazardly over the saddle and the horse's rump. She grinned a bit wickedly and hoisted her skirt to her knees. Men's heavy canvas britches showed beneath her petticoat. "'Course, I couldn't hardly tell you how to dress, considering. Sure am comfortable, though. A few miles with your skirts bunched up like that, and I bet you're one sore gal."

As Garrett swung up behind her, Abigail squirmed forward in the saddle, trying to avoid too intimate contact, but he wrapped one arm around her waist and firmly pulled her to him. She began to regret her decision not to wear a corset; every muscle in Garrett's lean chest and stomach seemed to ripple directly against her skin.

"Relax," he suggested as her heart thumped wildly.

"I'm being kidnapped, Mr. Garrett. Just how am I supposed to relax?"

"Your choice."

"Yep, one sore gal," the redhead repeated as they headed out. "But I can't say as I'll feel too sorry for you, *honey*."

Abigail Morgan was just the kind of woman Cam Garrett figured Tanner would pick for a wife. Good, solid stock to give Tanner the air of legitimacy he always aspired to. Well turned out. Respectable. Young enough to bear a few children. And as mean as Tanner himself, if the way she used her tongue and that purse gave any clue.

Handsome, too, in a rather sharp way, with her chestnut hair and wide-set hazel eyes. A person might call her looks patrician; her carriage clearly was. Taller than most, and slender, but with womanly curves that filled his arms nicely, especially with no corset confining them. He'd had to distract himself from that fact more than once already to avoid a reaction that would have been much too obvious to the woman sharing his saddle. Good looks were something Cam had hoped for but hadn't counted on. It would make the next few weeks a lot more pleasant and might even make up for that tongue of hers.

"Surely we've come far enough." Abigail shifted gingerly in the saddle. "You promised we would stop so I can change clothes. I want to change right now."

"Hannah was right, was she?" He was of a mind to make her ride a little farther, but he just couldn't do it. Cam reined his mount to a stop near a stream. "I suppose those bushes will make you a fair dressing room."

With little of his help, Abigail swung off the saddle. Digger Dunleavy, the man who had played Orris, held Abigail's things out to her. She jerked the bundle away and wobbled off toward the nearest brush.

"Hold on just a minute," Cam said as he dismounted.

Abigail ignored him and charged on. Cam was reminded of a stubborn cow after water.

"I thought we had this clear." Cam caught up and clamped a hand on her shoulder. "You listen to me, and you stay out of trouble."

"You're my only trouble, Mr. Garrett." The tangle of branches gave only slightly as Abigail leaned into them.

"Excuse me. I thought you might like to have one of us check for rattlers in there. But you go right ahead."

Abigail started backward with a gasp and landed in his arms. She didn't seem to mind at all, for the moment, and Cam certainly didn't. Yes, she was definitely curvaceous.

"Rattlers? You mean snakes?"

"Very big, very nasty snakes. The San Luis Valley is full of them. Most of the ranches hold snake hunts every year to get rid of some of them. Now, would you like me to find you a safe spot?"

"Is there such a thing with *you* in the vicinity?"

"You'll have to trust me," he said, releasing her. "Hannah, you come on, too."

Cam led the women down along the creek bank to a suitable opening in the bushes, where he poked around the edges with a branch fished out of the creek. Then he stretched tall and looked back toward the others. "Good, the men can't see you over here. You can change now."

Abigail stood with her bundle of clothes, waiting stolidly. It was clear she thought his precautions mere show.

"Go on. We don't have time to waste."

"Then you'd better give me some privacy, Mr. Garrett." A brilliant blush rose clear to her ears, but she made her point. "I need to do more than change clothes."

"I understand that. I'll turn away, and Hannah's along to protect your virtue."

Abigail glared sourly at Cam and held her ground.

"Go on, honey. Even if he peeks, you ain't got nothing Cam ain't seen before." Hannah's nasty smile revealed her delight in Abigail's predicament.

"I'm quite sure you can testify to that yourself. However, in New York a young woman doesn't undress before a man unless she's a harlot. But then, you are, aren't you?"

Abigail's taunt had a dangerous effect. The smirk froze on Hannah's lips, and her emerald eyes narrowed to catlike slits. "Cam honey, I think I'll just let Miss New-York-high-and-mighty worry about her own virtue. There must be some nicer company around here." She sashayed off down the stream, her hips swaying audaciously under the cotton skirt.

"You're a real prize, Abigail Morgan." Cam angrily slapped his hat against his thigh, and a thin cloud of yellow dust billowed around his legs as he glared at her. "There was no call for that."

"I really don't care what any of you think of me. Especially not that hussy." She plopped her bundle on the ground and quickly found the items she wanted. "Turn around."

"Just do what you must, woman. I'm not going to molest you."

Still mistrustful, Abigail risked the snakes to push a little ways into the bushes to take care of her more personal needs. Cam focused on the stream, watching the water swirl away toward the flats, where it would disappear into the sandy soil. Out of the corner of his eye he could see Abigail moving about. Somehow she managed to change without revealing so much as a flash of petticoat.

The sound of stomping as she set her feet into her boots made him turn around. Cam frowned. "That skirt's no better than what you had on."

"It will suit just fine." Abigail tugged on the side seams and revealed that what looked like a skirt was actually constructed like a baggy pair of pants.

"I should have known you'd be a Bloomer girl."

"Amelia Bloomer's ideas have a great deal of merit," Abigail retorted. "However, these are a design my dressmaker and I worked out."

"Looks practical. I half expected a formal habit."

"That's arriving later, with the rest of my clothes."

"The rest? You already have more than any three women in this valley. Here, let me see those." Cam strode over and, without her leave, bent to examine her boots. Soft as kid gloves, they came nearly to her knee. He could feel the warmth of her skin through the leather as he ran his hand up and down checking the fit. The sturdy heel was high enough to hold her foot in the stirrup.

"They'll do," he said softly, letting his fingers linger a moment high on her calf before he stood up. The surge of desire he felt as he looked down into those insolent eyes caught him off guard. *Slow down*, Cam warned himself, *there's plenty of time for that.*

"Of course they'll do. My father paid nearly seventy dollars for these boots."

"Tell me, do you calculate prices on everything?" She was definitely Tanner's type, he thought. "Is that how you decide what you like or don't like?"

"If it were, Mr. Garrett, I would surely like you. There must be quite a price on your head." Abigail picked up her bundle of clothes and gave him a tart look. "Shall we go?"

Dust billowed across the veranda of the Fidelity Ranch, churned up by men and horses in the ranch yard preparing to ride Garrett and his gang down. Franklin Tanner had given the order as soon as he'd read Garrett's damnable ransom note. Now something Orris Nagle was saying penetrated the fog of Franklin's rage.

"You're telling me Garrett kidnapped my fiancée off my own land?" Franklin Turner glared down at the Nagles from the steps of his house.

"Yes, sir, Mr. Tanner." Orris stood beside the buckboard with his pasty, sweating face, his fingers twisting the bowler hat in his hands. He licked his lips. "I'm afraid they have a good start, too. I . . . it took me a while to get out of the ropes and get the wagon hitched to get here."

"Orris worked just as hard as he could," Eleanor said on her husband's behalf. "His wrists are all shredded from the rope and—"

Franklin blocked out the drone of Eleanor's voice and turned to watch a man throw a saddle over a lanky buckskin. Franklin's foreman shouted orders for supplies and gear.

On my own land. The bastard.

Now he understood why last week's raid had been so brazen—it had been designed to keep him and his men here at the ranch, forcing him to send the Nagles on by themselves. Once again, Garrett seemed to know his plans in detail. His fingers tightened around the crumpled ransom note. Somebody had talked. He'd find out who and decide on an appropriate penance later, after he had Abigail safely in hand.

Franklin raked thick fingers through the shock of steel gray hair at his temple. He turned back to the Nagles, his expression a blank mask that hid his fury. His quiet stare brought Eleanor's chatter to a halt.

"Wait here a minute," Franklin said, striding past the couple. He motioned for his foreman and another man to join him at the side of the house. "How long will it be before you're ready to go?"

"About five more minutes, Mr. Tanner," the foreman answered. "Cookie's getting the grub together. I told him to make sure everyone had enough for three or four days."

Franklin nodded, then turned to the other man, his coyote-lean hired gun. "I have a special little chore for you, Stanton. You let the men know that you'll slit the tongue of anyone who mentions this matter to an outsider. I won't be the laughingstock of the whole valley."

"That's going to be a hard one, with that schoolteacher expecting Miss Morgan tonight," Stanton said. "Plus you got a bunch of folks coming for a wedding."

"I'll inform everyone that Abigail got a case of the bridal jitters and stayed in Denver for a few days. The Nagles remained with her to soothe her nerves and will bring her down later. That will explain everything for the time being."

"Yessir, Mr. T." Stanton spat, then scuffed a little dust over the damp spot with the toe of his boot. "We're gonna get that boy this time."

Franklin dismissed the two with a nod and headed back to the Nagles.

Orris cleared his throat. "I guess you don't need us any longer. Mrs. Nagle's had quite a rough time of it. I really need to get her home to her own bed."

"I have plenty of beds and a full staff to care for her. I'd be remiss if I let you take her another step." And besides, Franklin thought, if she goes to town, word of this fiasco will be in Denver by morning. "Meanwhile, you can show us precisely where Garrett kidnapped Miss Morgan and which direction they went. I'm sure you'd like to help us capture him, after what he did to the two of you."

"Well, of course, but I, uh, I don't really ride too well. I'm afraid I'll slow down you and your men." Orris spun his hat another time, clearly hoping to be let off the hook.

The man was a total idiot, Franklin thought. He'd have to take another look at Nagle's loan. Meantime, he'd give Orris a real reason to sweat. He met the man's frightened eyes and smiled. "Nonsense. You won't slow us down at all."

About the time the scrub piñon of the western foothills gave way to bull pine and blue spruce, Abigail succumbed to the crushing exhaustion of emotional letdown. Fighting it all the way, she finally sagged backward against Cam. His arms tightened gently, just enough to support her weight. Under other circumstances, she thought as her mind wandered, she might find his touch pleasant, even stimulating.

Abigail gasped as the bay stumbled. She must have dozed off. Strong arms caught her and steadied the horse.

"It's getting too dark to keep traveling." Cam's voice rumbled close to her ear. "There's a good campsite just ahead. We'll stop there for the night."

The site was level and just uphill from a noisy stream. Abigail peered around, trying to make out landmarks in the gathering dusk as the men picked out sleeping spots and tossed their bedrolls down.

"Want some beans, miss?" Digger held out an open can and a spoon.

"No, thank you. I'll wait for supper."

"This is supper, honey." Hannah strolled up and took the beans. "Think we're going to lay out silver and fancy white tablecloths for you?"

"Won't there be a fire and something warm to eat?"

"Wouldn't Tanner like that! Her Highness wants a fire, Cam honey. Wants us to cook for her, too."

"A fire could be seen for miles on a night like this, clear out into the valley." Cam took the spoon Hannah held out. "But you won't starve. There are beans, some sardines, and plenty of hardtack and beef jerky. Try some."

He held out something dark and stringy-looking. Abigail looked at it dubiously but accepted the leathery stick and gnawed off a bit. The greasy, peppery flavor mellowed as she chewed. She tore off another bite. "It's good."

"Don't sound so surprised. There's plenty more, so eat hearty. It will keep you warmer and make tomorrow's ride go a little easier."

Abigail ate standing up, the hard rocks offering no appeal after the long ride. Her appetite for the unfamiliar food astounded her. By the time she felt sated, most of the men were already asleep. She looked to Cam for direction.

"That one," he said, pointing to a bedroll laid off to one side. "You and Hannah are going to have to share."

"Now don't you wish you'd been nicer to me, honey?" Hannah purred.

"Be nice, Hannah." Cam looked at Abigail and shrugged. "At the time I thought you'd appreciate the warmth and the female company. You could share with me, I guess."

"I'd rather freeze to death," Abigail said.

"I wouldn't let that happen." Cam flashed a smile that made him look like a mischievous kid. "Just as a warning, we all sleep pretty lightly and have a tendency to shoot at things bumping around in the night."

"Shooting me would pretty much ruin your chance at a ransom," she said dryly.

"What makes you think I asked for a ransom? I'd stay in bed if I were you."

To Abigail's surprise, Hannah parceled out the blankets evenly. When Abigail mumbled a stiff thank you, Hannah just rolled over. She started snoring within seconds.

Abigail lay awake until the moon lit the peaks enough to recognize one she'd been using as a landmark. Even with all the circling and backtracking they'd done, they must have come a good twelve to fifteen miles due west. Along the way, riders had doubled up on horses, dropped away, and brushed tracks to further confuse the trail.

Franklin would have no idea where to start searching for her. The thought stopped her heart for a moment.

Abigail tugged the blanket up around her ears and ruthlessly pushed down the panic that threatened to overwhelm her. There was a solution to this predicament. Her father had seen to it she'd gotten the finest education available. She'd be damned if a common outlaw would get the best of Abigail Macaulay Morgan.

Chapter 2

She was still awake.

He could see the glittering white of her eyes in the moonlight, though nearly an hour had passed since she'd bedded down.

Cam Garrett leaned on his elbow, watching the dark mound made by the two women in his party. Hannah's determined snore kept rhythm with more raucous noises from Digger and Jesús. There wasn't a coyote worth the name that would come within a mile of that racket. If he hadn't experienced Hannah's nighttime chorale before, he'd swear she was doing it just to keep Abigail from getting a decent night's rest.

He'd have to see what he could do to get the two of them to make a truce—not that Abigail Morgan didn't deserve what she got, and in spades.

Despite her apparent mean streak, Cam had to admire any woman who could handle a kidnapping and most of a long day in the saddle and still be ready to scrap. City-bred or not, she was as tough as her words and certainly not the teary kind.

He flopped onto his back to find his special star, the one his father had given him for his tenth birthday. The steady twinkle reminded him of his mother's eyes—before Franklin Tanner had driven all the life out of her. The slow fire of hatred that smoldered within Cam flared briefly before he could bank it down. He reviewed his plan to get Tanner, step by careful step, until he dozed off.

The noise of someone moving around jerked Cam awake, and the brightening sky caught him off guard. He quickly sat up to check Abigail, chagrined at having slept so easily, and so soundly, after having bragged about how lightly he slept.

Hannah must have thought to include a hairbrush in the gear she'd picked out. Abigail stood by her bedroll, brushing her hair with long, smooth strokes that put a sheen like polished bronze on her chestnut locks. She'd taken down the intricate tangle of curls and braids she'd worn yesterday, and the loose hair spilled nearly to her hips. Cam suddenly ached to bury his face in the silky cascade.

She stopped in midstroke, wide hazel eyes meeting his with a challenge. "Am I to be shot for brushing my hair?"

"Not if I have a choice."

"Go ahead and do it for me. She let the cold in." Hannah flipped the blankets back with a flourish and stood up. Muttered complaints trailed her downhill as she walked toward the stream.

Abigail continued her brushing, drawing the thick hank of hair together on the nape of her neck. Cam lay back to watch her for a few more minutes, admiring the easy way she split the mass into three equal portions, then wove them into a neat braid as fat as her own wrist. She yanked a ribbon from her hat and finished off the end. Minus the fussy curls, she looked more at home in her riding gear. Prettier, too. Cam kept his opinion to himself.

He grew aware of other eyes watching Abigail with the same degree of interest and approval as she traded her blue jacket for one that matched her funny riding skirt.

Yearning for a fire and the smell of Digger's coffee, Cam tossed his blankets aside and stood up. "Gentlemen, get yourselves and your mounts ready to go." He turned to Abigail. "We'll be riding out within the half hour. Don't go far."

"You mean I'm allowed more than a yard away from you?"

"You couldn't get far up here now that daylight's come."

Nonetheless, he kept a close eye on her, even when Hannah reappeared somehow magically transformed. Cam wasn't sure what she'd done to the neckline of that dress, but the full glory of her curves now lay exposed to view, and her unbound hair ran riot. If Eleanor Nagle knew what could be done with cotton gingham and a little henna, Orris might be a happier man.

"Hannah, you're lookin' fine this mornin'," observed Digger.

"Surely are," agreed Lew. "We had a little more time, I might arrange some business with you."

Abigail's cheeks flamed, and her lips set into a line so thin and hard Cam thought it could cut Hannah's pretty white throat.

"You want to do business, you come on into town and talk to one of the other girls, honey. You know the rules." Hannah lifted her voice a little and directed it Abigail's way. "Cam doesn't want you fellas mixing business with his pleasure."

Abigail stomped off.

Hannah watched her go, then looked to Cam. "Nasty, self-righteous thing."

"You encourage her."

"The way she looks at me. She thinks she's better than me, just because she's supposed to marry that snake Tanner. She thinks rich makes nice."

"She'll know better soon enough."

Hannah sobered quickly. "She sure will. I'm worried about you, Cam honey. Taking a man's money is one thing, stealing his woman is another. You push Tanner too far and you'll get caught."

"I'll worry about how far to push Tanner. You just don't mess with Abigail Morgan. I'm the one who has to deal with her until Tanner comes up with the money."

"Oh, all right. I don't much like her, though."

Cam waited a decent interval to give Abigail enough time to get cleaned up, then rounded up a spoon and some food and hunted down his charge.

"Cold beans again, Abby," he announced as she eyed the can with dismay. "And to get the rest of the bad news over all at once, we'll be riding pretty much all day."

Abigail frowned, but she took the can. "The name is Abigail. Miss Morgan, to you."

"Does Tanner call you Abigail?"

"Yes, but he is my fiancé."

"Good. I'd hate to use the same name he does. Abby it is."

"You are altogether too forward, Mr. Garrett, especially for a common criminal and outlaw."

"Call me Cam. Outlaws tend to be a forward lot—it's hard to rob a stage if you're timid."

"I find it disgusting."

She apparently found beans for breakfast disgusting, too, the way she shuddered over each bite. Cam grinned. "It'll get better. The food I mean. Once we get where we're going."

"And where is that?" Abigail studied the beans with undue interest, arranging them neatly in the can with the spoon.

"You'd do better if you didn't talk with your mouth full," he advised with a grin. "It makes you seem too anxious."

"I usually have a decent poker face." Abigail scooped out more beans, then passed the tin back to Cam. "Why are you looking at me like that?"

"I was trying to picture you at a poker table."

"My father taught me poker. Plenty of women play cards."

"Bridge or whist, not poker. It's a man's game."

"There *are* women gamblers," Abigail insisted.

"They're a rough lot. Besides, most of them go in for faro or dice, not poker."

"I read about a woman named Poker Alice, who is reported to be very much a gentlewoman."

An image of the woman under discussion ran through Cam's mind, and he shook his head.

"Do the women in your social circle smoke cigars and pack a pistol. Alice Ivers proves the rule. Every woman I've met who plays poker worth a damn is mannish and argumentative."

"Really." The look she gave him could have scalded a cat. "Well, here's a picture that will be easier on your imagination: me in the witness stand when you're on trial for kidnapping." She turned away, dismissal as clear as if she'd been a French countess and he the lowest peasant.

Cam suddenly realized he'd trodden on a touchy area. Evidently Abby took pride in her poker playing—or someone had called her mannish and argumentative. Probably both, he suspected.

Mountain shadows dark as molasses still filled the bottom of the valley when they mounted and headed out. Abby felt so stiff and cold, Cam could have sworn he had a corpse riding in front of him. He waited until they'd ridden high enough to catch the sun before he ventured a few words, hoping the warmth would thaw her out, but only stony silence answered his efforts.

It was during lunch that Jesús motioned Cam over to where he and the other men squatted beneath a tree. "I . . ." Jesús glanced at Abby, pacing up and down the clearing a short distance away, and switched to Spanish. "I thought you should see what I found back at Mann Creek when I cleaned up camp this morning."

Cam flipped back the corners of the sweat-stained, blue kerchief that covered the object Jesús tossed in his direction. An appreciative smile touched the corner of his lips and eyes as he picked out the tortoiseshell comb, a scrolled AMM etched in gold on its back. "The little witch."

"Maybe she just forgot it, Cameron."

"Mighty convenient forgetting." Cam wondered if she'd left any clues behind when he had let her change clothes yesterday.

There was a lot more to this Abigail Morgan than he'd expected. Cam glanced over his shoulder. She was still mad, by god, and carrying herself like she'd trained at West Point.

"Good job, Jesús. I'll take care of this."

Cam tucked the comb deep into his saddlebags. She'd get the benefit of the doubt for now. Meantime, though, he'd keep a sharp eye out—and try to find a way to melt that ramrod straight spine.

"We can't go there." Abigail paled at the sight of the trail ahead, a narrow route clinging halfway up the side of a cliff.

"You *can* still speak. I was beginning to wonder." Cam offered the canteen to Abigail before he took a swig. "It's not often two people spend an entire day together on the same horse and one of them never says a word to the other."

"It's not often *one of them* is being kidnapped."

"True," he granted. "Actually the silence was a pleasant change from yesterday's diatribe. We ride this trail all the time. You have nothing to worry about."

"I know that," Abigail said, though she didn't remember anything like what met her eyes now. "Can't I walk?"

"If you're afraid of heights, you're safer mounted."

"I'm not afraid of heights." Abigail looked at the trail again, and sweat beaded across her upper lip. "I used to climb trees with my brother at my grandfather's house."

"Sure," Cam said, expressing doubt with that single word.

Abigail opened her mouth to argue, but he nudged the horse out onto the trail, and her insides pitched too wildly for her to worry about anything other than keeping her seat. She squeezed her eyes shut, but in her imagination the trail crumbled just ahead of them. *Just like the balcony had crumbled.* She jerked forward, one hand reaching out . . .

"Sit still." Cam knotted his arm around her waist and dragged her back against him. "If you want to kill yourself, fine, but don't take Billy and me with you."

"Damn you and Billy." Her flash of anger pushed the awful picture back, as anger always did. Abigail closed her outstretched hand around the saddle horn and searched for something else to think about, something else to drive off the horrible memories. She finally focused on the steady, firm pressure of Cam's arm around her. She felt the movement of his chest against her shoulders and tried to match her breathing to his, to draw on his calm confidence. She stared at the gloved hand with which he held the reins. It was a strong hand, one that could keep her safe. She let that strength surround her and seep into her being, and she pretended, just for the moment, that the arms belonged to someone who loved and cared for her.

"Don't be frightened, Abby, I have you. I won't let anything happen," Cam murmured, his warm breath gently stirring the fine hairs along the nape of her neck. A shiver traveled up her spine, one born not of fear but of some other emotion she couldn't quite put a name to. He continued talking, soft and comforting. "Now, we're going to make this little turn ahead. It might look a little scary, but the trail is wide enough. You'll be safe."

"I'm not frightened." She laid her arm over his and twined her fingers with those that curved around her waist, grateful when he snugged her a little closer.

The jutting wall forced the bay out toward the edge, until it seemed his broad hooves touched only air. Abigail pressed backward against Cam with all her might, willing herself not to scream.

"You're doing fine, Abby, just fine. We're almost there."

A twisted pine, clinging tenaciously to the outer edge of the slender trail, painted their legs with resin and a pungent scent. The bay stepped past it and off the cliff trail. Abigail gasped as the view opened up onto the long barrel of a rifle centered on her forehead from less than twenty feet.

"Be it ever so humble," Cam said. "It's only us, Charlie. You can stop scaring the lady."

"Just following your orders, boss." The youthful face behind the sights of the rifle lit up in a grin. The boy lowered his weapon. " 'The first thing anyone should see coming around that pine is the barrel of a gun between his eyes, I don't care who it is. You can ask questions later.' " The boy chuckled at his imitation of Cam. "Looks like hunting was good."

The words jolted Abigail into remembering her captivity, sending her as far away from Cam as the saddle would allow. The man behind her sighed.

After a quick exchange of news, Cam guided his mount down the slope into a narrow green valley that hugged the stream they'd been following. A handful of sturdy lean-tos were set up among the trees; the sparse gear inside spoke of human occupants rather than animal. What appeared to be a man-made shaft framed in heavy timber punched into the nearly vertical walls of the valley.

"Is that a gold mine?" Abby asked.

"Only in someone's dreams," Cam said. "Some prospectors a few years back got stuck here over the winter and drove a little shaft to occupy their time. Makes a good place to store things out of the weather."

Like a wagon. *Those poles angling down in the gloom could be wagon shafts*, Abigail realized with excitement. That could mean another route into this valley, one wide enough to bring in a wagon, with a road beyond leading toward a town. Probably wherever Hannah did . . . business, but a town where there might be help.

Not far beyond the mine stood a good-size cabin, its back nearly butting up against the steep mountainside. Open shutters beckoned in invitation. Cam pulled up in front of the cabin then helped Abigail down as the others dismounted nearby.

"Those prospectors built this, too," he said, pushing open the door with one booted toe. "It's not much, but it's snug enough."

Abigail stuck her head in just far enough to look around. A half dozen rickety chairs crowded around a table in one end of the dirt-floored room, and four army-style folding beds filled the other. A tiny cast-iron stove hogged the center of the room, its flat top holding a battered kettle. Useful items of all sorts hung from the open rafters and from pegs along the wall and filled plank shelves warped by weight and time. On one shelf small, tidy piles of clothing sat next to some canisters. Male clothing. Abigail immediately backed out of the cabin, right into Cam.

"This is becoming a habit," Cam said as he steadied her and stepped past. "Make yourself at home. Digger will bring your things in."

"Is there a second room that I didn't see?" She eyed the bedroll and saddlebags Cam carried, trying to ignore the warm, disturbing imprint his hand left on the small of her back.

"No. Just the one room. You and I will have to share." His eyes twinkled mischievously. Abigail was ready to snap her refusal when he continued, "That is, we'll have to share with Hannah. And Rico, when he gets here. He and I will take these two bunks." He indicated the two cots closest to the windows. "You and Hannah fight over the others."

"I'll take this one again, Cam honey. You know how I always have such cold feet." Hannah pushed past Abigail and plopped onto her choice, the bed closest to the stove—and to Cam, Abigail noticed. Fine with her.

Abigail was grateful for a bed as far as possible from both of them. It wasn't until she started putting her few possessions away that she noticed the decidedly flamboyant tangerine dress hanging from a peg in the dark corner nearby. Her nose led her to it, actually. It reeked of cheap gardenia scent, and its emerald trim and ruffles matched Hannah's eyes.

"This must be yours," Abigail said, carefully keeping the dress at arm's length as she removed it from the peg. "Would you mind putting it someplace where the stink won't be so overpowering?"

Hannah snatched the dress away, her green eyes flashing. "I suppose my perfume just ain't refined enough for you. Maybe you shouldn't have bought it for me, Cam honey."

"Perhaps you shouldn't bathe in it," Abigail advised between gritted teeth.

Digger, carrying in a couple of bedrolls, took one look at the two women. The bundles plopped in the dust as he retreated out the door.

Cam took the opposite tack, stepping smartly between the two of them as Hannah's open hand drew back for a slap. He backed her quickly toward the door.

"Why don't you hang the dress outside for a bit," Cam suggested. "You and it could both use a little airing."

Hannah looked like an argument, but she flung the dress over her shoulder and marched out.

Cam turned his attention to Abigail. "That was damned rude."

She suddenly wondered how she could have ever found those dark eyes feminine. They glittered like agates, and the firm set of his jaw was apparent even beneath the thick beard. She read the tightness in her chest as embarrassment but could find neither the grace to blush nor the wit to back down. "The dress stank. I couldn't possibly sleep with that smell in the room."

"You being such a fine, delicate creature yourself. That smell, as you call it, isn't the problem at all. You two have been at each other since—"

"Since she helped you kidnap me. In my book, that's reason enough to dislike her. And then there's the fact that she's a prostitute. I have no desire to associate with a woman like that."

"Well, now, that's understandable, Miss Morgan. We don't want those kind of women cluttering up the drawing rooms on Fifth Avenue, do we?"

Abigail swiped at the grit on her cheeks with her sleeve. "I realize prostitution is an acceptable female occupation to a man like you, Mr. Garrett, but it's not to me."

"You know, it's real easy to sit in judgment of someone like Hannah when you've never had to make any really hard choices in your life, choices like whether to starve in the cold or trade your body for a decent meal and a warm room. Whether to let that choice eat at you until you have no soul, or to try and make the best of things. I don't much care whether you like Hannah or not, but I expect you to treat her with as much respect as you would any other woman. You've thrown your last insult. Understand?"

"Don't worry, I won't call her a whore to her face again."

Cam stepped closer and looked down at her from inches away. "You're a handsome woman, Miss Morgan, but you have all the gentility of a drunken mule skinner."

"Then I should fit right into your gang." Her nails bit into her palms as she fought down the urge to slap him.

Cam turned away and Abigail thought he was leaving, but he stopped at his bed and ratted through his saddlebags.

"You'll be wanting these," he said, pitching something in her direction.

A pile of items landed at her feet: her comb, her monogrammed handkerchief, the label from her hat, a calling card, and her lace gloves. Abigail stared down at the clues she had so carefully planted along the way, all for nothing.

"You wretch." She scooped the comb off the floor and hurled it back at Cam, catching him square in the center of his chest. "You'd better pray I never get my hands on a gun. My father taught me to shoot."

"Your father should have taught you how to behave like a lady." Cam growled. "When you think you can, you come on down to supper."

Abigail turned away, her jaw clamped shut in anger. Cam's gaze bored into her back, but she forced herself to hold perfectly still until the wooden thud of the door told her he'd gone.

It was then, when she knew no one could see, that she permitted a single tear to slide down her cheek.

"One thing to say for Tanner, he grows good beef." Digger sliced another slab of steak off the well-aged carcass hanging from the branch of a big pine and slapped it on the huge iron skillet. The Fidelity brand showed on a ragged piece of hide pinned to the bark with a knife, advertising their reluctant supplier. As the meat sizzled, the old miner squinted at the cabin. "She comin' down?"

"It's up to her," Cam said, wondering himself how Abby could resist the aroma of prime beef and coffee after two days of canned beans. Vexatious creature.

"I hope she starves."

"Hannah, I told you this morning to ease off."

"If I hadn't been easing off, she'd need one of these steaks for her eye." Fists lifted high, Hannah danced around the fire like a prizefighter. "And I'll take on anybody here that doesn't like the way I smell."

"You smell fine," Digger said. "Mighty fine. In fact, I can't think of a girl that smells prettier."

The evening passed in familiar camaraderie, but Cam found his mind wandering in turns up the hill and back to the cliff trail. Lord, the woman had felt good filling his arms, pressed back against him as he talked her through her fear, his mouth barely an inch from that soft spot just behind her ear. It had taken all his will to keep from kissing her then and there. Only the thought that her reaction might have startled the horse right off the trail kept him from doing it.

How the fragile woman on the horse could become the arrogant shrew in the cabin was beyond him. The contrast was too stark, the change too abrupt. As Jesús fingered a melancholy tune on his battered old guitar, Cam's hand drifted to the tender spot on his breastbone where Abby's comb had caught him.

By the time Cam sucked the last sugared dregs of coffee out of a tin cup and strolled back to the cabin, Abigail was already in bed, the blankets drawn up around her head. Her uneven breathing gave lie to her pretense of sleep.

"You're going to be hungry by morning," he predicted to the stiff form. Hannah, for once, behaved herself and said nothing.

The first wash of morning light revealed no change in Abby's attitude. Cam let her miss breakfast as well, but at noon he heaped a plate with fried potatoes and onions, steak cooked to a turn, and some stewed dried apples thick with sugar and cinnamon, then filled a big cup with coffee and carried it all uphill. He took his time arranging things on the table before he finally sat down opposite Abby.

"Digger's quite a cook," he said around a forkful of potatoes sopped in drippings from the steak.

The silence dragged out interminably. Cam devoured fully half of his meal with her watching every bite before he decided to end her misery. He speared an enticing piece of steak and held it out. "Would you like something to eat?"

Apparently hunger pains won out over her pride. "Yes, I would," Abby admitted and leaned toward the fork with her mouth wide.

"Fine. There are beans on the shelf," he said, popping the steak in his mouth with gusto.

"Beans? I thought . . ."

"I don't wait tables, Miss Morgan. If you want to eat what the rest of us eat, go down to the campfire like everyone else. Otherwise, make do with beans."

To his surprise, it took only another minute for her to give in. Once she made the decision, she marched out the door and down to the fire without another glance back, her erect posture and those firm, set lips masking her feelings. Cam trailed after her, plate and cup in hand.

The men let Abby fend for herself. Unfamiliar as she must be with camp cooking, she soon had a healthy plateful of food. She hiked a few yards to where a granite boulder lay tangled in the roots of a pine and settled in well away from the others. Potatoes and meat flew into her mouth at an almost alarming rate.

"You can stop looking so smug, Mr. Garrett." Abby's fork paused momentarily as Cam picked out a seat on a flat spot on the edge of the same rock. "That was a very transparent ploy and only worked because I had already decided to come down for lunch."

"And pigs fly."

"Oh, they do, Mr. Garrett." She gave him a disingenuous look that almost had him believing her. "You see, I had already determined that I was being foolish. When I escape, I will require all my wits and physical strength to walk out over these mountains, so I will be eating quite well from now on."

"You do play poker, don't you?" Cam chewed the end of his fork thoughtfully. "That's a fine bluff, by the way, but you must have figured out I have men all around this valley. Besides, the cliff trail is the only safe route in or out. You're going to stay here until Tanner comes up with every penny of your ransom."

"We shall see who's actually bluffing. By the way, just how much did you ask for me?"

"Prices again? Never fear, Miss Morgan, I hold you in high esteem indeed. We asked for thirty thousand."

"Dollars?" The fork clattered on her plate as she stared at him in shock. "You expect Franklin to give you thirty thousand dollars in cash to get me back? He can hire an army to hunt you down like the beast you are for less than that."

"So you would think, señorita. But it seems he has other ideas." The familiar voice coming up behind them brought a smile of relief to Cam's face.

"Rico. What took you so long?"

"I had a little trouble gathering the news this time." He glanced at Abby, his expression questioning.

"Go ahead and have your little talk without me. I see no reason to listen to some tale you two concocted in an effort to demoralize me." Oblivious to the pine needles clinging to her skirt, Abigail swept away. Cam watched her go, amused and gratified that she took her plate with her.

"She walks like a queen, but she spits like a bobcat," said Rico. Removing his flat-crowned sombrero, he gave Cam a sound thump on the back and joined him beneath the tree. "You read Tanner correctly, *mi amigo*. He does not want it known that Cameron Garrett has his lady. He kept the Nagles with him at the Fidelity, where they talk to no one. He offers one thousand dollars to the first of his men who brings him the lady or word of her location, and he promises to kill anyone who passes word that she is missing."

"So only his men are covering the area."

"And they follow our false trail east through the lakes toward the Sangre de Cristos."

"People in Saguache were expecting her. What did Tanner tell them?"

"That she got nervous of the wedding and stayed in Denver to think about it." Rico rubbed the knotted veins on the back of his left hand with one stubby finger. "He makes her sound very foolish."

"She's going to appreciate that." Cam shook his head. "As well as I know that animal, he still amazes me. Any sane man would have called out the army to find us."

"It is said he already begins to froth like a mad dog at the very mention of your name. Do you still intend to go through with this plan of yours?"

"Even if she was fifty and looked like you." Cam laughed as he considered the possibility. "In fact, it might be easier if she was. Benjamin Franklin once pointed out that older women make good mistresses because they're so much more grateful for the attention."

"I am glad for your sake you do not have to test his idea. I worried that perhaps Tanner had found some fat *gringa* his own age, but this one . . ."

"It will be harder to make her fall in love with me."

"Is that necessary, Cameron?"

"That's not the kind of woman you just take, Rico. Besides, if Tanner's crazy now, just imagine him when he finds out I've seduced his fiancée, mind and body."

"*Sí.* It will drive him over the edge of caution, and the ranch will fall into your hands. Where it belongs." Grim satisfaction sparkling in his dark eyes, Rico gestured toward the fire and Abigail. "I see only one small problem. The lady hates you."

"I'm not so sure. You ought to see her with Hannah. If I didn't know better, I'd swear those two were jealous of each other."

Rico laughed. "Then it is good Hannah leaves us soon. How will you turn your bobcat into a purring kitten beneath your hand?"

"It's going to be a challenge. But before I trade her for Tanner's money, I'm going to take her from him in every sense of the word, just the way he's taken so much from me." Cam watched Abby as Digger poured her a cup of coffee, and he felt a sudden excitement that had little to do with revenge. "And I'm going to enjoy every minute of it."

Chapter 3

Fifteen. Abigail counted the men gathered around the noon campfire, then reviewed the faces of the others in her mind, ticking them off with fingers laid against her thigh. Yes, fifteen, counting the ones on guard above. Plus Hannah meant sixteen, if no one else rode in. After observing three men carry rifles out of camp at mid-morning and three come down a little later, she thought she had seen everyone at least once.

Aware of Cam Garrett's watchful eye, she rinsed her plate and fork in the stream and strolled back to the cabin. Instead of entering, however, she went on past the door and ducked around a corner. A quick peek back a few moments later revealed Cam more deeply in conversation with that Rico person, now that she was supposedly secure in the cabin. The others went about their business unconcerned about her whereabouts.

Abigail scurried around the back of the cabin, then walked calmly uphill toward the mine, keeping as much brush between herself and her captors as possible.

Once inside, the cool shadows of the tunnel brought both concealment and a sense of disappointment. The shafts that she'd thought belonged to a wagon were no more than long poles lashed together at one end with leather thongs. Maybe the cliff trail really was the only way into the valley. As long as she'd come this far, however, she might as well check for anything here that might be useful. Breathing harder than she should from the short climb, Abigail let her eyes adjust to the blackness and stepped in deeper.

It wasn't much of a mine shaft—less than ten yards deep. A neat row of bulky sacks stacked on top of kegs and boxes forced her to keep to one side of the tunnel. *Potatoes, beans, sugar, flour.* Abigail traced her fingers along the sides of the crates, barely able to read the stenciled letters in the dim light. *Coffee, Winchester .44/40.* Cartridges. That was more like it. The marks on the next crate down were illegible. With a sense of excitement, she shoved the sacks off onto the ground and pushed aside the cartridge box. She quickly dragged the box she wanted into better light. Square nails held the lid shut.

"Crowbar, crowbar." Abigail talked to herself as she hunted for something better to open it with than her bare hands. An odd hammer lay in a slope-sided pan; she grabbed it and went to work on the lid with the sharp end. "Please let this be guns."

"It's not," Cam said behind her. Abigail started guiltily and lurched to her feet. He steadied her with both hands around her waist. "Careful."

"Touch me again and I'll take this hammer to your head."

In answer, Cam twisted the hammer from her hand and tossed it behind him. Before Abigail could react, he locked his fingers around her wrists and tugged her so close she could feel his breath on her forehead. "That would be easier on me than the thirty tons of rock you're about to bring down on top of us."

Abigail settled instantly.

"That's better," Cam said. "See how that beam's propped? Knock that timber out and the whole front end of this mine collapses on our heads."

Abigail glanced at the timber, just a foot or so from where she'd been working. "A warning would have done. I was only—"

"You were only about to take that hammer to a box of dynamite."

"I don't believe you. This is all some excuse to manhandle me. Let me go."

"Fine. Get your little hammer and blow yourself to kingdom come. Just let me get out of here first." Cam set her loose as abruptly as he'd grabbed her and stepped toward the entrance. "I assume Tanner knows how to notify your parents. By the way, watch out for snakes."

"How convenient for you that there are always snakes where you don't want me to go." Abigail stepped beyond the propped timbers and pushed at a keg with her toe. "I'm not frightened this time."

"Sometimes rattlers like to nest up in dark places like this."

He sounded quite earnest. Abigail was about to think better of her expedition when, as if on cue, a nasty buzz sounded from somewhere to her right.

"*Stand still.*" The urgency in Cam's voice froze her in midturn. "Don't move, not so much as a breath. I can't see him."

Abigail searched the dark. What she first took as a knot of rope resolved into a snake, coiled about a yard away. She dared a whisper. "By that keg. Shoot it."

"Damn it to hell." Behind her, Cam crept around cautiously, a steady stream of curses against the snake and the mine pouring from his lips.

Abigail steeled herself for the roar of his pistol. The mountain pushed down on her more with every interminable second. Finally she felt Cam at her shoulder; he reached around her, some kind of pole in his hand, and stabbed downward like lightning.

The snake struck with such speed she hardly saw it. Something bumped her right shin, then a strange ringing sound echoed deep in the mine as Abigail waited for the pain of the snake's bite to reach her brain. Cam pushed her back and struck again at the rattler.

"Get out," he ordered.

She obeyed without question, the bright blue Rocky Mountain sky beckoning outside the entrance. Feeling oddly calm, she sat down in the dirt to examine the bite.

Her boot showed no sign of fang marks. Abigail stripped it off and peeled her stocking down to check her leg. Nothing.

A sound drew her eyes back to the mine. Cam stepped out into the sun, the writhing body of the snake coiled on the blade of the shovel he carried. Grimly he spilled it out onto the ground. The body continued to twitch as he buried the severed head deep in the rocky soil.

"God, I hate those things." Cam collapsed beside her. Sweat soaked dark stains beneath his arms and across his chest. "I swear, I didn't really think there would be a rattler in there. We cleaned out the whole valley a few weeks back, every snake we could find. Are you all right?"

"I think it bit me." Abigail noted a curious, shaking sensation as panic touched her at last. She held out her bare leg and pointed. "There. But there's no mark."

"Let me see." Cupping her heel in his hand, Cam examined her leg carefully. "If he'd gotten you, there'd be swelling by now. The shovel must have bumped your leg when he struck at it."

"The shovel." The ringing sound she'd heard. "It was the shovel." Her panic fled, and with it gone, modesty returned in a rush. Abigail pushed her riding skirt back over her knee and glared at Cam.

"I just saved your life three times over. Don't you think I deserve a little tolerance?" Cam traced a line down her shin with the tip of one finger. "Besides, you're the one that presented this beautiful bare leg."

"Limb. I can't imagine what I was thinking." Blushing, Abigail jerked her foot out of his hand and reached for her stocking.

"You thought you were dying, that's what."

Her stomach flip-flopped as the truth of his words struck her and her hands began shaking uncontrollably. Abigail let her stocking sag back to her ankle as she looked at Cam. "Why didn't you shoot it?"

"My preference, I assure you. I didn't shoot because that could have set off a cave-in just as easily as knocking that prop out. Mines are kind of finicky that way. Digger's lost two different partners through cave-ins. That was his rock hammer you were using. Digger's really a pretty interesting fellow. He could teach you a lot about mines and claims and claim jumpers. Don't tell my men, but snakes scare the wits out of me." He chuckled in honest good humor at himself, and the sound eased some of Abigail's fear. "They are good eating, though."

As he spoke, Cam rolled her stocking up over her calf, his fingers expertly gliding the heavy knitted silk into place. Distracted by his innocuous words, Abigail didn't realize what he was up to until his fingers brushed the soft skin behind her knee, at the bottom edge of her drawers. She gasped in shock as a rush of heat spread from that spot and jolted her into awareness.

She slapped him as hard as she could. Her fingers left vivid red stripes on his cheek above his beard.

"I suppose that means I'd better let you do the garter." Cam grinned as she bolted to her feet.

"You are loathsome." Boot in hand, Abigail hobbled down the hill, wincing as sharp stones bruised her heel.

Two hours later Abigail was still in a tizzy.

She flipped through a decaying magazine she'd found on the shelf with some of Hannah's things, trying to put the incident aside. She'd half expected Cam to come after her, either to harass her more or to apologize, but he hadn't.

Why that bothered her so much, she hadn't the vaguest idea. After all, he wasn't the first man to try to take liberties, although he was likely to be the last. As Franklin's wife, she'd hold a prominent position in Saguache, and no one would dare behave that way then.

Still, every time she thought of what Cam Garrett had done, her pulse raced as though his fingers still brushed against her skin.

She needed to find something to soothe her nerves, something familiar, calming. Abigail dropped the magazine on the chair and went in search of her hairbrush. Moments later she perched carefully on the splintery sill of the south window, undid her braid, and started brushing out her hair.

Outside, Cam's men moved about the camp freely, caring for their mounts, hauling wood, cleaning guns, performing the various chores needed in an active camp. Abigail watched them carefully, memorizing faces, putting names to them as she overheard bits of conversation.

As she watched, she brushed until her hair shone like polished wood in the sunlight, until the tension of the past few hours began to drain away. Below her, Rico lounged against the trunk of a bull pine, chewing on a long stem of grass. Wondering if he'd witnessed her stillborn attempt to escape, Abigail did her best to ignore him and began to reweave the long braid.

She couldn't ignore Cam, however, when he finally appeared. He came walking out of the thick trees at the far end of the valley, Hannah at his side. They walked in step, like lovers on a stroll through the park.

Abigail stopped braiding to watch them, the unfinished end of the plait in her hand.

They paused between some trees not far from the fire. Even at this distance Abigail could see the muscles tighten in Cam's arms and shoulders as his hands pressed against the trunks. The recollection of how those arms felt wrapped around her while riding along the cliff trail made her giddy.

She finished her braid blindly, disturbed by her thoughts.

After a time Hannah leaned toward Cam with a smile, laying a hand boldly on his chest. Cam laughed, then reached into his pocket and fished out a thick roll of money. He peeled off a few bills and tucked them into the deep décolletage Hannah affected, then patted her on the bottom as she headed on toward the fire, her skirts bouncing.

So that's what he'd been up to! The gall of the man.

Abigail shook with self-righteous anger. She'd heard of such goings-on, but that Hannah would sell herself so flagrantly came as a shock. Then for Cam to pay the trollop, right there where everyone could see! He probably used Franklin's money, too.

Cam turned uphill and headed toward the cabin. Abigail swallowed at a great choking lump wedged in her throat, and ducked away from the window.

When he entered a few minutes later, she was in the chair, hiding behind her magazine. She glared at the pages, trying to make some sense of them as Cam moved about the cabin. He settled onto the foot of the nearest cot and watched her.

"That must be quite an article," he said after a time. "You haven't turned a page since I came in here."

"I'm savoring the author's style." Abigail flipped a page. Her hands shook with anger, and she steadied the book against her knees.

"There's so much to be written about sanitary household management. I'm sure it palpitates with emotion."

"Circumstances force me to endure your company. I'd rather not deal with your sarcasm as well."

"So we're back to endure. I thought perhaps we'd gotten past that."

She stared at an illustration. "I have no idea what you mean."

"Stop hiding, Abby." Cam tugged the magazine out of her hands and tossed it aside. It flopped open to an advertisement and lay askew against the pillow. "Having her life saved would make any other woman happy, or at least mildly grateful. Instead you come up all sour and stiff again. Don't tell me that teasing you about your stocking—"

"I don't believe you! Your so-called teasing—and it was more than that—is the least offensive of your activities in the past few hours. I saw you pay that woman."

"Ah. So you jumped to conclusions."

"I know what Hannah is, Mr. Garrett."

"You have a very nasty mind, Abigail Morgan."

"You keep me prisoner here while you go off into the woods to carouse with a woman like that, and you tell me I have a nasty mind. Extraordinary."

"I haven't done any carousing since St.—" Cam bit off his sentence. "In a damned long time—not in the sense you mean. Look, I gave Hannah money to make up for the business she lost in going to Denver, and for the house split to her madam."

"I thought you were buying Hannah silk drawers."

"I am."

"Loyalty is certainly expensive in this part of the country."

"When doing a favor costs a friend something, I try to make it square."

"Out of Franklin's money, I suppose."

"Absolutely. I know you're—"

"You don't know anything about me," Abigail spat.

"Yes, I do."

Cam came off the cot onto his knees in front of her, bringing his eyes level with hers. "For instance, I know you're sitting in that chair like you have a board for a spine. It's a dead giveaway that you're angry."

His moustache danced as he spoke, drawing her eyes to its metallic sparkle. Her anger slowly dissolved, replaced by a subtle excitement that confused her.

"I know you're one of the toughest, brightest, most aggravating women I've ever met. I know you have beautiful, wide hazel eyes." Cam reached out, touched her temple with a callused fingertip and traced a line down the curve of her cheek to her jaw. He leaned closer; a slight pressure from his finger tilted her chin up, and he brushed his thumb over her lower lip. "And a tender mouth that can cut a man to the quick—which I've been wanting to kiss all day."

Abigail hardly knew where his words stopped and the kiss began, but it felt like the most natural thing in the world to part her lips for his gently exploring tongue.

It was a mistake. The pleasure that coursed through her veins when their tongues met swamped her good sense. Cam drew her tongue into his mouth, then let it escape. She had just begun to match his exploration with her own when he pulled back, rose and stepped away, leaving her wanting something more than what she'd received. A small noise of disappointment escaped her.

"What?" Cam asked.

"I . . . I, uh, was just . . ." She should be enraged. He was toying with her. She knew it. She searched for the spark of anger she was certain must be ready to burst into a full roaring blaze, but couldn't find it.

One corner of Cam's mouth lifted in a grin as he opened the door. He gestured toward the bed. "Maybe I should have Rico get you one of those things next time he gets to town."

Abigail twisted to see what he was talking about and went beet red: The magazine advertisement displayed Dr. and Madame Strong's Celebrated Tricora Corset in well-drawn detail. By the time she spluttered a protest, she was talking to the closed door.

The man was an utter cad, and the wicked sparkle of the evening fire in his eyes showed him unrepentant of the way he'd handled her earlier. Trying to ignore him, Abigail picked at the stew on her plate, suspicious that it contained the remnants of the snake.

Not that she was hungry, anyway. Her stomach had been queasy all afternoon, and she'd felt short of breath ever since hiking up to the mine. Abigail pushed the stew around a little longer, then gave it up. Even Digger's cobbler held no appeal. The first twinges of headache she'd noticed before dinner had grown into a steady throb of pain.

As they finished, the men hauled their own plates and cups to the stream to rinse them clean, then returned and piled them by the fire to dry.

One of the men reached for the big cast-iron stewpot. Cam stopped him, wrapped his own neckerchief around the handle of the pot, and held it out to Abigail. "Come on, Abby. We split chores pretty evenly around here."

"I'm not one of your gang, and I have no intention of doing chores."

"Think of it as payment for messing with Digger's gear up in the mine." Cam curved her fingers around the kerchief that cushioned the kettle's wire handle. The touch of his hand triggered another odd flutter of warmth in Abigail's blood. "I'll come and get that in a bit. I need to check on a couple of things. Go on."

Clearly, she wasn't going to avoid this chore. Behind her, Hannah laughed at some comment of Digger's. The sound brought back the image of Cam and the redhead beneath the trees.

None of my concern, Abigail reminded herself, but her chest felt unnaturally tight as she headed for the stream.

Burned stew and congealed grease made a blackened mess in the pot that the icy creek water wouldn't touch. She dropped Cam's kerchief in and scrubbed furiously, until her hands ached with the cold.

Eventually the kerchief shredded, and Abigail was reduced to scraping the crust free with a pebble. She thought again of Cam with Hannah, and the tightness in her chest grew more persistent.

About fifteen minutes later footsteps approached from behind. Abigail scrubbed harder.

"That thing's going to rust down to nothing before you ever get it clean that way." Hannah's voice was a mix of amazement and glee. "Lands, you don't even know how to wash a pot."

"Perhaps not." Abigail stood up and gave Hannah her most poisonous smile. "But then, I don't have *quite* as many skills as you do."

Either Hannah didn't get the message, or she chose to ignore it. She pointed at the kettle. "Fill that about halfway with water and bring it up to the fire. I'll show you the easy way."

The fire. Of course, a person needed warm water to wash up. Abigail felt like an idiot as she dipped the kettle into the stream and started after Hannah. Where was her mind? The headache must be making her slow-witted.

Even just half full, the pot seemed to weigh a ton. Breathing hard, Abigail dragged it and herself up the bank to the campfire, where she heaved the pot onto a rock at the fire's edge. Water sloshed over the side and hissed to steam on the hot coals.

"Where's that lye soap?" Hannah scavenged through Digger's cooking gear until she came up with a greasy brown bar. She shaved a few flakes into the water with a knife. "Now, let it sit there till it gets warm. It'll soften the whole mess up, and you can get it clean without wearing your fingers to a nub."

"If that soap of Digger's don't eat 'em," one of the men contributed as he got up and wandered off.

His departure left the two women alone, except for a threesome dealing stud poker on the far side of the fire.

It also left Abigail suddenly and uncomfortably aware of her dependence on the redhead. Prostitute or not, Hannah was the only other woman in a camp full of dangerous men. More to the point, Cam had been right: She'd behaved badly. It wasn't her position to judge Hannah.

"Thank you," Abigail blurted as Hannah began stacking dry cups and plates. "For your help, I mean."

Hannah waved her words off. "If it hadn't been me, it would've been someone else."

"After the way I behaved yesterday, I'm surprised you didn't leave me scrubbing all night." Abigail hesitated, then drew on years of social training to make herself go on. "I apologize for what I said about your perfume. It was uncalled for."

"Well, now," Hannah said, rocking back on her heels. A wry grin lifted one corner of her mouth. "When I got a better whiff of that dress, I started thinking maybe it was a touch strong."

"Maybe a little," Abigail admitted tentatively.

"See, in my trade, we girls get to trying to outdo each other, sort of to attract the customers, and living in the middle of it, a body gets used to the smell. Now that I been away from it for a while . . . well, it did stink."

"I still might have told you in a nicer way. I was rude, and I'm sorry."

"How did you manage to grow up without learning to wash a pot?" Hannah asked, apparently ready to go on to other subjects.

The question put Abigail off. "We had a cook. She did all of that sort of thing."

"And you never even watched her?"

"Father liked me to read to him after lunch, and after dinner we usually went out for the evening." Abigail slowly realized Hannah was gaping at her as if she had horns on her head. "I watched a few times," she said defensively. "I just didn't think of the fire tonight. Things are so different here."

"I didn't say nothin'," Hannah said. "Look, I got to go up to the cabin for a while. Cam's waiting for me. You going to be able to handle that?"

So they had another assignation scheduled. Barely able to restrain her tongue, Abigail focused on the dark water welling up from the bottom of the kettle as it warmed. "Yes. Thank you."

Humming a ditty that Abigail suspected had lewd words, Hannah strolled toward the cabin. The card players across the fire didn't even look up when she left.

With another reminder to herself that whatever activities Cam might or might not enjoy with Hannah were really none of her business, Abigail turned her attention to the kettle. True to Hannah's word, the combination of lye soap and warm water loosened the encrustation on the bottom of the pot. A swish with the remains of Cam's kerchief removed the mess. Abigail hauled the pot back to the stream to finish up the job.

She took her time at it, unwilling to go back to the fire, where she'd wind up staring at the cabin. Abigail propped the pot upside down on a rock to drain and meandered a ways downstream, enjoying the freedom of being alone for the first time since her hotel room in Denver.

Alone.

Abigail glanced around. There wasn't a man in sight, and night hid her from the ones on the ridge above. She could hardly ask for a better opportunity to escape.

With scarcely a second thought Abigail headed for the outlet of the valley. The creek's steady roar covered the noise she made as she crept through the willows and alders along its edge. A part of her wondered what snakes did at night, whether they curled up along stream banks waiting to bite unsuspecting city women. She kept going.

From back by the fire she heard a male voice call her name. Abigail pushed forward with less caution. Twigs snagged her hair, ripping it from the long, neat braid. More voices joined the first. She heard the alarm go up.

The cliff rose just ahead, jet against a star-sequined sky. Abigail paused to catch her breath. The trail along the cliff's face was out of the question, both because of the guard posted there and because of her vertigo. Night would make the dizziness worse, make the distance to the ground seem even greater and more horrifying. Since she hadn't been able to look down, she had no idea what the stream's course was like, but even if a horse couldn't travel that way, surely a person on foot could manage it.

The men's voices grew louder and spread out across the valley behind her. Abigail surged forward, a sudden, unreasoning fear filling her lungs with air. The bank grew steeper, the boulders along it, larger. The sound of rapids ahead muffled the footsteps behind her.

"Hold it," Cam said as he closed in from behind and laid a hand on her shoulder.

Abigail spun away, inexplicably terrified by his touch. Strands of hair, no longer contained by the braid, whipped across her face. She peered through the tangles, trying to find an opening in the brush.

There. Abigail dived for it as Cam reached for her again. Her foot caught a branch on a small log, and she fell flat.

"What's going on? What are you doing?" Cam's hand locked around one of Abigail's ankles. She kicked out. A grunt of pain rewarded her when her foot connected with something hard, but Cam held on.

"Rico, down here. That's enough, Abby."

"Turn me loose." Abigail clung to the nearest rock, then to the log as Cam dragged her backward. Cam shifted his hold to her waist and hips and heaved her to her feet. Several faces appeared in the surrounding brush.

Abigail rounded on Cam and swung, landing a fist square in his stomach. She heard laughter and raucous comments as Cam turned red-faced. Twisting Abigail away from him, he crossed her arms neatly over her chest and held her straight-jacketed in his embrace. Abigail raged at Cam and kicked at his shins with her booted heels. Every insult and vile name she'd ever heard rolled off her tongue until her lungs cried out for air.

"I'm telling you, she could take him," one of Cam's men argued over her yelling. "Probably could take you, too, Jesús."

"Shut up!" Cam roared, and everyone stopped at once. "I'm disgusted with the lot of you. What do you men think you were doing, letting her get away? Rico, make sure this doesn't happen again. I'll take care of Miss Morgan."

Bruising fingers clamped firmly around Abigail's wrist, and Cam stormed toward the cabin. Abigail fought him a few steps, then let him lead her, suddenly out of steam. Cam slowed as her weight dragged on his arm. For Abby every step became a mile run.

In the lantern-lit cabin, Abigail drooped onto a chair while Cam slammed shutters and dropped the door latch. Whatever he had in mind, he wanted everyone else left out of it. Abigail pressed the heel of her hand to her throbbing head and stared at the floor, braced for his explosion.

"I should skin you alive for that little episode. What on earth do you think you were doing? No, never mind, don't answer. You warned me you were going to walk out of here. I just didn't think you'd be so stupid as to try it at night without the vaguest idea of where you were going."

Oily smoke rose from the lantern. The air grew thick with its smell, sickening Abigail even more.

"You look like hell." Cam sloshed a little water into a tin basin and dunked a cloth. "Here," he said, dropping the cloth in her lap.

It felt cool, and she spread it across her palms and leaned her face into it.

"You have a heck of a right hand, Abigail Morgan. I suppose your father taught you to box, too."

"My brother," Abigail muttered into the cloth.

"Didn't your mother ever teach you anything?"

There was simply no more air. Her chest ached with the effort of breathing, and her head pounded. Abigail rose to her feet, wobbling, and stumbled away from the table, fighting the blackness that swirled over her eyes. She made it almost halfway to the door before she collapsed.

Chapter 4

"I seen somethin' like it before," Digger said. "Mountain sickness. Fellas come from back East on the trains and go right into the mines at Summitville. Some of 'em have trouble breathing. Not always right at first, but somethin' happens and they have trouble. Best thing to do is get 'em down for a time."

"How far down?" Cam asked. "Carnero?"

Rico vetoed the idea immediately. "By now Tanner has discovered we did not ride east. He will have his men turning the west side of the valley upside down."

Cam turned to the bed where Abigail shuddered with every hard-won breath. The tinge of blue around her mouth frightened him.

"Take her down to Noreen's. She'd give her a bed," Digger said.

"Oh, yeah." Hannah snorted. "Old Tanner would just love to find her in the next room when he comes in to see me. That'd be a wonderment."

"Hush," Cam warned, but Abby had her attention on Digger, who bent over her listening carefully.

"She's breathin' hard, but she's not bubblin' like with pneumonia. Does it hurt anyplace, miss?"

"Mostly my head," Abby whispered between pale, bluish lips.

"I think maybe you just need bed rest. Worked fine for some of the fellows that didn't have money to go back down off the mountain."

"We do not have to decide now," Rico said. "We cannot leave until first light anyway. Perhaps she will be better by then."

"Maybe," Cam allowed. "Meantime, you fellows get some rest."

"I will stay outside tonight," Rico said.

The two men headed for the door, but Digger stopped and motioned Cam over. He dropped his voice so Abby couldn't hear. "She's a tough one, but she's scared. That's makin' her fight every breath, and she won't get much rest that way. I got some laudanum in my kit."

Cam thought for a moment and nodded his agreement. Digger disappeared.

"Think that's a good idea?" Hannah asked.

"It's the best thing we've got right now, unless you're anxious to introduce her to the girls."

Hannah grumbled and plunked down at the table. A frown creased her pretty face as she stared at Abby. Abby stared back, her chest rising and falling too quickly.

Digger reappeared in a few minutes with a little blue bottle and a steaming cup of pine needle tea, so sweet with sugar it looked more like syrup.

"Already doctored it," he whispered, slipping the bottle into Cam's shirt pocket. "Only takes a few drops. The tea will do her some good, too."

Cam thanked him and sent him on his way, then turned back to Abby. She struggled to sit up.

"You're going to let me die up here, aren't you?" Her eyes were bright, almost feverish, but she met his gaze with the same challenge as always.

"Nope." Cam hooked one toe around a chair leg and dragged it over next to Abby's cot. He set the cup down on its seat for a moment, while he perched on the wooden frame of the cot. "First off, you're not dying. And second, if I thought you might, I'd get you down and to some help, even if I had to turn myself in to do it. Does that make you feel better?"

"Slightly," she admitted.

Hannah snorted again from her spot at the table. "You ain't exactly easy to please, are you, honey?"

"Right now you need to relax and get some rest." Cam gave Hannah a look that quelled her. "Digger made you some tea. Hope you like it sweet. I think he put half our sugar supply in it."

Abby accepted the cup and took a tentative sip. "It's fine."

As the pale green tea cooled, she drank more deeply. The laudanum began to work before Abby finished the sugary liquor at the bottom. Cam lifted the cup out of her fingers as she began to slump, and caught her with an arm around her shoulders.

"I feel so wobbly," Abby mumbled, trying to push him away. "Are you sure I'm not dying?"

"I'm sure." Cam eased her back as Hannah came to stand at the end of the cot.

"I'll sit up with her," Hannah volunteered.

Cam shook his head. "Thanks, but I brought her up here. I'll take care of her."

"You going to keep both these lamps lit?" At his nod Hannah grabbed for the blankets off her cot. "I'll sleep outside then. Never could get much rest with a lamp on."

"That's probably better for Abby anyway, the way you snore." Cam gave Abby a wink. She giggled sleepily.

"I don't snore," Hannah said. "You need me, you give a shout. G'night, you two."

"Tell Digger . . . kettle's . . . by stream," Abby muttered. "I left it . . ."

Cam carried the empty cup to the table, then went back to sit by Abby. She fought the drug as hard as she fought for breath, continually popping up with strange statements and bits of conversation. It took almost an hour for her to fall soundly asleep, and it was well past midnight before Cam saw any real change in her condition. Her breathing, while still a little too quick and shallow, finally evened out. Cam brushed a wave of chestnut hair off her forehead, and Abby sighed peacefully.

Pulling the little blue bottle out of his pocket, Cam tapped it thoughtfully. For all the trouble laudanum caused, it could work miracles.

Dawn found Cam dosing her again, a few drops on a spoon. Still groggy, Abby slurped down the bitter medicine without a protest. This time she curled against his chest like a sleepy child as the drug took effect. The scent of her hair wrapped itself around him, traces of lavender soap clinging to it despite the days in the mountains. Cam was still holding her when Rico came to the door with his breakfast.

"Well, if she's not better quick, it won't be Cam's fault." Hannah flapped at a no-see-um that buzzed around her ear and plunked down next to Digger's cook box. For some reason the bugs never seemed to bother Digger. Maybe it was the faded red long john shirt he wore every day. "He won't hardly let me in the cabin. Wonder what she'll think when she wakes up and finds out he's been doing for her. Bet she smacks him good."

Digger dumped a portion of cut oats into a pan and hoisted the bag up into a tree, away from rodents. "Miss kinda gets your craw, does she?"

"She started in on me from the first. You heard her."

"Might've been the sickness made her short, even then."

"Short, hell. Uppity is what she was. Still is, even if she did apologize to me last night—"

"See there, she ain't so bad."

"It was just before she ran off," Hannah said sourly. "I

should have known something was funny."

"Well, you won't have to bother with her much longer."

"Don't remind me. I ain't looking forward to going back to town. For a start, I'm going to miss this coffee of yours. Pour me a cup, please?" Hannah filched a cup off the stack of dishes and held it out for Digger to fill. "One thing I got to say, though, she's a tough cuss, for a city girl. That doesn't mean I like her, just that I hope Cam knows what he's doing. She's just the kind could turn things all around on him."

"You're still hankering for him," Digger said. It wasn't a question but a statement.

The fiery spots in Hannah's cheeks would have given her away anyway, so she went ahead and answered. "Not that it much matters. He doesn't feel the same."

"Don't make it any easier to watch him holding someone else's hand, though, does it? Even if it's just 'cause she's sick."

"Nope."

"Well, if you feel the need to talk, I got me a good pair of ears."

"Yes, sir, you do." Hannah leaned over and gave Digger a kiss on one ear. His face went as red as his shirt.

"There's my girl. Come on, take a little." Tranquil hands cradled Abigail's head and spooned warm ambrosia to her famished lips. In the distance, guitar music and feminine laughter tinkled on the air.

She knew this place, Abigail thought languidly. This must be heaven.

"You're an angel," Abby whispered with certainty.

A gentle, low chuckle. "Fallen angel, maybe. A little more . . ."

The midafternoon sun glared around the edges of the crude wooden shutter that covered the window, piercing the thick fur that seemed to fill Abigail's head. She squinted at the dust motes that swirled between the tools hanging in the open rafters and tried to figure out what had happened to the angel. The only person here was Cam Garrett, asleep in a chair tilted against the wall a few feet away, his hat on his knee.

And where was here, anyway?

She looked around the cabin, and slowly memories of the past few days drifted back.

Good lord. She was in bed wearing a man's nightshirt, and Cam Garrett was in the room. Abigail yanked the heavy wool blanket to her shoulders, then snaked an arm out to pitch a pillow at him.

Cam's eyes snapped open, and he grinned. "Back to normal, I see."

"I swear, if you come an inch closer, I'll scream. Where are my clothes, you ruffian?"

"I'm staying right here. Your clothes are being washed. And, no, I'm not the one who undressed you. Hannah and Digger did that."

Abby huffed a little, but his words relieved her major concern. "I remember thinking I was dying. Or had died."

"That little jaunt down the creek about did you in." Wrinkles pleated a notch between Cam's eyebrows. "You had me worried, Abby."

The honest concern in his eyes stirred a feeling inside her that Abigail didn't want to acknowledge. "Well, you don't have to worry anymore. I feel fine. Get out of here so I can get dressed."

"Sorry, no."

"I beg your pardon."

Cam shook his head. "I'm staying. And you're staying in bed."

"Keeping me unclothed will not keep me from running away from you at the first opportunity."

"I'm sure it won't, and I will take the threat seriously this time. But that's not why you're staying in bed."

"All right, Mr. Garrett. Say your piece."

Cam's explanation was brief and to the point.

According to Digger, she needed a good two or three days of bed rest before she could start moving around again. Half of one day was gone already. She'd see her clothes when Digger said she could be up—it seemed the old miner had confiscated every piece of clothing she had, just to make certain she stayed in bed. Meanwhile, when she needed it, Hannah had a wrapper she could borrow.

"Not that nasty orange and green thing, I hope," Abby said. "Oh, don't look at me like that. Hannah isn't around."

"No, not that one. Not that it will matter until at least tomorrow, maybe the day after. I don't want you to walk more than a few steps before then."

"What on earth am I supposed to do in the meantime? I can't just lie here."

Cam held a book up. "Have you read Hardy's *Return of the Native*?"

"No."

"Good. Then I'll read to you. And there are a couple more old magazines that Hannah packed up here. If that doesn't interest you, a few of the fellows need some mending done."

"How kind of you to think of me." Abigail allowed the sarcasm to drip from her voice.

"Such a change. You actually thought I was nice for a few minutes this morning. I fed you a little broth that Digger made, and you called me an angel." At her open-mouthed stare he added, laughing, "Of course, we had given you a touch of laudanum."

Abigail snapped her mouth shut firmly. "That explains it. I wasn't in my right mind."

"That's the end of the chapter." Cam slipped the ribbon mark in between the pages, closed the book, and laid it aside. "I don't think I've ever read aloud so much in my life. I'm getting hoarse."

"You don't need to do this, you know. I'm perfectly

capable of reading on my own. I'll bet I can even manage to hold the book up."

Cam smiled at Abby's snippety tone. "But then I'd have to find something else to do while I sit here with you. Idle hands are the devil's tools, you know. No telling what mischief I might think up."

Abby gave him a withering glance and tugged the ribbon off her braid. "Hand me my brush."

Actually, he'd already thought up plenty of mischief, all of which would have to wait until Abby was back on her feet. Seducing a hale and feisty woman was one thing, taking advantage of a sick one was another altogether. Still, it did no harm to daydream.

He very much wanted to kiss Abby again. That first time had been a lark, but it had whetted his appetite. Sitting a few feet away from Abby for nearly twenty-four hours had given him plenty of time to study her face, especially her lips. While the rest of her features might be sharpish—her cheekbones high and angular, her chin just a bit too strong to be completely feminine, her nose a mite too long—her mouth made up for the flaws with a lush fullness that Cam longed to sample at length.

After thoroughly brushing her hair, Abby began braiding it. Cam watched, as fascinated as he had been—what? three, four days ago? The lantern light glinted off something as her fingers worked through the tangles. Cam reached for her hand but pulled back when she glanced his way apprehensively. As she sat there, unmoving, he spotted what had been flashing in the light.

"Your ring," he said.

Abby held her hand out to look at her engagement ring, a large rectangular emerald set into a lozenge of gold pavéd with tiny round rubies. A greenback surrounded by drops of blood, Cam thought with a lurch of hatred for the man who'd put it on her. Appropriate.

"Quite a sight. I probably should have sent it back with the ransom note."

"Franklin wouldn't have recognized it," Abby said simply and went back to her braiding.

"A man remembers when he gives a ring like that to a woman."

"Not if he's never seen it. The man from Tiffany's brought over a selection of rings. I picked the one I liked best, and they billed Franklin."

"That's a damned cold-blooded way to get engaged."

Color mottled Abby's cheeks. "How I got engaged is none of your business."

"I hope you at least picked the most expensive one." He did, too, though not for the reason she would imagine.

"Why? Do you plan to steal my ring, too, Mr. Garrett?"

"I've stolen nothing of yours."

"Oh, that's right, you're only after Franklin's property. My, how chivalrous." Abby finished off the braid and flipped it over her shoulder. She stared up at him blandly, and her courage and control goaded Cam. Anger at Tanner and a simmering lust for his woman boiled up in him.

Cam dug deep within himself for the will to keep from pushing Abby down on the cot and demonstrating just which part of Tanner's property he wanted most at the moment. He rose and moved away, his hands held well away from his sides like a man backing off from a gunfight.

"If you don't mind, I'd like to go to sleep now." Abby clearly had no idea of the effect she was having on him.

For that matter, Cam barely understood it himself. He flexed his shoulders, trying to rid himself of some of the tension. "Me, too. Rico and Hannah should be coming up soon."

Aware that Abby watched his every move, Cam stripped off his shirt and hung it on a peg. He then took a moment to light a candle stub as a night-light for his friends, before he extinguished the lantern. The rest of the cabin faded into blackness in the dim flicker of the candle. In his mind's eye, the corner with the stove and table became a different room, one that was small, neat, simply furnished—the kind of house his mother had kept.

The sounds and sights of the distant past echoed in Cam's skull, and for a brief instant he wanted to ride headlong down into the valley and empty six chambers into Tanner's skull. No, five. He'd save one for Tanner's hired gun, Stanton. The idea surprised Cam, coming with such power. He'd set aside the possibility of murder years before, and planned better means of revenge, one of which was breathing softly just a few yards away.

Forcing his attention away from Abby, Cam slipped into his own cot. He was dog tired, with only that brief nap before Abby woke up. Still, his mind wouldn't let him sleep.

Less than a dozen feet away, Abigail lay staring at the back wall. She held herself stiff beneath a shielding layer of blankets clutched up to her chin, as if she suddenly expected him to lunge for her at any minute.

What would her reaction be if he did? Cam doubted she could predict it herself. Had she even been aware of the way she'd stared at him as he stripped off his shirt? If his imagination hadn't been playing tricks on him, something besides curiosity had shone in those eyes, a sort of hunger. He'd only caught a glimpse of her face before she'd rolled over in a huff, but the impression clung, sweetly seductive. The heavy swelling of his lust urged him to discover for himself, to bar the door and join her on the narrow folding bed, to make her feel the pleasure her body was designed for.

Cam grabbed the frame of the cot and squeezed until his knuckles ached.

No, he told himself, *not yet.* Her taking was to serve a purpose, not simply be an act of pleasure. This was Tanner's woman, Cam reminded himself once again, and it wasn't just her body he was after: It was her heart. When Abby knew she wanted him, that's when bedding her would do the most damage and give the most value in the long war with Tanner. That's when he would allow himself to enjoy her bounty. It wouldn't be long, but he had to wait.

Cam wondered for the thousandth time how Tanner had won her in the short space of a month-long trip back East. He couldn't picture Abby responding to the hearts and flowers of a traditional courtship. But then, he couldn't picture anyone courting Miss Abigail Morgan like that anyway. She'd cut them into shreds and toss the pieces out the drawing room window.

Maybe that was it. Maybe Franklin Tanner's innate meanness had made him proof against Abby's rapier tongue. Combined with the coat of manners the man seemed to put off and on at will, and his uncanny knack of hiding his nature when it suited him, Tanner might just have appeared the sort of man who could handle a woman like Abby. Or maybe it was because he looked rich and refined.

However Tanner had done it, Cam knew he had to offer something different to Abby. That shouldn't be too difficult.

The blood-and-money ring winked in the candlelight as Abby punched at her pillow. Cam smiled at the soft mound of blankets that covered her hips.

Yes, he told himself, there had been something more in her eyes. Getting her to realize it shouldn't be hard at all for a determined outlaw.

Chapter 5

It must be the aftereffects of the laudanum, Abigail decided. She shouldn't still be thinking about something so inconsequential as the man taking off his shirt, especially with him sitting right in front of her reading. It suddenly dawned on her that she was twisting the end of her braid around one finger, a habit she thought she'd abandoned at thirteen.

"I cannot stay in here another minute," Abigail said, dropping her braid. "I swear, I'm going to have a fit."

"You're already having one," Cam pointed out, snapping the book closed. "Makes me feel unappreciated."

"There's only so much bed rest and reading a body can absorb in one go, even if it's Thomas Hardy." In reality, she'd heard less than half of what Cam had said in the past hour.

"You've never been sick much, have you?"

"No. Not only am I bored beyond reason, but I'm certain my back has been deformed by the shape of this confounded cot. It sags. And just look out there." Abigail pointed toward the window. Glimpses of sapphire sky and the sound of Hannah and the others laughing as they went about their business made her imprisonment more galling. "It's beautiful. I want to enjoy it. Please let me go outside."

"Please? Excuse me." Cam tapped the side of his head with his palm as though he was trying to knock something out of his ear. "I must be hearing things. You didn't actually say please, did you?"

Abigail blushed. "I did, and I'll repeat it. Please let me out of here. Just for a few minutes."

"I can hardly refuse a 'please.' If you'll promise not to walk a step, I'll let you join the others for lunch."

"Promise," Abigail said, so relieved at the prospect of an outing she barely heard the terms. "May I have my clothes back?"

"Not until you're fit to move around on your own. Meantime, use this." Cam lifted the tangerine gown off a peg in the far corner and revealed a plain gingham day wrapper in an awkward shade of maize that probably looked wonderful on Hannah. He tossed it on the foot of the cot. "I'll be right outside. Holler when you're decent."

Abigail quickly donned the wrapper and sized herself up in the metal shaving mirror that hung near the basin. Though much more modest than any garment she'd have expected to see in Hannah's wardrobe, the borrowed wrapper was nothing to be seen wearing in polite company. It smelled of the sickeningly sweet gardenia scent Hannah favored, and its color gave Abigail's ivory skin an ugly yellow tinge that made her look sickly. But it covered what needed to be covered. She pulled on her boots, then took a few moments to brush out her hair and fluff out the fringe along her forehead and temples. A quick pinch gave her high cheekbones some color.

"I look jaundiced," she said as Cam entered.

He gave her a long, assessing look. Abigail tugged nervously at the securely tied belt. The way the flannel nightshirt bunched underneath, she felt positively matronly.

"Actually, I was thinking of a canary," Cam said.

"I don't sing."

"A shame. Come, pretty bird, and I'll take you down to eat." Without a warning, Cam scooped Abigail into his arms.

She shrieked and punched his shoulder. "Put me down."

"Don't hit my jaw," he warned, jerking his head back a little. "That's the side you clipped with your foot the other night. I thought you wanted to go out for a little."

"I did. I do. This isn't proper." Abigail started to squirm out of his arms, but that seemed even less proper, especially considering her deshabille. A disconcerting twinkle lit Cam's eyes, and Abigail's heart skipped a beat. "Set me down."

"Nope. You do need the sunshine, and Digger says you shouldn't move around much yet." Cam strode out the door and down the hill.

Abby tried to relax, tried to keep her mind on the humiliation of being carried down to eat like an invalid child, but she couldn't seem to manage it. All she could think of was how Cam had looked last night when he'd stripped off his shirt.

Lamplight had painted his chest and arms with golden highlights, defining each muscular ridge. He'd looked like a work of sculpture. A jagged scar marred his lean belly where it seemed the artist had refused to deal in perfection. Abigail knew he'd undressed like that before, but she'd stubbornly avoided even a glimpse of him. Last night the sight had taken her breath away and infuriated her all at once.

Now her skin tingled where Cam cradled her in those same muscular arms, and a neat diamond of fair, wiry hairs glinted within the open neck of his shirt, tempting her fingers to test their softness. An odd spark glowed to life deep in her belly.

The shuffle of men around the fire ended her ride. Abigail noticed a few men staring as Cam lowered her to her feet.

"Right here, miss," Digger said. He didn't seem to notice

a thing. "You can use this empty sack for a cushion."

To Abigail's conflicting relief and disappointment, Cam left her to her own devices during the meal, allowing Digger to entertain her while Cam spent his time in close conversation with Rico. More than once, however, she caught him glancing in her direction, his brown eyes narrowed speculatively beneath his hat.

Digger had just launched into a complicated tale about three brothers and their mules when Cam rose.

"Time for a nap," he announced.

"Have a good sleep," Abigail said.

"*Your* nap. We have a few chores to handle, so I'll take you back up now."

"I'm not a child, Mr. Garrett, and I don't need an afternoon nap."

"Digger?"

The grizzled miner squinted. "She's lookin' peaked."

"It's this dress," Abigail argued, but Cam stole her plate and tugged her to her feet. In seconds they were off to the cabin.

This time, without a parcel of men watching, Cam wasn't quite as quick to release her once they'd reached the cabin. His hands lingered on her shoulders after he set her down, warm even through layers of flannel and gingham. Conscious of the seconds that passed, Abigail held herself motionless.

The twinkle in Cam's eyes faded, replaced by something more intense. He dipped his head toward her mouth, his fingers tightening on her shoulders a fraction.

He's going to kiss me again, Abigail thought, and her heart thumped erratically against her ribs. She began to tremble. Her breath caught in her throat a moment, then her lungs filled with a rush like a gasp.

The sound broke the spell. With a shake of his head Cam stepped away.

"You shouldn't be up yet." He guided her toward the cot and tucked her in beneath the Union blue wool blankets. "I don't want you to move until supper. I'll be back in a little while."

Cam paused in the doorway a moment and tipped his hat before tugging it low over his eyes. Then he disappeared.

Would she have actually let him kiss her?

The question taunted Abigail as she lay there, staring up at the salty, cheesecloth-wrapped crust of a smoked ham that hung from the rafters.

There was something distinctly attractive about the man, despite his uncut hair and scruffy beard. He was clearly well educated, despite his current situation. She had the inkling that he would clean up nicely and look altogether too handsome in formal dress for a young woman's peace of mind. He had done extraordinary duty over the past two days, caring for her and entertaining her as though he was her personal nurse. Not at all the actions of an outlaw.

What if she'd met him under different circumstances, say the Ashfords' summer cotillion before she accepted Franklin's proposal . . . ?

But she *had* accepted Franklin's proposal, Abigail reminded herself harshly, and she had no business even contemplating another man's kiss, especially not Cam Garrett's.

Blast the man.

Abigail stuck a foot out from under the blanket and angrily kicked the chair Cam had tugged up beside her bed for reading. It tipped over and crashed against the wall. A cloud of dust billowed off the floor and swirled through a beam of sunlight, like dancers in a waltz.

She wondered if Cam could waltz.

"This is ridiculous," Abigail said aloud.

Why on earth was she letting that man—that *outlaw*—affect her this way? Why, she even let him tell her what to do. She felt fine, and she wanted to be up and about. Not that she could go far in a man's nightshirt and a cotton wrapper, but she most certainly didn't have to stay in bed mulling over nonsense.

Abigail tossed her covers aside and rose. A couple of minutes of work and she'd organized Cam's chair and a pair of empty crates into a rough chaise and a side table.

With one blanket as a shawl and the other as a lap rug, Abigail sat down by the window, smug in the fact that she wasn't the slightest bit out of breath, and went back to her reading. A breeze gently riffled the pages of the book.

Nearly an hour passed. The shadow of a cloud passed overhead, like a mourning veil caught on the wind. Abigail glanced out to watch the dark smudge travel up over the far wall of the valley and disappear. A big gray jay squawked from a branch just outside.

Altogether pleasant, she decided, for a kidnapping. She craned her neck a little to see down to the campfire.

What she saw lifted her clear off the chair.

Money.

Cam sat behind a crude table made from a board propped between two boxes. Stacks of bills were spread out like a fan in front of him, each pile weighted with a rock against the breeze.

Thousands of dollars.

No wonder Cam wanted her securely in bed, Abigail thought bitterly. They were dividing Franklin's money between themselves and didn't want a witness.

Well, she'd be a witness all right, and she'd have as many details as possible to tell a judge once the law caught up with Garrett and his men.

Cam argued somewhat intensely with Hannah and Jesús. Others chimed in now and again, but the distance, the background sound of rushing water, and the wind made it impossible to hear more than an occasional word.

Abigail leaned out. No better. She cursed the breeze roundly.

To Cam's right, Rico bent over what appeared to be a smudged piece of paper, the stub of a lead pencil gripped in his fingers. The entire gang, including Hannah, stared at the money so intently that no one noticed

Abigail hanging out the window.

Cam riffled the skimpy bundle remaining in his hands, then peeled off most of it and divided it into two fresh stacks, adding them to the fan of bills.

With a lick of his pencil, Rico bent and wrote. He shook his head and said something.

Heads nodded. Cam spoke again, waited, then folded the last few bills, tucking them into his shirt pocket. He rose and Hannah slid into the vacated spot next to Rico. They started wrapping the stacks of bills in sheets of old newspaper, making neat bundles that Rico labeled—each man's cut, Abigail assumed.

Abigail waited for the dole to start, for the first man to take his split. Instead, the men wandered off, each going his separate way. One by one, the bundles of cash disappeared into a pair of saddlebags at Rico's side.

That's odd. What on earth were they doing with the money? Abigail retreated to her chair before anyone noticed her at the window.

The Return of the Native languished on her lap as Abigail turned the scene over in her mind. She'd already known they had the money. Why was how they divided it such a secret, especially when not one of them took a penny? Except Cam, of course, who seemed to have kept enough to live comfortably for quite a while in this part of the country.

Exactly what she'd expect of an outlaw.

Still, when dinnertime rolled around, Abigail found herself once again fiddling with the belt of the wrapper, awaiting Cam's transport with a breathless impatience she had a hard time discounting.

She told herself it was the novelty of being carried that appealed to her. That was all. She'd never been carried like this, not as an adult anyway. If Cam tried to take liberties, she'd put him in his place.

Unfortunately, he never offered her the chance to do it.

Cam acted the complete gentleman, carrying her down to dinner without a single untoward look or comment. He carried on proper—if somewhat unexciting—conversation throughout the meal, and brought her back to the cabin with both Rico and Hannah as escorts.

Cam deposited Abigail by the cot, then went to work building a fire in the little black stove.

A deck of cards appeared from somewhere, along with a box of sulfur matches. As Hannah counted out some matches for each of them, Rico started dealing three hands of draw poker like he didn't have a care in the world.

Like he didn't have five thousand of Franklin Tanner's dollars in those saddlebags he'd just tossed over the back of his chair.

Abigail looked from the cards to the book and back, then drifted toward the table.

"You're supposed to be in bed." Cam pointed to the cot.

"Nonsense. I sat up all afternoon reading, and this isn't a whit more strenuous."

"She's old enough to know how she feels," Hannah said.

Abigail's choice of a vacant seat between Hannah and Rico didn't work to keep Cam at bay. He simply grabbed an empty chair and dragged it next to her, turning it so he could straddle it and lean over its back. The position put his face disconcertingly close, a mere twelve inches away. She could feel his breath warming her cheek and skittering down her neck. She had the feeling he hoped his presence would drive her away, and it made her all the more determined to stay.

"I'd like to play." Abigail flashed an ornery smile at Cam and reached for a handful of matches. "You can't tell me a woman can't play when Hannah's in the game."

Rico looked appalled, but Hannah jumped in. "She's got a point."

Cam lifted his hands in surrender. "Why not? Go ahead, Rico, deal her in."

Rico slid his chair around to make room for Cam, then scraped up the cards to reshuffle.

"I suppose you need to sit there to win." Abigail stared pointedly until Cam slid his chair over.

Two hours later she held a fat bundle of matches in the circle of her thumb and forefinger as Rico stared glumly.

"Never seen an actual lady play like that," Hannah said, folding her last hand and tossing it aside. "We've been suckered, gents."

"I think she speaks the truth, señorita," complained Rico. "You bluffed. You are not at all sick."

"*I* never said I was. Blame Cam and Digger." Especially Cam, Abigail thought, the way he sat there, watching her with eyes that glowed with the dark light of interest. She'd played more recklessly than ever in her life and had won several large pots on outrageous bluffs.

Cam scratched one of his remaining matches on the bottom of the table and watched it burn itself out between his fingers. "Sorry, *compadre*, I didn't think she could actually play. I seem to underestimate Miss Morgan continually."

"You make assumptions because I'm female," Abigail said.

Cam dipped his head, granting her the point. He studied her thoughtfully for a moment, his tongue curled against the center of his upper lip. Abigail felt it as though it touched her own lips. Cam smiled and turned to Rico. "Come on, let's go do a quick walk around."

"You boys watch your step out there," Hannah said.

The two men disappeared into the night. Hannah began piling personal items and clothing on one end of her cot.

Abigail's curiosity grew as she watched, and she finally asked, "Are you going somewhere?"

"Could say that."

"Back to, um . . ." Abigail didn't quite know how to put it.

"To work. At the whorehouse." Hannah said the word harshly, as though she was trying to shock Abigail.

It worked. Unsure of what to say, Abigail stretched the bound edge of the wrapper between her fingers.

"Yep, got to get back to work before my regulars start missing me," Hannah continued, watching Abigail for a reaction. "Claiming the monthlies doesn't work for more'n a week or so. Been longer than that already, but when you got sick, Cam wanted me to stay an extra day or two, in case you needed something it wasn't proper for a man to provide."

"Oh," Abigail said weakly. "That was considerate."

"That's Cam all over." Hannah fetched a worn carpetbag out of the corner and started filling it with the items on the cot. "Not like some of the men who come in. Tell me, do *nice* women like you ever wonder about the men who visit someone like me?"

Abigail decided the way to turn the conversation around was to stop being shocked. "I never had much reason to think about it before. I suppose they must be lonely."

"Doubt their wives would think so."

There went not being shocked. "Surely married men don't go to bordellos."

"A lot of my customers are married. Most of the regulars."

"But why . . . ?"

"Some like being with somebody different now and again. Some like things kind of nasty, if you know what I mean." Abigail had no idea what Hannah meant, but she nodded and Hannah went on. "Mostly they swear they don't get enough attention at home, but I know that ain't always true, 'cause I've seen too many fellows get married and keep right on coming in without hardly even a break for the honeymoon."

Abigail cleared her throat. "Well, I—"

"In fact, that's what I got to get back for." Hannah tossed in her hairbrush and latched the carpetbag. "I got a fellow been coming in twice a month for almost as long as I've been working. Last time I saw him, I thought it'd be the end of it, since he was getting married, but nope. He said he'd be coming in regular, didn't matter about the new wife. He did mention he wouldn't be in for a little while, since it'd interfere with the wedding. But seeing as the wedding's postponed for a while, Cam and I figure we'd best not chance it."

Hornets buzzed in Abigail's head. She sagged to the cot, and her voice came out in a ragged whisper. "Franklin?"

"None other."

"You're lying."

"If you say so."

"This is some story Garrett dreamed up for you to tell me."

"He doesn't even know I'm telling it. Probably wouldn't approve." Hannah shrugged. "This is woman to woman. Frank likes to watch sometimes, and he gets rough now and again, worse than most. I ain't sure what he'd be like with a wife, but I kinda felt like I ought to warn you."

"Franklin's not like that. You're lying."

" 'Cause I'm a whore." Hannah shoved the carpetbag off onto the floor and sat down across from Abigail. "Don't say I didn't warn you. Who else is going to tell you something like that?"

"Nobody, because it's not true."

"Then ask yourself this, honey. How did you know I was talking about Frank in the first place?"

Abigail still hadn't come up with a satisfactory answer to that question by the time Hannah and Rico rode out the next morning. Standing by the cabin door, swathed in a blanket, she watched Cam see his friends off. She missed Hannah's wrapper already. She was very conscious of her stocking-clad legs, left exposed by the nightshirt.

"You must play poker with me again when I return, señorita," Rico said before he rode off. "I must have a chance to win back my matches."

"If you think you can," Abigail replied, casting a glance Cam's way.

"In a few days, then. *Adios.*"

"*Adios.* Bye, Hannah." Cam watched them until they disappeared, then headed toward the fire, leaving Abigail behind. A few minutes later he came back up with a bundle of her clothes in his arms. "Digger said you can have these back, provided you take it easy."

"Thank you." Abigail reached for the clothes, but Cam dodged past her and set everything on the foot of her cot. The smell of coffee and frying bacon wafted up the hill. "That smells wonderful this morning. I can hardly wait to eat."

"I suppose Henderson brings you breakfast in bed every morning," Cam said.

"How do you know about Henderson?" Abigail asked cautiously, trying to recall if she'd ever mentioned the name.

"You were talking in your sleep last night. You mentioned him. You spoke like he might be a servant."

"She," Abigail said, worried about what else she might have said. She shook out her traveling suit. It was dusty and wrinkled, but it would do. At least the washables were all clean. She wondered briefly just who had laundered her unmentionables and where they'd been hung to dry in a camp full of men.

"Henderson is our maid," Abigail went on. "She only brings my breakfast up when I've been out late. I think I was dreaming that I was home. Everything was back to normal, and we'd been to the theater." A subsequent pair of dreams bore more significance, but she wasn't about to recount those. "Father bought us all subscriptions to a Shakespeare festival this summer."

"What play did you see? In your dream, I mean."

"What a strange question."

"Curiosity. Do you remember?"

"*Troilus and Cressida.*" It was a lie, but the name of

Shakespeare's most obscure play came easily to her lips. "This is a ridiculous conversation."

"We can talk about the weather, if you'd rather."

"I'd rather you step out so I can change." Abigail pointed toward the door.

Cam went obediently, but he waited just outside while she dressed. When she went to put her things away, Abigail noticed a pair of her drawers were missing.

They were in Hannah's carpetbag, no doubt. Well, she hoped they'd bind and be forever irritating.

Cam pounced as soon as she opened the door. "Why didn't you bring Henderson with you?"

"To keep you from holding two hostages. Really, Mr. Garrett, you are being nosy this morning." Abigail gathered her skirts close as she stepped past him and headed down the hill at a steady but careful pace. Despite her protestations of health, her legs felt a bit wobbly from lack of exercise. She nabbed a seat between two of his men. Safe between her buffers, she asked one to pass the biscuits.

"You don't have to tell me if you'd rather not." Cam nodded at the cowboy who passed a plate Abigail's way. "Want some coffee?"

"Yes, thank you. Henderson didn't want to come West. I'm afraid the poor woman pictured Indians behind every rock, ready to ambush her and steal her virtue." Abigail could have bitten her own tongue off. Instead she chose to scald it with a big gulp of the freshly poured coffee.

"If only she'd known," he said dryly, echoing Abigail's thoughts to a tee. "Ah, got it."

> For beauty, wit,
> High birth, vigour of bone, desert in service,
> Love, friendship, charity, are subjects all
> To envious and calumniating time.
> One touch of nature makes the whole world kin.

"*Troilus and Cressida,* Act Three, I think. Took me a minute."

The olive-skinned man on Abigail's right excused himself, and Cam plunked into the vacant spot next to Abigail, looking as if he'd staged a successful ambush of his own. "Don't gape like that, Abby, it's rude. Pass the ham."

Ingrained etiquette prompted her to reach for the dented tin platter and hold it up as he speared a thick, pink slab of meat.

Cam continued. "Very interesting choice of plays to dream about. Then again, maybe you were just hoping to flummox me with something obscure."

"It obviously didn't work," Abigail answered in as light a tone as she could muster, but she felt her cheeks burn as she belatedly recalled the heroine's behavior with men: Not a day after Cressida pledged complete fidelity to Troilus, she was kissing every general in the Greek army and batting her pretty eyes at Diomedes. Lord, why hadn't she picked something with a more uplifting female lead? By the sparkle of amusement in Cam's eye, he remembered Cressida's foibles as clearly as she did, and probably chose to attribute them to Abigail. Considering her behavior the past few days, she wasn't so sure there weren't real parallels.

"Delicious eggs," she muttered, stabbing a yolk.

With a laugh Cam turned his attention to Jesús. They talked of guard duties and Franklin's futile efforts to find them.

"Yep, sure going to miss Hannah around here," Digger said to no one in particular a few minutes later.

Several of the men nodded agreement, including Cam.

A spasm of uncalled-for jealousy gripped Abigail. How could a man capable of quoting Shakespeare associate with such a woman?

The same way Franklin could, a nasty, honest little inner voice interjected.

She knew then that she believed every awful word Hannah

had said. She squeezed her eyes shut against the sudden threat of tears.

"You okay, miss?" Digger asked.

"Hmmm? Fine, fine. I just got a little something in my eye."

Stretching his arms over his head, Cam inhaled deeply and allowed the past days' strain to fall away. The afternoon air tasted of summer dust and woodsmoke, but it was still the sweetest air he'd ever breathed. The mountains were bred into him, and all the forced years in the flat cities of the East hadn't changed that.

He glanced around for Abby and found her talking with Digger at the fire. She was so pleased to be up and around, she'd hung about all morning. He'd have to keep an eye on her for signs of the mountain sickness returning, but from the looks of her appetite, she was on the road to a full recovery.

"Watch out, friend," Cam warned Digger with a smile. "The woman plays a mean hand of poker and bluffs like a riverboat gambler. I've never seen Rico fold to a busted flush before."

Eating crow was worth the sparkle of satisfaction in Abby's eyes.

A few minutes later she hiked up to the cabin on her own. Cam followed at a distance. When he started in the door, Abby was headed for the stream, pail in hand.

Cam blocked her path. "You still don't follow instructions very well."

"I'm fine, really, I'm not short of breath at all."

"Fine. Let's keep you that way." Cam snagged the pail handle. Abby held on, and his strength pulled her close. Those beautiful, tempting lips hovered within reach. He started to lower his head, until the jingle of spurs warned him of an approaching audience.

"I'll get your water," Cam said. She just stood there,

all soft-eyed and stunned-looking, and a small part of him chuckled.

"Boss," Charlie called when Cam was about halfway to the stream. "Billy's busted out of the remuda again. He won't let me near him."

With a sigh Cam deposited the pail under a tree and went to round up his horse. The bay was a fine animal, but he had a tendency to ignore the flimsy rope corral and wander. Only occasionally would he let anyone besides Cam lead him back.

Cam's soft whistle brought a whinny of interest. He traipsed down through the brush to find Billy standing in the middle of the stream. The best part of an hour rushed past before Cam coaxed Billy back into the company of the other horses, and returned to the cabin with the water.

Abby was waiting. Cam no sooner stuck his nose in the door than she stood up. He knew he was in trouble from the board she'd apparently stitched into her jacket while he was gone.

"It has become clear, Mr. Garrett, that we have a problem."

Chapter 6

Cam deposited the pail on the crude slab that served as washstand and work counter, then faced Abby.

"We certainly do," he said. "Let's hear what you think it is."

"Chaperons."

"I beg your pardon?"

"We have no chaperons." Abby sounded as prissy as an old schoolmarm, and Cam had to work to keep the smile off his face. "Hannah and Rico are no longer here. If you think I'm going to stay in this cabin with you for a single night without a chaperon, you'd best reconsider."

"Rico and Hannah stayed outside the night you were sick."

"I didn't realize that. Nonetheless, I want someone to keep you in check. You've already proved how unreliable you are by stealing a kiss, and trying again just a little while ago. I cannot allow that to happen again."

"I don't need anyone to keep me in check. As for stealing a kiss, I warned you, and you didn't stop me. By the way, I enjoyed it very much. And you did, too."

"I didn't," Abby claimed, but her eyes fluttered shut for the briefest instant before she spoke, and afterward her shoulders slumped a little.

"You can do better than that," Cam chided her gently. "Rico never would have folded to a bluff that bad."

"You know it's improper. After all, I'm engaged to be married." Staring at her ring, she repeated firmly, "I cannot allow it to happen again."

"Then it's very simple. The next time I start to kiss you, all you have to do"—Cam stepped closer—"is look me in the eye . . . and tell me no."

For a long time Abby stared at a point on his chest somewhere around his third shirt button. Taking a deep breath, she squared her shoulders and lifted her chin to meet his gaze. Her lips parted, and Cam waited for his gamble to fail.

But no sound came. Eyes locked to Abby's in challenge and promise, Cam carefully lowered his head. He brushed his lips over hers in the lightest possible kiss. Still the word didn't come, and soon it couldn't as his lips closed over her mouth. He allowed himself a slow, thorough exploration, the kiss he thought she'd want, not the plunder he really wanted to wreak. She tasted like clover honey. When she swayed against him, he knew he'd judged right.

A soft moan fluttered in her throat, a sound that excited Cam but seemed to frighten Abby. She stiffened in his arms and began to struggle.

Cam broke off the kiss instantly and released her. His regretful sigh came naturally, more naturally than the discipline required to step back. "I'll take that as a no."

"I cannot believe you did that."

"That I kissed you, or that I let you go?" Cam asked, his voice a bit more ragged than it should be.

"Either . . . I mean, neither . . . I mean, I was right. This situation is intolerable. I insist you produce a suitable chaperon or arrange separate sleeping quarters."

"I'm telling you, you're as safe in this cabin with me as you want to be. Besides, we're a little shy on old maid aunts around here."

"A couple of your men will do."

"Most of them would be, I'm certain, quite willing to crawl into your bed if the opportunity presented itself." That shook her, even if it was an exaggeration. Cam pressed the point: "Or to ignore me if I chose to do so."

"What about Digger?"

"All right, I'll ask him at supper. Meantime, I want you to take it easy. That means a nap. No water hauling."

Defiance written on her face, Abby lifted the pail.

"Abby," Cam warned.

"Just washing up first." She poured a generous amount of water in the basin and set the pail back. "Even prisoners are allowed to do that. Get out."

The afternoon shadows that come so early to narrow mountain valleys had already crept over the cabin. Cam stood with one foot on an upended log beside the door, shaping the brim of his hat and listening to the vigorous splash of water inside. He wondered if its coolness could wash away the smudge of his lips from around Abby's mouth.

It probably could, he decided as he walked down the hill.

Abigail accepted her second piece of coal-baked gingerbread from Digger with chagrin. She seemed to be consuming as much as any of Cam's men, probably a result of the mountain air.

"Delicious," she said around a mouthful of gingerbread. She turned to Cam. "Ask him."

Cam explained the situation succinctly to Digger but without mention of the incidents that burned so clearly in her mind. "So Abby would like you to bunk in the cabin."

"I really don't like sleepin' inside any time the weather's half tolerable," Digger said. "Makes my skin crawl. Maybe one of the other fellas'll do it. Sorry, Cam. Miss."

He wandered back toward the fire, and Abigail glared at Cam. "You knew he wouldn't agree when I suggested him."

"You can still pick someone else," Cam offered. "While you do, I have some things to take care of."

He disappeared into the blackness beyond the fire, taking his gingerbread with him, and Abigail turned a critical eye on his men. After Cam's earlier, shocking comments concerning the others, she spied shortcomings in every man she considered, the most common being youth or a leering cast of eye.

Her choices seemed slim. Abigail quickly counted the men and added in the watchers she assumed stood guard up the mountain. Four men besides Rico were absent. She'd been too distracted to notice.

"Where is everyone?" she asked Charlie, who sat nearby.

"Fellows come and go a lot."

"With the money, I suppose."

"No, ma'am. The money don't have nothing to do with it. Why, we don't even keep more than what we need for supplies and such."

"Why on earth would you steal it, then?"

"To helps folks out." The freckled face split into a grin, and Charlie flicked a strand of reddish-brown hair away from his mouth. "And to aggravate old Tanner."

"You make it sound as if you only steal from him."

"Well, him and the Fidelity, but that's all out of the same barrel, way I see it."

"Why?"

"To make him pay." Vehemence cracked Charlie's voice, reminding Abigail just how young the boy was. The flickering campfire picked out a halo of peach fuzz along his jaw and upper lip. "Tanner's hurt every man here, one way or the other, and plenty more that aren't able to ride with us. We're all helping Cam even things out with the old snake.

Beggin' your pardon, miss, but him being your betrothed and all, you must know how he is."

"I thought I did," Abby muttered, half to herself, then she turned a brittle smile in Charlie's direction. "But apparently I was mistaken. I'd be very much obliged if you would tell me more."

Charlie suddenly looked uncomfortable. "Cam'd be riled if he heard me talking out of turn."

"Nonsense." Abigail took her gingerbread and scooted over to a rock next to the boy. "You're not going to give away any secrets or plans. Just tell me what Franklin did to you that would make you want to steal from him. Please."

Loose scree shifted under Cam's boots as he cleared the top of the ridge. A low voice challenged him from the inky shadow of a boulder. Cam froze, his hands well out from his sides.

"It's Garrett. Evening, Ephram. Brought you something from Digger." Cam held out the gingerbread.

"Thanks, boss. This stuff's almost as good as my Louise's." The man relaxed. "Fine night. Not a sign of trouble."

They sat in silence for a while as Cam scanned the nearly invisible slopes of the mountains beyond the valley, looking for any trace of campfire or other light. He turned full circle, peering into the black, so any odd form could penetrate his brain. Nothing. After a brief word with Ephram, he headed back down the slope.

From a clear vantage point just above the mine, he noticed Abby had moved to sit closer to Charlie, who sat there looking way too serious, his head bent close to hers in conversation. Abby listened intently, nodding. Their proximity made Cam squirm, especially when she patted the boy's arm.

Where the blazes was Digger, letting her work the boy for information like that?

Cam lengthened his stride. The scree tumbled away in miniature landslides, carrying him downward an extra yard or so with each step, but by the time he reentered the circle of light, Charlie was walking away. Cam thought he caught a glint of tears in the boy's blue eyes.

Abby, on the other hand, was dry-eyed and thin-lipped, perched so stiff and still on her rock that she looked like a statue. Cam sat down beside her. Just above the lace trimming of her collar her pulse beat quickly.

"I saw you with Charlie. What did he tell you?" Cam asked.

"Nothing." Abby looked up at him, a strained half-grin tugging at her lips. "At least nothing for you to worry about. He knows better than to give away your secrets, Mr. Garrett. He admires you a great deal."

"I imagine that goes against your grain."

Not a rise from her. Cam stared at the fire, trying to figure out what Charlie might have said to put Abby in this mood.

"Excuse me," she said a time later, rising. "I'd really like to be alone for a few minutes. And then I think I'll go to bed."

Without a fuss over a chaperon? Now he knew something had happened. Cam watched Abby make her way up the hill, then went in search of Charlie.

"Naw," the boy answered. "She didn't want to know about anything except me and why I ride with you."

"Just what did you tell her?"

"Mostly about how I'd like to string the son of a bitch up, but you won't let me." The tremor of pain in Charlie's voice told Cam he'd been right about the tears. "Are we going to get him, Cam?"

"We are."

"You know, I ain't seen Pa since he went off to that sanitarium. Are you sure they're taking good care of him?"

"The best care Tanner's money can buy. When this is all over, I'll take you up to see him, myself. Did you tell Abby about your father, too?"

Charlie nodded. "She's a nice lady. Pretty, too. I guess I kind of rattled on, but I swear, I didn't say a thing that could hurt anybody down the road. Sorry."

"Nothing to be sorry about." He squeezed the boy's shoulder and headed uphill toward the light that leaked out around the cabin's shutters. Cam rapped on the cabin door to warn Abby he was coming in, then pushed. The door gave a fraction of an inch, then stuck.

He tried again, rattling the door thoroughly just to be sure it wasn't jammed, then knocked harder.

"Abby." A shadow passed by the crack of light at the edges of the door. "Abby, I know you're in there. Open up."

"No." Her voice came crisp and clear and certain. "I told you, Mr. Garrett, I am not sleeping in this cabin alone with you."

"Well, I'm not spending the night out here."

"You should have considered that before you treated my request for a chaperon with such a cavalier attitude."

"Granted. But it's too late to find one now." Lowering his voice so his men wouldn't hear, Cam wheedled, "I proved earlier that you're safe with me."

"Oh, is that what that demonstration proved?"

"Come on, now, open the door."

"No."

"I'll be damned if I'll sleep on the ground without so much as a blanket."

"You won't have to. I threw your bedroll out before I barred the door. You're practically standing on it."

He looked down. Sure enough, there it was. Cam cursed, then stepped over it, heading for the window.

"I barred the shutters as well, so don't get any ideas about coming through the window." She sounded so blasted smug, he wanted to throttle her even as he laughed.

"Okay, Abby, you win. I'll sleep out here for tonight, but I want you to answer one question. Is it me you're afraid of—or yourself?"

Out beyond the cabin the underbrush crackled with the movement of some night creature. Cam listened to it, and to the sound of the creek below, and waited for Abby's answer. It never came, but the silence was an answer in itself.

Abigail paced back and forth in front of the door, stopping occasionally to survey the flimsy latch. It was nothing more than a stout branch dropped into crude brackets, designed to keep the door shut against weather and curious small animals. A determined man could kick it open easily enough or come through the loosely hung planks that shuttered the windows. That Cam didn't could only mean that he didn't really want to, and for that she was currently grateful.

Too many thoughts whirled through her mind to have to worry about Cam Garrett or her reactions to his attempts at seduction. She just didn't have the energy, mental or physical, to keep pushing him away right now. She needed to figure out the truth about him and Franklin Tanner.

Every time she put her mind to the problem, her world flipped upside down. The gentleman she'd planned to marry turned into a fiend, and her kidnapper became a hero.

Or did they? She just didn't know anymore.

She couldn't have been that wrong about Franklin, Abby told herself. She simply had to look at this logically.

Most of the things Charlie attributed to Franklin, from missing sheep to soured wells, could be accidents or acts of nature. The resulting foreclosure was almost certainly legal. The father's breakdown happened almost a year later. If Franklin ended up with the property, it might just be good money sense, like her grandfather had shown in building his business.

Then again, Charlie's tears were real; Abigail was certain of that. If Franklin had done half the things the boy had described, he deserved his hatred. According to Charlie, the rest of the men had equally valid reasons to despise Franklin—reasons that some sense of propriety or privacy unfortunately kept the boy from discussing them with her.

On the other hand, Charlie claimed that Cam paid for his father's care, and hinted that the money they stole went to help people fight off Tanner, as if Cam were some kind of Robin Hood, with a mob of cowboys as his Merry Men. What if Rico had taken all those packets of money to families in the valley?

It made sense, but Abigail's pride fought that conclusion. She could not have misjudged Franklin so badly. These men were outlaws and thieves; they were lying to her.

Hannah didn't lie. Abigail had no evidence, but she knew it as surely as she knew her own name. Franklin paid Hannah for her favors, and he intended to go right on doing so after he was married. What's more, he apparently hurt Hannah somehow. A man like that might be capable of almost anything. Heartsick and disgusted, Abigail collapsed onto a chair and stared into the steady flame of the lantern.

If I were a moth, she thought, *I could fly into that beautiful light and let the heat consume me.*

Or she could open the door and let Cam in, which would have the same effect.

"Just look me in the eye and say no," he'd said. "That's all it takes."

That's all. Just look into his mesmerizing eyes, then escape a kiss as potent and habituating as laudanum, and tell him you don't want any more of his drug. The only reason she'd escaped this afternoon was her instinctive reaction to the sensation of drowning, and the fact that Cam Garrett was good to his word—something she had trouble saying for herself these days.

Embarrassed, Abigail twisted at her emerald and ruby engagement ring. Whether or not Franklin Tanner was the man he presented himself to be, he most assuredly was her fiancé. She owed him some scrap of faithfulness, at least until she sorted the whole mess out.

How on earth could she manage that, stuck here in the mountains with these men? For all she knew, every time

Cam Garrett kissed her into stupefied confusion, he was laughing at Franklin. The idea infuriated her nearly as much as the idea that Franklin might have fooled her.

Abigail finally blew out the lantern and crawled into bed. The darkness surrounding her only made matters worse. The two men duelled in her thoughts, Cam constantly assuming the role of hero, beating Franklin back into the shadows where he suddenly seemed at home. She drifted off with Cam Garrett's bearded face laughing at her.

The next thing she knew, she smelled coffee. Cam's image had long since vanished in the piercing light that sliced through the cracks around the door. The sounds of men moving about and calling to each other drifted up the hill. Bracing herself against the chill that still permeated the cabin, Abigail dashed the blankets back and scrambled into her clothes. She started for the washbowl, anxious to get down the hill for a hot cup of that coffee and some warming sun.

Then she spotted it. She froze in midstep.

A battered tin cup sat on the rickety table, steam rising off the rich brown liquid it contained.

Impossible. Abigail surveyed the shutters and the door. All the bars rested in their brackets. There was no sign of disturbance. No one could have been in this cabin, yet a fresh cup of coffee sat on the table.

She touched the cup. The morning air had taken the scalding edge off, but the coffee's warmth held. Not more than a few minutes had passed since someone—Cam, of course—had put it on the table, only a few feet from where she'd slept.

Abigail headed for the door, primed for battle, ready to skewer Garrett with words in front of his men. Her hand on the latch bar, she stopped as another possibility struck her. She returned to the table.

Drinking the coffee gave Abigail time to consider her next step. For once, she wasn't going to play the game Cam's way. She stood a better chance at getting more information about the nature of the trouble between him and Franklin if she stayed calm. Maybe if she assembled the scattered pieces of the puzzle that linked the two men, she could find some way out of this situation. At the very least she'd have the tools to deal with Cam, and then with Franklin once he ransomed her—although the thought of seeing him again made the hairs lift along her arms.

Abigail dunked the empty cup in the pail, wiped it dry, then placed it on a shelf behind a pair of similar tin cups. If the gods smiled on her, Cam would never spot it and would be left wondering what had become of his little joke.

Let him wonder.

Garnering the confidence of another of Cam's men presented some difficulty. It would take more than the touch and warm smile that had primed Charlie. Abigail brushed out her hair and smoothed her skirt. A few quick pats brought a rosy glow to her cheeks.

"Just call me Miss Pinkerton," she whispered as she strolled down the hill to breakfast with her unsuspecting informants.

Digger scooped coals around the Dutch oven and piled more on the lid. "Works better than any ol' cookstove. You sure you want to be doin' that, miss? You sure don't look like you're enjoyin' it."

"I'm fine." How anybody could possibly enjoy skinning a rabbit escaped her. Abigail gritted her teeth and slipped the knife along under the skin of the belly and back legs the way Digger had shown her. At least whoever shot it had gutted it. "What next?"

"Now you grab it there"—Digger indicated an area near the back legs—"and pull. Just strip it off like you'd skin a cat. Aw, hell, I mean heck, miss. Just let me do it."

Seconds later the poor denuded bunny joined his brother on the slab of pine Digger used for a cutting board. Abigail hurried off to wash the blood from her hands, feeling like a Judas to the little cottontails she'd enjoyed chasing around her grandfather's lawn during the summers.

Still, she'd learned something. If she ever escaped, she'd need to eat, and skinning a rabbit was a first step.

A full morning spent loitering around the fire had paid off after lunch when the old miner accepted her offer of help. Clumsy as she was with the unfamiliar kitchen work, Digger seemed pleased to have her company. It gave her the perfect excuse to ignore Cam. He'd eventually wandered off to take care of whatever it was outlaws took care of—but not before she'd caught him watching her in a puzzled way. She thought of the cup and smiled.

Digger had ample time to finish his butchering before she drifted back.

"Got something a little easier." He held out a bowl containing some flour and lard, plus a pair of butter knives. "Mix that all up till it makes—"

"Pea-size pieces." Abigail grinned at finding something familiar at last. She held the two knives parallel between her fingers and began cutting the lard into the flour. "My brother and I used to sneak down to the kitchen when Cook made pies. If we helped, she'd bake the scraps up for us with cinnamon and sugar."

"My ma did the same thing. Guess kids is kids, no matter how rich they be." Knees creaking, Digger squatted to check the Dutch oven and its mess of cornbread.

"Father always wondered why our appetites were off." This was finally getting somewhere. Maybe now she could get a word or two out of the old fellow. Abigail decided to jump in. "Mr. Garrett says you're a miner."

"Was."

"Didn't you find any gold?"

"Plenty. That was the problem."

"I don't understand."

"Well, you see, me and Griff—he was my last partner—we had ourselves a claim up in Lake City awhile back. We barely had color at first, but . . ." Digger continued his story, losing Abigail in the talk of color and quartz, assays, lodes, and rockers. Then a too-familiar name yanked her attention back. "Yep, a few years back, ol' Tanner offered us five thousand apiece for our rights to the Becky Ann. I wanted to sell, but Griff didn't, and we'd made a deal never to sell without the other, so I stuck."

"I'm sure he appreciated it."

"Not for long, he didn't. See, that's when things started happening." Digger's gray eyes took on a faraway look. "Accidents, like. Rocker table collapsed. Pumps went bad from one day to the next. Replacin' and fixin' things ate up every penny we took out. Then we got bushwhacked on the way to town. The more gold we took out of the mine, the more problems we got. Tanner kept comin' back. Griff got more stubborn. Took to sleepin' right there at the claim, with a shotgun across his belly."

A coal tumbled off the fire. Digger flicked it back with a heavily callused finger. "Shotgun didn't do him no good when twenty yards of slope landed atop of him."

"Surely you don't think Franklin did that!"

Digger's eyes snapped into focus, and he stood up. "I shouldn't be talkin' about this with you, miss."

"You cannot make an accusation like that and then walk away from me."

After a long, hard look at Abigail, Digger nodded. "Nope. Suppose I can't. You already heard it this far, you might as well know the rest. Tanner showed up at Griff's wake with two thousand dollars cash money and a couple of boys lookin' serious enough to make a body think twice. I signed the Becky Ann over to him on the spot. Over the next few months he got the claims on all four sides, then he brought in some Welsh boys to drive a shaft. He was clearin' better'n three thousand a month up till late last year."

"What happened?"

"Seems there's no more gold." A thin grin tightened Digger's cheeks, and he moved off toward the box of cooking gear he kept off to one side. "Yes, it does seem that way."

Poking at the crumbles of dough in her bowl, Abigail considered Digger's story and tried to ignore the hollow ache deep in her chest.

Sleep came hard that night. The morning light rattled her awake to find a gaudy yellow feather, from one of the little canarylike birds that flitted around the stream, lying where the coffee had been the day before. Again Abigail checked the door and windows, and again she shook off the discomfort of knowing Cam was able to slip in and out while she slept.

The feather secreted inside the lining of her handbag, Abigail went down to breakfast. She greeted Cam amicably, noting with amusement the creases between his brows as he looked at her. Throughout his breakfast of biscuits and a spicy concoction Digger called redeye gravy, he looked somewhat confused by her mood.

When Cam finally strolled off, she went to talk to Lew.

"My fences kept getting knocked down," Lew said over a leftover piece of peach cobbler Abigail dished up for him midmorning. "We lost cattle every time. When my little girl took sick, the doc said she had to be someplace warm, so I sold out. Tanner gave me a middling decent price, but I know it was his men tearing the fences down to begin with. My wife's down in Tucson with little Melinda, staying with her kin. I surely do miss her, miss 'em both."

"So why are you here, doing this?"

"A man can't let himself be done bad like that without getting a few licks back."

The hollow ache spread inside her.

"My brother went to bring in the sheep," Jesús told her that evening when she caught him alone feeding the horses. "His little son found him the next day at the bottom of the arroyo, his neck broken. The earth had not yet settled on his coffin when Tanner bought our note from the bank and called it."

She went straight to the cabin, though the hour was early, and locked herself in. The more she learned about Franklin, the more disgust she felt for him—and for herself, for letting him take her in so thoroughly. Whatever Franklin had done to Cam, it must have been horrible. She paced the dirt floor of the cabin well into the night. Cam knocked once, late, but went away when she did not answer.

The next morning the table held a thumb-size crystal of translucent amethyst, still warm from Cam's hand. Abigail tucked it deep in the pocket of her skirt and started for breakfast.

Chores kept the men busy all morning, but after lunch she plunked herself into the middle of a group of men sharing a smoke beneath a tree.

"Why do you ride with Cam?" she asked.

Several hats got pulled down to shade suspicious eyes. Boots scuffled in the dirt as two of the men rose to leave.

"I've already discovered that Franklin Tanner isn't the man I thought," Abigail said. "I'm engaged to him. I think I have the right to know just how bad he is. Please."

Antonio, dark eyes flashing in anger, walked away.

The other man looked around the rough circle, shrugged, and sat back down with the others. "My only spring went sour," he started off. "Right in the middle of summer, when the creeks ran dry. Cattle took sick and I lost better than three-quarters of my herd. The bank took my place, and Tanner bought it from them."

His words seemed to stir the other men's anger, and their stories began to tumble out.

" . . . Pa got gunned down . . . never found out who . . ."

" . . . accused of stealing Fidelity cattle. My wife was scared off our property while I was in jail. We forfeited."

" . . . prize bull broke out of his stall. Found him mired up to his eyeballs. Watched him die along with my dreams . . ."

The litany of misfortune went on and on. Abigail dug her fingers into her palms and forced herself to hear it all as Franklin's handsome, square-jawed face, smiling at her as he had the night they'd met, swam in and out of focus.

"That's the way it is, miss," Pete finally said. "Fidelity just keeps growing and growing, eating up the little ranchers like we was pancakes on Tanner's table. We all know he's behind the trouble, and not one of us can prove it."

"The sheriff might as well be some fancy watch fob, the way he dangles out of Tanner's pocket," added Ephram.

"Surely someone has stood up to him."

"Nope. At least nobody who's had much luck outside of Cam."

"Why is Cam in the middle of this?" An uncomfortable silence met Abby's question. She waited a moment, then asked again, "What did Franklin do to him?"

They all looked at each other, and finally Ephram straightened up. "Sorry, miss, but if Cam wants you to know, it's his business to tell you, not ours. Let's just leave it at this. We all give it up till Cam showed up with everything all figured out, how to get—"

"That's enough," Pete interrupted. "You'll be excusing us all, miss. We got chores to do."

Seconds later Abigail sat alone in the shade, the final pieces of the puzzle still out of reach.

Frustration added to the turmoil in her belly. The gnawing felt enough like hunger to lead her toward Digger, who put her to work so quickly she barely had time to grapple with the facts of the stories she'd just heard.

Skirt gathered well back from the glowing coals, Abigail bent over some chunky applesauce with a long wooden spoon. Skin from the dried apples swirled through the cinnamon-laced mixture Digger had prepared.

"You been askin' a lot of questions the past couple of days," Digger said as he sawed at a big ham. "You gettin' the answers you want?"

"No, but they're what I need."

Digger tossed a slab of meat on his big black skillet. "You still planning to marry Tanner?"

Abigail lifted her chin to stare at Digger across the fire. His eyes said he already knew the answer, just as she did. It had been clear to her for days now, even if she hadn't wanted to admit it to herself. The fatty, salt-encrusted edges of the ham danced and popped with the heat. She heard the slight jingle of spurs behind her and knew it was Cam before he even spoke.

"That's an answer I'd like to hear, too."

Chapter 7

Abigail continued stirring, moving the spoon in precise figure eights that kept the applesauce from sticking to the bottom of the cast-iron pot. Her fingertips turned white where she gripped the handle.

"Can't you just leave me alone?"

Cam squatted beside her. "I've done just that for several days now, if you haven't noticed."

"Of course I have, and if I had been less concerned with being secretive, I'd have noticed it sooner. You wanted me to talk to your men. You wanted me to hear all those stories."

"It wasn't in my plans, but once you started, I figured you might as well hear it. You'd never get the truth on the Fidelity."

"The truth. For all I know, every one of those stories was complete invention for my benefit."

"Why would we do that?"

"To make me a more malleable hostage. To win my sympathy for your crimes."

"You looked every one of those men in the eye. Do you really think any of them lied to you?"

The faces reeled through Abby's mind, the agony of loss clear on each one, but the truth she'd been willing to admit to Digger a moment earlier promised to make her more vulnerable before Cam. She dug in her heels stubbornly. "Franklin's involvement is all circumstantial. Not one of your men presented any concrete proof that Franklin was involved in their trouble."

"Fifteen years ago every one of these men ran a successful ranch. Then Tanner landed in this valley like some bloated locust and started devouring them, one by one." Cam's face reflected some of the pain she'd seen in his men.

"Did he devour yours, too?" Abigail asked quietly.

Like smoke wafted away on the wind, the pain passed from Cam's face, replaced by something dark and forbidding.

"He did, didn't he?" Abigail prodded. "That's what's behind this war."

"At least you understand what it is."

"I'm a prisoner of your infernal war; of course I understand it. Why don't you ever answer a question?"

"I take after you. Are you going to marry Tanner or not, knowing what you do about him?"

"That's between Franklin and me. I don't care to discuss it with you."

"Well, if you have any doubts, talk to Hannah the next time you see her. He goes whoring at the drop of a hat. She can tell you things about him that would turn your stomach."

"She already has." Sickened, Abigail dropped the spoon beside the pot and walked away. Cam scrambled after her. Behind them, Digger fussed about people who didn't finish what they started.

"I'm sorry," Cam said when he caught up with her by the stream. "I had no cause to be that vulgar."

Franklin is the vulgar one, Abigail thought. She marched past a tall clump of white bitterroot growing by the stream. She decided to follow the tumbling waters upstream, toward the peak in the near distance.

"Where are we going?" Cam asked.

"To see if there's another way out of this little prison camp of yours," Abby said. She wanted to be anyplace but with Cam. He was more dangerous to her than Franklin, by any measure.

"I already told you the cliff path's the only safe way in or out."

"You don't mind if I see for myself."

Cam shrugged and kept following.

The stream's course climbed the length of the valley. Abigail traced her way along as it curved left, past the rope corral, and out of sight of the cabin. She slowed as the path grew steeper.

"Take it easy," Cam urged. "You're still supposed to be resting."

The stream curved back to the right, hooking around behind a wall of rock Abigail had thought formed the upper end of the valley. Instead, and to her surprise, the valley continued behind the ridge, widening into a small but relatively flat area covered evenly with aspen. The paper white and black trunks were interspersed with wispy grasses and a scattering of flowers. Her anger vanished, erased by the unexpected beauty of the place.

"Oh," Abigail sighed. Above her head the spade-shaped leaves of the aspens quivered nervously. A moment later the barest breeze grazed her cheek. "For a minute I thought I made them quake," she admitted when Cam raised an eyebrow at her delighted exclamation. Another stirring of breeze set the aspens shivering again. "They're wonderful. The whole place is."

"You should see this country in the autumn. Whole mountainsides turn gold, and when the wind comes through, it's like the sun has shattered and fallen onto the trees."

Something akin to awe tinged Cam's voice.

"I can almost see it, when you say it that way." Abigail threaded her way into the stand. Beyond the trees a nearly vertical slope of ground rose toward the sky. Midway up, the water poured into the valley through a narrow cut, roiling down in a series of small waterfalls that beat a fine mist out of the water as it fell.

A thin, barely discernible trail zigzagged up a few yards from the stream. Abigail followed it upward with her eyes. It petered out somewhere shy of the ridgetop, or perhaps just grew too faint to see. Depending on what was on the other side of that ridge, it might be worth the climb—to someone who could handle the height.

As she groaned in temporary defeat, she heard humming behind her and glanced over her shoulder.

Cam leaned against a tree, an "I told you so" look on his face. "Even the deer have enough sense not to use that trail much. Once you get up top, you have your choice of breaking your leg in a field of boulders the size of a Conestoga or dropping over a cliff worse than the one you like so much."

"What about the other side?" Abigail asked, surveying the west wall.

"More of the same, roughly."

"Plus three men on guard around the rim of the valley, just in case I decide to try anyway."

"There is that," Cam agreed amiably. "Actually, they're mostly watching for people coming in, but I'm sure they'd notice if you headed out. Anyway, the walk up here wasn't a waste. Come on, there's something else you might as well see while you're here."

Without so much as a by-your-leave, he steered Abigail back toward the water's edge, the flat of his hand a firm, persuasive pressure on her shoulder.

"That looks like a columbine." Needing a diversion, Abigail darted away toward a lacy plant on the verge of blooming.

"It is."

A few heavy buds, partly unfurled, drooped at the ends of long stems. Abigail touched one. "These look like they'll be blue. I've only seen red and yellow."

"Blue for the Colorado sky and white centers for the snow, or so they say. Up higher the blue fades out almost white, then they really do look like doves. The name, columbine, comes from—"

"*Columba*, for dove," Abigail said, proving she'd studied her Latin, too, and wondering once again about his education and how easily he could throw her off balance. She hardly remembered what they'd been talking about. "You never did say where you learned those lines from the play."

"An instructor of mine held the benighted opinion that *Troilus and Cressida* was old Will's unsung masterpiece. I had to recite Ullyses' speech once for punishment. Part of it stuck."

"What had you done?"

One corner of Cam's mouth twitched up in a grin. "Nothing too terrible. Come see what's over here." Cam directed her on through the trees to the stream's edge.

Following the lay of the land, the stream also broadened here among the aspens. While the main force of water continued its rush down the valley, a portion of it swirled out of the channel to form a shallow, clear pool. The gravel bottom sparkled in the few rays of sun that spilled over the ridgetop so late in the afternoon.

"I come up here most mornings to wash off," Cam said.

An image of Cam by the pool—stripped to the waist, drops of water scattered like diamonds across his bare chest and shoulders—strayed into Abigail's mind. She tried very hard to stop the blush that rose up from her collar, but failed.

A dull, brick-colored pebble lay at her feet. Abigail stooped to dip the stone into the pool, hoping the water's sheen would reveal a richer color—and provide a needed diversion for her thoughts. Seconds later, biting cold sunk into her joints like fangs.

She jerked her hand out, her blush disrupted by the shock. "If you bathe in that, you're a lunatic!"

"You're the maiden who makes me sleep in the moonlight." Cam reached out and cradled her hand in his, massaging her fingers to restore their warmth.

"I thought water got warmer in pools," Abby said.

"Only if it sits. Besides, this comes right off the snow up on top of the peak. It's really not so bad, once you're used to it. You ought to come up some morning. I'll arrange some privacy, and you can take time to explore after you're through with your bath. It's an interesting pocket of treasures."

As he spoke, his touch grew less therapeutic and more personal, his fingertips drifting across her palm and over the smooth flesh on the inside of her wrist. A shiver ran up her arm and across her shoulders. Abigail tried to credit it to the water's chill, but her pulse fluttered from the sheer pleasure of his touch.

"In fact," he added with a smile, "occasionally a person can find a few crystals of amethyst in the pool."

"You found it—er, really? How interesting." Blast it all, he'd almost caught her out while she was distracted. Even worse, he'd distracted her in order to catch her out. But what a lovely distraction, she thought, almost worth losing the game.

"You and amethyst share certain qualities: all points and hard edges, but beautiful to look at and smooth to the touch."

Ignoring Abigail's halfhearted efforts to free her hand, Cam continued tracing patterns on her palm, spirals that expanded outward like the sensations they created through her body. The reaching edge of the pattern touched the hollowness deep inside Abby, promising to fill that place with light and movement as heady as any waltz. With a shock she realized she wanted Cam to kiss her.

He wanted it, too. His eyes had that look, the one she was coming to recognize, to anticipate.

Abigail swayed forward slightly, leaning into the kiss she knew was coming. She watched as Cam's head dropped, as his lips parted slightly.

Her breath caught in her throat as he bypassed her offered mouth. He lifted her hand and kissed her palm instead, moving his lips over the sensitive skin, repeating with his tongue the spiral his fingers had traced moments earlier. His full beard and mustache dusted over her palm around the edges of the spiral, enhancing its effect. She watched him, mesmerized. Meeting her eyes, he paused to nip at the full mound at the base of her thumb, and her gasp, not of pain, but of pleasure, brought a low chuckle from Cam.

He kissed her hand again, then curled her fingers shut, trapping the warmth of his kiss in her grasp. Cam tugged her toward him. A slight shift, and she went into his arms, her mouth searching for his lips.

Cam obliged, thoroughly, dipping his tongue into her mouth in a long, lazy foray that set her mouth afire. His whiskers smelled faintly of soap and of pine smoke from the fire, and as she reached up to run her fingers through the scruff, Abby wondered inanely if the golden dusting of curls across his chest would carry the same scents, and if they would tickle her cheek quite the same way.

As much as she wanted to know, she had no chance to find out. Cam began to ease back, but Abigail moved onto tiptoe, following him, trying to extend the exquisite contact. With a final, gentle nibble at her lower lip that made her catch her breath once more, Cam firmly gripped her shoulders and set her away.

"Digger will be frying our ham into saddle leather," he said. He held her a few inches away, close enough that the heat of his body spanned the distance. "He's likely to send somebody looking for us. We'd better go."

Abigail nodded reluctantly.

"The offer holds. Anytime you want to come up here, let me know. I'd suggest early morning. It can be magical, Abby." Cam brushed a tendril of hair off her temple, his fingers lingering on her skin a moment longer than necessary.

"Magical," he repeated, and she felt sure the word contained an offer to act as her personal magician.

The first hues of sunset tinted the sky just a shade pinker than the crystal of amethyst hidden in her pocket. With Cam's arm around her waist, they made their way back downstream. Her left hand still protected the kiss he'd given her. She dared a glance sideways, caught the edge of a smile tugging the corner of Cam's eyes, and her heart stumbled like a drunkard.

In that instant Abigail knew that her decision not to marry Franklin Tanner had nothing to do with what he'd done to Charlie and the others.

It didn't matter if every grimy story she'd heard about Franklin in the last two weeks turned out to be an out and out lie; it didn't matter if every scene in the past week had been staged for her benefit. Somewhere along the line, and without realizing it, she'd concluded she could never marry a man she didn't love. Therefore, she couldn't marry Franklin; she knew she didn't love him.

Because I'm falling in love with Cam. The thought ricocheted through Abigail's mind like a bullet in a barrel.

Impossible.

Absolutely impossible. She wouldn't allow herself to feel this way. Not toward a man who was using her for revenge, not toward a common outlaw.

The trouble was, there was nothing common about Cam Garrett, from the poetry he quoted, to the way he kissed her.

Just the thought of those kisses made her feel as if she'd downed an entire magnum of champagne. She placed her feet very carefully as she walked beside him down the hill.

Amethysts were supposed to protect the owner from drunkenness, Abby recalled as she fingered the stone hidden in her pocket. Pressing her thumb into the sharp, crystalline point, she hoped fervently that hers would work against the potent wine Cam Garrett brewed.

Maybe he'd been a fool to break off that kiss. Maybe he should have gone ahead and kept her up by the pool, seen what might come of that amazing desire he'd felt in her.

Cam sat across the fire from Abby, watching her poke at her beans. Sometime on the walk down, her mood had changed. He wasn't sure what it was, embarrassment over how freely she'd kissed him, sadness—or anger—over Tanner, or something else. She'd crawled inside herself, though, and now Cam wondered if he'd have to start all over again to seduce her.

Digger ambled over, interrupting Cam's thoughts.

"My thumb's hurtin', boss. Trouble comin'."

"It already has." Cam grinned at his friend. "Most likely a storm is coming. You know it's just rheumatism."

"Trouble ache's different from the weather ache. I can tell." Digger waggled the predictive digit, his right, a scarred mess ever since Cam had known him. Cam put little stock in its portents, but Digger and half the outfit swore by it. "Bet Tanner's up to somethin'. When's Rico due back?"

"Two, maybe three days. Oh, no, I recognize that face, Digger. Don't you go spouting your gloom to anyone else."

"Wouldn't do that. Already too quiet around this fire tonight, Cam, and New York'd be the worst of the lot, all turned inside out." Digger's eyes accused Cam over the rim of a plate as he scooped beans and crumbled corn bread into his mouth. Cam wondered just how much the old man had guessed about his plans for Abby.

"You're as much at fault as anybody," Cam replied. "You told her about Griff."

"'At was two days ago."

"But it made her curious. She heard the rest of Tanner's sins today. I think it's all just sinking in. Plus she's probably tired out. Stubborn little fool had to go see the top end of the valley for herself. I'm still not all that easy about her lungs."

"She'll be fine, but I sure do hope she don't stir the men up no more. Can't stand a fire this quiet." Grumbling, Digger went back to his favorite spot.

Bad memories being no friend to a pleasant evening around the campfire, the men drifted off almost as soon as they finished eating. After a time only a couple of them remained in the circle of light—one of them being young Charlie, who'd grabbed a place at Abby's feet and had spent the meal staring at her with something suspiciously like adoration.

Curse it, the kid had gone sweet on the woman. It was a wonder more of the men hadn't joined him, seeing how long they'd been stuck up here in the mountains. Cam tried to ignore the knot he got in his gut at the thought of Abby with any of his men.

After topping off his coffee, he headed Charlie's way. "Digger needs help with wash up."

"But I—" Charlie protested. Cam jerked his thumb over his shoulder, and the boy flushed. "Uh, sure, Cam. Come on, Jesús, give me a hand. It's your turn anyways."

Abby looked up as Cam requisitioned Charlie's spot. Was that embarrassment or desire coloring her cheeks? Cam couldn't tell by firelight, but it didn't much matter; he wasn't going to push her tonight—or so he told his body as it reacted to her presence.

"Digger's going to think you don't like his food," Cam said, pointing at the nearly untouched plate in Abby's hand.

She stared at it blankly.

"You're lost somewhere, Abby."

"I was just thinking what a laugh my brother would be having about now, if he'd heard the stories I have about Franklin. When I got the letter with his proposal, I waved it in Mac's face as proof that a woman can have a strong will and still be loved." Bitter laughter twisted Abby's lips. "Franklin dances beautifully, you know."

"So I've heard."

"I met him at a ball last year when he was back East on business. We ran into him a few times at the theater and about town. He came to dinner once or twice. We had some lively discussions and debates. I really didn't think he thought much of me, but every time we got a letter over the next few months, he included a greeting to me. The notes were just cordial, the kind that keep acquaintances in touch. In February or March he suddenly began writing to me directly. He said he'd been thinking about me all along. Each letter was more personal than the one before, full of poetry and descriptions of the ranch."

"When did he propose?"

"The end of April."

Just after the last visit from his financial men, Cam recalled. He nodded, and Abby went on.

"Most men don't appreciate my 'blazing tongue and opinionated ways,' as my brother puts it. Franklin said he admired my independence, that it was a necessity for a woman in the West. He even said he liked the fact that I play poker and shoot skeet. Anyway, I accepted. The man from Tiffany's came a few days later." Abby scratched absently at the emerald with a fingernail.

Blood and money, Cam thought again, and wondered just how Tanner intended to pay for the ring. He knew for a fact the Fidelity didn't have that kind of cash left. Tanner had taken a loan to make the reward money, just as he would take a loan to ransom Abby, the straw that would, at long last, break the camel's back.

"There's one point I haven't heard you mention in all this," Cam said. "Did you—do you—love him?"

Abby rose and scraped the remains of her dinner into the fire. The beans sizzled and popped as she walked away. Cam followed a few feet behind.

They were nearly to the cabin before she stopped and turned toward Cam. The distant fire was reflected as small golden flames in eyes bright with anger and hurt.

"No," she said. "I don't love him. I thought I respected him and that respect would be enough. I settled, you see. I never even had a serious beau before Franklin. Imagine, at my age."

"Then the men in New York are idiots." Cam cupped her cheeks in his hands and kissed her firmly on the lips. Her response excited him, and he accepted the invitation of her parted lips to taste her more deeply, careless of the eyes that might be watching them in the dark. Coaxing her desire, he feathered kisses over her cheeks and eyes, trailed his hands across her shoulders, and down her arms. She lifted up to him hungrily, her breasts firm and round against his chest, her nipples hard as pebbles. The layers of cloth between them cried to be torn away.

The cabin stood there, a few feet away, its privacy beckoning. Instinct guided Cam toward the door, but a fragment of good sense held him back, told him to leave her excited and reaching for him, just this one last time. He twined his fingers through hers and pulled her close enough so that she could feel the hardness centered between his thighs.

"I want you, Abby," he whispered against her lips. Her eyes flew open. "You'd better go on inside and lock that door before I can't help myself."

The mix of desire, confusion, and relief on Abby's face made him thankful for that little scrap of logic. She bolted into the cabin, slamming the door behind her. He heard the bar drop into place.

Cam fetched his bedroll from where he'd stashed it in a box. He paused a moment, leaning against the door. By standing very still, he could hear Abby's quiet breathing just on the other side. He could almost feel the weight of her pressing against the door, wanting to come to him.

"Abby?"

A long silence. "What?"

"Sweet dreams."

No response. Cam smiled.

He unrolled his blanket on the flat spot he'd staked out at the corner of the cabin and stretched out. The glow of a match, then of the lantern, seeped out around the shutters. Cam closed his eyes and enjoyed a night full of erotic, tumultuous dreams of his own.

As he lay half awake in the quiet just before dawn, guilt slithered across Cam's belly like a small, black snake and lifted its triangular head to stare him down.

You're as bad as Tanner, the snake hissed. *Using her for your own purposes.*

Impatient, Cam flipped the blanket aside.

A fly tickled Abby's cheek.

The touch jerked her away from the dreams that had tantalized her all night. Somewhat grateful, more regretful, she swatted at the insect. It ignored her, and the tickle quickly grew to infuriating proportions. Abby snatched at the creature again, and her fingers closed around a lock of her own hair, waving in the cool morning breeze.

In the pewter-gray of first light, she could barely distinguish the window from the walls of the cabin. It took her a moment to realize that the breeze came through unimpeded. The shutters on the north window stood open. She came awake in an instant.

A quick glance around the cabin showed her alone. Abby slipped out of bed and hurriedly donned her skirt and blouse waist. She was wrestling with the last few buttons down her back when she spotted the morning's gift, a single, perfect columbine lying on the table like a resting dove. Whether Cam had found it in the grove or someplace else, she knew he meant it as an invitation. Even the window he'd left open pointed her in the right direction.

"No," Abby said aloud. "Absolutely not."

When Cam strolled into sight a half hour later, his hat in his hand, his shirt hanging open, and his hair and beard still wet, she still stood at the window. He looked wild and untamed, a little terrifying, and he walked straight to her.

Feeling safe within the confines of the cabin, Abby dared a smile.

"I dreamed about you," Cam said. He hopped over the sill as if it were no barrier at all. Before she realized he was in the cabin, he had her in his arms.

Cam's kiss was fiery and intense, and left no doubt as to the content of his dream. Abby put her hand up to fend off the rush of desire, but found instead the wall of his chest. Her fingers knotted into the damp, golden curls as her other hand slipped willfully under his shirt to caress his smooth back.

"You dreamed about me, too," Cam whispered. "You want me, don't you, Abby?"

His hands wandered as freely as hers, his fingers skimming beneath the hem of Abby's blouse. He found the few loose buttons at the back, and worked the others free. The garment slipped forward over her shoulders, and Cam tugged it lower, exposing the lace of her camisole and the full upper mounds of her breasts. Abby heard him catch his breath.

"I knew it. You do want me." Cam tugged at the thin fabric that obscured his goal, finding the erect peaks by Abby's gasp of pleasure. Watching her face intently, he continued the provocative motion, alternately kneading and drawing at the taut, sensitive points until Abby moaned in agonized delight.

"You do want me," Cam repeated. "Say it, Abby. Tell me you want me." His voice carried the urgency she felt, but the words jumbled and knotted inside her. Only her hands seemed to work properly. She laced them around Cam's neck and pulled him to her. His kisses trailed down her neck and met his fingers at her breasts. Cupping her breasts, he suckled each one in turn through the thin cambric of her camisole. Fire raced to a secret spot deep in her belly and exploded into a blazing furnace, and she fought to keep from melting to the floor.

"Tell me you want me, Abby," he urged again.

"Cam. Cam." The voice sounded very far away, and Abby didn't recognize the sound. She buried her face in the pale streaks of gold that covered his head. Cam nibbled at the tiny bows and buttons holding her camisole closed, taking an occasional, incredible nip at her breasts.

"Cam honey. Yoo-hoo!"

"Cameron?"

Cam froze, a length of ribbon in his teeth. "Damn it all to hell." Slipping Abby's blouse into position, Cam began buttoning buttons as quickly as his fingers would work.

"What is it?" Voice and wits returned to Abby at the same instant. "That sounds like Hannah and Rico."

"It is, and if she's back up here already, it means something's gone wrong. I'll head them off. Get yourself together and come on down." An easy hop took Cam back out the window, but he leaned back in and pressed a searing kiss to Abby's lips. "That's to let you know this is not over. Your body says you want me, Abigail Morgan, and I intend to get you to admit it."

Chapter 8

Abigail stuck her fist in her mouth and muffled a scream of frustration. Frustration at the circumstances. Frustration at the interruption.

Most of all, frustration at her body and the ease with which she succumbed to Cam every time he touched her.

Still, inexperienced as she might be in physical love, Abby understood that they had been far too engrossed with each other for Cam to walk away for anything trivial. The excited timbre of Hannah's voice and the more serious rumble of Rico's confirmed the urgency of the situation, though Abigail couldn't make out the words.

Stuffing the hem of her blouse into her skirt, Abigail hurried downhill before anyone might realize what she and Cam had been doing.

"... and he spooked me," Hannah was saying as Abby walked up. "I had Cheng's little brother keep an eye on him till he headed for the ranch, then I hightailed it out of town." Hannah pointed at Abigail and frowned. "We've got ourselves an eavesdropper."

"We're not saying anything she can't hear," Cam said. "I don't understand. If Stanton was in town, where was Tanner?"

"At the ranch." Rico shrugged. "I know, it is unusual, but our *compadre* said Tanner had some problems that could not wait. He took the men but told Stanton to keep looking. I discovered Hannah at Juanita's last night—"

"Night before," Hannah corrected.

"*Sí*, night before," Rico agreed. "We have ridden straight through. I did not want to leave her within their reach, so . . ."

"And I laughed at Digger's sore thumb," Cam mumbled to himself.

"You'll learn," Hannah said.

"I sure as hell hope all the girls can keep their mouths shut."

"Nobody at Noreen's is going to admit anything to those skunks, don't you worry about that, but I'll tell you, this plan of yours better work. I'm getting to the age where it's a little late to be starting over again in a new town with no money."

Abigail might have missed the warning look Cam shot in Hannah's direction if she hadn't been watching him closely. She assumed it was because Hannah had just given away the name of her employer. He shouldn't worry. She'd never give Franklin a scrap of information that might hurt anyone.

Hannah turned back to the subject at hand. "Anyhow, I swear Stanton *knew* I'd been with you. He didn't say it in so many words, but he knew it just the same."

"Come on, Hannah, how could he know?"

"I don't know, but he did."

"I think I might know how he found out." This should feel better, Abigail told herself. She'd nurtured the secret hope for days, and now that it paid off, she wished it hadn't.

Three pairs of eyes accused her of treachery.

"Abby?" Cam demanded.

"Don't look at me like that. I didn't do anything," Abigail said defensively. "My clothes all have New York labels, and my initials are worked into the lace of my underthings."

Hannah looked ashen. "Jesus. And I thought it was just fancy work."

"Tell me you didn't," Cam said.

"Those drawers were so pretty, Cam honey. I just thought I'd sorta borrow them. Figured I could give them back when this was all over." Hannah winced. "I sent them to the laundry the first day back."

Cam whipped his hat against his thigh. "Damn it, Hannah. You know Tanner owns a piece of Soo Ling."

"He would not necessarily know Hannah was with the *señorita* just from her things showing up in the laundry," Rico said, trying to put a better light on the situation.

"Besides, I had on that ugly old bonnet when I was around the Nagles. Fat old Orris didn't see enough of me to give a good description," Hannah countered.

"But you went on about her drawers." Cam paced back and forth, working the crown of his hat back into shape. "If Orris or Ellie mentioned that and then Stanton heard about the laundry, he might have put it together and figured you'd helped yourself to her things."

"Seems like he'd have just dragged me off to Tanner."

"He might not be absolutely sure it was you, or he might have decided to wait and see what you did. Are you sure Stanton headed toward Saguache?" Cam asked.

"Well, I didn't see him with my own eyes or nothing, but I was real careful, and so was Rico."

"We rode like ghosts who leave no trail, Cameron. I also watched for riders behind us. We were not followed." Rico sounded positive, but Cam still looked worried.

"Still, we'd better tell the men to watch for trouble. No more hunting for a few days, everybody stays close to camp."

"That's for me," Hannah said. "I could sleep through a

gold rush, the way I feel. A night in Juanita's root cellar didn't do a thing for me. Say, I want to scrub down first. Anybody care to join me?"

"I'll get Charlie to haul you some water," Cam said.

Abigail wondered briefly if he would have ignored Hannah's blatant invitation if she hadn't been around.

No matter. In the few moments free of Cam's seductive influence, common sense had returned. Whatever he thought, the unfortunate activity begun in the cabin most certainly was over.

Hannah was back. She might not be Abigail's choice of companions, but she would do as a chaperon.

The afternoon brought with it a change in the weather. Dark, smoky clouds exploded across the sky above the narrow valley with astonishing speed and sent streaks of lightning dancing along the peaks. As the claps of thunder rattled closer and closer, Cam called the guards in, and they came skidding down off the exposed ridges gratefully. Minutes later a thunderbolt shattered a boulder on the west side, sending pieces tumbling down into the valley. For all the fury, the only moisture the storm brought was a few kernels of hail.

A dozen people crowding into the cabin made for lots of noise and a certain number of bawdy jokes, most of which came from Hannah. Embarrassed, Abigail scrounged a needle and thread and retreated to a corner to catch a loose button on her jacket and tack some lace on her camisole.

The hail passed quickly, leaving barely a trace of white on the ground, but the lightning storm continued for most of the afternoon.

Tucked away in the corner, almost invisible in the rowdy group, Abby absorbed bits and pieces of cowboy and mountain lore. Digger hung about just outside the door, contributing his share of wild stories and gossip. After a time the talk turned naturally enough to Franklin Tanner.

At least Abby thought it turned naturally. She hadn't

noticed Cam steering the conversation along, concentrating as she was on her sewing, though she wouldn't put it beyond him. She glanced up at the first mention of Franklin's name and pierced her index finger with the needle. A stain like a red poppy bloomed on the front of the camisole she was mending, and she quickly stuffed the garment behind her and sucked the injured finger. She avoided Cam's curious gaze.

As soon as the storm petered out, which it did nearly as abruptly as it had rolled in, the cabin cleared. Cam strolled on out with Hannah, but reappeared before Abby even had a chance to put away her mending.

"Is your finger okay?" he asked.

"Fine."

"Your clothes aren't." Cam dragged the camisole off the bed with a hooked finger.

"Put that down." Abby snatched at the garment, but Cam lifted it up over his head, out of her reach. When she gave up, he held the camisole out for inspection, stretching it out by the narrow, lacy straps.

"What a shame. This is the one that you had on when you got sick. I recognize it."

Abby colored. "You said Hannah and Digger undressed me."

"Oh, they did. But I caught a glimpse. About this much." Cam indicated a crescent that included much of the bosom. "And there are your initials, bold as life. I sure didn't notice them. Must have been distracted at the time."

Cam turned his eyes straight to the source of distraction, letting his gaze wander deliberately over the high, round outline of her breasts. Abby felt her nipples pucker, as though he'd caressed her again. While she stood there enthralled by her response, he held the camisole up to her, matching it to the curves of her body.

"Look at that, right over your heart," Cam taunted, tracing a line that skimmed the deep valley between her breasts and came to rest over the stain.

Abby closed her eyes, focusing all her senses on that one spot where Cam's finger rested. If he pressed a bit harder, she thought, he could touch her heart. Self-preservation made her tug his hand away.

Cam didn't resist. The stained camisole slipped to the floor.

"Maybe we'd better go on down by the fire," Cam suggested.

Abby nodded, not quite trusting her voice. She retrieved the camisole and carried it over to the basin, where she slopped a little cold water out of the pail and put the stain to soak. Still wordless, she grabbed her jacket and hat and headed out the door. The pressure of his fingertip over her heart clung, warm and persistent.

"Who's gonna take Lew his supper?" Digger asked.

"I will," Cam volunteered. "I want to do a good walk around since everybody was down during the storm."

He piled a plate high with ham, rice thick with gravy, and stewed dried apples, then tossed enough johnnycakes on top to make the mess unstable. Making a show of balancing the awkward pile, Cam poured some coffee. A good half cup sloshed out, sizzling on the hot rocks ringing the fire.

"Let me do that," Abby said. She grabbed the pot away and topped the cup off neatly. "Does he like it sweet?"

"Very. Two big spoonfuls. Um . . . I could sure use some help carrying it up."

"You are quite transparent," Abby said.

Hannah apparently thought so, too, Cam decided, noting the redhead's frown. "I guess I'll have to ask someone else, then."

"Oh, I'll do it," Abby said quickly. "You needn't bother Hannah, she's had such a long ride."

She sounded so put-out and so eager at the same time. Cam suppressed a grin until the darkness beyond the fire hid his face.

Shadowed bowers and discreet niches beckoned to Cam. He could lead Abby into any one, he thought, and kiss her into willing submission, overcome those last fragile threads of resistance. The enthusiastic stirring in his loins reminded him of the way she'd felt pressed against him that morning, on the verge of admitting her desire.

On the way back we could stop there among those willows, he thought, then rejected the idea. Exciting as it seemed to him, the crudity would never appeal to Abby. A little more spooning would have to do for now, before he left her to climb up to check on the men guarding the ridge. He knew just where to take her for that.

The craggy line of the cliff rose ahead. Cam whistled softly to let Lew know they were there.

The creek splashed below, the water tumbling between boulders the size of a horse. That, and the rustle of small animals in the underbrush, were the only sounds.

"Lew." Cam called the man's name and waited.

"Maybe he had to . . . use the necessary," Abby suggested.

"Shh. Stand right here. I'm going to look around, and I don't want Lew shooting you for a stranger." Cam tugged Abby out into a patch of moonlight where her dress would show up clearly. He handed her the plate and took off to find Lew.

A quick search turned up no traces. Cam hustled back to Abby, who for once had followed his orders.

"Can you find your way back to the fire?" he asked.

"Certainly, but—"

"Leave that stuff here. Get straight back to Rico and tell him Lew's gone missing. I want him and at least two others up here pronto, and three extra men up top. You and Hannah get in the cabin and bolt everything up. Charlie and Digger will stay with you two."

"You think someone's here, don't you? In the valley."

"Maybe, but it's more likely that Lew's taken a fall in the dark. I just want to be careful."

"If he has fallen, Hannah and I can help look as well as the others can."

"I don't want to worry about you two. Now go on. And be careful."

Cam watched until Abby became part of the shadows, indistinguishable from the trees below. She's safe, he told himself. It was only a few hundred yards to the fire. He debated just for an instant calling her back and firing a shot to summon help, but anyone within ten miles would hear it on a night like this. If someone had followed Hannah and Rico, he didn't want to alert them.

Drawing his pistol, Cam wedged himself into a narrow slit at the head of the cliff trail. This spot protected his back and offered a clear view of the trail opening. No one would get in or out.

In just a few minutes Rico would bring help. Cam settled in to wait.

Without Cam's surefooted guidance, the route back seemed steep and full of hazards. Abigail picked her way along in the dark, holding the line between speed and caution.

The trees to her right appeared taller, thicker, different than they had going up. Convinced she'd taken a wrong turn, Abigail paused to reconnoiter. It took her a long moment to spot the faint glow of the fire on the trees just ahead, and another to make out the scraggly line of the game trail that led to the fire circle. She was right on the path. Blotting at her forehead with her sleeve, Abigail sighed with relief and hurried on.

In the next step her feet went out from under her. A rough hand clamped over her mouth, another slipped around her waist. Kicking and raking at the man who held her, Abby felt herself dragged backward, down the hill into a thick, musky clump of currants at the edge of the stream.

"Settle down, missy, settle down," the oily voice whispered in her ear, barely distinguishable from the stream noise. "I can get you out of here. Settle down. I'm not going to hurt you, missy. I'm here to help."

Gradually, and against every instinct, Abigail forced herself to calm down. The man loosened his hold but kept her held up against him so closely she could feel his sweat seeping through her clothes. The hand over her mouth smelled of cheap tobacco and overheated horse.

"I'm Liam Stanton. You know the name?" When Abigail nodded, he continued. "Then you know I'm working for your man. Mr. Tanner's mighty anxious to see you, little lady. You calm enough now to keep your voice down?"

Abigail nodded again. As soon as Stanton released her, she spun to face him.

"Is Franklin here, too?" she demanded in a hoarse whisper. The thought disturbed rather than comforted.

"Nope. Found you on my own."

"How?"

"One of our Chinee at the laundry spotted your fancy knickers, and I figured out Hannah must've been the one playing like Ellie Nagle. I set a match to her tail to spook the lyin' bitch, then just trailed her. She and that Mexican about lost me, but I stuck."

Just as Cam thought. Abigail stared at Stanton's hooded eyes, glittering coldly beneath the brim of his hat. "What did you do to Lew?"

"Don't you worry about him, he's not hurting any. Time for us to get out of here. Where's that fellow you went up with?"

"Cam's looking for Lew. You won't be able to get out that way."

"*We* will. That was Garrett, huh? Thought it might be, but I've never seen him up close. Makes no difference who he is, though," Stanton continued, "so long as I know where he is. I want you to go back up and distract him a little while I move around."

"I won't help you hurt anyone," Abigail said.

"Don't you worry none. I'll just crack him up back of

his head like I did that other fellow. Once I take care of him, you hustle down that trail right quick."

"We can't do that. I mean, I can't handle the cliff path. I'm afraid of heights." *And I don't want to go with you.* If she told Stanton that, Abby suspected those glittery eyes would go even flatter and more dangerous.

" 'I can't. I won't.' You're being rescued, missy, let's have some help. Besides, there's a big reward on you, and I intend to earn it. You'll do whatever it takes." Stanton's tone was light, but a knife suddenly appeared in his hand, and the coiled tension in his body reminded Abigail of the snake, ready to strike. The coppery taste of fear flooded Abby's mouth.

"You can't kill me," she whispered. "You won't get your money."

Stanton's lips moved against her ear. "I won't get it if I'm dead, either. Now, my horse is tied at the other end of that trail."

"They'll come after us."

"There's a bunch of our men over Long Park way. We'll ride for them. Don't you worry, missy, I plan to be alive to enjoy my thousand bucks."

"Only a thousand?" Abigail whispered to herself. A paltry fraction of the ransom. Her surprise at the discrepancy must have registered in her voice.

"What?" Stanton demanded.

"Oh, nothing. I was just thinking what a tremendous bargain that is for Franklin—considering Mr. Garrett wants thirty thousand for me."

"Huh?" Stanton looked genuinely surprised, then his lips lifted in a feral grin that exposed the tip of his tongue flicking over his teeth. "Guess I'd better have myself a talk with the boss when we get back. Now, if you really don't want anyone hurt, you just do like I say."

A spider dropped off the rock onto Cam's sleeve. He brushed it away and shifted slightly.

"Hurry, Abby," he whispered to the night. The breeze drifting down the valley carried no sound of anyone coming, and he began to regret sending her back alone. There'd been no choice, Cam reminded himself, short of leaving the trail unguarded. She'd be fine. He shifted again.

Five minutes later, with no sign of either Rico or Abby, Cam aimed his gun skyward and squeezed off a single, echoing round.

Within moments Rico and half the others joined Cam at the trail head. Cam barked out orders, and the men scattered. Holding his position, Cam watched his men work through the shadows.

"Over here, Cam," Antonio called from along the trail. Cam headed around the corner, Rico close behind. With Antonio's pointing finger to show the way, it took Cam only a few seconds to spot the broken form on the rocks below. Cam stared down at Lew, noting the odd angles of neck and limbs.

"It looks like he fell," Antonio said. "I think he is dead."

"Lew?" Cam shouted. The figure didn't stir. Antonio was right, almost surely. But they had to know positively. "We can't tell from here. Rico, you think we can get a man or two down there?"

"We can, *sí*. I will get what we need." His friend hustled back along the trail like a much younger man.

"You take the watch until Rico gets back," he ordered Antonio. "I'll be up top."

After a quick survey of the shadows around the trail head, Cam headed for the ridge. Halfway up, he stopped to survey the inky valley below. From his position, about twice tree height, any motion in the shadows stood out more clearly. He picked out most of his men, now far up the valley, with no trouble, but hesitated over the irregular shape of a downed log. Too bulky. As Cam stared, trying to figure out why it looked odd, the shape moved and split and resolved into a log and two standing people, one wearing a skirt.

Abby. And someone, a man, who moved dangerously and had his hand at her back. Hairs prickled along Cam's neck.

Cam moved back down the slope silent as a cougar, his mind racing to identify the foe. Too small for Tanner; it must be Stanton. Anybody else? Cam reached into the dark with his vision and decided the man worked alone—unless Abby had decided to work with him.

The man prodded Abby forward, then ducked into the blackness between the trees and was lost. Cam reached the bottom of the slope and dodged into a shadow of his own just as Antonio called out.

"Who is there?"

"I am. Abigail Morgan. Don't shoot." If Stanton had a gun on her, she sounded pretty natural, Cam thought.

His rifle gleaming dully in his hands, Antonio stepped out into the patch of moonlight. "Cam was worried, *señorita*. Why did you not call out?"

"I felt so foolish getting all twisted around like that. Wandering around in the dark like a ninny."

Come on, Antonio. He's moving around behind you. Cam strained to place the thought in Antonio's skull.

"Anyway, when I heard that shot, I decided to follow the sound back this way."

"Cam fired to summon us. Because you did not do as you were told, our position may now be known to Tanner's men. But of course, that is what you wanted, is it not?" Antonio flipped the rifle up onto his shoulder and strode toward Abby, biting off the words. "You are very much trouble. If it was my decision, you would be tied up and kept in the cabin. Then there would be no running away, no sickness, no getting lost. What are you doing?"

A blur of motion flew out of the darkness behind Antonio. Cam had an impression of polished steel held low, and of Antonio turning too slowly.

"Stanton." Cam roared the name and stepped out into the moonlight.

The wildness of a trapped animal lit Stanton's eyes. He changed direction in mid-dive, twisting toward Abby, reaching under Tony's descending rifle.

Suddenly Stanton's path reversed. He rose backward, flapping his arms like some bizarre bird. The knife tumbled out of his hand and spun lazily to the ground. A ragged hole exploded a hand's width above his waist. A second shot tore through Stanton's shoulder and flipped him at the last instant, so he landed facedown in the dust.

In the silence after the gunshots' echoes had died, Cam waited for Abby's scream. There was only the sound of the stream.

Within seconds half a dozen men appeared out of the night and surrounded them; half a dozen guns trained on Stanton's twitching body.

"Nice shot, Tony," said Pete.

"Only the second one." Antonio cleared the chamber on his rifle. "I do not know where the first one came from."

The men looked at each other in confusion. No one owned up.

A weight dragged at Cam's arm. He looked down, noticed for the first time the pistol in his hand. Years of imagining Stanton dead, and he hadn't even been aware of drawing on him. All that had mattered was Abby and Antonio—and Lew, lying broken at the bottom of the cliff. Shock's protective numbness flowed through his being and across his face.

"It came from me," Cam said, stepping into the circle. He carefully slid his pistol back into its holster, then bent over Stanton. "Help me get him over."

Ungentle handling brought a moan from Stanton. Air left in the lungs, Cam thought, then he heard the rattling intake of breath. Rico grabbed Stanton's pistols and tossed them aside.

Stanton opened his eyes and met Cam's hard-won even gaze. "Son of a bitch."

"Get Digger," Cam said calmly to the nearest man. "We'll get you some help, get you patched up."

"No good. Tell Hannah . . . see her in hell. You, too." Stanton held his hand up, covered to the elbow in blood and dirt. His eyes rolled up and he whispered, "Shot me good."

"Damn good," one of Cam's men said.

"Shut up. The rest of you, get back to what you were doing. There's no guarantee he didn't bring friends along." Cam stayed at Stanton's side until Digger arrived, then pulled Abby well aside, where the gore and Stanton's moans seemed less obtrusive.

"What happened?" he asked.

"He . . . he caught me, back there. I couldn't get away."

"So you decided to set Tony up for him?"

"He promised he wouldn't hurt him. I tried to . . ." No tears came, but Abby's voice sounded as brittle as her expression looked. She took a deep, shuddering breath. "I tried to signal Tony. Stanton said he was alone."

"Of course he did."

"He didn't want to share the reward for finding me. I think he was telling the truth."

"C'mere, Garrett," Stanton gurgled. "C'mere."

Cam glanced toward the wounded man, then back to Abby's tight face, glad she didn't reach out to him. He had nothing to give her right now. "Antonio, get her out of here."

"No. I shot him, too, Cam. I will stay." Antonio held his ground.

"Rico, then. Go on, get her out of here." Cam turned away from Abby before her presence undermined his control. "Okay, Stanton, what do you want?"

The roar in Abby's ears grew and grew, just like the shots had seemed to magnify with every repeating echo. She pushed the sound back, stuffed it into the place she kept all her worst secrets from herself. The night grew painfully silent.

Abigail allowed Rico to guide her back to the fire, feeling cold and numb, as if she'd been out in a blizzard. Once there she huddled into a tiny knot, not far from Hannah.

Digger trudged back into view a half hour later, looking gaunt.

"He's gone," was all he'd say. He pulled a pint bottle of whiskey out of his cook box and spilled a healthy slug into his cup. Rico held out his mug and accepted a dose.

A long time passed before the others trickled down. Cam came last, a long while after the others, looking pale in the firelight. A dark stain of sweat ringed the crown of his hat and streaked patches beneath his arms and down the front of his shirt. He looked at Abby, then at the grim, tense faces around the fire.

"We're moving out of here," he said. "I want this camp broken apart by dawn. Clean it up so nothing's left to show we've been here. Not a trace."

Chapter 9

It wasn't the temperature that made the morning so unbearable, Abigail thought, scrubbing at her aching eyes: It was the sunlight.

It scorched down on them, the white hot sun determined to burn the color out of the heavens. A huge wedge of sky in the east rose over them, bleached a powdery shade that was barely blue. Snow-capped peaks scalloped the edge of the horizon all around, offering a sense of coolness combined with ever more blinding light. Abigail pulled her hat lower against the blazing intensity.

Her mount plodded along steadily, following the rump of Cam's horse ahead. Abigail absently thumped the animal's neck, encouraging its patient surefootedness, and turned her attention back to the erect back of the man leading the little group. The man she'd thought she could love.

Cam Garrett. Outlaw.

Killer.

The image of Liam Stanton dying in a growing pool of his own blood clung tenaciously to the edges of Abigail's consciousness, despite all her efforts to dislodge it. It didn't help that, in the twelve hours or better since he'd shot Stanton, Cam had not shown one sign of remorse. In fact, he'd been a model of coolness and almost military efficiency as he and his men had prepared to leave the valley.

Standing before the cabin in the ashen gray light preceding dawn, Abigail had barely recognized the place. During the night every lean-to had been demolished, every piece of usable equipment loaded onto packhorses and mules. Then men began stripping the cabin of every sign of human occupancy.

By the time Abigail tied off her bedroll and carried it outside, flames had devoured the scraps of the camp. She watched three men extinguish the campfire and erase the pit as thoroughly as a student would erase a blackboard, right down to dumping the fire-scarred rocks into the creek, black side down. Under Digger's direction, food got divided between saddlebags and packs. A few items, too heavy to permit rapid flight, were dragged up to the mine. According to Hannah, the two bodies and Stanton's saddle and gear already rested there. His horse had been set free outside the valley to fend for itself.

Cam led his gang toward the upper end of the valley, Abigail mounted before him. His arms felt like a stranger's.

A muted roar rumbled up behind them, followed shortly by Digger and two men brushing tracks.

"She came down real easy," the old man said. "It'll take about a week to dig out."

They had collapsed the mine, Abigail realized, recalling the propped timbers Cam had pointed out.

"But it can be done?" Cam asked.

"When it's time," Digger replied. "Then I'll see to it myself."

With a nod, Cam faced the others.

"Everybody knows where we're going. Once we're over the top, split off into groups of two and three. Half of you go on around and come back at the trail from the north.

Take your time, make sure nobody follows you."

Then Cam had turned his mount toward the slender deer path Abigail had seen earlier, the one he'd said led nowhere. He met the question in her eyes with a shrug. "I said it was dangerous, not impossible."

Now, safely over the precipitous trail and mounted on the Appaloosa left free by Lew's death, Abby wondered what other facts Cam had manipulated to control her. Every doubt she'd ever had about him and his motives grew to elephantine proportions.

She could not be in love with Cam, not with someone who could shoot a man down like that.

As they rode into the blessed, cool shade of thick spruce along a north-facing slope, the previous night replayed itself again and again in Abby's mind: Stanton rushing forward; Cam's firm, deliberate voice; the shot; Stanton's blood, black and oily in the moonlight; and the scream that never escaped her lips and still sat there, lodged just at the back of her throat.

No, the worst wasn't Cam's detachment. The worst was her responsibility in the matter. One yell would have brought every man in camp to her aid; instead, she'd let Stanton convince her he'd just knock Antonio out.

"Campfire?"

Abigail started at Cam's voice. It took her a moment to realize he was talking about the faint scent of smoke wafting through the trees.

"Possible," Rico said. "If so, we need to keep the *señorita* well away."

An open patch in the forest revealed smoke rising skyward in a broad funnel of gray and white that linked sky to ground. Cam wheeled his bay off the trail and up to a treeless ridge.

"Wildfire," he called as Rico and Abby caught up. "Probably flared up from the lightning yesterday."

The fire appeared to be some distance away, west and a

little to the north, behind at least a couple of ridges. A sudden breeze scudding along the ridge tasted of pine smoke and heat. Whinnying nervously, the Appaloosa tossed his head and jerked against the reins.

"Let's go. We can't sit here." Abigail felt the hairs on her arms rise. If the fire ran with the breeze, the grass beneath them would soon be black tufts, or so she assumed from the way the smoke drifted their way. Watching the gardener burn off weeds in the garden each fall hardly made her an expert on wildfire. Her horse squealed again and danced sideways a couple of steps.

"Keep that animal under control. You're going to need him as soon as we figure out where we're headed." Cam scanned the area thoroughly, as did Rico.

They exchanged views while Abby silently fumed and fussed, trying not to let her horse feel her agitation. When Cam finally led them down off the ridge and turned back to retrace their path, she sighed with relief.

"We're going to outflank it," Cam explained to her. "The breeze is holding steady, so we'll ride back a few miles. When we're well clear, we'll cut around the back side of the burn. We'll be fine."

"Just let's go."

Shortly after noon they veered due west and soon put the line of fire behind them. It was about then that Abigail spotted the road, a thin brown line sketched against the blue-green forest in the middle distance. Its sight triggered an enormous longing in Abigail, an ache to be away from Franklin Tanner and Cam Garrett, away from outlaws and ranchers, away from all the lying and stealing and killing and forest fires. That road could take her away.

It disappeared from sight as they dropped into another wooded stretch, but its position remained locked into Abigail's senses.

That road could take her home.

She stared at Cam, a few yards ahead. The breeze shifted to curl around them from a fresh direction, suddenly lacing smoke through the trees where it had been clear moments before.

Eyes rolling, her Appaloosa hopped sideways and skittered off the trail and deep into the trees. By the time Abigail fought him to a standstill, the laces of smoke had turned into thick, billowing sheets that choked out all the air and turned the trees into dark ghosts around her.

"Abby." Cam's smoke-muffled voice came from somewhere nearby, but she couldn't make out his form. "Abby."

She started to answer, then bit her lip as she saw her unexpected chance to put an end to this travesty. Getting to that road became the most important thing in her mind, much more important than the fire burning behind them.

The Appaloosa responded, albeit reluctantly, to her signal to back away.

Back. Back. A thick layer of needles silenced the horse's hooves. Abby stifled a cough. Back just a little farther. Tears streamed down her cheeks. The smoke, she told herself.

"*Señorita.*"

"*Abby!*"

Orienting herself by their shouts, Abby deliberately turned her mount away. The barest touch of her heels sent the animal toward the distant road. Their voices quickly faded as she rode away.

"*Abby!* Damn it, Rico, you were supposed to be right behind her."

Rico shot Cam a sideways glance but otherwise ignored the accusation and continued combing the ground for signs of Abby's passing.

In its vagaries the breeze had switched at least a half dozen times in the few minutes since Abby disappeared, whipping the smoke over them and away again. Nonetheless, they hadn't been able to spot her during the breaks, and the choking smoke raised tears which made tracking difficult.

"This way," Rico said at last, and they started off.

"The Lake City toll road's ahead," Cam said when he realized the general direction of Abby's trail. "I noticed it from back a mile or two. She must have spotted it at the same time."

"I thought you said you had your bobcat tamed."

"We'll worry about that later. I'm not losing her, Rico. I've worked too hard to let her get away from me now." *I took a man's life to keep her.* Bile ate at Cam's stomach.

The smoke whipped around them again, thicker, hotter, driven on a more insistent wind. Palms suddenly damp with sweat inside his gloves, Cam searched for an opening in the trees and found one a few dozen yards away.

A moment later the smoky haze soared above them on the wind to reveal a tremendous cloud that billowed skyward on their right flank, the lower portions glowing dirty red. A tree just inside the cloud exploded. Sparks and burning debris flew high, arching ahead of the fire. Seconds later flames as brilliant as Christmas candles lit the top of the next ridge.

"*Madre de Dios,*" Rico whispered beside him. "It is turning."

Cam realized each candle was a tree, its top burning like a torch. With each erratic gust, the flames spread. A patch of grass a hundred yards ahead of the burning trees turned black, and a bush at its edge roared into a new torch. The body of the fire rolled up to meet the newly charred patch, urged forward by the changeable wind.

"If she has half the sense I think she has, she'll head straight for the wagon road."

"I know a faster way," Rico said. "It will put us on the road a little east, between her and Saguache. We can keep her from reaching Tanner."

"Go on ahead. If you run into any of the others, have them help you cover the road. And if you happen to find Abby, fire off a couple of shots, then get her to the dugout. Tie her up if you have to."

"And you?"

"I'll do my best to find her, and then get out of here before I end up a roast."

As the Appaloosa skidded down a steep, brushy embankment on its haunches, Abigail realized she was in trouble. Not only was she lost, she couldn't even tell where the fire was anymore.

The wind continued to shift, angling back and forth between the mountains. Chased by smoke, reprieved, and chased again, Abigail had tried to keep herself to her general course, but someplace along the line she'd lost track. She no longer knew in which direction she was heading. Clouds of smoke obscured every landmark, as well as most of the sky. Even the sun was reduced to a thin glow behind the smoke, and it hung so nearly overhead it gave no clue as to west and east.

Another gust of smoky wind roiled among the huckleberries along the stream. The Appaloosa whinnied fretfully and flared its nostrils as Abigail tried pointing him up the streambed.

"Come on, boy, keep calm. I need you now. Don't go all milk-livered on me." Abigail cooed to the frightened beast as she reined him around in a tight circle to get him back under control. "We're going right up this stream a bit, and then over the ridge. I bet we can see the road from there, if the smoke lets us. Settle down, boy, settle down. It's not much farther, and once we get to the road, you can run as fast as you want. We'll put miles between us and this silly fire."

Abigail once again guided the Appaloosa upstream. He balked, tossing his head in refusal.

"Curse it, go." Fear sharp in her voice, Abigail dug her heels into the Appaloosa's side. He went.

A few yards upstream, a jumbled tower of boulders stood on one side of the stream. Again the horse balked, and again Abigail applied her heels.

A scream tore the air. For just an instant Abigail thought it was the horse, then a sleek, tan shape darted off the rocks and leapt across the narrow stream. The creature stood for an instant, looked them over with startled golden eyes, then vanished.

Mountain lion, Abigail registered in awed terror, just as the Appaloosa shot straight up. He locked his knees, landing with the force of a steam hammer. Abigail's jaw snapped at the impact. The horse shot up again, then twisted sideways.

Abigail lost all contact with the saddle. Flailing at the air, she crashed down into water and rocks. Pain flashed through her hip and elbows. The horse splashed a cautious dozen feet away and waited for her.

Icy water drove Abigail to her feet in seconds. Ignoring the pain in her hip, she slogged toward the nervous horse, chatting in an easy voice. He let her come within inches of grabbing his bridle, then wheeled and disappeared downstream in a froth of water. Abigail chased him a few yards, then realized the futility.

"I hope the glue factory gets you," she called after him.

Another wave of smoke, hotter yet, drove Abigail out of her fantasy of vengeance. Weighted by yards of soggy fabric, she clambered out of the water onto a warm, flat boulder. The urge to stay there and dry out was strong, but the unrelenting smoke argued against that. The fire must be coming nearer. She turned upstream. The sight of the rock tower made her stop. That mountain lion was around someplace, probably up this draw.

Downstream was fine, Abigail told herself, seeing as she didn't even know where she was going anymore. Maybe the horse would calm down and she could catch him.

Realistically, though, there wasn't much chance of that, and the smoke seemed so much thicker down that way. She needed to get up high enough to see the road and the flames, get herself back on track.

Abigail squared her shoulders. Uphill it was, mountain lions be hanged.

"There we go." Cam spotted a slightly darker slash in the soil angling down the hillside a few yards ahead. The clear imprint of shod hooves stood out in the disturbed earth.

Encouraged, he urged his mount down the same loose slope. At the bottom he found where she'd gone into the stream. The opposite bank showed no signs of her coming out.

He wondered if Abby was clever enough to ride in the stream. He wouldn't put anything past her, city-bred or not.

She'd go downstream, toward the road, Cam told himself, provided she still knew which way she was going. The way she'd been wandering the past couple of miles, he suspected she was lost. He turned downstream.

A few hundred yards along, Cam found where Abby's horse came out of the stream. The first quick surge of elation turned to caution as soon as he noticed the animal's stride: the Appaloosa was running straight out. The fire had gotten to her, and it looked as if the horse had spooked.

Cam rode a little farther, then pulled up with a funny feeling in his gut. A quick check up the draw wouldn't hurt.

Cam whirled the bay around and gave him the spurs.

Abigail scaled the last few yards of the hill on her hands and knees, clutching at whatever stray bushes and clumps of grass provided decent handholds. A final heave put her over the top, and she lay on the ground panting. It seemed as if half the mountainside had combined with the water in her skirts and turned to mud. Every movement wrapped the sodden mess around her legs. Her hip ached.

Surrendering temporarily to the handicaps, Abigail propped herself gingerly on her bruised elbows and peered around, trying to get herself oriented.

She saw no sign of the road, but that said little. A sea

of smoky haze obscured every detail within a few hundred feet and rendered everything beyond that all but invisible. Abigail rolled to her back and saw nothing but smoke and more smoke. Or maybe some of it was clouds—she couldn't tell anymore. The dim saucer of light that marked the sun's position, however, had slipped off center.

"West! So I want to go that way." Abby's triumphant smile faded and she sat up. "That way" was back downstream.

She'd come the wrong way and wasted the better part of an hour at it, too, not to mention letting the fire come an hour closer. Reluctant to give up the ground she'd gained, and even more reluctant to move a single step closer to the fire, Abigail convinced herself the top of the ridge was a fine place to walk. It was even wide enough to keep her from getting dizzy.

A shadow stirred in the smoke below. Abigail held her breath, certain it was the mountain lion. But she quickly picked out the indistinct shapes of a man leading a horse.

Cam.

She scrambled back from the edge. A few stones tumbled down the slope and she stifled a curse.

"Abby?"

She kept silent a long moment, until the sound of the bay's hooves drifted up the slope, and then Abigail was up and gone, pelting along the ridge. Her muddy skirts flapped and clung to her legs as she followed the curving ridge around and down through a clump of trees.

The ridge played out far too soon, ending in a promontory of tumbled rock. Abigail halted well back from where it jutted out into smoky space, and assessed her position. To her left lay a reasonable slope, one she knew she could handle but which would keep her in the fire's general path. She rejected it out of hand. To her right, another feasible slope, the one that led back down to the stream—again, in the path of the flames.

In fact, as she debated her options, the fire crested the nearest ridge and the freshening wind sent burning embers tumbling down the slope. For the first time she wondered if a person on foot *could* outrun a fire, if *she* could outrun a fire.

She didn't have to. Cam must be coming. She could turn back and find him. She didn't want to, but she could.

If she headed back and didn't find Cam, however, the fire would have her.

Her stomach rolled in a series of warning flips, but Abigail knew she had few choices left. Nothing to do but scramble down whatever slope lay beyond those rocks. If it matched the one she'd come up, it would be easy enough, and at least she'd be moving away from the fire. She just might be able to get away.

Abigail sidled over to the edge. When she was sure she had a good footing, when her stomach told her it was okay, she dared a glance down.

The balcony crumbled and she reached forward, grasping for the dark gown as it billowed in the wind.

Swaying, Abby clutched at a thin young pine that twisted up out of the rocks. Hot wind whipped around her, tugged at her soggy clothing, and tried to pull her over the edge. The little tree pitched with the wind and the weight of her body.

The gown slipped through her fingers, leaving traces of blue-green velvet under her nails, just the shade of the branches below.

"No!" she screamed.

A bolt of self-preservation streaked through Abigail, and she hurtled backward, away from the beckoning drop. She curled into a ball and lay there for a few moments, until she found the energy, the anger, the brute force of will to beat the images back.

Across the draw an ancient, resinous tree exploded like a bomb; a few sparks leapt downhill and smoldered near the stream. The fire could cross within minutes, then it was a clear, uphill race to where she stood.

Fresh fear replaced the old, familiar terror, and Abigail pushed to her feet and turned back along the ridge.

Cam was there, watching her grimly from the back of his long-legged bay. He held out his hand. Shaking with fear and relief, Abby reached out, and he yanked her into the saddle in front of him.

"I want an explanation, but right now we need to get out of here," Cam said, some barely contained emotion roughening his voice. His arms were secure around her; a lover's arms, a killer's arms.

Whichever he was, whatever she thought of him, Abby realized, her life was in this man's hands—just as a life had been in hers once. She had to hope he did a better job of it than she had done.

Another tree exploded somewhere in the near distance, and this time the wind lofted the sparks high overhead. They drifted down and lay on the hillside just below like so many lovely, deadly gems. The bay snorted and pawed.

"You're not going to like this," Cam said.

"I know," Abby mumbled. She squeezed her eyes tight. "I'm ready."

They plunged down the hill.

Over the years Cam had had many reasons to praise Billy's heart, but never so much as today. The big bay never let the fire intimidate him, despite the way it jumped and popped up all around. Any other horse would have refused the things Cam asked, especially when the flames licked at the edges of the trail. Billy just forged ahead, shaking off sparks as if they were deerflies.

On the flats they could have outrun the fire easily; in the rugged terrain of the La Garitas, they barely stayed a step ahead, and that wouldn't last much longer. Strong as he was, Billy couldn't keep up the pace forever, not carrying a double load. With few choices for shelter, Cam picked the closest he knew.

The wind and flames chased them up one draw and down the next, and up and over ridge after ridge, like some living being in pursuit. Cam pushed Billy, gained the narrow lead he needed, then turned the horse to race along a parallel to the fire's leading edge, only a few hundred yards before it. Whipped by the wind, flames streamed off the highest trees like pennants. Cam gave Billy his head, and together he and Abby leaned forward, aiding his flight across a small, tinder-dry meadow, over the ridge on the other side, and down into a deep gulch.

Now came the gamble.

Cam turned Billy toward the fire, Abby tense but silent before him. The horse churned upstream as smoke poured down the channel, so thick Cam nearly missed his mark.

The overhang was just as he remembered it, a healthy scoop taken out of the very body of the mountain. A yard of solid stone capped the wedge-shaped hollow with a roof more secure than any man might build. The floor consisted of gravel and silt that supported little plant life.

More important, the cut bank across the stream rose a good dozen feet high before it softened into a brush-covered slope. The fire would come close—it was only yards away now—but the overhang would shelter them. The flames would not touch this place.

He hoped.

Cam swung off the horse and led Billy into the cavity, out of reach of the approaching fire. Shunning his help, Abby dismounted and scooted over to the back wall. With a rush of guilt Cam looked at Billy's foam-flecked hide and heaving sides. The animal sorely needed some attention.

"Sorry, boy. People first." Cam took a pull from his canteen, passed it to Abby, then turned to hobble and blindfold the horse to keep him from running when the fire rushed the draw. Then he took a moment to flick open his bedroll. From the clothes inside, Cam picked out a well-worn red shirt and some canvas pants and held them out to Abby.

"Here. You need to get out of those wet things."

Abby shook her head. "I'm fine."

"You're wet to the bone and tired, to boot, and you'll freeze when it cools down later. Go ahead. Quick."

With an odd, questioning look, Abby accepted the clothes and moved a distance away to change. At least her willful streak didn't extend to senseless stubbornness. Cam managed to get their limited gear secured and still allow Abby some privacy. It wasn't even too hard keeping his eyes off her as she slipped out of her clothes. The middle of a forest fire just wasn't the time or place to get excited. Abby's emotions were just too unpredictable, the situation too volatile, to risk letting his guard down again. Cam checked that his rifle and hunting knife were well out of Abby's reach.

Overhead, pitch bubbled out of trees with a high whine that pierced the crackling roar of the flames.

A few hot embers tumbled over the lip of the overhang and splashed into the water. The hiss of steam startled Billy, and he rose onto his hind legs and laid his ears back flat along his neck.

"That's a boy. You're entitled. Just remember you're not going anyplace without us."

Cam cosseted the bay until he calmed down, then led him as far under the overhang as he could and, as an extra measure of safety, tossed a rope over the horse's head and tied him to a sturdy snag half-buried in the gravel. Careful of the erratic shower of burning debris from above, Cam fetched Abby's bedraggled blouse and dunked it in the water, then joined Abby where she had retreated into the deepest corner of the wedge.

"Try breathing through this. It'll make the air cooler and a little cleaner."

"You're coughing, too," Abby said, but she took the garment gratefully and held it over her nose and mouth as she sagged to the ground. "It's getting hotter."

Cam nodded as he ratted through his saddlebags for his spare neck scarf.

"Are we going to be safe here?"

A facile yes was on Cam's tongue, ready to assure, but Abby's piercing eyes demanded the truth. "I don't know. The fire won't come in here, but when that brush across the stream catches, well, it all depends on the wind. This overhang isn't that deep. It could get pretty warm."

Abby stared at the waves of smoke rolling down the gulch and nodded.

The wind continued to blow fitfully, like the blasts of a bellows through a smithy's forge. The fire raced onto the opposite slope.

Billy finally lost his tolerance for the sparks that drifted across the stream and stung his rump. He screamed and fought the rope with every gust of wind.

"Why don't you wet the blanket and put it over him?" Abby asked.

"We'll need it later tonight." Cam said, but the suggestion inspired him, and he grabbed Abby's muddy riding skirt and draped it over the animal's hindquarters.

Flames twined through the willows on the creek's far edge, and the overhang heated like an oven.

"Face the wall!" Cam shouted to Abby over the crackling roar, and when she did, he curled around her to make a hollow place for her against the cool clay and pulled her soggy jacket up to make a tent over their heads and shoulders. Over that he draped his heavy yellow rain slicker. In the rough shelter of the jackets, the air stayed fairly breathable, but Cam's exposed shins took the brunt of the heat. More than once he brushed at his legs, convinced his pants were on fire. Each time he was gratified to find himself physically intact. Billy's screams tore the air.

It seemed that at least one of them had some luck due. The wind finally decided on a single direction—straight down the gulch. The hottest part of the fire blazed by in a little under an hour, having consumed the ready fuel, and the flames diminished to a spotty and much cooler fire. Abby soon pushed the long slicker aside.

"Can we get out of here now?"

"Some of the standing wood's still burning and the ground will be hot for hours yet, maybe days. Things could flare up. We'll take our time, make sure we don't get caught again." Cam let Abby's jacket, now stiff with dry mud, slip to the ground. "I need to take care of Billy."

Her face glowing cherry from the heat that still washed across the creek, Abby watched quietly from the cleft as Cam checked Billy over.

"Thanks to your skirt, he's in pretty good shape."

"I'm sure Madame Chloe would be delighted to hear that."

"For all the abuse, he'll carry us out just fine." Cam scratched Billy's favorite spot, just behind his right ear. "I owe you, boy. A whole bag of peppermints next time we get to town."

"We've got to set up camp or something," Abby said.

"There's not much to set up. I don't suppose you want a fire."

A rueful smile touched her lips, and Abby shook her head. "I can't just sit here."

"Then fill up the canteen and figure out what we've got to eat."

"Do you have some suspenders for these things?" Abby asked as she rose.

Cam turned, and the sight of her shook him to the core. Ill fitting as they were, his clothes revealed Abby's charms most effectively. The red shirt drew his attention to the full breasts barely hidden by its thin, worn flannel. She'd apparently stripped to the skin, for there was no sign of camisole restraining the soft sway of her flesh as she walked toward him. Cam caught his breath in wonder.

"Suspenders?" Abby repeated, and he finally noticed she was holding his pants up by a fistful of excess fabric.

Where had his mind been the past hour? Even a fire shouldn't have made him miss this.

"Not exactly tailored for you, are they? Let me get some rope." Cam cut a yard or so from the end of the rope holding Billy and handed it to Abby.

Trim as he was, she was slighter still. If she turned loose, the pants would probably slide around her ankles. The idea of her dressed in nothing but a worn red shirt held a certain appeal. One tug would send the shirt buttons flying . . . .

Somehow Cam kept his mind on business. They soon had a decent, if minimal, camp set up and enough food in their bellies to hold them till morning. He got Billy resettled at the far end of the grotto, well away from where they'd sleep.

Abby didn't say anything about the single bedroll, but Cam caught her staring at it as night approached.

"How could you do it?" she asked.

"We don't have much choice," he began. "If you hadn't lost your mount—"

"No. I mean Stanton. How could you shoot a man and then just keep going like this, like nothing happened?"

"Same answer. I don't have much choice. Is that what this afternoon was about?"

"I got too close to the edge and got dizzy, that's all," Abby said casually. She scooped up her blouse and carried it to the water's edge.

Cam followed her and stood over her as she began rinsing the mud out. "That was more than dizziness, but that's not what I'm talking about and you know it."

"When that smoke came around us, my horse got spooked. The next thing I knew, I was lost."

"You rode off deliberately, and you were headed for the Lake City road until you really did get lost."

"Was I? Just where is Lake City?"

"Knock it off, Abby. Were you running back to Tanner?"

"Hardly. I don't know why you find it so difficult to believe I might want to get away from you. You're an outlaw, for heaven's sake. You kidnapped me."

"I was an outlaw yesterday, and the day before, and the day before that. You didn't seem to mind then."

"Or so you thought. I guess I'm at least as good an actress as Hannah."

"Crap. Did you take off because of what happened with Stanton?"

Abby froze, the white blouse drifting in the shallow water at the stream's edge. "You shot him in cold blood."

"It's not cold blood when he's about to kill someone else." Cam grew abruptly angry. He grabbed Abby's arm and jerked her to her feet. "My god, he'd already slit Lew's throat."

"You didn't know that then."

"But I knew about others before that. And let's not ignore the part you had in his death, either, my little Judas goat. 'Oh, help, I lost my way in the dark.' If you hadn't set Antonio up, Stanton wouldn't have gotten the drop on him, and I wouldn't have had to shoot Stanton."

"Don't you think I know that?" Anguish born of guilt replaced the sarcasm in Abby's voice. "I told you I tried to signal Tony. I didn't know what else to do."

"Neither did I."

"You wanted to kill them, Stanton and Franklin both."

"Maybe I did at some point in my life, but not anymore. I've had half a dozen chances to kill either one or both in the past five or six years, and I didn't do it. I had to shoot him. You and he forced me into it. Besides, if I did everything I wanted, I'd have been in your bed two weeks ago."

Abby opened her mouth, but the roar of avalanching debris drowned out her denial.

"Watch it!" Cam reached for Abby just as a burning log rocketed over the ledge above and splashed into the water behind her in an explosion of sparks and steam. The shock threw her against his chest, and Cam caught her and held her there, safe.

In the next breath Abby's arms were around his neck. Her fingers threaded into his hair, tugging his head within reach.

She touched her lips to his hesitantly, then more surely, her tongue questing, probing. Her impatient hunger inflamed Cam, changing his anger to something even more primal. The feel of the red flannel beneath his hands wiped out any vestigial impulse to do the honorable thing.

"Abby."

Chapter 10

It was dangerous, this ferocious need, more dangerous than the fire that still scorched the mountains all around them. It verged on insanity.

Abby knew it, knew what meeting her need would mean, and still she pressed Cam for more, demanded his response with every skill she'd absorbed from his efforts over the past fortnight. Cam grabbed her wrists as though to free himself. A low growl rumbled in his throat, and he wrested control of the kiss, bruising Abby's lips with a hunger as sharp as her own. Cam twined his tongue with hers, licking at her, devouring her, arousing her as he slipped his hands along her arms and down the length of her body to her hips. Abby raised on to her toes, and he pulled her to him.

The quick tightening low in her belly defined Abby's need even more clearly, erased the last shreds of society-bred propriety and self-control. She moved against Cam, brazen as Hannah ever could be, feeling his stirring hardness trapped between their bodies, and needing him even more.

His eyes coal dark in the deepening twilight, Cam set her back from him, scanning Abby's face intently.

Whatever he saw must have satisfied him, for his gaze dropped lower, into the shadows of his red shirt. Hooking one finger in the vee of the neckline, he tugged the material out from her skin. Warm air swirled over Abby's breasts, and her nipples tightened in anticipation.

A smile curved Cam's lips as he lifted the weight of her breasts in his palms, rubbing the velvety cloth over the sensitive peaks until Abby ached for the touch of flesh against flesh. She arched into his hands, his touch a gentle torture, inviting him to strip away the fabric, but he continued to use it to tantalize her. When she thought she couldn't bear it any longer, Abby began to unbutton her shirt.

"No." Cam pulled her hands away.

For one frantic instant Abby thought he was going to walk away again, leave her aroused and unsatisfied, but Cam lowered his head for another series of kisses that said he was far from through, kisses that covered her face and pushed the collar of her shirt aside to nibble at her neck and shoulders. Kisses that promised and enthralled, cajoled and seduced.

Abby caught her breath as he recaptured her breasts and resumed his merciless teasing. His thumbs traced circles around her nipples, flicking back and forth over the crests until every tingling nerve in her body seemed to focus in those two incredibly swollen points.

Nearly swooning with the sheer pleasure of it, she steadied herself against Cam's chest with one hand, her fingers splayed across the open collar of his shirt. The sudden recollection of his bare torso, sculptured by lantern light in the cabin, blazed into Abby's mind. The triangle of feverish skin beneath her palm emboldened her. Trapped still by Cam's lips, by his deep, soul-racking kisses, she made short work of the long line of buttons and slipped her hands inside his shirt to explore his form by touch. His square shoulders, the broad reach of his back, his narrow waist and flat belly, his muscled chest, each came in turn under her searching hands. But it wasn't until her fingertips skimmed over his nipples that Abby discovered her power.

Cam shuddered; one spasm rippled through the muscles beneath her hands, and another, lower, where his loins brushed against her.

Abby ran her fingertips over the flat buttons of his nipples again. The same reaction. With delicate, deliberate vengeance, she duplicated the flicking motions Cam made at her breasts, until she coaxed his nipples erect.

"Be careful, woman," Cam warned in a voice ragged with desire.

"I'm tired of being careful. I want you. I want you to teach me, Cam." She dipped her head to touch her lips to one coppery circle.

With a growl Cam locked his arms around her, crushing her close so she could do no more damage. "You're learning fine on your own. Come here." He drew her toward the recess where they were to sleep, stopping at the edge of the blanket. "Take your boots off."

He nibbled at Abby's neck enticingly as she obeyed and kicked her boots aside. Spurs jingled as Cam's heavier boots landed in the gravel next to hers.

"I'm not stopping this time, Abby." His fingers worked at the knotted rope at her waist. "We could burn alive and I wouldn't be able to stop."

In answer, she pushed his shirt off his shoulders and down his arms, and stripped the long shirttail out of his pants. As she unbuckled his gunbelt, Cam shook his arms free of his sleeves and went back to untying her makeshift belt; a moment later it dropped away. Abby felt the pants shift and hang on her hips.

Mischief mixing with the dark desire in his eyes, Cam took her hands and stepped backward a long pace forcing her to follow. The pants slithered over Abby's hips and landed in a bunch around her ankles. Following Cam, she stepped out of them and onto the blanket before it hit her what he'd done, before her skin suffused with crimson at the realization that her drawers were in the sodden pile of clothes she'd shed earlier, and she was standing before him naked from the waist down.

"I've been imagining you like this since you asked for that damned rope," Cam admitted in a raw whisper. "I just had to see it for myself."

His crooked smile faded to a look of smoldering heat, and Cam reached for her. His hands played freely over cloth and skin, unbuttoning the top few buttons of her shirt as he plundered her mouth once more, briefly, then trailed kisses down her neck and into the valley between her breasts. Abby ran her hands across Cam's bare chest. But when he pushed aside the shirt at last and scooped one breast into a ripe mound in his palm, ready for the warm wetness of his mouth, she could manage only to clutch at his shoulders and toss her head back in a pleasured sigh.

He suckled and nipped and tongued and teased, then switched to the other breast for a time. Eventually he left them both behind to follow the path of buttons down the length of her body. Unfastening them one at a time, he placed long, delicate kisses at each newly revealed spot, until he reached the final button and the shirt fell open.

As Abby stood trembling, heart racing, in the dim glow of the dying sun and fire, Cam's heated gaze skimmed over her body. She heard the sharp intake of his breath, felt the trace of Cam's fingers over the hollow of her belly and down. Unhesitating, he slipped his hand between her thighs. Abby gasped as warmth flowed to the spot where he touched her.

All the exquisite, torturous sensations lingering in her breasts tumbled downward to join those created by his fingers as Cam stroked and probed with deliberate enjoyment. A sheen of perspiration slicked his skin beneath her hands.

"Please, oh, please," Abby breathed, wondering how long

she could remain standing under Cam's assault. She heard him chuckle as his kiss returned to her breasts, and then her limbs turned to jelly as he mirrored with his tongue the wicked, delicious things he was doing with his hand. She sagged, and Cam caught her with a strong arm around her waist, lowering her to her knees without ever interrupting the fluid dance of his fingers among the folds of dewy skin. Still gripping his shoulders, she tried to pull him down to lie with her, but he held her upright.

"Oh, please, Cam, please now," she begged again.

"Not quite yet." Cam smiled and steered her hands down, over the diamond of golden hair on his chest, across his flat belly to the waist of his pants. With no words of encouragement needed, she stripped open the button fly, helping him peel the pants away. "See what you do to me?" With gentle firmness, Cam guided her hand to him, curling her fingers around his taut, heavy flesh.

Again Abby felt power as her touch caused a stir of life and heat. Tentatively, then with growing sureness and excitement, she explored the length of him, discovered the incredible juxtaposition of hardness and delicacy. She was surprised when Cam pulled her hand away.

"You do learn too quickly. Come here." Cam sat back, made himself comfortable against his saddle and the wall of the grotto, then pulled Abby astride his thighs. Her confusion must have been evident. "Too many rocks. If we do it the usual way, you'll be all bruises tomorrow." His fingers slipped into her moistness, found a spot more sensitive than most and stroked it gently. With a cry of pleasure, Abby arched into him, her nipples brushing the curls that sprinkled his chest. "Besides, I want to watch you give yourself to me."

A rush of liquid heat drenched Abby as Cam dipped the tip of one finger inside her, and his exclamation of discovery matched Abby's soft, shuddering moan. Instinctively she pressed into his hand, felt his finger slide deeper.

"So warm, so tight," he whispered. He withdrew his

finger partway and inserted it again. "Open for me, Abby. Let yourself open." Eyes bright with desire, Cam slipped a second finger alongside the first. The fullness enchanted Abby, the churning of his fingers within excited her. She pressed down again into his palm, letting him ready her. Her hips squirmed softly as she tried to pull his fingers deeper.

"You need something more, don't you, love?" Cam teased, releasing her. "What do you need, Abby?"

"You." Restless, she reached for him. "I don't know what to do."

"Let me show you." His strong hands cupping her bottom, Cam tugged Abby closer, lifting her above him. A slight shift of his hips brought his shaft against her soft, heated core. "Take me into you," he urged, holding her there, just touching him. "Slowly, a little at a time."

Abby drifted onto him, Cam coaxing her along with his voice and touch. His sure hands guided her, never forcing her down but refusing to let her back off more than the merest fraction. When the stretching pain of his entry made her want to lift away, he held her locked in position, calming her with quiet praise. He told her of the pleasure to come in words that made her hot and slick and ready to take him deeper. Inch by inch, her path eased by her own moisture, Abby slowly accepted his length.

As she hesitated at the last, convinced she could contain no more of him, Cam raised her a fraction and settled her back, then pressed her hips down as he lifted into her and buried himself completely. A hoarse whisper echoed in the dark, "You're mine."

Abby clung to Cam, adjusting to his male size as he caressed her breasts, coaxing them to still harder peaks. His hands wandered over her possessively, pushing the red shirt aside, and the soft stream of air he blew over her breasts raised prickles of flesh that left her even more sensitive. Cam placed one hand low on her belly, and moving it downward, he brushed through the soft triangle of hair. He moved directly to that sensitive spot he'd found earlier, circling it, then trapping it against the fleshy pad of his thumb.

Instinctively Abby pressed against his thumb, slid against it in the slow bucking motion that brought her pleasure. In doing so, she moved along his length. Cam shuddered beneath her. An exclamation of understanding escaped Abby, and she began to experiment, using her own pleasure and the tortured groans of the man beneath her as the measure of her success. Her movements grew bolder, more certain, as she climbed toward some unknown goal. Then abruptly, without warning, she reached it and shattered into a million starlit pieces.

Abby cried out in wonder as Cam, far beyond reason, plunged into her, thrusting upward until his body arched and tensed. As he pulsed into her, Abby's body tightened, welcoming his seed. She collapsed, gratefully spent, against his chest and they clung to each other.

"You're mine," Cam whispered again, shaking his head as if to rid himself of a haze.

"What?" Abby asked.

"Nothing. I just didn't think it would be like this." He held her for a long time, their bodies trembling and spent, before he invited her, "Come lie beside me, my beautiful wanton."

You're mine, Cam thought again, much later, as they lay fitted together like two spoons in a drawer. He traced the curve of Abby's hip, careful not to waken her. *All of that passion, all of that glorious, erotic delight in your body is mine.*

The memory of his driving desire as her silky sheath enveloped him was enough to harden him again, and with her bare buttocks tucked up against him, he soon found himself a hair's breadth away from entering her from behind. Abby stirred sleepily in his arms.

It would be so easy, Cam thought. He could sink deep

within her before she even awakened, enjoy her heated arousal from beginning to end.

Stop acting like a buck in rut.

With an effort of will, Cam pushed away from Abby and slipped out from under the blanket. Moving quietly, he donned his pants and boots and went to check his horse. Kneeling by the stream, he splashed frigid water over his head and shoulders.

When he cooled down he went back to Abby, sat on a rock and watched her sleep.

What he'd told her was true: He didn't think it would be like this.

Revenge wasn't supposed to be *this* sweet. His sense of victory wasn't supposed to get swamped by desire. He wasn't supposed to ache for her.

Abby wasn't meant to be his lover, after all, but when he had his arms around her, she felt like a lover. Cam tried to distance himself, to remind himself why he had done this thing, but only one answer came into his mind: because he wanted to, because he wanted Abby. Tomorrow, he promised himself, tomorrow he'd remember its purpose and figure it all out.

Abby rolled onto her back, her breasts rising and falling gently with each breath. "Cam?"

"Right here." Cam kicked his boots free and slipped beneath the blanket. She burrowed into his arms, a warm bundle that aroused and soothed with her nearness, and drifted back to sleep.

"You're mine," he whispered again.

The words were still in Cam's mind when he awoke hours later to bright sun and the sight of Abby standing by the stream, staring out at the blackened slopes. At the sound of his rising, she turned and met his eyes. A blush suffused her cheeks and seeped charmingly down the neckline of his oversize red shirt.

"I should have rinsed out my clothes last night. With

the air so warm, they'd all be dry by now and I could return your things. I suppose I'll just have to beat the mud out and see if they'll do. When I see how severely burnt everything is and recall how quickly that fire traveled, I am truly grateful to you. Really, we are so lucky to be a—"

Cam cut her off with a kiss. With one hand he cupped the back of Abby's head; with the other he teased her mouth open with a gentle tug to the chin. When she sighed, he dipped his tongue in slow reminder of the previous night's delights.

"—alive," Abby finished a bit breathlessly when Cam released her. She slipped her arms around his waist, and he gathered her to him. "Oh, my."

"Oh, my, indeed. I didn't think you were the kind to get embarrassed."

"I'm not. That is, I . . . oh, well, yes, I am embarrassed. What does one say the morning after . . . something like that?"

"Thank you?" Cam suggested with a smile.

Abby pinched him. "I'm serious. I feel so awkward. All day long I was furious with you and this insane situation you've dragged me into, and suddenly all I wanted was for you to hold me."

"You wanted a little more than that," Cam corrected gently. "It wasn't all that sudden. We've both been wanting it for days." The clear flare of remembered desire that lit Abby's eyes pleased him more than he'd have thought possible, and he ignored the nagging voice that asked what those hazel eyes would hold when she discovered how he'd planned all along to use her.

"Katherine Braddock—she's a friend of mine back home—intimated that . . . something like that was a woman's duty. She didn't seem to like it very much. Maybe her husband isn't very adept," she said quite deliberately, a slight, suggestive smile on her lips.

"Your awkward feelings disappear quickly, don't they?" Cam chuckled at the fresh pink that spotted Abby's cheeks.

If he didn't get his hands off her, he'd have her back on that blanket in seconds. Cam set her away and smudged at a dirty spot on her nose with his thumb. "You'd make a lovely chimney sweep. Wash your face while I water Billy."

"I certainly smell like a sweep," Abby groused as she knelt by the stream. "Of course, so do you. I can't imagine you found that attractive."

"I found everything about you attractive last night. In fact, I have a feeling I will appreciate the scent of woodsmoke in an entirely new way now. Every campfire is likely to send me in search of you."

"You are an unrepentant cad, Mr. Garrett," Abby's tone scolded, but her eyes smiled. "Now, what did you do with my blouse?"

"You had it last."

"But that was before . . . oh, no."

"You left it in the water," Cam recalled.

"It's probably in Mexico by now."

"More like Utah, from here. Look, I need to check things out anyway, see if we can get out of here safely. I'll see if I can spot it snagged downstream."

"I thought we'd be stuck here for a while."

"No longer than necessary. We've got plenty of people food, but all I have for Billy is a few handfuls of oats. We need to find him some decent grass."

"Do you think there is any?"

It was hard to fault her skepticism, Cam thought, staring out at the smoking, black landscape. The aftermath of a war could hardly be worse. *Heck of a place to take a virgin, Garrett.* No wonder she called their lovemaking "something like that."

"There will be, someplace. We may have to ride a ways."

What does one do and say the morning after such an experience? Abby wondered again as they rode out of the gulch. She tried to imagine a normal morning after, after a night spent with a man in a proper marriage bed—the kind she was to have had with Franklin, something she now had a great deal of trouble even comprehending, much less imagining without disgust.

How could a woman sit across from a man at breakfast, sipping at coffee and reading the morning mail, after the sort of thing that had happened last night? Of course, it apparently wasn't always such a cataclysmic experience, if Katherine was serious.

Riding in Cam's arms was easier than facing him back by the stream, maybe because his arms felt so right around her, or maybe because she didn't have to meet the gleam of desire in his eyes. They rode out from the gulch, as close to due north as the terrain would allow, across acres and acres of devastation. Here and there a dim red glow lingered under layers of ash. These areas Cam gave wide berth, but he always turned back north.

What astonished Abby was the randomness of the burn, the way the flames seemed to have hopscotched through some meadows and bypassed certain trees, or even entire stands. Some areas had enough grass intact that Cam let his horse snag a few mouthfuls as they traveled.

"How did you know about that cave?" Abby asked.

"My father and I came hunting up here when I was a kid. We stumbled across it during a snowstorm and liked it so much we came back every fall after roundup. It's been years."

"I didn't know you grew up around here. I don't know very much about you at all, considering."

"There's not very much to know."

Oh, yes there is, Cam Garrett. Abby would start with the basics. "Does your family have a ranch?"

"We did."

Two words, calmly said, and in them, Abby suspected, the key to Cam's vendetta against Franklin Tanner. She laid her head back against Cam's shoulder and pulled his arm tighter around her waist.

"Franklin," she said. "What did he do?"

Every muscle in Cam's body tensed, but his voice remained calm, collected. "He took it all."

"How? What did he do?" she repeated.

"He took everything. My father, my mother, the ranch. Every single thing that ever meant anything to me. He even tried to take my life. Just leave it at that." Cam's clipped tone allowed no further probing, but Abby felt the shuddering movement of his chest, as if he was holding in a sob, or swallowing enough hatred to choke a man, and suddenly she was very frightened for him.

"Revenge won't bring any of it back."

"We'll see."

"It won't make you feel any better, either."

"Now, there you're wrong. It already has."

Franklin scrawled a few notes along the edge of the map, then sat back to take a broader look. It contained too many blank stretches, unmapped or roughly mapped areas that could hide an army. He'd have to find a couple of scouts who knew the high mountains better, who could find the kind of hideouts Garrett and his men would be likely to use. He flipped through his journal, hoping to see some clue he'd overlooked.

Two weeks. Two damned weeks Abby had been in Garrett's hands. If he'd so much as touched her . . .

Knuckles rapped sharply on the door. Tanner flipped the map over. "In."

Hawkins pushed the door open and stepped through, followed closely by Domingo, the half Comanche hand Tanner kept around for his unique usefulness. "Got some news on Stanton, boss. You ain't going to like it."

"Go on."

"Seems the last anyone saw of him, he was at Noreen's. Talking to Hannah. That'd be three, four days ago."

"He wouldn't have gone off without reason. She probably had some information for him." Franklin rolled the pencil between his fingers.

"I don't think so, Mr. Tanner," Hawk said reluctantly.

Franklin glanced up. "Spit it out."

"Well, sir, Hannah's gone, too. Noreen's pissed as all get-out. She says Hannah left an hour or two after Stanton was there, without saying a word."

"To meet him?"

"Noreen didn't likely know, but she sure as hell would like to get her hands on either one of them. Nobody bought out Hannah's contract. We found a couple of boys said they saw the two of them headed north off the road. They weren't together at that point, but . . ."

Tanner looked to the other man. Domingo shook his head silently, and Tanner knew there had been no trail to pick up. Suddenly the days of frustration threatened to spill over.

"Get out of here," he ordered, and the men disappeared without question. The front door slammed and heavy boots tromped across the porch and down the steps.

Something cracked sharply. Franklin looked down, found the splintered remains of the pencil in his fist. That's what he'd do to them. First Garrett, then Stanton, then delectable, red-haired Hannah. He'd break them into little pieces, every one of them, and then he'd let Domingo have them for sport.

First he needed to get Abigail back. She'd bring him everything he needed to get those three. Franklin dumped the broken pencil into the wastecan near his feet, then reached for his pen and a sheet of stationery. He felt the splinters in his palm as he carefully composed the telegrams to St. Louis and Denver.

First he'd get Abigail, then he'd track the others down and break them, no matter what it took.

"This is it. We'll stop for lunch here and give Billy a chance to graze." Cam dismounted.

Abby slipped down into his waiting arms, then dashed off into the center of a meadow brilliant with fireweed and scarlet gilia. Arms wide, she spun around in delight. "It's glorious. Beautiful, green grass and all these flowers. I didn't think we'd ever get out of the ashes." She found a spot amid a swath of fireweed and flopped onto her back. She pulled one magenta stalk to her nose and inhaled. "I'll be right here, enjoying the smell."

A few minutes later Cam stood over her, grinning. "You present a sore temptation, Miss Morgan, lying there like that. 'Many a green gown has been given; Many a kiss both odde and even.' "

"I'm sure any education that presented archaic poetry must have taught you self-control as well," she scolded. He'd piqued her curiosity once again, however. Abby sat up and assumed a less wanton pose. "Where did you study?"

"Back East."

"That's not an answer," Abby said in exasperation. "Doesn't being your paramour grant me at least a few privileges?"

"One time, my sweet, does not a paramour make." Cam dropped to his knees next to Abby. "Did you give yourself to me to get 'privileges'?"

"Of course not. I wish you'd just tell me about yourself."

"I've spent nearly thirteen years figuring out what to do about Tanner, and almost that long watching every word I say, just to make certain I get my chance. That's not going to change any time soon, and certainly not before I move on him. It's not easy for me to let anybody get too close, Abby."

"After last night you should realize I'm not going to use every scrap of information against you."

"I wouldn't have thought you'd take off on me yesterday afternoon, either, but there you went."

Was that just yesterday afternoon? It seemed like a different year, different people. "I saw the road. I was in such a state, I couldn't think."

"Well, the road's just the other side of this hill, not more than a couple of miles. Turn left for Lake City, right for Saguache."

Abby stared at him, stunned. "Are you sending me back?"

"Hardly. Just letting you know where you are. I intend to keep you close by, and I will undoubtedly take every opportunity to encourage you to repeat our actions of last night. Including right here, right now."

He proceeded to do so, with a long, persuasive kiss and an intimate caress that shackled Abby to him as surely as chains.

"Very encouraging," Abby said, her lips moist from his roving tongue.

"I'm glad." Cam plucked a single fairy trumpet from a nearby gilia and drew it across Abby's lips. The nectar flowed, tasting sweet as honeysuckle. "This would have been a better place for your first time. Beautiful, quiet, safe. A place where we can take our time."

"But I needed you last night." She wondered if Cam's outlaw ways had rubbed off on her somehow. Every time he took her in his arms, she grew bold, her words and actions reckless.

"And now?"

"I think," Abby whispered, looking him straight in the eye, "that I may need you again."

"Do you still think I'm a cad?"

"Definitely. Without a single redeeming quality."

"And do you know what you are?"

"What?"

"Delicious." Cam tasted the flower nectar on her lips, then whispered an absolutely shocking suggestion into her ear, a suggestion that made heated excitement flow to exactly the spot he proposed tasting next. Abby felt certain that the merest touch of his tongue there would make her senses explode. When Cam worked his knee between her thighs, she felt her anticipation grow.

"Do two times make a paramour?" she wondered aloud

as Cam pressed her down into the grass and reached for her rope belt.

"No, but it's much closer."

The high-pitched whinny of the bay and the answering neigh of an approaching horse made Cam lift his head. Fingers touching his gun, he scanned the area quickly, then relaxed. He raised a hand in greeting.

"It's Rico," he muttered, sounding acutely frustrated. "A thousand square miles of wilderness and he finds us here and now."

"The man has impeccable timing." Abby quickly adjusted her clothes and sat up. "This is the second time he's interrupted us."

"That's what chaperons are for," Cam reminded her in a low voice, and she felt like swatting him. "I can always send him away."

"Heavens, no. If you do that, he'll figure out exactly what we are . . . were doing."

"I'd say he's already guessed."

Abby twisted to see him. Sure enough, Rico exhibited the unfocused gaze and set smile of a person pretending not to see something private. He reined in his horse down at the stream next to Billy and dismounted.

Abby tried to compose herself as Cam helped her to her feet. "Well, if he can pretend not to notice, I certainly can."

She started off, but Cam stuck a finger in the waist of her pants and tugged her back.

"We may not be able to finish what we started here for a few days, but I promise you, we will finish it. You keep in mind what I intend to do with you, and remember that I'm as anxious to do it as you are to find out what it's like. Now let's go tell the man hello."

Chapter 11

A day and a half later, beneath the crystal blue sky of late afternoon, Cam pointed to a stand of big timber just the other side of a strip of open park.

"We're headed for that saddle between those two peaks," he said.

Abby peered at the ridge. "I don't see anybody there yet."

"You wouldn't. Nobody would. That's the point." Cam doffed his hat and waved it a couple of times as though signaling someone. "The trees are thick enough up there to hide Hannibal and his elephants. The other side's about as open as this. Short of crawling over the top of the mountains, there's no way anyone can get near us without being seen. To top it off, enough game uses the trails over that saddle to keep us fed without much trouble."

As they neared the foot of the ridge, two men with rifles stepped out into the sun.

"I think they're curious about your clothes," Cam said after they'd exchanged greetings with the two and ridden on into the trees. "There's our new place."

"Where?" All Abby saw was a mound of dirt, indistinguishable from the rest of the mountain. A short distance away, Digger bent over a pan, peeling a few potatoes.

"About thirty feet over that way," Cam coached. "Look for what doesn't belong. Nature tends toward curves and angles. She doesn't draw straight lines very well, especially on the horizontal."

"The door," Abby said, finally spotting the hard black edges of a doorway leading into the mound. "That's a cabin?"

"A dugout. Kind of like a soddy with no sod. Of course, it's not as comfortable as the cabin. And the whole situation does lack a little in privacy."

A surreptitious squeeze let Abby know that Cam had no more forgotten the unfinished business between them than she had. Forgotten? She could scarcely think of anything else. There had been times in the past day when she wished for another fire, or at least some minor diversion that might separate them from Rico for an hour or two, long enough to experience Cam's suggested delight.

Abby wondered just how she'd turned into such a libertine in a matter of days.

"Got any coffee?" Cam asked as he helped Abby down.

"Just some cold," Digger said. "We ain't had a fire but at night and early mornin' before sun's up, just in case Tanner and his bunch is around. Want me to pour you some?"

"No, I need to check things out first. I'll wait for supper."

"Who is here so far?" Rico asked.

"Everybody but Charlie and Tony. I 'spect they decided to come around the long way after that fire. You folks look like you come out of it a bit worse for wear, if you'll pardon me, miss."

"And I thought I looked like a fashionable belle from Paris." Abby pulled the oversize pants out skirtlike and curtsied to Digger. "I'm afraid I lost Lew's horse and everything I own. I was trying to get away from Cam and a mountain lion spooked my horse, and I ended up in a stream."

Digger's mouth dropped open, and he looked from Abby, to Rico, to Cam and back again.

Cam looked nearly as shocked. "I never heard about any mountain lion."

"Didn't I mention that? I suppose by the time I was in the mood to volunteer anything, it just didn't seem to matter anymore." She gave Cam a meaningful look, grinning at his slightly fevered glance back. She was beginning to discover the fun in being able to twit him like that. "I'd like some of that coffee, Digger, cold or not."

Digger glanced toward Cam again, this time his bushy eyebrow curved up in question.

"Don't ask me," Cam said blandly. "I have no idea why she does the things she does, or says the things she says."

"Don't suppose you do." Digger pointed Abby toward his grub box and makeshift kitchen, chuckling to himself as he poured her a tin cup of coffee. "Dare say you're a-startin' to like it, though."

As she sipped at the bitter, cold coffee with nonchalance, Abby was intently aware of Cam's long, assessing look. When he turned his mount uphill and rode off with Rico, her gaze traced the line where his neck curved into his shoulders. Her fingers curled around the smoothness of the cup.

Digger fussed around his pots for a few minutes, getting things ready so the fire could be kept to a minimum. "Guess you'll be sleepin' in there," he said, gesturing at the dugout. "Go in and take a look around."

Abby tossed the dregs out of her cup onto the ground and took Digger up on his suggestion. She opened the door and stared around the gloomy interior of the hut. Crescent-shaped spade marks still showed in the back wall where the earth had been chopped away. The supports for the dirt roof consisted largely of saplings small enough to have been chopped down with the same spade and woven together with their branches still intact. She stepped in. Hannah lay on one of the familiar army cots, a blanket pulled to her chin and her arm over her eyes.

"Who made this?" Abby hesitated to use the word built. Hacked would be more appropriate.

"Some fellas a while back was robbin' payroll wagons and stages and such," Digger said from the doorway just behind Abby. "They hid out in this place for a couple of summers till they got cocky and decided they liked life in town a little better. Kept doin' their business from right in Alamosa. One of 'em's dead now, and at least two're in state prison. They should've stayed up here."

"I think I can see why they didn't." A tangle of brittle twigs barely skimmed Abby's head. A man of any size, like Cam, would have to stoop. "It's not much more than a cave."

"It ain't so bad. Down in the prairies in the old days, they sometimes dug down in a flat field and just sodded over the hole. Every time it rained, the whole mess filled up with water."

"Why would people live like that?"

"Because they couldn't afford better." Raising up on one elbow, Hannah gave Abby a pointed stare. "Like my folks. Ma used to pile all the kids on a bed to get them out of the muck. They had a real wood house by the time I came along, but it wasn't much better."

"And where you live now is?" Abby asked.

"Noreen's is a damned palace compared to my house." Bitterness shook Hannah's voice and she flopped onto her back. "Get your self-righteous pity out of here."

"Hannah, I—"

"Shut up. I can see it in those big round eyes. You're about to say how sorry you are that my life was so rough. No maids to bring me breakfast in bed. Well, take it someplace else. I'm trying to get some sleep."

"Aw, Hannah," Digger started, but Abby pushed out past him, and he abandoned his scolding and followed. "Don't take her to heart, miss."

"I don't." Abby strolled over to the big pot of water that held the potatoes for supper and prodded one floating slice with a finger. "And I don't feel sorry for her, either. I'll talk to her later. We'll work it out."

Digger shooed her away from the pot and started arranging the kindling and wood for the evening fire. "Hannah's as tough as they come, but she told me on the way up here—"

"You two rode together?"

He ducked his head a little shyly. "Yes'm. Anyway, she mentioned how much she misses all her family, her ma, especially. She took off hopin' she could send some money back to help out, but they won't take it, seein' how Hannah earns it. She's kind of proud of 'em, even though she'll tell you it's foolishness. Same time, it hurts her that her ma and pa are ashamed."

"At least she has a mother to be ashamed of her," Abby mused. Digger gave her a quizzical look that she chose to ignore. "Is there anything I can do to help you with dinner?"

"I been meanin' to tell you, miss, around these parts, what a body eats at night is supper. Dinner's what you eat at noon. Just hand me them matches there."

The odd thing was, Cam thought as he rode the perimeter, Digger was right. He did like Abby's quick tongue and disconcerting way of telling the truth just when you least expected it.

Like in the middle of a fire.

Cam shook aside the blistering memories and concentrated on the task at hand.

Jesús had everything in order: guards set, men assigned to hunt, and a couple of riders sent into Lake City for grain and a few supplies.

Cam nodded his appreciation. "Couldn't have done any better myself. You up to a ride into town?"

"I think I could force myself." The man's dazzling grin nearly split his face. With a wife as pretty as Maria, Cam could hardly blame him.

"While you're home, I want you to nose around a little, find out what Tanner's up to and what his plans are. See if he knew where Stanton was headed. Check on Juanita, see if anyone's watching her place. If you can get to her safely, you might suggest she leave town for a few weeks. Arrange a telegram from a sick cousin if she needs a good story."

"Should I tell our other friends how to reach us?"

Cam considered the risks and rejected the idea. "Not at this point. Have them go back to using the drop in Tracy Canyon. We'll check it whenever we can."

"As you wish. How much time do I have?"

"As long as you need. By the way, I want you to pick up a few things to bring back." Cam dictated a brief list and handed Jesús the necessary cash.

"I will see you next spring, then. Ah, Maria . . ." Jesús gave Cam a wink and headed off to get his gear together.

Cam laughed, confident that Jesús would be back within the week, saddle sore, full of news, and strumming nothing but love songs on his guitar for a month.

"What about Tanner?" Rico asked when they were unsaddling their horses and no one else was within hearing. "If you cut off our contacts, how will we know when he is ready to pay the *señorita's* ransom?"

"We'll hear eventually. He'll just have to wait."

"Tanner is not a patient man. When we do not answer quickly—"

"I'm not running this outfit for Tanner's convenience," Cam growled, tossing his saddle onto a fallen log next to Rico's.

"You cannot delay too long. Willem is due soon."

"He can postpone his trip. In fact, before Jesús leaves, I'll tell him to wire Uncle Karl to arrange the delay."

"Why? You've spent years getting to this point. You can have Tanner by the end of the month."

"Or he can have us. I'll worry about taking Tanner's money when I'm convinced we're all safe. I'm not going to lose another man by getting slack or by hurrying into something we're not ready for."

"Three days ago you said we were ready, before you spent the night alone with the señorita. You have not said what happened, but now your eyes are full of lust and you find these excuses for delay."

Cam waved the idea aside. "I'm just being careful."

"You have always been careful, but never have I seen you reluctant to do what needs to be done."

"I never had one of my men killed before. And I never had to shoot a man down, either. I discovered killing doesn't sit well with me, Rico. Daydreaming about it is one thing, but pulling the trigger . . ."

"But you did it, thank the saints." Rico crossed himself.

"And I'll do it again if I have to, but I want to make sure I *don't* have to. That means being very certain of every step against Tanner from this point on. Waiting will just make him that much crazier, make it that much easier to put one over on him. He'll expose himself for what he really is, and that's the only way we can really cripple him. Abby is the key to that, nothing more." *Convince yourself, too, Garrett.*

Rico gave Cam a long, hard look, then sighed. "I am being a foolish old man. We have spent years planning this together."

"And we'll finish it together, too. Just like we planned."

Easy enough to say in the light of day with Abby out of sight. It was a whole different matter at night, with her sleeping a few feet away, and when all he could think of was burying himself in her warmth. He wanted to wrap his arms around her for as long as he had strength.

But that required time and privacy. As he tossed and turned on the uncomfortable camp bed, Cam plotted to find both. Even if Abby were willing to slip out of the dugout in the middle of the night to get away from Hannah and Rico, a dozen men slept just outside the door. He couldn't very well announce, "Oh, just ignore us, I'm taking her off into the woods now for a tumble."

A tumble. Cam's groin tightened as he imagined spilling Abby into the grass in some high meadow and falling on top of her in delighted abandon. He lay in the dark for what might have been hours, aching, until he finally drifted into a restless sleep that lasted until the aroma of coffee overwhelmed the earthen smell of the dugout.

"I am *not* sleeping in there again," Abby announced at breakfast. Slight blue circles beneath her eyes spoke of a night as restless as Cam's. "Bugs kept falling out of that trash heap that passes for a roof. Plop. Plop." She shuddered, and Cam got the impression it was at least partly for dramatic effect. "I barely kept from screaming."

"I didn't have any problem with bugs," Hannah said.

"Your snoring probably scared them all over to her side," Cam said.

"I don't snore."

"Yes, you do." A chorus of male voices ended the argument before it got going. Hannah pouted.

"Those were probably just little beetles," Rico said.

"I don't care what they were," Abby said. "I will not have another one landing on me. I'm sleeping outside."

Anticipation made Cam's pulse race. "Remember, it's not as warm up here as it was down in the middle of that fire."

"Frostbite is better than bugbite any day." Abby brushed a wisp of hair out of her face and helped herself to a rasher of bacon and another flapjack. Poking at a drop of grease, already congealed to lard in the frosty morning air, she met Cam's eyes with a look that made a tight knot form in the middle of his chest. He suddenly knew Abby wasn't the least bit afraid of bugs. "I do reserve the right to change my mind, however," she added.

The double meanings were not lost on Cam. He knew what she was playing at and understood her unwillingness to let the others know what had passed between them. He smiled. "Of course, but I have a feeling that once you get used to lying under the stars, it will be hard to go back."

For both of them. She looked so beautiful in that damned red shirt. Quickly excusing himself, Cam headed off to his chores before the urge to rip those buttons open made him do something crass.

Reluctant as Cam was to admit it, even to himself, Rico was right: He found it harder and harder to even consider sending Abby back to Tanner, much less stay callous about it. When Tanner realized she'd taken a lover, and who that lover was, he'd go berserk. Cam had planned the kidnapping in the first place because he knew Tanner would react that way.

It had seemed so clear at the time, using some faceless pawn to set the final steps in motion. But now the pawn had a face, and flashing hazel eyes, and lips sweet as wild berries. Now the musky female scent of Abby blended with the smell of smoke in Cam's mind. How could he put her back in Tanner's hands? Yet how could he keep her and let his men down, betraying the promise he'd made them? He had to figure out a way to keep both Abby *and* his promise.

He grabbed his tack and headed for the stake line. Ten minutes later Cam slipped his rifle into the scabbard on his saddle and wheeled out of camp.

"Going hunting," he told the man watching the north approach, but he wasn't sure for what.

"I can't believe you found him!" Abby dashed to meet Antonio and Charlie as they rode into camp at long last. Behind them, on a long rope lead alongside their pack horses, trailed Lew's Appaloosa, his head drooping in dejection.

Charlie hopped off his horse, a big grin turning his round cheeks to apples. He shook Abby's hand like he was priming a pump.

"I sure am glad to see you, miss. When we found your pony, I was sure you must be around someplace. I made Tony search and search, but we couldn't find any trace of you. I was awfully worried, with that fire going. How did you lose him?"

He got an abridged version of the events, minus the part about trying to escape and what had happened between her and Cam, but including the mountain lion and the race up the gulch, which Abby knew would give the boy a thrill. "And then we met Rico," she finished.

"Where did you get thrown?" Charlie asked.

"I'm not really sure. Maybe Cam or Rico could tell you. All I know is, I'm certainly glad to have some of my own clothes back." Abby started toward the Appaloosa before she noticed that his saddle looked sadly empty. "Where's my . . . Oh, no."

"The animal carried nothing when we found him," Antonio said.

"It kind of looks like maybe you didn't tie things on so good," Charlie added. "Or he might have tried to roll the saddle off."

"Oh, no," Abby repeated, staring down at the dirty knees of her borrowed pants. She'd spent a good portion of the day scrubbing out her riding skirt and jacket, but she had little faith they'd be in wearable condition once they dried. Hannah was in no better shape, having left her clothes behind when she fled Stanton.

Oh, well, fortunately she had her underthings. She could always borrow clothes from the men on occasion, at least so she could launder Cam's clothes.

Abby turned back to Charlie. "Maybe after you take care of your horse, you could teach me how to tie a better knot."

The boy fairly leapt to get his work done. He then returned with a length of rope and sat down with Abby on a log and started showing her his best knots. Within minutes Digger was contributing his opinion, followed quickly by Pete and, eventually, Rico.

Thoroughly bewildered by the scattered, contrary instructions, Abby left the men to their haggling and wandered off to practice on her own.

"Over, then around," Abby muttered, twisting the rope ends the way Charlie had done.

"Actually, it's around, then over." Cam's strong arms slipped around Abby, and he took her hands.

A familiar shiver ran down her spine. "Must you sneak up on me?"

"I wasn't sneaking. Everyone else saw me." Sure enough, her group of would-be instructors drifted back to their business, sideways glances showing their nosiness. "You were just too busy tying this backward. Let me show you." Cam guided Abby through the motions, his beard brushing against her neck as he worked.

"Around, then over," repeated Abby mechanically, more interested in the feel of the man than of the rope.

"Let's try it once more." Cam stripped the knot out and started Abby through the pattern again. She watched his hands and remembered the feel of them against her skin, so powerful, so gentle. "There. Now you do it."

"It's easy once you know how," Abby marveled as the rope practically fell into place.

"That's true of a lot of things," Cam said dryly, then grunted as Abby jabbed an elbow into his ribs. He caught at her wrists, which had the effect of wrapping her more tightly in his arms. "I see you're still as genteel as the day we met."

"And you're still every bit the outlaw," she retorted, trying to sound casual when all she wanted was for him to pick her up and carry her off to do the wondrous things he'd promised. "Where have you been all day?"

"Hunting. Checking the area out. While I was out, I discovered I barely know how to ride anymore without you in front of me." Cam brushed his lips along her cheek as he released her, barely a kiss but enough to tell Abby he'd understood her rather obscure offer at breakfast.

Anticipation bubbled through her veins as they walked down to the campfire together.

"I cannot believe it. Why didn't you head Hannah off?" Cam demanded in a barely controlled whisper.

Rico grinned. "She has her own mind, and to tell the truth, I think it is funny."

The two men shared a bucket as they washed up in the early light of the following morning. Cam splashed an abundance of icy water over his face and shoulders. What he really needed was to strip down and dump the bucket over his head, force the heat of sexual frustration from his body and get himself back under control. But he didn't want to give Hannah the satisfaction of seeing the state he was in. And she would see, because she was parading back and forth not a dozen yards away, her hips swinging like she was working the parlor at Noreen's.

Cam had watched Abby subtly throughout the evening, just as she'd watched him. The more their eyes met, the more hers glowed with mischief and desire, and the more he wanted her.

So it had come as no real surprise when, as the men started drifting toward their bedrolls, Abby marched into the dugout and carried out an armload of blankets.

"Where's a good spot?" she asked the crew in general, but Cam in particular, her voice light.

"There's a pretty flat area up just above those two trees. Just uphill," Cam said. Just close enough so as not to raise too many suspicions, but isolated enough that they might manage—what? His mind raced through the possibilities as he made his own bed up a few yards away.

"Must you?" she asked sourly.

"You didn't really think I'd let you sleep out here alone, did you, with your habit of running off?" Cam asked loudly enough for half the camp to hear, and when Abby bit her lip to kill a smile, he knew he was playing the game correctly. "And don't give me any nonsense about chaperons."

They were about to settle in when Hannah appeared out of nowhere and dumped a wad of blankets between Cam's bedroll and Abby's.

"It's such a nice night out, I thought I'd join you two. This is a real fine idea you had, getting away from all those bugs."

"You said there weren't any bugs," Cam said.

"I saw some when I was combing my hair. Besides, I heard what you said about chaperons and started thinking about how it'd look to the biddies down in the valley if they found out you two had been sleeping out here alone. Wouldn't want Abby's reputation ruined."

Hannah wouldn't budge. Short of announcing to the whole outfit just why he and Abby didn't want any company, Cam could think of nothing that would shake her loose.

Through the whole scene, Hannah had remained totally relaxed and guileless, but then she probably acted the same way around Tanner. She still looked innocent, even as she wiggled her fanny in front of Digger. Cam couldn't figure out if she was honestly jealous or just out to tweak him and Abby a little.

Meantime, Abby sat with her back all stiff again and glared at Cam as though the whole thing was his fault, which it was. He never should have put her and Hannah in the same state, much less the same camp.

Cam dunked his head in the bucket and held it till the cold made his temples throb. It didn't do a thing for his libido.

"You don't know a thing. Poco can run circles around any horse here," claimed Charlie.

"Put your money on it then," Ephram said. "My mare against yours, for a dollar."

A dozen faces looked to Cam for permission. "Go ahead. If anyone was coming, they'd have shown up by now."

Men leapt for their saddles, and the camp emptied in minutes. Even Hannah, caught up in the excitement, rode off with the others. Half-eaten plates of food lay scattered around.

Abby stared after them.

"Foolishness," muttered Digger. "Lookit this mess."

"I'll help you clean up," Abby said. She grabbed the bucket and headed down to the tiny stream of water that trickled down off the snowy mountaintop.

With the bucket full, the thin wire handle cut into her fingers. Abby stopped about halfway back to switch hands, when she heard a horse coming up fast from in back of her. She turned to see Cam wheel his mount to a stop a few feet away. Against the sun he made a towering shadow atop the big bay. He put his hand out to her.

"Still having problems riding alone?" Abby asked, her heart thumping so loudly she feared it would spook his horse.

"Uh-huh."

"Digger's waiting for his water," she said.

Cam leaned down and took the bucket easily on two fingers. Water sloshed over the toe of his boot as he nudged Billy up the hill. He was back in moments, the bucket gone.

"I told Digger I was taking you to see the race," Cam said as he lifted her into the saddle. They rode to the top of a clear rise, where he stopped for a minute and pointed at a distant cluster of horsemen. Two of them galloped madly toward the rest. "There, now you've seen the race."

Cam then wrapped his arms around Abby and turned north. Billy's ground-eating canter quickly carried them across the open field, bright with aromatic bee balm and classic blue flax, and onto the forested shoulder of the mountain beyond.

"You are a wicked, wicked man, Mr. Garrett," Abby scolded solemnly. "If we get lost, how will anyone find us?"

"I don't want anyone to find us." He pressed his lips to a spot just behind Abby's ear, tracing small circles with his tongue over the sensitive skin.

"Neither do I." Abby felt the wild recklessness rush through her veins again. "I suppose it ought to bother me that everyone's going to know, but you have a terrible influence on me. All I've been able to think of is what you told me you wanted to do, what you started to do before Rico found us. I want you to do that to me, Cam, and the rest of the world be damned."

The sturdy wall of his chest behind her shuddered like a leaf in the wind. "Oh, woman. Do you have any idea what it does to a man when you say things like that?"

"Other men, no. You, yes." She had a very clear idea, seeing how closely he held her, and her imagination stirred up reciprocal responses deep within her own body.

A few hundred yards later the bay threaded his way into a grove of aspen. They spilled down the slope like the stately columns of an ancient temple, the green-gold leaves a rippling canopy overhead.

"Here we are," Cam said.

She noticed the flowers, then.

Huge purple asters, thousands of them, rippled beneath the trees. Throughout, bright clumps of arnica dotted the sunnier patches with yellow. A scattering of columbines, each plant covered with multiple spurred blossoms, added a touch of blue and white to the mix.

I love him, Abby thought as she realized this incredible gift was for her. The tenuous patience of the past days vanished like smoke. "Haven't we gone far enough yet?"

"Not nearly." Cam jerked the bay to a standstill and swung to the ground. He held his arms up, beckoning her to join him. With a sense of deep delight Abby slid into his grasp, slipping down the length of his body until she hung suspended in his arms, her toes a few inches above the flower-covered ground, her breasts crushed against his frame. With a groan Cam accepted the kiss she offered and returned it twice over before he abruptly set Abby down and led her a few yards away to a tiny, grassy hillock where the sun warmed the earth.

They tumbled into the grass together and stripped each other in moments, fingers flying deftly over buttons, lacings, and boots like they were hateful shackles to be removed. As the last garment dropped away, the frenzy receded, and they began to move more slowly. Their hands drifted over each other, brushing a shoulder here, cupping a breast there, stroking the curve of a waist or the length of a thigh. Gradually Cam added kisses to the play, and when he reached her breasts and teased first one nipple and then the other to straining points, Abby uttered a sigh of such delighted surrender that Cam laughed aloud. A slight pressure from his fingers tilted Abby onto her back; another moved her thighs apart.

"Oh, yes," Abby breathed.

"Oh, no," Cam answered. "Not yet, my sweet. I've waited too long. I'm not going to be rushed, and neither are you." He proceeded to kiss every inch of her sun-warmed skin, covering her in a deliberate and descending pattern, slipping back occasionally to nibble at her ears or suckle at her breasts, bypassing the sensitive juncture of her thighs to skim down her legs. Feet, ankles, calves, knees felt his lips as he worked his way back up, and all the while Abby lay open to him, exposed to the devilish, dark gaze that devoured her most secret places, as palpable as a touch.

Suddenly reticent, Abby tried to cover herself. Cam pushed her hands away and shifted to kneel between her legs, forcing her thighs even wider apart. His eyes never left his goal.

"You're beautiful," he whispered. "Like a flower opening just for me." Touching the edge of one petal of skin with a fingertip, Cam smiled at the shudder that racked Abby. He dipped his finger into the moisture that flooded there at his touch. "Full of nectar and just as sweet. Let me taste you, Abby."

Chapter 12

As often as she'd tried to imagine it, as much as she wanted it, Abby was utterly unprepared for the sweet, wild shock of Cam's mouth closing over her. When he dipped his tongue where his finger had been, Abby thought she would quite simply die. She arched to meet him, to submit for her execution, her fingers knotting in the grasses and flowers that cushioned her.

That first turbulence was only the start. Cam explored those few square inches of delicate flesh as thoroughly as he had kissed her entire body. All the sensation focused into a finer and finer point, until he flicked over the exact spot that sent Abby into a convulsion of release. Her cry of surprise turned to exaltation, and the sound spun up through the trees as Cam drew the pleasure out of her deliberately and skillfully.

Cam shifted to cover her with his body, the long, hard length of him slipping home easily in her moisture. He began to move in long even strokes that set the muscles deep within her pulsing anew.

Surrendering to her body's knowledge, Abby hooked her

heels around Cam's back, begging him to appease this fresh need. His meaningless, heat-soaked words lured her along as Cam glided in and out of her with ever increasing urgency. When he finally spilled into her with a hoarse shout, the excitement of feeling his climax carried Abby along to the same peak again.

They lay entwined for a long time, absorbed in the power of what had passed between them. Abby clung to Cam as the tremors went on and on deep within her, until she shook with the pure exhaustion of pleasure.

"*Now* we've gone far enough." Cam collapsed next to Abby and lay on his side tracing circles over her belly and breasts with one fingertip. "Much as I hate to move, we're going to have to get dressed."

"Mmm, why?"

"The sun's awfully strong up this high. All your beautiful, creamy flesh will burn to a crisp if I keep you naked so I can enjoy you again." He reached behind and dragged the red shirt over to cover Abby's torso. "Then you won't want me nibbling all those delicate areas that I so enjoy nibbling. Like here, and here, and most of all, here."

"It's not fair to tell me to get dressed and then do that." Abby pushed Cam's hand away from where it covered the downy vee between her thighs. "Can't we just move under the trees?"

"You'll still burn."

Abby sat up reluctantly and pulled the shirt over her arms. "Hand me my drawers."

"Just a minute." Cam got up and ran down to where Billy munched lazily on tufts of sweet grass. Abby began to laugh. "What?" he hollered.

"I've never seen a man running around nude before," Abby answered honestly as Cam returned with his canteen. "It's nothing at all like the Greek statues at the museums."

"No fig leaf," Cam said. "Try this." He held the big round canteen before him like the classical foliage and struck an heroic pose.

"Much better. I can just picture you bounding around the groves with Artemis." Abby dissolved into a giggling fit.

"You sit there with weeds in your hair, wearing nothing but my shirt, and you think *I* look funny? I'm crushed." Cam rifled through the scattering of clothes until he found his kerchief, then knelt by Abby and pushed her gently back. "Let me clean you up, sweet."

"I'd rather you didn't," Abby protested shyly, trying to push Cam away, but nothing dissuaded him. He soaked the cotton square with water from the canteen and gently performed this most intimate service as she scolded and blushed.

"Now admit it feels good," Cam coaxed. "Cool and clean on your skin."

"Then I get to do the same for you." Abby grabbed for the cloth, but Cam playfully jerked it out of reach.

"If you touch me like that, we'll never get dressed, and you'll have to spend the next week soaked in rancid bear grease or some such nonsense that Digger will come up with for the burn."

"Disgusting thought." Abby reached for her pants.

Later, when they had tugged their clothes back into order and lazed beneath the trees, Abby closed her eyes. The entire scene played through her mind, right down to the reflection of leaf-scattered sunlight in Cam's dark eyes as he filled her.

Abby nestled into the crook of Cam's arm as he brushed a kiss across the sunburned tip of her nose, contentment a warm shawl around her shoulders. His chest moved in lazy swells against Abby's cheek, lulling her into a drowsy state of half awareness that lasted until the tickle of his beard on her forehead made her eyes pop open. Amused, she tickled back, riffling her fingertips through the tangle of gold and silver just under his chin.

Cam came awake with a start and raked vigorously at the furry underside of his jaw. "It itches enough without you doing that."

"Why do you have it, then?"

"The usual reasons a man grows a beard."

"I hope you don't think it makes you more handsome, because it doesn't." Abby stroked at his beard, smoothing the wiry hair down to have a better look at the line of his jaw. "At least I don't think it does. I can't really tell what you look like under all this brush."

Laughing, Cam captured her fingers and pulled her hand away. Abby wrenched her hand free easily, but she didn't reach for his face again, electing instead to flatten her palm across the firm stretch of belly just above the waistband of his trousers. She traced the ridge of white scar tissue with her fingertips.

"I don't know a lot of things," she whispered, "like where you got this scar, and what you mean to do with me now. I realize you originally intended to ransom me back, since that's what you took me for, but things have obviously changed. I won't go back to Franklin even if you—"

Cam's face darkened and he rolled across Abby, pinning her to the ground. "Don't say his name, not here."

"But I—"

"Not here, Abby. This place is just for us. Just for this." His kiss was fierce, possessive, as he ran his hands freely down her body.

"Not here," she agreed softly. Cam held her gaze for a long moment, some ferocious, unspoken emotion wrestling for control of his features. He took a deep breath.

"There's a tremendous view from a little farther up the hill." Suddenly his weight was gone, and he was up and off through the trees.

Abby lay there for a moment, stunned by the swiftness of his departure, then rose and spotted Cam moving up the mountain, already a distance away. She found her boots behind two different bushes.

"I will know what happened between you and Franklin," she vowed quietly as she followed Cam. "You will talk to me."

The aspen petered out as she came to a jumble of huge boulders. Intent on talking with Cam, she pursued him out onto an undulating stretch of granite. He stood there like the figurehead on the bow of a stone ship.

"Magnificent, isn't it?" Cam gestured toward the long range of blue and white mountains, indicating the farthest peaks. "Those are the San Juans."

"You can't keep avoiding my questions," she said, glancing down to check her footing.

Twenty feet. It must be at least that far to the crumpled figure below. Abby stood in the open French doors, broken notes of harp music from the conservatory below discordant on the night air. Someone started screaming.

"Abby. Abby." Cam's voice summoned her back to the present. She left the nightmare and bolted away from the ledge of rock where he held her, back toward the safety of the aspen grove.

"You led me out there on purpose," she raged when he caught up with her at the grove's edge. She whirled on him. The fury it took to push the images away hung about her, fueling the blows she rained on his chest with knotted fists. "Damn you. Every time. Every time I have to see her again, lying there. Damn you. You did that to me on purpose."

"I didn't." Cam took her pummeling without protest, fending off only the worst blows until she gave out and crumpled to her knees. He knelt beside her. "I swear, Abby, I didn't intend . . . I wasn't paying attention. What happened?"

"She was listening to the music, dancing around in a little circle on the balcony. I was watching her. The balcony collapsed."

That was the part everybody knew, the part that was easiest to say. Abby stared at her knees. Nobody, not even her brother, Mac, knew the rest. Suddenly she wanted Cam to know, to show him she trusted him even if he couldn't trust her yet.

"The sound was so strange, just a little tiny crack. She looked at me, and we both knew it was terrible even before she started to fall. I tried to grab her." Abby held out her hand, her fingers clenched into a fist, nails biting into her palm as if she still gripped the fabric. A dry sob escaped her, but she held back the tears. "I even got hold of her dress. The next day I had to scrape the threads out from under my nails."

Cam's comforting arm slipped around her shoulders, making her feel safe. "Who was it, Abby?"

She could see the face in front of her, eyes wide with terror, and couldn't believe she hadn't spoken the name. Suddenly years of unspoken self-recrimination slipped out. "If I had been stronger, I could have held her. If I'd been a man, she'd have been safe. I was too weak, and she died."

"Who?"

The name balled in her throat and tears burned like acid in her eyes. Abby swallowed hard, fighting the choking sensation in her throat. "My mother."

Cam glanced away, a pain beyond words searing his face. "So you've spent years blaming yourself for letting her die."

He understood. Tears scalded Abby's cheeks, and she pushed to her feet, and slipped away from Cam into the aspen grove.

He came after her, the pain still in his eyes. "I'm sorry. I didn't mean . . ."

She laid a finger over his lips. "No. You were right, not here."

After the smallest hesitation Cam nodded, then he gathered her into his arms. "You need this place as much as I do, don't you? A place where the demons can't find you. It's safe here, sweet wanton. Just you and me."

"Just you and me."

Other than poor Charlie, who blushed so fiercely that Abby caught his embarrassment, the only signs that Cam's men had even noticed they were gone were a few knowing smiles on discreetly turned faces as she and Cam approached the evening fire. As randy as this bunch could be with Hannah, they seemed to have the cowboy's famed deference for a respectable woman.

So-called respectable woman, Abby amended. She hardly fit the category anymore, and if she'd had any pretensions, the afternoon with Cam beneath the trees had disabused her of them.

Only Rico stared blatantly at her and Cam over his steaming coffee, his eyes flat, black coins in an unreadable face. Abby glanced toward Hannah, expecting no quarter there, either, but the redhead was strangely subdued. Hannah let the opportunity pass with neither a giggle nor a snipe. Abby began to relax then and dished herself a hearty supper. Cam chose a spot at her side, where his rock-hard thigh warmed hers and he could steal an occasional bite of stew off her plate.

"You're making quite a show," Abby pointed out under her breath.

He licked a dab of gravy off his finger and gave her a wink and a grin, and Abby felt a surge of pleasure totally out of proportion to his act.

A few minutes later Cam disappeared on his rounds, Rico at his side by an order barely disguised as a request. Abby hoisted a half-empty bucket and slipped off to wash up. She'd just set the tin washbowl out when Hannah slipped into the cabin behind her and pulled the door shut.

"Hannah, I don't really think—"

"I ain't in here to mouth off. Dang, you can't see a thing in here." Seconds later Hannah had a lantern lit. She held it up and considered Abby carefully. "I never took a real honest look at you. I guess you're pretty enough."

Backhanded as it was, Abby realized Hannah meant it as a compliment.

"But I ain't in here for that, neither," Hannah continued.

"What do you want?"

"It's just, well, the fellows told me you asked all of them why they ride with Cam. You never asked me."

"I just assumed because you and Cam . . ."

"Well, yeah, but that came after. Remember how I said before that Frank gets kind of rough?" Hannah hesitated, clearly uncomfortable. "Well, he hurt me. I mean, whoring ain't easy, and you expect some of the customers to get a little out of hand sometimes, but he did something even Noreen never heard of before. Aw, hell. Here."

With no further preamble, Hannah lifted her skirt to her waist, quickly undid her drawers, and dropped them.

Abby gasped, not at Hannah's immodesty, but at the pale scar high on her inner thigh. Interlocked, one-inch high letters that read *FT*.

Just like the mark on Franklin's stationery.

"Fideli-T," he'd told her one night over sherry. "I mark everything that's mine."

"He's got a little old iron he uses for his books and such," Hannah mumbled as she readjusted her clothes.

"Iron," Abby repeated dully.

"Branding iron."

"My god." Abby collapsed onto the edge of a cot, her hand over her mouth to hold back the bile that rose in her throat. In an awkward gesture of comfort, Hannah patted her shoulder and sat down beside her.

"Someone like you doesn't have any business hearing this, but here goes. Franklin used to have these poker games. He'd buy one or two of us off the floor at Noreen's, and we'd go out to his place for the night. Sometimes he'd make us the prize for the final hand."

"That's disgusting."

"That's business, honey. Nothing to get upset about. Anyway, he took a shine to me, I guess. One night I was working the room like I was supposed to, getting his friends all worked up so they're ready to . . . well, Franklin won the hand and we went off together like usual, except this time he wanted to tie me up. Now that ain't so odd, but when he got done, he got up and started poking around in the fireplace and the next thing I know he's marked me like some cow, the bastard. Then he starts telling me how every time a man's with me, the whole rest of my life, he'll know I'm Franklin Tanner's favorite whore, like it's some goddamned honor."

At some point, Abby wasn't quite sure when, her hand had slipped around Hannah's.

Hannah sucked in a deep, shuddering breath. "Noreen stopped letting him take anyone for parties, but he still comes around like I said. Every couple of weeks."

"Why are you telling me this now?" Abby asked.

"I was going to tell you before, but when you called me a liar, I . . . Anyway, I wanted you to understand why I feel like I do, about Tanner and about Cam. Cam Garrett's the best man I ever met, and I've met a lot, honey. Why, when he first saw this brand, I thought he'd go out and kill Tanner right then."

When he saw it. Jealousy ripped through Abby like a hot knife, and she dropped Hannah's hand. "I think I've heard enough."

Hannah smoothed at the ruffle on her sleeve and stood up. "It's not that way between Cam and me anymore. If truth be told, it never really was. You ought to know that, too."

"But you . . ." Abby stopped herself. No more accusations. She gathered herself a moment, then said quietly, "Thank you, Hannah."

Hannah accepted the thanks with a nod, then turned away and took a deep breath. "You know what the strangest part of this is? I like you. For all the grief we give each other, I actually like you. You take pretty much anything a body gives you without folding."

"I guess we're not so different," Abby said.

Cam took her off again the next day, and the day after that, and by the fourth day, they stopped inventing excuses to cover their escapes. They simply slipped off during the drowsy period just after lunch. Apparently the other men thought nothing of it.

Jesús rode back into camp just after sunset five days later, his mount showing signs of hard use. He barely acknowledged the men around the fire before he drew Cam and Rico aside.

"From our friends," he said simply, fishing into his vest pocket for a folded piece of paper the size and shape of a telegram.

He held it out. Cam accepted the message and headed for the dugout and some privacy. "Rico, get us some light."

It took a few moments for Rico to rustle up a match and get the lantern lit. All the while Cam stood just outside the door, the telegram burning in his fingers. A few yards away a lock of Abby's chestnut and bronze hair caught the firelight. Cam turned away and went inside.

"How did it go?" he asked Jesús.

"Everyone is safe, even Juanita. No one has bothered her since Rico and Hannah left. Stanton must have been riding alone."

"Good."

"Our friends say Tanner believes Stanton and Hannah ran away together. He intends to hunt them down. I think it will be a long hunt, no?"

"Yes." The door was closed and barred before Cam opened the telegram.

"He's taken the loan." Cam barely kept his voice from cracking. The prospect of Tanner's impending ruin danced in his skull. "John sent the full details."

"There was this, as well." Smiling, Jesús fished out an envelope and passed it across. "When I saw it, I decided not to send the telegram to St. Louis. If I am mistaken . . ."

"I don't think you are."

Definitely Fidelity stationery, Cam thought as he broke the seal on the envelope. In all the times he'd handled it, he'd never gotten over the peculiar texture of Tanner's ivory paper; nothing felt quite the same way, except maybe a brand new greenback. Cam read the note through twice. Impatient, Rico leaned over his shoulder and grabbed the paper away as soon as he saw that Cam had finished.

"He's accepted our terms," Cam said.

Rico's weatherbeaten face creased into a smile as he glanced up from reading. "Excellent. His venom for you is clear, even in his writing. It poisons his judgment. It will not take much more to push him over the edge."

Cam nodded and accepted the paper back, with fingers suddenly as clumsy as sausages.

Not much, just Abby.

"We'll go over this again tomorrow when we're fresh," Cam said. "I want to compare what he's agreed to with a copy of what I sent him. Hope you had some time with Maria."

"*Sí.*" Jesús bobbed his head. "She put together the items you wanted. She says you must thank her by eating at least a dozen *sopapillas* the next time you visit."

"With any luck, that visit won't be too far away."

"She also fears you have ruined me for sheep ranching. Perhaps we will have to find other game to keep us in the mountains, heh?"

"Naturally," Cam agreed, and then both smiled with the knowledge that it was the very last thing either of them wanted.

"Ah, yes. The Nagles are now back at their store." Jesús reached for the door. "I will go to eat now. The others will be happy to hear the plan is working."

"I don't want you spreading any of this around yet."

"But the news is good!" Jesús protested. "Your plan is working. He wants his *señorita* back."

"And I want to go over everything one more time before I tell the men it's a go-ahead. We're not going to bury anyone else because I overlooked something. Keep it to yourself for now."

Hands out in surrender, Jesús shrugged. "As you say."

Cam followed him to the door. "I'll get those things from you later. Oh, and Jesús . . . good job."

This was it, Cam thought, standing there in the doorway, the chill night air washing over his face. A thirty-thousand dollar loan was enough to put Tanner on the edge of financial disaster, and the lever for tilting him over the edge sat by the fire, laughing at one of Charlie's unlikely stories.

Abby. The only thing he wanted in the whole world was to strip off his clothes and lie with her in the dark, not even make love to her, just hold her, skin to skin. Cam's palms tingled with the remembered feel of Abby's silken flesh beneath his hands. His hands pressed against the crudely planed beams framing the doorway until the old wood groaned.

"Why do you keep this secret?" Rico's question, soft and full of accusation, came from the dugout behind Cam. "You must share the beginnings of our victory with your men this night."

"It isn't victory yet." Cam pushed the door shut again and turned to face his friend. The dark stain of emotion in Rico's olive cheeks caught him off guard.

"The next steps are simple," Rico said.

Cam shook his head. "Straightforward, maybe, but hardly simple."

"You think of the señorita."

"Of course I do."

"Her betrothed sits on his rancho—*your* rancho—like some great maggot devouring everything. Every day he infests other lives, ruins other men. But you, you can stop him. That is what you took his woman for, Cameron. Remember that. Always remember why you do this thing. Remember what he did to you."

A face, searingly beautiful but twisted by shame and grief, wavered on the edge of Cam's consciousness, then flooded forward. With her memory came the old resolve, bitter but familiar from years of nurturing it. Cam felt his heart harden all over again, a physical pain that threatened to drive out any emotion but revenge, and he fought it.

"We're figuring out another way, Rico. I'm not sending Abby back."

"Bah." Rico spat the word out. "Months. Years we have worked for this, and now you would give it up."

"I'm not giving anything up."

"Just because the little p—"

Cam's dark glance cut the crude Spanish word off. "I don't care if you are like a father to me, if I hear you use that term about Abby or any other woman, I will take you apart."

"Because the little *princess*"—Rico gave Cam a sour look—"grants you her favors, you're going to ruin it all."

"It's not like that. I don't want her to go, and she doesn't want to, either. Even if she was the harridan of the hills, I couldn't send her back. It wouldn't be right, Rico. You know it. It was stupid of me to hang so much on being as big a bastard as Tanner."

"It was a good plan."

"Then we've got to come up with a new one that will do the same damage to him, without lowering ourselves to his level."

"There is no time. We only have a week, less, before Willem is due from St. Louis. You must leave tomorrow if you are to be ready."

"I know, so let's get busy. I have a couple of ideas. Let's see that copy of the note we left with the Nagles."

"Bah," repeated Rico, but he produced their sheaf of maps and notes and smoothed them across his knee. "I suppose I must keep you from killing yourself."

He should have expected the dream. It had been months since it had come, and he seldom went so long without it, even after all these years. With Rico dredging up the memory, it was bound to happen.

It started the way it always did, the way it had for year

upon endless year. Cam walked up to the house, a neat, whitewashed structure that seemed as familiar as the back of his own hand. A climbing rose vine, redolent with scent and deep scarlet blossoms, twined up a rough trellis by the front door. His mother had coddled the plant for years, claiming its perfume made her less homesick for Switzerland.

The door stood half open. Cam slipped through and walked silently across the room. The people in the bedroom didn't even notice him when he pushed the curtain aside with one finger and stood there watching.

Broad, muscled back to the door, the man worked at the buttons on the woman's dress while she held herself still as death, her eyes squeezed shut as though she wanted to block out the man's presence. Her lips moved, but Cam couldn't hear the words over the roaring that filled his soul, a roar like a freight train barreling through a cattle stampede, the loudest sound he'd ever heard. The man answered roughly, then released the woman's hair to tumble over her shoulders. He pulled her camisole open with greedy quickness and kneaded at her breasts through the cloud of white-blond hair that covered them, his hands cruel.

Cam wanted to turn away, but his limbs had grown wooden. So he watched as the man knelt and lowered his head to the woman's breasts. Something, perhaps the creak of his disbelieving body sagging against the wall, made the woman look up, and Cam met his mother's eyes.

Except this time they weren't his mother's. Instead of clear blue, the eyes that filled with shock were hazel. He looked at the woman's hair and found chestnut instead of blond.

The man suckled once more at Abby's breast, hard enough to draw a gasp of pain from parted lips, then released her to rise and face Cam.

Victory twisted Franklin Tanner's lips into a parody of a smile. A knife flashed deadly silver in his hand.

*   *   *

A loud cry of pain and fury jerked Abby from the depths of sleep. She sat bolt upright, eyes wide, searching for the source.

Cam was on his feet, Rico already at his side.

An accident, Abby thought, but sleep still deadened her limbs, and she had trouble freeing herself from her bedroll. She finally struggled upright, the blanket around her shoulders, and pushed past Hannah.

"Are you all right?" she asked.

Strain tightened the skin around Cam's eyes as he met her concerned gaze. "Mother of god," he groaned, then stalked off into the night.

Abby started after him.

"No," said Rico, and his stubby fingers closed tightly over Abby's shoulder to stop her. "He does not need you, señorita."

"Nonsense." Abby knocked Rico's hand away and started forward again. Suddenly she found herself facing Rico, who'd darted in front of her like a man years younger.

"No. It is only a bad dream, señorita, a very old one." Rico's voice grew suddenly venomous. "It comes back to him because of you."

A sharp crack echoed from higher on the mountain, wood against wood. Abby yanked free of Rico. "I don't know what you think you're doing, but I'm going up there to talk to Cam. Now let me past."

Rico moved to block her again, and when Abby cut around the other side of him he wrapped his arms around her waist and bodily carried her downhill a few steps.

"Damn you, Rico, he needs someone," Abby pleaded. Another cracking blow rolled down the hill, then another, and she flinched inside with each one.

Even Rico looked disturbed at the blows. "Hannah will go."

"No, she won't," Digger said, and his matter-of-fact tone drew their attention from each other. The rest of Cam's men watched from the shadows around the closely banked fire, their eyes intent. Digger turned to Hannah and laced his fingers through hers. "Never been you he's needed, girl, not that way."

Hannah looked at Rico and shook her head. "He's right, Rico, and we both know it. I'm not the one to help Cam with this."

"Then I will go," Rico said.

"No." Two voices chimed almost in unison, and Charlie and Antonio stepped forward to flank Digger.

"It should be Abby. I mean, Miss Morgan," Charlie said.

"The señorita," Antonio agreed.

Rico whirled on Antonio. "You speak for her, Antonio. The *bruja* set you up for Stanton, almost got you killed."

The man shook his head. "She tried to signal me. I was so intent on berating her, I refused to see it. Just as you are so jealous now that you cannot see Cameron needs her. I do not like her, either, but—"

"I do," Charlie interrupted.

"I do not," Antonio said, giving the boy a sideways glance before he faced off with Rico and continued. "But what we like is not important. She is what Cam needs."

"I will go," repeated Rico. "I have dealt with these dreams of Cameron's for years."

"Now it is time for someone else."

"Set her loose, Rico." Jesús had hung back, but now he stepped up beside Antonio, and Abigail felt the power of the four men united against Rico. "Now."

Slowly, unwillingly, Rico's arms relaxed, and Abby wriggled away. A dozen pairs of eyes watched in expectation as the crack of another blow rolled down the mountain. Concern, outright fear, made her muscles tight. "I don't even know what his dream was about. Rico?"

Rico snorted and walked away, giving Antonio and Jesús the evil eye as he went. They turned and followed him, taking Charlie and the rest of the men with them.

Except for Digger. The old man stood in the moonlight

in his baggy, worn clothes and his shaggy silver hair and half-grown beard, looking wise and gentle.

"Help me, Digger," Abby begged, pulling the blanket around herself.

He shook his head. "To do hisself any good, he's got to be the one tells you why he's hurting. Don't you worry miss. You just love him, you'll both be fine."

Chapter 13

Cam threw the full weight of his body into the swing, shattering the wrist-thick branch against the big pine, showering his forearms with splinters. The nightmare image still clung; Tanner's face still mocked him. Already sweating hard, he stripped off his vest and shirt and reached for another branch off the deadfall nearby. He growled as he faced the hapless pine, then he swung again, twice as hard as before, and continued swinging, blow after blow, until a white scar of damaged bark revealed the tree's heart.

As he hefted another branch he saw Abby, watching from the deep shadows a few yards away, her face pinched with concern. Cam barely paused when she stepped out into the moonlight.

"Go away."

She flinched as he hit the tree again. "No. Stop it."

"Go away!" Cam roared as he flung the branch aside.

In one abrupt motion he pulled Abby against his chest. His hands spanned her waist roughly, and she gasped as his weight carried her back against the tree. The shock of the contact rippled through his body with startling force.

They stood there a moment, eyes locked in challenge.

"If you're trying to frighten me, you may as well stop," Abby said with a calmness that belied the rapid pulse dancing in her temple. "I stopped being frightened a long time ago."

"You shouldn't have." Cam covered her lips with brutal pressure, contempt for himself making his kiss rough. The thought that he could ever have considered sending her back into that monster's hands made him sick inside. He was as depraved as Tanner; neither one of them deserved her.

"But I did," she whispered when he lifted his head at last. She stroked a finger along the edge of his beard, soothing a twitching muscle there to stillness. "As much as I tried not to, as often as I told myself that you were dangerous, that I should keep you at a distance, I did stop being afraid. I guess I kept seeing the gentleman behind the outlaw."

Bitter amusement twisted Cam's lips into a half grin. "A gentleman would never think of doing the things I've done to you."

"I know. But then a lady would never let you do them." With a sigh of surrender Abby stretched up to brush a kiss across his lips. Her fingers played across his chest with seductive skill.

"God, woman, don't do this to me." With a moan of guilt Cam buried his face against Abby's shoulder. The faint scent of smoke that clung to her clothes wafted over him, stirring his body to that powerfully familiar need that demanded Abby, and only Abby, to fulfill it. The rhythm of his hands changed against her flesh, no longer rough, but cajoling, seductive. He found the fullness of her breasts beneath the soft flannel and easily coaxed her nipples erect. Her sigh of pleasure stirred softly against his neck.

"I shouldn't want you like this," Cam whispered. "I have no right to feel this way, to expect you to feel it. But God help me, I do. Say it's all right, Abby. Tell me you want me, too."

In impatient answer, she stripped open the button fly of his pants, releasing the velvet hardness of him to her searching fingers. "Of course I want you, you silly fool. I love you."

In the fever that drove him, he took Abby standing there against the tree, cradling her in his hands as they joined, as she coaxed him along with touches and sounds that echoed his own urgency. He had no will to hold himself back, needing her, needing the sanctuary of her delicate warmth so desperately that the first spasm of her completion sent him spinning out of control. Muffling his shout of release against her mouth, he emptied into her, and then spent, sagged to the ground, carrying Abby along in a tangle of limbs and half-removed clothes.

Later, when they lay with legs entwined, the blanket wrapped tight against the night chill, she asked him about his dream.

"Shhh," he whispered. He couldn't tell her. Not yet.

For now he had to let it stay there in his gut, let it fester, use the pain to hone a fresh strategy against Tanner. For thirteen years the fury had powered his life. Once he shared the story with Abby, Cam felt with deep certainty, the drive for revenge would vanish. He came perilously close to losing his edge every time he held her, just as Rico warned.

Rico.

He'd have to prove to Rico the gambit could still work, without their pawn. Rico would forgive him if the change of plans still won the war against Tanner.

After they'd beaten Tanner, after they were all safe, that's when he'd tell her all of it. And maybe, just maybe, Abby would be able to forgive him, too.

"You really are mine," Cam breathed in disbelief as early sunlight touched the hollow where they lay.

"I always have been. You just didn't know it." The boughs Cam had gathered into a makeshift bed prickled

Abby, even through the heavy blanket and her clothes.

Cam wove his fingers into the gleaming mass of her hair and pulled it across his chest to make a silken coverlet. "As you pointed out, I'm a fool—though I'd pick a stronger word."

"They'll be wondering about us in camp," she said a time later, listening to the noises that drifted up from the men below.

"I'll give you a few minutes of privacy, then we'll go on down together."

Abby was crawling around on her hands and knees when Cam returned from his short hike through the brush.

"One of my buttons popped off last night," she explained, glancing up.

A wry, knowing smile touched Cam's lips. "Just one?"

Hunt unsuccessful, Abby scrambled to her feet, her hand resting on the broken skin of the pine he'd attacked. Pitch coated her fingers like blood, fragrant and sticky. "Was this you or Franklin?"

"I'm not certain."

"Will you tell me about your dream?"

It seemed to take Cam a long time to fill his lungs, as though steel bands bound his chest. His pain brought a tightness to Abby's throat.

"Yes. But not now, sweet. After."

"After what? After Franklin pays the ransom? He's offered, I take it. Don't look so shocked—that's the only reason I could think of why Jesús would come back so early." Abby swallowed hard and plunged on through Cam's pensive silence. "You never have said whether you still plan to send me back."

"I don't."

More than the words, the husky break in Cam's voice told Abby what she wanted to know: the man returned her love, even if he couldn't put a name to what he felt.

"Then we're going to have to come up with a very good plan to get the money anyway."

" 'We' won't do anything." Cam grabbed the heavy blue blanket and gave it a shake. Pine needles flew through the air. "This is my war, Abby."

"That may be, but you're going to need me to win it. You can't very well expect Franklin to hand over thirty thousand dollars if I'm not at least in the vicinity. He's got to think he's getting me back, or you'll never see that money."

"I said no. We'll come up with another way."

"But—"

The blanket hit the ground again, and Cam smothered her arguments with a kiss so persuasive, she was almost tempted to surrender to his opinion. Almost.

Abby tried to wrestle away, words of protest forming. Cam's arms went around her more firmly, his kiss deepening, until she couldn't find the breath to argue.

Never mind, she decided, returning his kiss with equal vigor. There was plenty of time to fight later.

"Now, are you ready to go down and have some breakfast?" he asked, and Abby knew he'd taken her response as acquiescence. Fine. Discretion was often the best way around a useless argument—that and a plan of one's own, which she lacked at this point.

"I'm not sure which I want more, food or hot water," she said.

"I almost forgot. There's a package waiting for you. I had Jesús bring back some clothes for you and Hannah. I'm not sure if they'll fit, but—"

"Oh, Cam! Thank you, thank you, thank you." Abby flung her arms around his neck and gave him an enthusiastic hug.

She'd gotten Cam Garrett's heart and clean clothes, all in one morning.

The world couldn't get any sweeter.

"That'll go easier with some help," Hannah said.

Abby glanced up through soapy, streaming locks of hair that hung over the bucket. She and Hannah had agreed to share the dugout to get cleaned up, but despite their last few discussions, Abby wasn't sure they'd come quite far enough for this much trust.

Her doubts must have shown. Hannah tossed her towel over her shoulder and put her hands on her hips. "I ain't going to drown you, honey. Just give me that cup."

With so much hair to handle, it really was a problem to wash it alone. Abby handed over the cup she was using. To her everlasting relief, Hannah just rinsed.

A few minutes later Abby wrapped one of Digger's cleaner muslin towels around her head. "Now I can do you," she offered.

"That'd be fine." Hannah flipped her hair over the catch bucket, and Abby began scooping fresh water.

"You ought to see the fancy bath Noreen put in at the house last year," Hannah said as she worked up a lather. "All tile, and with a pump that brings the water right into the tub. She even has a little old stove in there, with a tank on the side, so Cheng don't even have to carry kettles during the winter."

"How convenient for all of you."

"She didn't put it in for us girls, honey, it's for the customers. But two people get as clean as one. Noreen calls it the 'salle de bain.' "

Abby cringed, both at Hannah's pronunciation and the turn of the conversation.

"Cost her a mint, too," Hannah continued. "I thought she was wasting her money, but you know, we get a fellow just about every night wanting his back scrubbed. Two or three on Saturdays."

"I can imagine." Abby could, too, though it would have been unthinkable a few weeks ago. In fact, her imagination carried her right into a big claw-foot tub with Cam. The warm water. The slick feel of his body.

"Rinse me," Hannah said, ducking her head again. Abby shook herself and began dipping. "I'm going to miss all that. Well, maybe not all of it, but that bath. I'm surely going to miss that bath. Bet Cam will, too."

Abby studied the vulnerable curve of Hannah's neck, ready to squelch the surge of jealousy, but it didn't come. "You have a little bit more soap over your ear. Let me get it."

This time it was Hannah who glanced up dubiously through streams of water.

"It must be hard, knowing you can never go back," Abby said gently, and suddenly Hannah was no longer a threat. Whether the redhead had ever shared a bath with Cam or not, it didn't matter. That was the past, and Cam was the present and the future.

Hannah accepted a towel and scrubbed at her hair with the nubby muslin, then dropped onto one of the makeshift stools. "It was a sight more fun when I could shock the drawers off you."

"Not for me." Abby smiled and shook her head. "For what it's worth, I'm grateful to you for telling me about Franklin at the beginning. When I think I might have gone back to him, ended up married to him . . ."

Hannah's head popped up. "You know, we got a hell of a problem. Tanner won't turn loose of that money without you."

"I know. I offered to help, but Cam won't even discuss it with me." Abby unbuttoned her old camisole, now gray from wear and stream-water washings, and poured a little warm water into an empty tin basin.

"He's stubborn that way. You going to keep trying?"

"Absolutely. I'm scared for him, Hannah. He's so determined to get to Franklin, he may try something foolish. I need your help. I know it's asking a lot, but—"

"This is Cam we're talking about, honey. What did you have in mind?"

After a night's sleep a fresh plan should have come easily, but here they were, five hours later, still skunked.

Rico rubbed a gritty, lead smudged finger over his cheek.

"I told you. We must send her back."

"No. I am not giving that monster the slightest chance to do to her what he did to my mother." The nightmare image welled up like a sob, and Cam's voice trailed off.

"That won't happen. Arrange witnesses, tell her to refuse to be alone with him. Her public refusal to marry him will be almost as humiliating for Tanner as learning you seduced her, and she will be in no danger. She can go home to her family. Then you can find your *gringa* later, if you wish."

"If I wish?"

"You may discover that when she is removed from you, she is not nearly so attractive. I know you are concerned, but the *señorita* will not give Tanner a chance to harm her. There is no other way to convince Tanner to release the money, and if he does not, the past months of work go to waste. We will have to start over, almost from the beginning."

"No, we won't. We'll come up with something. I want a council after supper. You, Jesús, Antonio. Digger, too. We're going to work this out, one way or the other."

As he walked down to the campfire, his thoughts remained on the problem.

"What do you think?" Abby popped out from behind Digger and spun around, yards of crisp forest green calico sweeping a wide circle to reveal a flash of sparkling white petticoat and a glimpse of booted ankle. "I believe my card has a space, sir."

All Cam's concerns evaporated with her smile. With Abby safe and in his arms, the rest of the world would fall into place. Grinning like a schoolboy at his first dance, Cam twirled her once around the fire. Her braid lay in a clean line down her back, the damp end tickling the back of his hand where he held her waist.

"Well?" she asked.

"Clearly the belle of the ball." Cam leaned closer to whisper in her ear. "Although I've become quite partial to faded red flannel. As a matter of fact, now that you have some other clothes to wear, I may just indulge a whim of mine and rip open that shirt just to see the buttons fly."

"My, sir, such talk could give a lady the vapors." Abby fanned herself with exaggerated style, then spun around before him again. "I'm amazed this fits so well. Hannah's does too. Jesús must have an eye for women's clothing."

"His wife does. I just had Jesús give her the name of someone in town about the same size as each of you. She sews for half the women in the valley, but I think this is store bought."

"Undoubtedly. She wouldn't have had time to sew for two of us. But I don't care. I'm so happy to be clean all the way through, I can hardly bear it."

"Is that all it takes to make you happy?"

"Let me see." Mischief lit Abby's eyes as she chewed her lip in contemplation. The pressure left her mouth the shade of a perfectly ripe strawberry. Cam couldn't resist, and he kissed her.

The taste of her sang through his veins. He held the kiss a long time, too long, considering how many of his men lingered about watching. Finally a slight noise behind Abby made Cam look up.

"Got to get started on supper." Digger shifted one suspender and scratched his shoulder. "You're kinda in the way with whatever that is you're doin' there."

"Just staking claim, friend. Something you ought to understand."

Digger nodded and slipped his suspender back into place with a brisk pop. "'Bout time. Yessir, it's about time."

The lantern in the dugout threw a rectangular wash of yellow light over the ground as Hannah slipped outside.

Abby barely let the door shut before she pounced. "What are they planning?"

"Craziness. Not here. Let's talk somewhere else."

"What?" Abby repeated when they'd found a spot private enough to satisfy Hannah.

"Cam wants to let Tanner keep the money for the time being, then steal it before he can get it back to the bank."

Abby felt a sinking anguish. "That's insane. Franklin will have every man on his ranch standing guard."

"Told you it was crazy," Hannah said glumly. "Somebody's going to get killed over this one. But if they don't somehow clean him out now, they might not get another chance for a while, and meantime, Tanner'd just get cockier and take over more of the small ranches. I've seen the man do it for too long to think it won't just keep getting worse. The only reason we have a chance now is because of the storms last winter. And because of you."

"That's what worries me. This all started because I came out here. If someone gets killed, if Cam gets killed . . . Do you know anything about where they planned to pick up the ransom?"

"Sure. We all know. Cam made us act out the whole thing a dozen times before he worked it out so he was happy. I was you."

"What's the area like?"

"Nice little flat spot, pretty broad, clear views. A steep cut toward the west end."

"Do you know it well enough to draw a map?"

"Sure, but—"

"Then let's find some paper and a pencil. If we can figure out how to work it, I may have an idea."

They wound up using a flat rock and some charcoal from the fire, but Hannah's sketch provided the information Abby needed to see if her plan could work. She smiled in satisfaction and picked up the rock.

"Let's go."

With five male bodies and a lantern crowded into a room the size of two large bedsteads, the air in the dugout was filled with heat and scent. Perspiration beaded across Abby's forehead as soon as she pushed through the door. Hannah followed close on her heels.

"Gentlemen."

"Señorita. Hannah," said Jesús.

"What do you want, ladies?" Cam stood up, his jaw already set with that stubborn look of his.

It put Abby's back up immediately. "To save you from yourself. You can't steal the money. You need my help."

"Spying, Hannah?" Cam gave the redhead an accusing look before he turned his attention back to Abby. "We've already been over this."

"*We* have been over nothing," Abby snapped. "*You* decided I had nothing to contribute. *You* decided I need your absolute protection from Franklin. And *you* are in here deciding on ways to get yourself and your men killed accomplishing what could be a rather simple task. *I*, on the other hand, have a plan." She carried her rock into the center of the group and plunked it on the floor. "Is that a good approximation of where you intend to trade me for the ransom money?"

"Intend*ed*. It's fair. This hill's a little farther west." Cam smudged the mark out with his thumb and sketched it back in with Abby's piece of charcoal. "Tanner would come in front down here, and we were planning to use this trail in."

"And the exchange takes place here." Abby marked the spot with a dollar sign. "One of Franklin's men is supposed to bring the money and leave it here on a rock."

"*Sí*," said Jesús and Rico simultaneously as Cam frowned.

Rico continued. "Then we are to ride across. There. As you ride over to Tanner's man, I come the last few yards and pick up the money."

"Then it's easy. We do it just the way you planned."

"Damn it, Abby," Cam began, "I have no intention of letting you—"

"*Except*," she shouted him down. "Except instead of passing by the money, I'll reach down and take it myself. We'll have the money, and Franklin will have nothing."

"And you expect he will give up you and the money, just

like that," Rico said sarcastically.

"She's not stupid," Hannah interjected. "He'll try to chase you all, but Cam figured he'd do that even if he got Abby and kept the money for himself. You know you all worked that out before we even decided to kidnap her."

"She's got you there." Digger leaned back, a smug, proud smile on his face as he eyed Hannah.

"Abby will be right in the middle of a gunfight," Cam said.

"I don't think so," Abby said. "Whatever his other faults, Franklin apparently bears enough honest affection for me that he's willing to spend thirty thousand dollars to get me back. I doubt he'll let anyone shoot at me." Abby gave Cam a tight smile, more bravado than anything. "Besides, he still thinks I want to marry him. He expects me to come straight to him and throw my arms around him in relief. Given a fast horse, I can be away and through this gap with you before he figures it out."

"And the rest of the gang can back them up," Hannah finished. "He'll have to ride all the way around, just like you planned. We can do it, Cam."

"What if she falls off her horse again?"

"That isn't fair," Abby said. "I was in the middle of a forest fire and a mountain lion jumped out in front of us. I've ridden my whole life. I can sit a horse just fine under normal conditions."

"These will hardly be normal conditions. Men will be chasing you." Cam threw his hands in the air. "The whole thing's insane."

"Odd. That's just what Hannah and I thought when we found out what *you* were up to. It seems that short of giving the whole thing up, you have two choices: Keep me safe while you get yourselves killed, or let me help you accomplish exactly what you want to do, what you set out to do at the start."

Cam stared at the floor, a haunted look in his eye. "Tell her this is crazy, Rico."

"No," his friend said softly. "She is right. When Tanner realizes she ran away on her own, and to be with you . . ."

"It'll drive him loco," Digger said.

"Damned right. It'll drive all of them loco, and some hothead on his side will shoot *at Abby* before Tanner has a chance to rein his men in," Cam said.

"Cam, that's a chance we'll have to take. This is the only way."

Abby's argument quelled the last of Cam's protests, and the conversation went on. Abby knew her point was won when the men began reviewing how they'd put the entire gang within reach of the ransom site without being spotted. She listened intently, aware that her own safety depended on understanding every detail of Cam's original plan and the amendments he made to ensure her escape.

"When this is through, the final steps will fall into place," Rico said after Hannah and the others had drifted out.

"We're going to arrange a delay. Willem will postpone his trip for now," Cam said.

"You cannot! We must strike while Tanner is—" Rico cut himself off. "We should not discuss this in front of her."

"Rico's right on this one, Abby. Wait for me outside. And no eavesdropping."

"None," she promised. She was sorely tempted, standing at the edge of the campfire's circle of warmth, not to sneak back and press her ear to the wide cracks around the door. Finally the door opened again, and Rico came out wearing a satisfied expression. She hurried to rejoin Cam.

"Can I come back in now?"

He slipped his arms around her and gave her a quick hug. "Sorry, sweet, but this outfit has had a rule from the start: No one knows any more than he needs to. It keeps us all safer."

"I understand."

Cam cleared his throat. "There is one thing you do need to know, though. I have to leave tomorrow."

"Why?"

"We have a lot of arrangements to make for a certain caller Tanner's about to have, and I have to go to Colorado Springs."

"You mean you won't be with us when Franklin comes."

"No, which is part of the reason I was so dead-set against having you involved in this. If I could figure out any other way, we'd do it. Rico pointed out a few things just now that I was trying to ignore. If I don't go to Colorado Springs, the whole plan will have been for nothing. Rico promised me he'd take care of you while I'm gone."

"Who's going to take care of you? You said 'we' had arrangements to make."

Cam's silence grew to awkward length, and Abby had a flash of intuition. "Hannah."

"She's going with me," he admitted reluctantly. "She has certain skills I need."

"I'll bet she does."

"Not like that. I'm sorry I have to be so secretive with you, Abby. Only three people in camp know the full plan for Tanner. I swear, I'll tell you as soon as it's over."

"I'll hold you to that."

"You really don't have to worry about Hannah," Cam said. "She used to think she was in love with me, but I think her attention's turning elsewhere these days. I see her sitting with Digger a lot."

"How about you—were you ever in love with her?"

"No."

"Have you ever been in love with anyone?" Abby pressed, suddenly very much needing to hear the words from Cam, needing his reassurance before she let him ride off with Hannah, before she faced Franklin.

"Once." The barest hint of a smile curved Cam's lips, and he tugged her a little closer. His kisses drifted across her temple and past her ear to the soft spot just behind it that made her shiver.

"Did you ever tell this woman how you felt?"

"No. But she is about the most intelligent creature I've ever come across. I think she figured it out."

That was as close as he'd come to saying it. It would have to do for now.

Abby nodded sagely. "Probably so."

Cam only allowed himself to look back once, from far across the meadow, and it almost ruined him.

Abby had run out from the trees to watch them ride away. Her deep-green dress blended into the shadowed forest behind her, but her hair, unbraided and tousled from a restless night's sleep in his arms, caught the early light like a halo. Eyes locked, neither of them waved, neither of them moved, until Hannah finally put out her hand and touched Cam's arm.

"We've got to get going. I need every minute to get you looking like you belong in a bank, and you're going to have to do some fancy talking to get Lil to let us use her place."

"Yeah." He said it, but he didn't move. He couldn't, until Digger came down from the trees and led Abby back. The two of them turned, one last time. Digger lifted his hand in a wave, which Hannah answered. Abby simply looked across the distance into Cam's soul, then disappeared into the trees. He recalled the red flannel shirt folded into his bedroll, hoping that the scent of her still left on it would let him sleep without her nearby.

Hannah sat a moment longer. "You really ready for this, Cam?"

"I don't have much choice."

"Rico will take care of her. He might not like her, but he'd never hurt you."

"I know. Let's go get Tanner."

They turned toward Salida.

"She won't try to mess with him anymore," Digger said. "Not that Cam'd do anything, but Hannah told me herself she don't want to come between you and him. She's kinda come to like you, she says."

"She apparently likes you, too."

"Nah." The old miner reddened around the collar, but Abby noted the hopeful look in his eyes.

"Think about it, Digger. She already told me herself that she wasn't interested in Cam anymore, but she came to you, too. I think she wanted *you*, more than anyone else, to know she's getting over Cam."

"Why, I suppose you're right at that, miss. I sure do hope so." Digger straightened up, a hopeful smile crinkling his worn face. "You know, I always felt that girl had something special to her."

"So do you," Abby said. "So do you."

Four long days passed in camp. Abby spent that time fretting over Cam and reviewing the exchange with Rico until it scorched itself into her memory. Then it was time to start riding down the mountain to the meeting place. That morning Abby slipped on the jacket from her riding suit, the only garment of her own not lost or ruined beyond wear. She then joined Rico and the others outside.

"You will ride the Appaloosa again for now," Rico said, "but Ephram will give you his horse before we reach the site tomorrow."

"I thought Charlie's horse was the fastest."

"He thought so also, but the race proved otherwise."

"Oh." Memories of what she had done during the race tinged Abby's cheeks with embarrassment, but in the pink light of dawn, no one seemed to notice.

"Do you have everything?" Rico asked as she prepared to mount.

Abby held out her arms and looked down at the dress Cam had bought her, which already showed the effects of five days and nights of continuous wear. "This is it."

Rico nodded. "Then we shall go. Charlie, Antonio, you make certain the camp is clean. Leave no traces to show that anyone was here in the past six months."

"Sure, Rico."

"*Sí*."

"Where will we go afterward?" Abby asked.

"We have one more camp, señorita." Rico swatted his horse's belly and pulled the cinch tight when the animal blew air. "It is better hidden even than the little valley. The men know it. I will tell you where it lies when we are away from Tanner."

"You still don't trust me."

"No," he said, but then a quick smile brightened his face. "But I am beginning to understand what Cam sees in you, Señorita Morgan. I think trust will come after I see Tanner's money in your hand."

Chapter 14

"There they are."

Rico tilted his sombrero back and stabbed a finger toward a boulder-studded stretch of yellow dirt and gray-green brush. Just beyond its far edge, four horsemen approached.

"Franklin." Abby peeked out from behind the boulder they were using for camouflage, and recognized his stocky figure instantly. He dwarfed his horse, a big, yellow dun stallion that he sat like Caesar. His clothes looked plain compared to the men behind him, but Abby knew his coat and pants would be of the finest cut, like the tailored evening clothes he'd worn in New York. Even at this distance he made a compelling figure; however, if the dangerous-looking men behind him weren't enough to make her uneasy, all Abby had to do was recall what Franklin did for amusement.

"The rest of them will be just beyond that rise," Rico went on, apparently unaware of how white Abby's knuckles turned as she clenched her fists. "Our men will move into position within the next few minutes."

"I'm not as worried about the ones behind the rise as I

am about those four," Abby said.

With a nod, Rico identified two of the three other men as Franklin's foreman and his new hired gun.

"But Liam Stanton's been gone less than a month!"

"A man like Señor Tanner cannot afford to be without protection for long."

"And the other one?" Abby asked.

"The sheriff. He will make anything Tanner does look legal. Pay no attention to them for now. I am most concerned that you know exactly where our escape lies. We will have only a few moments from the time you take the money. You must ride straight for those rocks without hesitation. If there is trouble, lie flat on your horse and do not look back. Ride as fast as you can. Jesús will see you safely to Cameron."

"I understand."

"Will you recognize the path from below?"

Abby assessed the area once more. "I think so."

"You must be certain." Dusting off his pants, Rico started back down toward their horses. "I will point it out to you before you start toward Tanner."

That moment came far too soon. As her mount shifted from foot to foot, Abby tried to find a source of calm within herself.

"She does not look like a prisoner," said Jesús. "Tanner will suspect something."

Reins dangling across his palm, Rico squinted up at Abby. "Perhaps we should tie her."

"I won't be able to get the bag," Abby protested.

"I will not really do it, señorita, but we can make it appear you are tied." Rico cut a length off one of the rawhide ties dangling from his saddle and demonstrated. "Cross your arms and loop this around, so. When you are ready, you can drop it, but from a distance, you will look indeed like our prisoner."

"Let me muss up my hair a little, too." Abby quickly loosened her braid and raked her fingers across her scalp to loosen a few wisps. With the rawhide looped neatly over her wrists, she submitted to Rico's inspection.

"*Muy bueno,*" Rico said. "You appear an excellent hostage. Are we ready?"

He swung up into his saddle and gave the signal to move. Antonio, Pete, and Ephram fell in behind, and they entered the valley.

"I wish Cam were here," Abby said aloud.

"I, also, but it cannot be." Rico hesitated, then added, "Even if circumstances did not require his absence, he could not ride with us now. Tanner has not seen his face in years, not since Cameron was a boy. It must remain so for now."

"But surely you can't have been robbing the ranch without Franklin ever seeing you."

"We have taken great pains to keep Tanner and his crew from identifying us, in order to protect the families and friends of those who ride here."

Abby glanced over her shoulder. Sure enough, the other three men had pulled their kerchiefs up over their noses, just like the outlaws in Portia Goodman's illustrated books.

"Franklin's the one who should be hiding his face. He's the criminal."

"Perhaps you should tell the sheriff that."

Abby and Rico quickly found themselves facing Franklin Tanner from some fifty yards away. Their respective escorts stayed some distance behind. Abby stared at Franklin with what she hoped appeared to be anxious longing, all the while sensing his examination like bugs crawling over her skin.

Strange, she thought, what knowledge of a person could do to one's perceptions. Suddenly the pattern of lines around his pale blue eyes made him look dissipated, and the salt and pepper mustache she'd once admired seemed as hateful as the rest of him.

"Where's Garrett?" Franklin shouted across the expanse of low-growing bitterbrush. "Is he still too much of a coward to show his face?"

"He watches from a distance, you can be sure," Rico answered.

"That's not part of the deal, Padilla."

"Neither are the men you have in the arroyo, señor, but we all make accommodations, no? Show us what you have in the bag."

Franklin opened the carpetbag and tilted it toward Rico, then lifted two fat bundles of cash aloft while Rico rode out several yards past Abby to get a better view. Rico nodded.

"*Excelente*. The rest had better match it, señor, or we will come back to carve the balance out of your skin." Rico turned his mount back toward Abby, spoke in a voice so low she could barely hear. "Señorita, look over your shoulder. You will see a large boulder with another on top. Just to the right is your goal."

Abby followed his instructions and easily spotted the gap that marked their escape route. "I see it," she murmured barely moving her lips.

"Have those animals harmed you, Abigail?" Franklin called.

About time you asked about me, you wretch, and don't call them animals. Abby held her face in that hopeful half-smile. "No. I'm fine, Franklin. They treated me quite well under the circumstances. Just make this be over, please."

"It will be shortly, my dear. Whenever these gents are ready."

"We have been ready for weeks, señor. We were only waiting for you to decide the señorita was worth the expense." Rico crooked his finger, inviting Tanner to ride forward.

In Franklin's substantial fist the beige and maroon carpetbag appeared no heavier than a woman's purse. Abby tried to estimate its weight, not wanting to be caught off balance as she snatched it up. The height of the rock where he set the money was about right: She'd barely have to lean over to reach the handle. That would make her escape that much quicker.

Franklin deposited the bag and backed his horse away, his icy-blue eyes never leaving Rico's face.

"There's your money, you thieving bastards. Send Miss Morgan over."

"Move a little farther back, I think," Rico said and waited for Tanner to comply. "Are you ready, señorita?"

Swallowing one last lump of anxiety, Abby nodded. "Here I come, Franklin."

As she nudged her mount forward, the men behind Tanner straightened. She heard Rico fall in a short distance behind her and knew Cam's men held themselves as ready as Franklin's. A silent plea for luck flew skyward as she rode out.

The rock loomed on her right, the patterned satchel nearly within reach. Abby gripped the reins securely and assessed the distance, preparing herself. Her eyes locked with Franklin's. *Someday it will be my pleasure to tell you what you are*, she thought.

Now.

Abby leaned forward, letting the rawhide tie slip away from her wrists as her mount gathered himself to respond to her growing tension.

A cloud of dust billowed up between Abby and Franklin, jerking her attention away from the bag of money. To her astonishment, a man sprang out of the center of the cloud. He held a rifle pointed straight at Rico.

Spooked, Abby's horse reared onto his back legs, neighing in distress. In the seconds it took her to fight him to a standstill, every man present drew his gun.

"Hold your fire! Hold your fire!" Rico and Franklin shouted over and over.

Only Abby's presence in the field of fire kept the men from blowing each other's brains out in the first seconds.

Now she realized she held this tentative truce in her hands, along with several men's lives. An absurd calm flowed through her and clarified her thinking. She blessed whatever providence had guided her startled mount into a direct line between Rico and the man on the ground, making a clear shot impossible. She held the animal still, shielding Rico.

"What is he doing here?" Rico demanded of Tanner, pointing toward the man with the rifle. "You value her so little, you would risk her life with your trickery?"

"Back off, *amigo*, or he'll drop you and your men like the dogs they are." Face taut with fury, Franklin stood in his stirrups, towering over everyone, his voice commanding. "Pick up the satchel, Abigail, and bring it back to me. You will be safe. Domingo will only fire if one of them tries to detain you."

"Does she have your word?" Rico asked derisively.

"Now, Abigail," Franklin ordered.

If she moved, either to take the money or to escape, the man with the rifle would have a clear shot: Rico, and possibly the others, would be dead in seconds. There was only one real choice.

"I can't. Make him put his gun down—please, Franklin." Abby allowed every ounce of the terror she felt for Rico and the others to color her voice. She sounded pathetic, even to herself, but her thoughts remained calm and precise. "I can't bring you the money. I heard Mr. Garrett tell that man with the big hat to shoot me first if you tried to take the money back."

Franklin's glance swept over the men behind Abby. She could only hope Antonio was aiming more or less in her direction to lend her ploy some validity.

Behind her, Rico cursed in vehement Spanish and called to her softly, "You need not do this."

But Franklin's demeanor had already changed. He settled back into his saddle, a conciliatory expression on his face, and Abby knew she'd hit the right key. Maybe he actually did care for her in some perverse way.

"Please, Franklin," she begged. "Make him go away."

"Of course, my dearest," Franklin said. "After all, it's only money, not worth your life. Domingo, throw your gun down and back off."

The man obeyed, his actions deliberate.

"The next move's yours," Franklin said.

"As we planned it," Rico answered.

"I'll stay right here," Abby called out. "You can all see me. I won't move until you and your men get away safely. Just, please, don't shoot me."

Moments later Rico hung the bulky satchel from the horn of his saddle. Catching Abby's eye, he tilted his hat slightly with one finger. She saw a flash of admiration there she'd never seen before.

"*Hasta la vista, señorita.*"

Until we see you again—a promise Abby clutched to her heart as she turned back to Franklin. Behind her, four horses galloped away. She sat stock still, listening to the thundering of hooves fade. Franklin lifted his hand, ready to signal his men.

With a moan and a flutter Abby tumbled off the saddle. She hit the dirt with a thump and lay there, arm aching, trying to pretend she'd fainted dead away.

Her swoon distracted the Fidelity men and bought an extra few seconds for Rico and the others. Franklin leapt from his horse and ran to gather her into his arms.

"Get them!" he ordered, his voice as hard as Damascus steel. "I want every one of those bastards dead by sundown. The man who brings me that satchel and Garrett's body won't have to work for the rest of his life."

Franklin's words froze Abby's heart to stillness. She forced herself to breathe, trying to fight down the shudder that racked her as the riders raced away.

"Abigail, are you all right?" Chafing her wrists between his broad palms, Franklin bent over her with the solicitude any man should have for his betrothed. "Wake up, my dear."

"Franklin? Oh, Franklin, are they gone?" Abby threw her arms around his neck, choking back her panic as he wrapped his thickly muscled arms around her.

"Gone, and well rid of the vermin. Let me take you home, Abigail."

"Yes. Oh, please, Franklin. Get me out of here."

Cam, get me out of here.

"I want tea with honey. Now. And a blanket. You, get a hot bath going."

Franklin burst through the front door of the Fidelity ranch house, carrying Abigail and shouting orders. With no more than a cursory glance at his burden, his staff jumped to obey. Abby felt like a fraud. Her shoulder hurt from that phony tumble she'd taken, but that was her only physical complaint.

Mentally, emotionally, that was a different matter. With every breath Abby ached for news that Rico and the others had escaped safely. Cam was safe, somewhere, but fear for his men far outstripped her personal concerns. Franklin hardly seemed likely to hurt her at this point.

Abby accepted his help into the parlor, then insisted she be put down. He settled her onto an overstuffed chaise and was tucking a lap robe around her knees when his cook came in to deposit a tea tray on a nearby cabinet.

Franklin immediately went to pour a cup.

"Here you are, my dear," he said, returning. The translucent Limoges cup and saucer looked doll-size in his grip. "Drink this. It will do you good."

Abby took a sip and gasped as the liquid burnt its way down her throat. "This tastes like whisky."

"I added a little, my dear. You were so silent on the way home, I thought you must be in shock."

"It's just that so much has happened. I suppose I'm still trying to digest it. Why did you ever try something so"—underhanded, she thought—"bold?"

"I could hardly trust Garrett to simply release you, money or no."

More than they could trust you. Abby had to bite her tongue. She sipped at the doctored tea, trying to appear more like a newly rescued victim. "You must have known how dangerous those men were. You might have been killed. And where on earth did that Domingo person come from?"

"As soon as I had the other details of the ransom arranged, I had the area scouted. There wasn't anyplace for an ambush, so I put a man in a shallow pit, put an old carpet over the top, and covered it up with dirt."

"But we—I mean, they watched everything for hours. Since dawn."

Franklin chuckled proudly. "That's the beauty of it. Domingo's part Comanche. He crawled in there last night, after dark. It would have worked, too, if that nag they put you on hadn't spooked. It's a shame we didn't manage to capture at least one of Garrett's men. Then we'd have him. You're looking pale, darling." Franklin went to the door and bellowed down the hall, "Is that bath ready yet?"

"Yes, sir, Mr. Tanner," came an answer. "Just taking the hot water up."

"Now, I want you to take a good hot bath and go to bed. The whisky will help you sleep."

"I'm not that tired. It's not even dark yet. Why don't you take me on into town. It's really not proper for me to stay here alone with you."

"But we aren't alone. I invited Mrs. Nagle—the real one, this time—for a visit and to act as our chaperon."

"And I will be more than happy to stay to get you well settled here, Miss Morgan," Ellie Nagle said as she appeared in the open doorway. To Abigail's eye, she looked little changed from the horse-faced bundle tied by the stream. "I'm sorry, I was just changing for dinner. I hope that nasty, abusive man did not harm you in any way."

Abby shook her head. "They took good care of me. I suppose I was valuable."

"Mr. Tanner cannot, of course, leave you in town where they might assault you again."

"Of course," Abby surrendered as the numbing effects of the whiskey seeped out to her fingers and toes. As much as she wanted to be away from him, slipping out of Franklin's grip tonight seemed out of the question. She'd have to work it out tomorrow.

"I took the liberty of having your trunk opened," Mrs. Nagle said. "I put all your things away. Of course, if they're not to your liking, we can rearrange them tomorrow. Would you like to go up?"

"Not quite yet." Not until some word came about Rico and the others.

"Don't be stubborn, Abigail." Franklin joined her, perching on the end of the chaise, a tumbler of whiskey in one hand. His fingertips showed white where he gripped the heavy leaded crystal.

"I thought you liked my stubbornness."

"Only when it makes sense, but right now it doesn't. You're exhausted."

"But I'm still too excited to sleep. Let me just rest here." Abby ignored the roil of disgust in her stomach as Franklin patted her hand. "I've been in the mountains with those awful men so long, I really would enjoy just sitting here with you for a while."

"And I'd enjoy having you here. It's been much too long." Franklin lifted her hand, and for a moment, Abby feared he was going to kiss her fingers. She steeled herself, but he only gave her a fond look and released her. "Would you care to join us, Eleanor?"

"Yes, certainly. Just let me get my sewing."

Ellie Nagle embroidered half an eagle on a pillow cover before the sound of a horse broke Franklin's steady pacing. A dust-coated rider knocked on the door and stood there, hat in hand.

"You'd better have good news," Franklin growled, but the man just shook his head.

"We were right on 'em, Mr. Tanner, sir, but they closed off the gap with a rockslide. The rest of the crew's still after 'em, but Walters said I ought to come back and tell you they're goin' the long way around."

Leaded crystal shattered into blue sparks as Franklin pitched his empty glass into the hearth. "I told you to get them!"

"I did, sir, at least one of 'em. Looked like a kid. Clipped his wing pretty solid, so it ain't all bad news."

Abby jumped to her feet, Charlie's name on her lips, but Franklin's exuberant response silenced her. He strode over to the door and clapped the man on the shoulder. "Extra fifty in your next pay envelope."

"Thank *you*, Mr. Tanner. Anything you want me to take back to Walters?"

"Nope. You might as well sleep in your own bunk tonight. Walters and the others will be back come daylight. We're not going to catch them this time out."

"Yes, sir. I, uh, I'll stop by the kitchen, have someone clean up that glass if you want."

"Fine." Franklin waved his hand in dismissal, and the cowboy clumped off down the hall. Franklin turned to Abby, his eyebrow lifted in a question. "You seemed concerned that someone had been shot."

"Did I? Oh, Franklin, you must be terribly upset with me. If I hadn't fainted out there, your men might have done more than shoot one boy." She wondered if Franklin could detect the irony in her words.

"Don't be harsh on yourself. From the sounds of it, they were prepared for anything I could throw at them short of a troop of the U.S. Cavalry. Besides, the knowledge you can give us about Garrett's hideouts, his habits, the identities of his men, will all make up for today. I promise you, Abigail, we'll run them to ground. Garrett and his men will pay for what they've put you through."

Abby felt herself blanche at the idea. Fortunately, Mrs. Nagle mistook her distress for exhaustion. The woman hustled her away from Franklin and into a tub of steaming water. An hour later Abby lay in a huge double bed beneath a down comforter.

They were all safe, for now. Even poor Charlie would be in Digger's capable hands.

Tomorrow, Franklin would ask her to betray them all.

"Shall I read aloud to you, Miss Morgan?" Ellie asked when she had shaken out Abby's clothes and hung them to air. "I have been enjoying *Return of the Native* by Mr. Thomas Hardy lately."

The book Cam had read her in the cabin.

Abby saw Cam's face, the way he twisted one strand of his beard between thumb and finger as he read, and smiled to herself.

Later, when the house slept and she had time for planning, she'd decide how to protect his men and their families. She'd figure out what lies to tell Franklin, and more important, how to get out of this house. For now, she needed Cam's reckless strength. Whatever reminders of it lay in the book's familiar tale might help her.

"That would be lovely, Mrs. Nagle. You may continue wherever you left off in your own reading."

For the third time Cam guided his hands through the familiar but unpracticed motions of tying a tie. The tails came out uneven again, and he ripped the knot out. "Blast it."

"Set down and let me fix that thing." Hannah pushed him down onto a sateen-covered chair and sat on his lap. "Don't get your dander up. This is the only way I've ever done it."

She worked the tie for several minutes before finally patting it down. "Perfect. Abby's fine, you know. She's a gutsy thing, and Rico'll take good care of her for you, even if he doesn't think much of her yet. By now they're probably sitting around counting all that money into nice neat little piles."

"Keep telling me that."

Rising, Cam reached for the coat draped over the end of the bed. Hannah took it instead and helped him into it. A quick, fussy brush at the lapels, and she turned him toward the long mirror in the corner.

"Very natty," Hannah said.

A stranger stared back. No, not a stranger, just a friend he hadn't seen since early last spring. He was wearing a severely tailored black serge suit, polished black Wellingtons, and a starched collar. Cam shook his head at the sight.

"What?" Hannah asked.

"You're amazing. Every time we do this, it takes me by surprise."

"Me, too, even though I see it happening." Hannah stepped up beside him to look at his reflection in the mirror. "I don't know which makes the biggest difference, shaving you or dying your hair brown."

"It's definitely the brown hair." Cam smoothed at the shorn, dyed remnants of his locks. His fingers came away slick with oil. "Or maybe all this macassar."

"You're the one said to put it on so thick. At least the hair dye matches what we had before." Hannah eyed his reflection more critically. "But your face still looks awfully dark to me, and your cheeks don't quite match your chin. I should have put some more of that bleaching cream on you. That stuff Lil gave us don't work like what we kept at Noreen's."

"You're seeing red, not brown, from where that concoction's peeling my skin off. Do you women really do that to yourselves voluntarily?"

"I'll bet you a double eagle it's the first thing Abby asks for when she gets to town. She's getting dark as a walnut, and not just on her face, or so I noticed the other day when she was climbing into that new dress. You really ought to find a place out of the sun."

An overpowering need for Abby swept over Cam, and he stood there like an oaf.

"You got it bad," Hannah said, then she turned solemn. "I sure hope you can keep it together around Tanner. He's bound to bad-mouth her now."

"I can," Cam promised himself as he loaded his pockets with the essentials. He packed a neat black leather valise with the balance of his city clothes. His own dusty clothes and gear lay in a pile in the corner.

Hannah began gathering them up. "I'll get these washed up and pack them away for you. This'll probably be the last chance I get. I reckon it'll be Abby's job from now on out."

"I haven't thought much beyond the next few days. Abby and I will have to work a few things out." He watched Hannah fold a shirt. "You're taking this pretty well."

"Heck, what am I supposed to do, rip her hair out?"

"Kind of looked like you would for those first few days. How come you're not mad at me?"

"For what, falling in love with a real lady? I knew all along I didn't stand a chance—hell, honey, I'm a *whore*."

"Don't ever believe that, Hannah. You may do the work of a whore, but in the ways that count, you're as fine a lady as any woman I've ever known."

"Keep saying stuff like that, and I may decide to wrestle Abby for you. Anyway, it was a pretty good dream while it lasted. And I still got the best part of it: We're gonna get Tanner."

"And after that?"

"I been thinking I might get out of the business. Maybe start a boardinghouse or somethin'. Kinda depends on whether I get any better offers."

"Want me to put in a good word with Digger?"

"Now, what would I want with that old rat?" But her eyes were bright as she said it, and Cam grinned. Hannah glanced around at the baroquely decorated room. "I guess I'd better keep my mouth shut about where you've been the past couple of days. I doubt Abby'd like to hear you were in a whorehouse with me, even if it wasn't for the usual business."

"No, but she's going to hear it anyway, and from me."

Lips pursed, Hannah whistled long and low. "Brave boy. But first you've got to finish off Tanner. Let's get you to that train. I'll come back and square up with Lil for the room, then I'll head for the hotel. You be sure to wire me when everything's done."

"Absolutely. Remind me again that Abby's safe."

Hannah grinned. "She's safe, and right now she's probably eating enough of Digger's johnnycakes to stuff a cow. Never did see a woman could put down so much food."

"Abigail, you've got to give us more."

Franklin paced a tight circle around his leather-topped desk, a sharp contrast to the laconic man who sat next to Abby. Jacob Walters, the gunman who replaced Stanton on the payroll, was a study in self-control despite the dust and sweat of hard pursuit that crusted his shirt and jacket.

"I'm sorry, Franklin, but they moved me around so much, I have no idea where their camps were." Abby twisted her neck to follow his pacing as he looped behind her. "We slept someplace different every night or two."

"Are you telling me you don't even remember one of those places? What the mountains looked like, or the trees, or a stream?" Walters stared at her with open curiosity—and doubt. "There's got to be something, Miss Morgan."

"Nothing of consequence."

"Try us. We might recognize something. Describe the very last place they held you up in the mountains."

"Well, I'll try." A picture of cooperation and concentration, Abby combined features of both camps and embellished them. She then tacked on an outright fabrication.

"I do recall there was a stream, with a waterfall about two stories high. That was about a mile from where we stayed."

The two men looked at each other, frowning.

"No bells here," said Walters, "but you know the area better."

Franklin shook his head. "We'll come back to it. How about names?"

"I thought about that all night," Abby said. That much, at least, was true. "I'm afraid I'm not much more use there."

Eyes narrowed with suspicion, Franklin stopped in front of Abby, staring down at her. "Why are you protecting them?"

"Protecting them? Good heavens, Franklin, you can't imagine—"

"I do."

"Well, you're mistaken. It's just that they all used nicknames, excepting Mr. Garrett and that Rico person. There was one man they called Ranger, and a Bully. There was even a Mac, just like my brother. You remember Mac, don't you, Franklin?" At Franklin's impatient nod, Abby continued, listing the names she'd assigned to each man, based on characteristics she'd remember and keep straight. Mac was young Charlie, so much like her own brother during his youth. Along the line she tossed in Digger's name, since he had no family she could endanger.

"Digger Dunleavy." Franklin jumped on the name. "He's one of the ones I told you about, Walters."

The gunman nodded.

At least dropping Digger's name had given her fabrications the ring of honesty. Abby spent another few minutes evading the truth for their benefit, then Franklin sent the other man packing.

"Go over everything she said with the men," Franklin said. "See if any of them recognize that campsite."

With Walters gone, Franklin finally sat down, taking the vacant chair in front of his desk. He was so close to Abby that his knees brushed hers. She tugged the dove-gray skirt of her day dress close and smoothed the fabric over her knees.

"It is so good to have you here at last." Franklin leaned over and folded his hands over hers, a confident smile curving his lips. "I took the liberty of rescheduling our wedding to Saturday noon. The new invitations went out early this morning. We will be short a few guests, but—"

"Franklin, you can't!" Abby sprung up, pushing her chair backward so hard it fell over. "We can't, I can't, I don't want, that is . . ."

"What, my dear? If you are concerned about the arrangements, I assure you, three days is more than ample."

"It's not that." Time to put an end to this farce, Abby decided. She took a deep breath. "Franklin, I probably should have told you this last night, but there was so much going on and with Mrs. Nagle right there, I just couldn't seem to get it out. The past month has given me an ample taste of your West. It is a violent, violent place."

"You were among a group of hellions, their captive. Life on the Fidelity will suit you better." Franklin righted the chair.

"It wasn't just Cam Garrett's men. Everyone, everything here is violent: the land, the weather, even you. The man I met in New York didn't seem the sort who could keep a man in a hole for a night and a day just to trap someone."

"I'd have kept him in there a week if it meant getting Garrett."

"You see what I mean? This is a hard land; it breeds hard people. I find I don't want to become any harder than I am. I want to go home."

"Nonsense. I think I know what's behind this. Did Garrett or any of his men molest you? Force themselves on you?"

Anger suffused Abby's skin with red, anger that she had to swallow back before it betrayed her. *You could ask that*, she thought, staring at the man who'd marked Hannah with his brand, *when you do the things you do.* Unexpressed loathing trembled through her frame, but once again, Franklin's own expectations protected her.

"I'm sorry, my dear," he said with all sincerity. "I know how embarrassing this kind of question must be for you."

"But, of course, you must ask it." Be *softer, Abby, more contrite*. "The answer is no. No one forced himself on me.

They were all perfect gentlemen, to the last man. I even had a chaperon of sorts."

"Ah, yes, that woman who impersonated Eleanor Nagle. You could hardly call her to testify to your reputation." Franklin rubbed his chin thoughtfully. "That's it, isn't it? You're concerned about your reputation among the townsfolk, worried people will believe the worst. Rest assured, it will be no problem. No one knows you were with Garrett."

"What? Franklin, that's impossible. I've been missing for a month. You had to cancel the wedding. You must have told someone."

"I announced you had some second thoughts, that you had decided to stay in Denver for a few weeks to adjust to Colorado and to reconsider. Now they all think you came in unannounced yesterday, ready to marry me. Only my men and the Nagles know the truth, and you'll find them exceptionally discreet. Your reputation is, and will remain, intact."

"My reputation is not the issue here: I simply want to go home." Home to Cam's arms, she wanted to scream, but Abby kept her tone polite, her words logical. "I'm sorry if this will cause you any embarrassment in the community. If you like, I will announce the cancellation myself. I can say I came to tell you in person and you misunderstood my arrival. If you'll have someone take me into town this afternoon, I can speak to the minister and arrange a wire to my father."

"I'm afraid that wouldn't be wise. You are clearly still in shock from your ordeal. Given a few days' rest, I'm sure you will see I'm right about this."

He trapped her hands again, the sheer physical power of him barely restrained. It occurred to Abby that he could crush her without raising a sweat.

"You're my fiancée, Abigail. On Saturday you'll become my wife, and then everything will be just fine. I'll do whatever I can to keep you here, and we'll live happily ever after, as they say."

How could he give her that ridiculous speech and stand there with blue eyes full of affectionate concern? Abby's discomfort grew to desperation as she began to feel trapped.

Anxious to be away from him, Abby pressed a finger to her temple, as though she had a headache. She needed to escape to the haven of her room where she could think.

"We will have to continue this discussion later," she said, looking pained. "I very much need to lie down for a spell."

"Of course, my dear. This must have been a very trying morning for you. I'll have someone call you later for lunch." Franklin released her hands, but not before he lifted each one to his lips for a tender kiss. "I am so very glad to have you here at last."

Later, in her room, it took five solid minutes of scrubbing before Abby was satisfied her hands were clean. It took her longer to set aside her disgust and fear of Franklin enough to think.

She checked the illustrated linen calendar tacked inside the tall wardrobe. It took some calculating, but she finally figured out the date:

Wednesday, August 11. The wedding would be Saturday. She had three days to slip this trap.

Chapter 15

As she had the first day in the valley camp, Abby went reconnoitering after lunch. No goal as clear as the mine shaft tempted her, so she wandered from room to room, memorizing the layout of the house and noting the tasteful quality of its furnishings.

From the ornate wooden bedsteads and marbled dressers of the bedrooms upstairs, to the handsome pianoforte in one corner of the parlor, Abby spotted few items that would look out of place in her father's home. Franklin's study even included a pair of glass-fronted bookcases five shelves tall, where classical dramas and modern novels shared space with Franklin's texts on animal husbandry. It was clearly a man's house, lacking the gimcracks and lush draperies popular among women back East, but if she had come here directly, without learning Franklin's character, she might have thought to make herself very comfortable.

Instead, Abby felt like a rabbit, wandering through the wolf's den looking for bolt holes.

Even if she found one, she wasn't certain where the nearest shelter lay. Abby decided her next move was to figure out just where Saguache was.

Fortunately, Franklin had made that considerably easier by posting a framed map of the Fidelity holdings in the downstairs hall just outside his study. Franklin's pride of ownership showed clearly in the heavy black hash marks that marked a huge portion of the northwest corner of the San Luis Valley. Abby noticed where a previous line had been scraped off the parchment and a new parcel recently added to Franklin's holdings.

Had that ranch belonged to Charlie's father, or to Lew? Those little brown dashes, mostly around adjacent properties, must indicate his next targets. Abby had to clench her fists to keep from slamming the frame to the floor.

Franklin's thievery, however, wasn't her immediate worry. Right now she needed to get herself oriented and find Saguache. Abby studied the map carefully, then walked to the front door.

"Howdy, Miss Morgan," said a hand lounging on the front stoop. She recognized him as one of the wrangler's that had backed up Franklin at the ransom exchange. "Name's Hawkins. Anything I can do for you?"

"As a matter of fact, there is. I pride myself on my sense of direction back home, yet I find myself so turned around by all these mountains, I'm not even sure which way's north."

"That away, ma'am. Just remember that there's no mountains to the south and you'll be okay."

"That big peak there must be . . ."

"That's Storm King."

"Oh, of course. Franklin mentioned in one of his letters that he could see it from the veranda. Thank you." All right, if that was Storm King, then according to the map, Saguache lay angled off to the northwest, about seven or eight miles away. "I do admire this land of yours."

"Not mine, ma'am, Mr. Tanner's. And yours, too, pretty quick."

Perhaps, but not via Franklin Tanner. Abby stood for a moment longer, letting the landmarks sink into her brain and sizing up the possibilities.

"Something else, ma'am?" Hawkins asked.

"What are all those buildings?" She gestured toward the outbuildings, nearly a dozen in all, every one neatly painted and well kept.

"Bunkhouse. Tack shed. Smokehouse." Hawkins pointed to each as he listed them off. "That yellow one's the cookhouse."

"I thought the kitchen was inside."

"It is, ma'am, but that's just for Mr. Tanner and his guests. And you, now, of course. The rest of us eat plain grub. That big red building's the horse barn."

"I think I'll walk out there. Franklin wrote so much about his horses."

"I don't think that'd be such a good idea right now."

"Oh?"

"No, ma'am, you feelin' so poorly after all the excitement yesterday. It'd be better if you just stayed here at the house. I'm sure Mr. Tanner will take you around when he thinks you're up to it."

"Mr. Tanner does not decide when I'm capable of taking a walk. You may tell him I've gone out to the horse barn."

Hawkins straightened up, effectively blocking Abby's progress. His face remained cheerful, but Abby could feel the threat in his stance. "Begging your pardon, ma'am, but around here, Mr. Tanner decides everything. Best for you if you learn that right away."

Cam's train traveled from Salida to Pueblo, then headed on north toward Colorado Springs. They'd arrive in another hour. He had to meet Willem there to get the new contracts and then be ready to catch the two A.M. southbound to Alamosa.

Cam creased the railroad schedule into precise quarters and tucked it into his card case. He settled back to watch the middle-aged woman sitting across from him. She fanned herself vigorously, despite the distinct chill in the Pullman car. Cam considered pointing out to her that her paper fan carried a watercolor image of Lydia G. Pinkham's rosy-cheeked grandchildren; surely she didn't intend to advertise a remedy for female complaints. Instead, he excused himself and went out to stand on the platform.

The circuitous route and backtracking aggravated Cam as it never had before. He spent every mile second-guessing his decisions, wishing there had been some way to confirm the exchange—and Abby's safety—before leaving Salida.

Still, he recognized the necessity of leaving a convoluted trail: If Tanner ever checked, he'd be able to trace Willem Friederich's travels all the way back to St. Louis in an unbroken line. Tomorrow night Willem would leave his hotel, and a short while later he'd board the train for Alamosa, wearing the same black suit he'd been wearing at dinner in the Broadmoor's elegant dining room.

Except the man on the train wouldn't be Willem. He'd be Franklin Tanner's nemesis, come for one final visit.

About midafternoon, after Ellie Nagle had dozed off over her sewing, Abby knocked on the door to Franklin's study.

"Come in, my dear, come in." He slipped a sheet of blotting paper into a red-bound ledger, snapped it shut, and folded his arms across the book. The scented pomade in his graying hair caught the light. "You are a pleasant interruption to a tedious chore."

"I doubt you'll think so when I've had my say. We really need to finish the conversation we had earlier."

"I was perfectly satisfied with the conclusion."

"Well, I wasn't. I made my position perfectly clear, and you refused to understand, so I will say it again: I do not wish to stay here. I do not wish to marry you."

"It's not at all unusual for a young woman to have second thoughts a few days before her marriage, especially after an experience as trying as what you've been through."

"You're not even hearing me."

"Yes, I am." Franklin gave her a paternal smile. "But I've told you, my dear, your concerns are absolutely groundless. You'll realize that, once we're man and wife. You'll see, Abigail, I am right about this. Now, I have to go over a few things with my foreman. When I'm finished I'll have time to take you on a tour of the barn, if you like. Hawkins said you were asking about the horses earlier."

Though his voice was devoid of any overt hostility, Abby's flesh chilled: So his man was watching her, and this was Franklin's subtle way of letting her know it. Instinct warned her to back down for the time being, to take this opportunity to gain a little more knowledge. "I was. You wrote me so much about that stallion of yours, I wanted to take a better look at him. I'm afraid I wasn't paying much attention yesterday."

"That's understandable. I'm glad you're taking such an interest. I expect this business will take a half hour or so. You go put on your boots and something that won't suffer from the dust. I'd hate to see that lovely gown ruined."

Seething, Abby went through the motions of excusing herself. She stopped in the hallway and surveyed the map again. She could walk the distance to town easily enough, she decided, but a horse would make her chances of escaping better. Either way, she still had to figure out a way to get past the front door.

A half hour later, still stewing over a way out of this predicament, Abby knocked oncc more at the study door.

No answer came. She checked the parlor and dining room and found them empty as well. A glance through the leaded-glass panes of the front door showed Hawkins soaping a saddle at the bottom of the steps. She went back to the study to wait.

Franklin certainly kept a neat desk. The red ledger had disappeared, along with the blotting paper. Other than a pen and a brace of pipes in a carved antler holder, only a simple date book rested on the desk, Franklin's bold hand scrawled across its pale blue lines.

Yesterday's schedule simply read, "Abigail."

Abby snorted. She might have dropped in for a social visit, for all his schedule gave away. That in itself would make a nosy person look twice.

"And I'm nosy," Abby said aloud.

She slid the book around, and began flipping back and forth through a few pages, reading the entries. Everything, from the half hour with the foreman today to the upcoming wedding, was listed methodically and in detail—everything except the ransom. Abby continued reading, a bit puzzled by this omission.

Tomorrow, Franklin had meetings scheduled with three gentlemen, business associates by the look of it, and then a meeting with all three in the evening after dinner. According to his notes, two of the men were arriving in Henry by train in the morning, the third riding in from Del Norte. A tiny dollar sign, barely bigger than an apostrophe, appeared after one Germanic-looking name.

She turned the pages back to today's date and pushed it back into its place on the desk.

"Did you find what you were looking for?" Franklin asked.

Abby jumped up, flushed. "I didn't hear you come in."

"Apparently." He stood just inside the door, his bearing and voice cold and suspicious. Abby decided to disarm him with confession.

"I hope you don't mind. I'm always so curious about people's desks and appointment books. The way they're kept is so revealing about the person's mind. Yours is organized, precise, just as I would have expected."

"I recall your own writing desk as very tidy."

Abby smiled ruefully. "Only superficially, I'm afraid. The drawers and pigeonholes are always chock-full of bits and pieces needing sorting. I imagine your drawers are as neat as the top." Without waiting for Franklin's permission, Abby stepped around the desk and yanked open the center drawer. "See. Pencils, ink bottle, rubber eraser, notepaper. Not an item out of place." She pushed the drawer shut again and slipped out from behind the desk just as quickly. "Which way to the horses, kind sir?"

The last few crystals of ice in Franklin's manner vanished as Abby accepted his arm and let him lead her out to the barn.

As much as it galled her to see all those fast horses—including Ephram's prize mare—standing there just out of reach, she actually managed to enjoy the animals.

"He's a handsome thing," she said of Franklin's favorite, a big yellow dun stallion.

"Thunder could carry both of us all the way from South Fork to Fort Garland at a dead run," Franklin bragged. "But I have a special treat for you over here."

A big corner stall held a hot-blooded mare, a dish-nosed, pearly gray creature with two white half stockings on her front legs and her belly swelled with pregnancy.

"She's beautiful," Abby said in all honesty.

"Come here, sweetheart." Franklin dug into his coat pocket and came up with a lump of sugar to offer the mare. "This is my best brood mare. That's Thunder's foal she's carrying. It's going to be a hell of an animal, Abigail. She's yours. The foal, too."

"I can't—"

"And why not? You're going to be my wife. I've been planning this all summer, just waiting for you to get here. By all rights, I should wait until Saturday to give her to you, but you look so charming today, I just cannot resist."

"Franklin, stop it. I am not staying. I am not—"

"Hush." Though the word came out gently enough, his fingers closed around her upper arm in a grip that brought tears to Abby's eyes. Franklin's voice dropped to a low rumble, and he started for the door, dragging Abby along. "There's no reason for my hands to hear your flights of fancy, Abigail."

"Turn loose of me," Abby demanded as they entered the sunlight, but Franklin seemed oblivious to her words. He looked perfectly calm and reasoned, but the bruising crush of his fingers around her arm told her otherwise. She dug in her heels and repeated, "Release me, or your men will hear more than a flight of fancy."

"Am I hurting you, my dear?" He eased the pressure, but kept his hold firm. His eyes, paler by far than the sky above, glittered beneath the brim of his Stetson. "I do apologize; we will keep this particular topic of discussion, however, to ourselves from now on. You must realize, of course, how inappropriate it is to raise personal matters in front of the hired help."

"Of course," Abigail said, echoing his hollow insincerity, but he accepted her words at face value.

"Now, have you ever seen a good cutting horse work? No, of course not. Hawk, go turn that bunch of steers out of the holding pen into the main corral, then take them back one at a time. I'll take Miss Morgan around so she can watch."

"Yes, sir."

Leaning against the top rail of the split-wood corral, Abby watched the rider and horse separate out a young longhorn from its fellows. The animal dodged this way and that trying to escape the rider and get back to his group, but the horse seemed to outguess the creature at every turn. The poor steer grew more frantic at each pass, until it finally turned and bolted into the chute. The gate dropped behind him.

The next steer went in as quickly, but the third, a rangy creature with scars all over his hide, gave them problems.

Abby had noticed him watching the cutting horse work his companions. Now he used what he'd seen. He eluded the horse easily, feinting in one direction and then slipping around behind to rejoin the little herd. After it happened a second time, Hawkins turned his attention to a different target. The steer hung well back within his group, out of the man's reach, watching.

Impressed by the horse's training, Abby applauded along with Franklin when the rangy old steer, the last in the corral, finally trotted into the chute without challenging the horse.

"Clever thing," she whispered, watching him join his friends. She also silently thanked him for an old lesson he'd just reinforced.

Panicky, random efforts didn't pay. Carefully sizing up your opportunities did. So did bluffing.

Franklin's unholy blend of charm and evil had put her off the track. Trapped, she'd acted just like one of those other steers and tried to take him head on. She'd forgotten her father's most important poker lesson: "*Just because the other player has a few better hands, it doesn't mean you can't win in the long run. You just have to wait your chance.*"

The old steer had known it, had made things go his way.

"I had no idea how exciting moving cattle could be." Abby smiled up at Franklin, as though the wonder of the West had just struck her. "I mean, you wrote me about it, but actually seeing a horse do that. It's amazing. Please show me more."

She curled her fingers through Franklin's and saw him puff up a little with a misplaced sense of victory. She recalled the second part of her father's lesson:

"*Of course, if he cheats, that's a different matter.*" In her mind she could see Papa's sideburns wiggle as he grinned. "*Then you have to outcheat him.*"

She found Ellie Nagle crying.

Not that Ellie wanted to be caught, but Abby roared into her bedroom so quickly after she finally got away from Franklin that the woman didn't have time to shut the adjoining door.

"What on earth?" Abby led the woman back to her chair and sat down on the petit point footstool in front of her. "What's wrong, Mrs. Nagle?"

"N-nothing," Ellie sniffled into her lace-edged hankie.

"You hardly seem the sort to cry over nothing. Tell me what's wrong."

"I'm homesick. I miss Orris—Mr. Nagle, so much. I'm not used to being away from him. Three weeks is just too long."

"Three days," Abby corrected, but Ellie repeated her statement. Abby stared at her, stunned. "You don't mean . . . You haven't been here the whole time I was with C—gone, have you?"

"Oh, please don't mention this to Mr. Tanner. I wasn't supposed to say anything." Ellie's tears trickled off to nothing as fright widened her eyes. Her voice was little more than a whisper. "Oh, dear lord, if he should call our note, I don't know what I'd do."

"Has he threatened to take your business away? I want you to tell me the whole story."

"Oh, I can't. That's why he kept me here in the first place. All my friends know I'm such a chatterbox, I can't keep a good story to myself. Mr. Tanner didn't want anybody in town to find out that Garrett person had you, so he had us visit here so it'd stay private till they found you. When a whole week went by, he had to let Orris go back and open up the store."

"Why did Mr. Nagle leave without you?"

"A person doesn't always have a choice."

"Did Franklin threaten you?"

"Well, no. Not in so many words." Ellie blotted at her nose again. "But it was very clear to Orris he wasn't to say anything. He's been telling people I'm in Denver trying to convince you to come. I have family there, a sister who's a little sickly, so it seemed reasonable that I might stay.

That way, when you arrived and I came home at the same time, it would look all right. Oh, listen to me, I've told you everything. That's why Mr. Tanner wanted me here until after he got you back. He said once he married you and captured Cam Garrett, it didn't matter what Mr. Nagle and I said."

"But he didn't get Garrett." Abby put her arms around the woman's bony, fleshless shoulders. "Calm down, calm down. I'm sure Franklin is doing everything he can to find those outlaws. Once that's all resolved, you won't have a thing to worry about."

"You think he'll catch Garrett?"

"I know he's trying." Abby crossed her fingers against the possibility of success. "We'd better dress for dinner, don't you think? You needn't worry that I'll say anything to Franklin, but you really mustn't say anything, either."

"Oh, thank you. You've been a great comfort, Miss Morgan. It's so good to have another woman here."

Back in her own room Abby pitched a pillow against the wall in frustration and disappointment. The one person likely to help her get away from the Fidelity, and Ellie could be trusted with nothing but trouble.

Where was Hannah—tough, resilient, resourceful Hannah—when Abby really needed her? With Cam, wherever that was. Abby pitched the pillow again.

Dinner was medieval.

That was the only word to describe the scene, Abby decided later as she lay in bed watching the moon through her window. There stood Franklin, the lord of the manor carving the roast, his knife flashing arcs of light across the spotless linen. His henchman, Walters, guarded his right, while the ladies watched and listened, decorative chattel with no say in their fates.

Through it all, Abigail kept up a patter of bright, meaningless conversation, designed to keep Ellie Nagle's mind off their earlier discussion and to put Franklin off his guard.

Later, when they'd shared a glass of amber sherry, she even managed to apologize to Franklin for giving him such a fit about the wedding. She barely held her tongue when he gloated once again about knowing best.

"Eleanor said your wedding gown is magnificent," he went on as she stared at the fire. "I haven't seen it, of course, but I'm glad you went all out. I want to present you to the valley in the grandest style, and every man and woman within a half-day's ride will be here Saturday."

"Here at the house? I thought the church . . ."

"Too small." Franklin waved the idea off. "Especially for the reception. I'm having the damnedest party this valley's ever seen, just to let everyone know how glad I am you're marrying me. I'm surprised you haven't smelled all the baking going on."

"I have. I just thought everything would be taken into town. It would be so much easier for people."

"Not for us. Especially not after what you've been through. I'm keeping you safe under my wing, Abigail, until Garrett's either in jail or six feet under. Then we'll go to town whenever you like. We'll take trips into Del Norte, too. I've a habit of going down there every few weeks for dances and the like."

Dances. Dances! *You go whoring, you pig, and in the most despicable style!* It had taken every ounce of Abby's will to keep from screaming at him.

But she hadn't, and she wouldn't, not until the right time came, no matter what he did or said.

Abby pushed the coverlet aside, fully awake and charged with the pure energy of righteous anger. The chilly night air, rich with the scents of hay and cattle, poured through the open sash of the window and rolled across her bare feet.

Arms folded across her bosom to ward off the chill, Abby padded over to the window. She had no trouble approaching it. The veranda roof angled out just below her room, holding her vertigo at bay, but the drop off the edge of the roof was a good ten or twelve feet. To make escape more impossible,

Hawkins or one of the other men waited there. She'd seen the glow of a cheroot through the front door's glass as she'd come up.

The breeze lifted the hem of her nightgown, sending a chill up her legs. Putting her weight into it, Abby pulled the sash down.

A few nights ago she would have welcomed that breeze across her skin, delighting in the coolness after the heat of Cam's loving. She stood there, lost in the memory, absorbed in the wanting.

A soft click, and the faint aroma of cognac and tobacco tugged Abby out of her reverie. She turned, Cam's touch so fresh in her mind that for the first instant she thought it was him, almost said his name and ran into his arms.

"You are exquisite." Franklin's voice rasped across the silent room, husky with desire.

Abigail froze. "Wh-what are you doing in here?"

"Watching you. Don't be afraid. I watched you last night, too, while you slept. But tonight, with the moonlight behind you . . ."

The moonlight, showing him her body through the thin muslin nightgown. Abby fought down the nausea. "You must leave now. It's not proper for you to be here." *Wake up, Ellie.*

"You are a treasure, a treasure beyond value. I cannot believe you'll be mine."

"But not until we're married."

"I know, pet. As much as I want you, as beautiful as you are, standing there like a goddess, I won't touch you tonight. Our wedding night will be special, Abigail. I promise you."

"Good night, Franklin." She said it firmly, and to her shocked relief, he left, slipping back into the dark hallway like a specter.

Abby stood there by the window, shaking, for a very long time, then found the basin and vomited until her stomach was empty and nothing but bile came. When the retching stopped, she rinsed her mouth and changed her nightclothes. She dug into the drawer for a heavy flannel gown that enveloped her from neck to toe.

She spent the night huddled in the center of the bed, as she used to when she was a child afraid of the dark and her parents wouldn't come anymore. But when the bell rang for breakfast, she arrived at the table at the same time as Ellie and Franklin.

Reaching deep inside herself for the strength, she faced them and Walters across the table, no sign of strain on her face. Evidence of the night's damage lay hidden beneath a judicious layer of cosmetics. The bright patter of the previous evening still flowed across her lips.

They were almost finished when Mrs. Nagle asked for more coffee. An unnatural tinge of color lit Ellie's cheeks when Abby passed the silver carafe, and Abby realized that the woman knew about Franklin's visit last night. Ellie had been awake, and she'd stayed in her own room, probably cowering in her bed, the whole time Franklin was there, the whole time Abby was sick.

"After breakfast I'm taking a quick ride out to the holding pens," Franklin said. "Would you like to come along?"

Abby looked from Ellie to Franklin, debating which one she despised more. It was a close call.

"Yes, of course, Franklin, I'd love to have a ride with you before your guests arrive."

The transfer at Alamosa behind him, Cam stood on the rear platform all the way to Henry, passing the time and a flask of brandy with Tanner's attorney from Denver. As far as the man was concerned—as far as he'd known for nearly six years—the dark-haired German man before him *was* Willem Friederich.

They'd be riding out to the Fidelity together, and Cam looked forward to the trip. It gave him plenty of time to get Willem's mannerisms and high-pitched, accented voice ginned in solidly.

Also, the attorney could be an amazing source of legal and financial gossip with a little alcohol in him, and Cam pressed the brandy on him with a generosity born of necessity. The information in Willem's notes was skimpier than Cam had been led to expect. He needed just a few more details on Tanner's latest transactions to make sure the trap, once sprung, held until Tanner either died or gnawed his own leg off.

Lucius Beebe, Jr. could provide those details, doze off along the way, and wake up to look perfectly sober in all senses of the word by the time they reached the Fidelity. The real treat was, he never seemed to remember a thing he said while drunk and went along with whatever anyone claimed. Cam had often wondered how the man ever achieved such prominence in the law—until he found out that Lucius Beebe, Sr., ran the firm and actually handled most of the business. Junior, it seemed, largely made the social calls and toted papers around. He and Tanner got along famously; it made Cam wonder about Beebe's more private tastes in entertainment.

The liveryman in Henry had their buggy waiting, "as Mr. Tanner ordered." Cam tossed his satchel in back alongside Beebe's and hustled the man onto the seat.

The few minutes in town were always nerve-racking. A few men in Henry knew Cam Garrett on sight. Disguised or not, he didn't want to risk being seen as Willem. Even his own men had never seen him without at least a partial beard.

Within ten minutes they hit the outskirts of town; within twenty he had Beebe talking. By the time they reached the south end of Fidelity holdings shortly after noon, Beebe had long since succumbed to the brandy and dozed off.

Without letting the horses slow their even trot, Cam removed a packet of papers from the snoring attorney's portfolio. A quick check proved the documents matched the ones Cam carried in his own valise, except for a few crucial passages buried deep in paragraphs of legal verbosity. He made the switch, then sat back to enjoy the rest of the trip.

A little later they passed the rough track where Digger had turned off the road with Abby that first day. Kidnapping her right on Fidelity land had been designed to add to Tanner's aggravation. Tanner should be on the brink by now, ready for the slightest shove to send him over.

Cam flicked the reins across the livery horse's rump, and the animal picked up its pace. He could hardly wait to turn down the lane that led to the ranch house. "Awaken yourself, Lucius. We are there."

"Mmmph? Uhm, yes. All right, I'm awake. Nothing like a good nap before a man starts serious business, eh? Look, there's that wrangler of his." Beebe waved.

"*Ja*, Mr. Hawkins."

Hawkins fell in alongside the buggy. "Howdy there, gentlemen. Mr. Tanner's waiting for you up at the house, along with Mr. Evans. If you want to just follow me up, I'll see to your buggy, and you can go on in."

This was the part Cam hated the most of every trip, the first sight of Tanner's big white house, sitting where his father's house had stood. He'd had to learn to use that anger to sharpen his performance.

This time the hackles went up on his neck higher than usual. Cam hesitated, checking the yard before he dismounted, but found it normal. The house looked fine, too, all the curtains wide open, no concealed gunmen, but something was wrong and he couldn't quite put his finger on it. He longed for Rico or Jesús at his back.

"Welcome, gentlemen." Tanner greeted them at the door, looking altogether too composed for Cam's peace of mind. "You missed dinner, but there are sandwiches for you, and some coffee and pie in my study."

"Good, we can eat while we talk," Beebe said. "Sounds like plenty to hold me until one of your beef suppers. Hello, Evans." Tanner's other guest stepped up to shake hands.

"Sandwiches are fine for me, also," Willem said. "I have waited a long time for another Tanner feast. My father is very jealous he could not come this time."

"No feast tonight. We'll be eating pretty simply until Saturday. But then, by god, Willem, you'll eat like you've never eaten in your life." Tanner's joviality grated on Cam's raw nerves.

And then he knew what was wrong.

Whatever possessed Abby to laugh at that moment, he'd be grateful forever. It gave him the seconds he needed to prepare himself, to freeze his expression into immobility, to find a distracting book in Tanner's case so that he wasn't facing her when the door opened, to absorb the shock before their eyes met.

"And here's the reason for our delayed feast. My dear, this is Mr. Zebediah Evans, my geologist, Mr. Lucius Beebe, my attorney from Denver, and Mr. Willem Friederich, a broker friend from St. Louis. Gentlemen, my fiancée, Miss Abigail Morgan, late of New York City. We will be married Saturday."

"Ah, at last we meet her. Congratulations!" Beebe cried.

Don't give me away, sweet. Cam put on his best Willem expression, a bit prissy and extremely rigid, as he slipped one hand into his pocket to cradle the little two-shot derringer Willem always carried when he came West.

"On behalf of our firm, we wish you many happy returns," he said as he turned from the bookcase, a volume of Shakespeare in his other hand.

Chapter 16

Abby stood there in the doorway, her fingertips resting lightly on the polished brass doorknob, staring at Cam. Her eyes rounded with shock, and Cam could see her begin to form his name.

For one hellacious instant his gut told him she was here of her own free will, that she'd somehow slipped away from Rico to be with Tanner, that she was going to betray him.

Then her mouth snapped shut, and he saw, really saw, the look in her eyes, the same trapped look that had been in his mother's eyes those years ago. But he saw something else there, too—a stubborn strength his mother had lacked.

Wrenching his gaze away, Cam confronted another threat: Ellie Nagle, standing on tiptoe to peep over Abby's shoulder. Damn the woman! She was supposed to be with her husband.

The whole thing had fallen apart, that was clear.

In his pocket the little derringer warmed in his grip. Cam eased the hammer back slowly as he tipped the book into its slot on the shelf. Abby continued to stare.

"Come, come, my dear. Say something to our guests." Full of exuberant good spirits, Tanner lifted Abby's hand onto his arm as though she belonged at his side. "What is the matter with you?"

"I'm sorry, Franklin." She shook herself as though she was coming out of a reverie. "For a moment I thought one of my former suitors had come back to haunt me."

Cam levered his thumb over the hammer of his pistol, but Lucius Beebe, still flush from the half bottle of brandy he'd downed, stepped forward to take Abby's hand.

"I assure you, dear lady, if I had been he, you would not be marrying Tanner here."

"Ah, but Mr. Stevens lacked your easy way with words." Without so much as a flicker, Abby allowed Beebe to assume he was the look-alike. "He also lacked your head of hair by over half. He became quite upset when I told him he ought to consider a wig."

Her comment brought laughter from Tanner and the others. Cam joined in, his relief and delight with Abby's quickness making it easier than he'd have thought possible.

"Hhh-mmm." Ellie cleared her throat, and Abby turned to her at once.

"Franklin, you've been remiss in your introductions."

Tanner went through the rudiments, and to Cam's further relief, Ellie seemed more curious about Beebe than himself. Abby stepped in before that changed.

"Please excuse us, gentlemen, but we have some sewing to do." Abby looked up at Tanner, a smile of appeasement on her lips. "I'm afraid my gown is so loaded with *passementerie* that Mrs. Nagle's dress looks altogether too plain. We're going to alter her skirt and add some lace and ribbon contrasts. I happened to bring a reel of maroon velvet ribbon that—"

"What you do to Eleanor's clothes is of no concern to me, so long as you are both happy with the result," said Tanner.

"Fine." She herded Ellie out the door and turned back to say, "I hope you will all be able to attend the ceremony on Saturday."

Saturday. Two days to get Abby out of this.

"Certainly, certainly," said Beebe. Evans concurred.

"And you, Mr. Fredericks?" Abby turned to Cam.

"Free-der-ick," he pronounced clearly, and the hint of a smile lifted the corners of Abby's mouth. "I would not miss it for any price."

"Wonderful. Gentlemen."

Tanner watched Abby leave, going so far as to step out in the hall to observe her on the stairs. Cam watched him watching, hating the greedy, possessive glint in Tanner's eyes, ready to drive a fist into his smug face.

Bring it to heel, Cam ordered himself, easing the hammer of the derringer back into place. The only way to keep Abby safe was to go through with this charade for now. With deliberation he pulled a spotless white handkerchief from his pocket and took off his glasses.

Willem made a ritual of polishing his glasses: two careful puffs of steamy breath on each side, then neat circles with one cloth-covered finger. He always completed the inside surfaces of both lenses, then the outside, then as a final step polished the brass wire frame until it gleamed. He'd done it that way since the day Cam had moved in with his uncle.

Now Cam followed the same steps, concentrating to make certain he did it exactly the way Cousin Willem did. By the time he slipped the curved wire temples over his ears and tucked his monogrammed kerchief back into his pocket, he was back in control, back in character as Willem Friederich and ready to eat and sit down to business with Tanner.

"Damned fine beef," Beebe said around a mouthful of sandwich. "Now, you want to tell us what this is about, Franklin? I thought that girl was supposed to be here a month ago."

* * *

Cam.

Abby dragged Ellie Nagle up the stairs. "Go get your dress and whatever petticoat you're wearing under it so we can see how much we need to do. I'll find the ribbon."

Cam.

Her mother's chest stood in one corner of the room, open and mostly empty. Thanks to Ellie, the neatly packed clothes now filled the massive wardrobe, but miscellaneous items still lined the bottom of the chest. Abby dug down for her sewing kit and the box of trims she'd tucked in for fashion changes.

Cam.

No, don't think about it, or you might say his name aloud, sing it out the window.

Brown hair, no beard, ridiculous glasses making his eyes watery, skin somehow bleached to near pallor: She had still known him on sight, had still felt his presence sweetening the room as soon as she opened the door.

And then she'd almost given him away to Franklin.

Abby sorted through the box of trimmings, scolding herself for being caught off guard. She'd expected some kind of rescue. She should have been ready for anything, including Cam, looking like a New York banker, in the same room as Franklin.

Cam.

No, Willem. Willem Friederich.

He had to be Willem in her every thought in order for them both to stay safe, just as she had to stick to the part of the willing bride. Whatever he was doing here in this house, she had to help him by keeping Franklin content and off guard.

He had to be Willem, because if he was Cam, and Franklin touched her in front of him, she would scream.

Willem Friederich. Abby repeated the name to herself, over and over, even when Ellie came in with her mousy pink dress and they started pinning folds and tacking the costly silk velvet ribbon into bows and swags. Every time she placed a pin, she said the name. Every time she tucked a pleat, or snipped a thread, or gathered a bit of lace, she repeated, Willem Friederich.

But it was still Cam Garrett downstairs, and she still wanted to run into his arms. And in a couple of hours she had to sit down at a dinner with him across the table and keep Ellie Nagle from noticing just who he was.

One thing about Tanner, Cam thought as he listened to the man's explanations all afternoon, he lied consistently.

He lied about Abby, about the wedding, about why he'd borrowed a total of forty thousand dollars in the past three months, and about his profits, both on the ranch and in the mine.

What's more, he did it convincingly. A man without the complete story would undoubtedly believe him. Since Willem wasn't supposed to have the whole story, Cam pretended to believe.

Cam chewed his lip thoughtfully as Tanner talked. "Your explanation sounds quite satisfactory. My father is simply concerned that we do not place our company at risk because of your activities. Your investments in Europe have accrued handsome dividends in the past year, but since it will be some time before you see that money . . ."

"You want to make certain about the ranch, naturally."

"The storms last winter caused many ranchers hardship."

"We did fine, however, and the mine's in good shape, isn't it, Evans?"

"Yes, sir." Evans sat up, obviously ready to do his part. "We lost the vein temporarily, but I figured out where it dove. We'll hit it a few yards down."

"At which point I can pay off all the loans with interest."

"And even if you don't, you've got Miss Morgan's trust funds to look forward to," Beebe said.

"What trusts?" Cam demanded, nearly forgetting Willem's accent in his shock.

"Miss Morgan's grandfather established a sizable account for her." Beebe missed Tanner's warning glance and prattled on. "All very tidy. It comes payable on her thirtieth birthday, or upon her marriage. Her mother also left her a small trust."

"An heiress, then." Cam's mind whirled, but he carefully maintained Willem's demeanor of distant interest. "Well, your good fortune is ours. To be perfectly honest, my father, my brothers, and I wish to become neither cattle ranchers nor miners. We wish only to make money."

"That's the business, my friend," Tanner said. "You stay out of my way, and I'll make us all wealthy men."

"Then we are ready to sign this new agreement. Lucius, do you have the papers?"

"Right here." Beebe reached for his portfolio.

"It's too close to dinner. We'll sign off tomorrow." Tanner rose to pour himself a whisky from the crystal decanter on the table by the window. He offered drinks to his guests.

"No, thank you." He's not anxious enough, Cam thought. He should be ready to sign anything, to eat bricks if that's what it takes—he would be, if things had gone as planned. As it stood, Tanner needed the money only until he could get his hands on Abby's trusts. He lacked that crucial edge of desperation and jealousy Cam had counted on for the next step. Why the Sam Hill hadn't Abby mentioned a trust? Because, you idiot, you didn't trust her enough to tell her what you had planned.

"You don't want to be thinking about contracts the day before your wedding," Beebe said, accepting the shot Tanner poured for him. He waved the documents around his head. "Father went over this deal with a fine-tooth comb. He says it's tight. Go on, get it out of the way now."

Staring into the fire, Tanner swished a mouthful of whisky through his teeth before he swallowed. "You're right. Let's do it."

Good boy, Lucius.

Impatient now that the decision was made, Tanner bellowed out the window for his foreman to come in as a witness.

In moments it was done, and they each had their copies. Cam tucked his securely into an inner pocket. "I will now put this away safely and take my walk before changing for dinner. You will come also, Lucius?"

Beebe declined, pleading business which probably had more to do with Tanner's liquor supply than the practice of law.

"Go ahead, Lucius. I'll be changing, as well." Tanner bent to his big floor safe, contract in hand, and started twirling the dial. "With Abigail in the house, I find myself behaving like a gentleman again."

Like hell.

Cam breathed a sigh of relief as Tanner shoved the contract into the safe and spun the tumblers to lock it. At least he wouldn't be reading it over any time soon.

One step closer, Cam kept repeating to himself. He just had to keep himself together for a few hours, see where Tanner's men were, get through the evening, then he could figure out how to get Abby out of here. When he had her safely away, *then* he'd find a way to turn this mess around.

Somehow, using every skill her father and Mac had ever taught her at the poker table, Abby made it through dinner, but Ellie didn't help at all.

Try as she might, Abby could not steer the woman away from Cam. Not only did Franklin seat the two of them across from each other at dinner, but Ellie refused to take the conversational bait Abby tossed her way. Every time Ellie asked Cam a question about St. Louis or watched him pass the bread and butter, Abby was sure she'd recognize him. How could she not?

A three-layer chocolate cake was half gone before Abby began to relax. However obvious Cam seemed to her, Ellie just didn't seem to connect the clean-shaven broker before her with the scruffy outlaw in the arroyo. Abby still tried to excuse the men for after-dinner drinks and cigars—trying anything to separate Ellie from Cam.

"I'm sure we can forego that formality tonight," Franklin countered. "The four of us usually stay up for a hand or two of poker. We can wait until then for a smoke."

"Absolutely," agreed Mr. Beebe.

"That would be better, I suppose, considering what a small group we are," Abby said. I can face this without so much as a flicker of distress, she told herself as she entered the parlor on Mr. Evans's arm.

She'd just managed to engage him and Ellie in a spirited recounting of the final Ute uprising six years earlier, when Franklin interrupted. "May I have my fiancée for a moment?"

Taking Abby's hand, Franklin tugged her away from the group, to where the light of a tall oil lamp fell full on her face. He stroked a fingertip along her cheek, curling a ringlet of her hair around his finger. "You are radiant, my dear. That is the bridal glow I've been waiting to see."

"Thank you, Franklin." Actually, the primrose silk ottoman gown she wore reflected against her skin, so she appeared to have a healthy flush. The beige bombazine she'd first put on for dinner had given her the complexion of a consumptive factory girl. After catching a glimpse of her sallow face in the mirror, she'd stripped down and started again. Apparently she'd chosen well enough to fool Franklin.

At the edge of Abby's vision Cam rolled an empty whisky glass between the fingers of one hand. He stuffed his other hand casually into his jacket pocket as he studied the portrait on the far wall with the rapt attention of an art critic, but Abby felt every iota of his attention on her and Franklin.

The image of the tree, its bark beaten off in fury, flashed in her mind. Cam's eyes narrowed with the same rage, and a fine dew of perspiration collected on his forehead. She had to get Franklin away from her before they both broke.

"I'd like a sherry," she said. "Would you get one for me, please? Just a small one."

The errand carried Franklin to the opposite corner of the room, leaving less than a dozen feet of open space between Abby and Cam.

Their eyes locked for an instant, then Abby forced her gaze back to Franklin just in time to see him glance up from the leaded-crystal decanter.

Cam turned back to the painting.

"Eleanor, I'd like you to show off your singing for my guests," Franklin said when he'd handed Abby her drink.

"I really couldn't, not without Orris to play for me."

"I'll play." Unbuttoning his jacket, Franklin sat down at the piano and reached for a sheet of music from the stack nearby. "Do you know this tune?"

To Abby's surprise they were quite good, at least up to the quality of amateur duets she'd heard in the city. Ellie possessed a rich alto strictly at odds with her appearance.

When his guests applauded, Franklin smiled at Abby and sailed into another tune without pause, then another. As he and Ellie became more involved in their performance, Abby drifted away and began admiring Franklin's paintings and *objets d'art* for herself. Eventually she reached Cam.

"I'm not certain I recognize the artist of that piece, Mr. Friederich." Abby indicated the landscape that held Cam's attention so completely, a pair of children playing in the sand. "Perhaps I'll have to ask."

"Not necessary, Miss Morgan. I have admired this painting each time I visit the Fidelity. It is a Cassatt. See. Here." With a helpful smile, Cam reached across the divan to point out the artist's mark. "A minor work, but still quite nice." His voice dropped to a murmur, barely intelligible over the pounding piano and Ellie's vocal embellishments. "I'll come to your room later."

Abby leaned forward, squinting and shaking her head. "That can't possibly be."

"I'm quite certain. My room, then. Late."

"Oh, yes. I make it out, now." She gave Cam a nod, then sailed off. "Franklin, why on earth didn't you tell me you owned a Cassatt? She's becoming quite the rage among my friends in the city."

Franklin came to her room again that night.

This time Abby expected it. If she'd had the key, she would have locked the door, but Franklin hadn't left her that choice. Cursing softly, she donned her heaviest flannel nightdress, then stood near the open window, listening to the raucous laughter of the poker game below as the sound drifted up from the parlor. When the card game broke up, she tucked herself deep into the bed, fluffed the featherbed around her to hide the shape of her body, and waited for Franklin's heavy steps to come down the hall to her door.

Feigning sleep was harder than she expected. The regular, shallow breaths didn't give her taught muscles enough air. Abby felt she was slowly suffocating. She ached for a deep, lung-filling gasp.

Franklin stood at the foot of her bed for a good ten minutes. Even when she sensed him move away, she wouldn't permit herself the luxury of that breath, not until she'd heard the soft click of her door and, a moment later, the muffled latching of his own a few rooms away.

Run to Cam, every sense shrieked, but Abby stayed in her bed, warm, shielded from Franklin and his obscene lust, for as long as she could hold herself still. She lay there for an hour, maybe longer, until she felt certain Franklin must be asleep.

Her hand bumped the nightstand as she rolled out of bed, so she stood there motionless in the dark as the mantel clock ticked off another few minutes, making sure he hadn't woken. The cold seeped through her flannel gown, raising gooseflesh along her arms and legs.

Shivering with cold and tension, Abby gathered up her wrapper and listened at the door.

Not a sound.

The handle turned easily, releasing the latch without a sound. Well-oiled hinges whispered open and closed again—*thank you, Franklin.*

Abby stood in the windowless hall, adjusting to the blackness. The rough nub of the hall rug prickled her bare feet as she swept a hand in a careful circle, hip high. There was the table, with its little bust of Franklin's first wife. She stepped around it.

Seconds later she slipped through Cam's door and into his arms. He kissed her roughly and set her down, then took a moment to stuff a rolled towel under the door to muffle their voices.

"What happened? Where's Rico?" Cam demanded.

It was hard to keep her voice to a calm whisper, when all she wanted to do was run shrieking from this insane asylum, but somehow Abby managed it. She ran through the scene at the ransom exchange briefly. "They all got away, except Franklin's man said someone was wounded. I think it was Charlie."

"Damn. At least you're okay."

"I'm fine, except for being here. I hope you have a plan."

"I do, sort of, but it doesn't look good for tonight. I checked things out before I came up. Tanner's got men on both doors." Cam moved to the window, staring out into the night. "I think I just saw another one light up out by the barn."

"The guards are my fault. I made the mistake of telling Franklin I didn't want to marry him. He was quite . . . put-out."

"That little display downstairs could have fooled me." An uneven tremor shook Cam's voice, and Abby's heart shattered at the sound.

"Don't." Abby tugged him away from the window. No longer softened by the heavy beard, Cam's face was all lines and sharp, pain-filled angles in the moonlight. She touched his cheek, tracing the unfamiliar smoothness of his jaw, now only slightly marred by razor stubble. "Don't. I had to—have to—convince him I've come around. That's all."

"God, I hate this." His hand closed around hers, and he pressed a kiss to her palm. "I don't want you *convincing* him of anything."

"I know that, but we don't have much choice. If we can't get out of here before the wedding, I can at least act happy until there's a minister and a crowd of witnesses around. You'd have to keep on as Willem, but Franklin can't very well hold me here if I tell fifty people I want to leave."

"Don't count on that. It depends on whether he owns all fifty of them." It seemed to Abby that Cam started to ask her something, but he stopped and shook his head resolutely. "No. We're not staying that long, and we're leaving together. I'll have a better chance to look things over tomorrow, work something out. I have a few resources that Tanner doesn't know about. We'll be okay."

"I've known that from the minute I saw you in those ridiculous glasses. Who are you supposed to be?"

"My cousin. We've been working on this for years."

Abby reached up and ruffled her fingers across his cropped brown hair. "Is this Hannah's work?"

Cam nodded.

"Too much oil. I do like you without the beard, however." She stood there, her fingers twined in his. "I love you."

Cam swallowed hard and released her with a tiny push toward the door. "You'd better get back to your room."

"Not yet," she said, ignoring the frown on his face as she leaned into his arms. Her words were a bare whisper against his ear. "Don't make me go, Cam, please. I need to be with you."

"Abby, we can't. It's too dangerous."

"That's why I need you. Please, just for a while. Kiss me."

With a low, unwilling growl, he lowered his lips to hers. She felt his need flare as quickly as her own. His hands brushed over the soft, white flannel of her gown, fitting her curves to his tall, strong body. She drank him in through parted lips. The buttons of his shirt separated easily under her fingers, as easily as those on her nightgown opened for him, and Abby felt wiry hair spring up against her breasts. She swayed softly, letting her nipples trace gentle arcs across his chest.

"Stop," Cam whispered. "This is insane."

"This is necessary," Abby answered, the conviction deeper than any fear. "For both of us." She twisted her hands into the loose fabric of his shirt and tugged him toward the bed. Suddenly the room swirled around her as Cam scooped her up and lowered her to the thick rug.

"It squeaks," was his hushed explanation as he reached for the hem of her gown.

Their joining was quick, quiet, desperate, and enough to last Abby through the next day. She carried the bright, liquid fire of him inside her, letting the knowledge of it warm her every time Franklin came near, drawing strength from it every time she had to smile at Franklin and approve some detail of his arrangements for the wedding.

Wagons loaded with tables, chairs, and wooden kegs of beer creaked up the road just after noon. Franklin called Abby out of the house to help supervise. Cam was with him. She avoided his eyes.

"It's your wedding, too. Tell them where you want these things. Where's that idiot with the flower garlands? Al!" Franklin stomped off toward the barn, Cam at his heels, and for one fleeting instant, Abby thought she'd been left alone with strangers. Then Hawkins appeared from behind the wagon.

"I think the pavilion would look nice under that tree," Abby told a workman blandly. "How many tables are there?"

It seemed the impending wedding emboldened Franklin. As the day progressed, he found excuses to touch Abby at every turn, brushing against her as they passed through doorways, allowing his hand to linger on her arm or shoulder as he escorted her around.

Buoyed by her time in Cam's arms, Abby withstood the assaults well enough, even when the contact lingered.

Cam however, grew darker and darker, and she could see his hold on Willem Friederich's persona growing fragile. When Franklin pulled her into his unoccupied study late that afternoon and pressed an aggressive kiss on her, she put her foot down.

"You overstep yourself, Franklin." Abby pushed him away and reached for the brass doorknob.

"I'm only beginning to exercise my husbandly rights."

"We are not married yet."

"Ah, but the ceremony is less than twenty-four hours away, and frankly, this coldness you show concerns me. Of course, I understand that the distance of our courtship didn't allow you to grow accustomed to my presence. I simply seek to make up for that a bit, my dear wife-to-be, so you can be comfortable joining me in my bed tomorrow night."

"Gentlemen do not speak of such things. I will not tolerate it." Only the sure knowledge she wouldn't be anywhere near his bed kept Abby from slapping him.

"The subject will not come up again today," Franklin agreed amiably, giving her a knowing smile. "I will suggest to you, however, not to lay any bets on what you will or will not tolerate, Abigail. You never know when your limits might be tested."

A wave of fear washed over Abby, and she dug her fingernails into her palms to hold the nausea down.

Cam peered around the door, every feature controlled. Only his eyes blazed with the fury she knew ate at him. His right hand rested in his pocket, his fingers curled around something.

A gun.

Abby suddenly knew it was a gun, and she grew frightened beyond anything Franklin made her feel.

"I believe I hear another wagon coming," Cam said helpfully. "Perhaps some guests are coming for the wedding early."

"Thank you, Willem. Come meet them, Abigail." Franklin tucked her hand into the crook of his arm and started down the hall.

Abby glanced over her shoulder, gave Cam a quick reassuring smile. "I'm okay," she mouthed silently. She saw his hand relax.

I can do this. I can do this.

Abby paced back and forth along the foot of her bed, hugging herself tightly as though she could physically keep herself from falling apart. After the blunt way Franklin had stated his intentions, the thought of letting him walk in and stare at her again while she lay in bed terrified her.

If he decided to do more than watch her sleep, she'd scream. Cam would come running, and that would be a disaster.

That thought forced her beneath the covers as Franklin's footsteps approached. That thought made her lie there while Franklin loomed over her, the smell of cognac and tobacco swirling over her like a dank cloud.

She'd always liked the scents when they clung to her father after an evening with guests. Now they nauseated her, stinking of something overtly masculine and threatening. Franklin reached out in the dark to lift a lock of her hair. Abby sighed and stirred away from the touch as though in her sleep.

"Only a dream, dearest," he whispered. A few moments later the door opened and closed again, and she was alone.

Abby lay in the dark awhile, but she couldn't keep herself there as long as the previous night. The instant she felt it was safe, she got up and left the room.

She dashed past rooms now filled with wedding guests, and slipped through Cam's door with a sigh of relief.

She sensed him behind her before she heard anything. She turned to find him staring at her in the pale moonlight, his face a stark, drawn mask.

"What was that bastard doing in your room?" Cam demanded in a raw whisper that ripped into her soul with its pain.

"Nothing. You weren't supposed to see that." She stepped forward and laid a finger across his lips to silence him. The smoothness of his upper lip still astonished her. "No. Because I knew you'd take it wrong. He just watches me sleep."

"Watches?"

"Every night since I got here. That's why I didn't want you to come to me. I didn't want you killed over something that . . . stupid. It makes my skin crawl, but I'm all right."

"Are you sure he hasn't touched you?" he asked. A shudder of revulsion rattled through Abby at the thought.

"Franklin asked me the same thing about you. I lied to him. I'll never lie to you. No, he hasn't touched me. He's waiting for our wedding night." Another shudder rocked her, and Abby threw her arms around Cam's neck. "Please kiss me, and then tell me you figured a way out of this mess."

With a sharp intake of breath, he complied to the first part of her request with a brief, fierce kiss. He pressed a dark shirt and pants into her hand. "Put these on. You'll have to go without boots. A couple of heavy pairs of socks should do instead. You won't be walking far."

"I'd go naked if I had to." Abby shrugged out of her nightgown and reached for the shirt.

"I have a friend here," Cam explained as he fished a bundle of papers out of his case, jammed them into his boot, and pulled his pantleg down to hide them. "Doesn't matter who. He's got a horse staked in a gully in back of the barn. He's arranged a little diversion that should pull the guards over to the other side of the house for a few minutes."

Abby pulled his pants on and buttoned the fly. Cam had brought suspenders this time, and she accepted them with a touch of distant amusement. "What about the man by the barn?"

"Asleep. Tanner's cook keeps a convenient supply of laudanum," Cam said as she slipped on two pairs of his heaviest socks. "There's one part that might be a little hard for you."

"What's that?"

"We're going out the window."

"What?" Her stomach twisted and Abby groped for the chair. "I can't."

"You can." Fingers digging into her arms, Cam yanked her to her feet. "You can. If I can watch you let that scum put his hands on you—watch him march into your room like he owns you, for god's sake—without killing him, you can go out that window. You're tougher than I am, Abby Morgan. You've proved that over and over."

"I'm not tough about this."

"It's less than twelve feet. I have a rope."

"A rope? What good will that do?"

"As much as you let it. Now, come on." He dragged her to the window, raised the sash high. "Look, Abby. *Look*."

"You're going to wake up the whole house."

"Then look."

She looked. Only Cam's firm grip kept her from falling over.

"I can't do it," Abby repeated. Somewhere in the distance a cow lowed sullenly. "I can't."

"You don't have a choice. That's our signal." He picked up the twin lengths of rope, already secure around the leg of the big marble-topped dresser, then swung his legs over the windowsill. "We have about two minutes. I'm going. Either you come, or we're both dead. Come on, sit here with me. Straddle it, that's a girl."

"Cam, I can't put my head out the window."

"Then you'd better be ready to put it on Tanner's pillow," he said harshly and lowered himself over the ledge.

He didn't mean it. Abby knew that. Cam would kill Franklin before he let that happen, even if he died himself doing it. But the joint images of herself in Franklin's bed and Cam lying dead shocked her out of her immobility.

She heard the soft crunch of gravel below and swung her other leg out. Her head swam with dizziness. The rope bit into her belly as she rolled over on the ledge and let her legs dangle.

"That's it. Come on. I've got you."

Abby clutched the rope, lowering herself slowly into space, her terror almost overwhelming her. Her hands burned as she slipped down the rope. The thudding of her heart drowned out every other sound. Abby felt as if she was going to pass out.

A pair of strong hands caught her ankles. Abby eased down a little farther, felt the hands support her with confident strength. Down, just a bit more, and he caught her hips. She released the rope, ecstatically sliding groundward. Finally she felt the blessed, uneven solidity of earth beneath her feet. The hands held her as she found her purchase.

It was then she saw Cam, standing a few feet away, the long blue barrel of a pistol pressed against his temple. Domingo smiled at her.

The aroma of cognac and tobacco wrapped itself around her like iron bands.

Chapter 17

Cam's fists came up of their own accord, ready to beat Tanner into a bloody pulp. Domingo pressed his pistol harder against Cam's skull and clicked the hammer back another notch. Cam froze, helpless, watching Tanner's hands on Abby's body.

Her feet touched the ground and she looked at him, and the glow of victory that lit her face solidified into a mask of uncomprehending shock. Tanner loomed over her, a demon, ready to carry her to hell.

"Not a word," Tanner warned softly, releasing Abby to draw his pistol from the waistband of his trousers. "Not one word form either of you. I don't want my guests to know what vipers I have in my household. We'll go to the smokehouse to discuss your treachery. Lead the way, Abigail."

"Franklin, I—"

Tanner whipped around and shoved his revolver into Cam's belly with jarring force. "Your choice, my dear—silence or one very loud noise."

Abby bit her lip and backed away a few steps, then turned and walked toward the tiny, unpainted building at the back corner of the ranch yard. Cam followed a few steps behind, Walters and Domingo on either side of him and Tanner behind.

Abby disappeared into the smokehouse's dark interior. At the not so subtle pressure of Tanner's pistol, now pressed into the tender area just over his kidneys, Cam followed her inside.

"Get that lantern," Tanner ordered Domingo. "Shut the door first. I don't want anybody knowing we're out here."

A moment later the lantern flared into brilliance. Cam squinted his eyes against the light and quickly found Abby. Tanner saw the look and punched Cam low in the stomach. The blow doubled Cam over and left him sucking for air, eyes watering.

"Tie him to that post," Tanner said. "Facing this way, since he wants to look at her so badly. What about you, Abigail? Do you want to look at him, too?"

Face pale but emotionless in the harsh light, Abby stared at a point somewhere high on the opposite wall. "I don't care one way or the other."

Good, Abby. Good. Tanner was baiting her, watching to see if he could use them against each other.

"That's a poor attitude to take toward your . . . friend. Where were you going, Abigail?"

"Mr. Friederich agreed to help me get as far as Denver, since you refused to respect my wishes."

"For a price, I assume. Like a little romp in your bed."

"Don't be coarse! He's more mercenary than that. I offered him a thousand dollars."

"Indeed."

"I was forced into this drastic measure by your refusal to let me go back to New York." She hesitated. "I suppose you must allow it, now that my reputation is so obviously damaged."

The noise started low, like a rumble of anger, then burst

out of Tanner, a full-fledged laugh. He stepped around to face Abby, wiping the tears from his cheeks, and tucked his pistol back into his pants. "You really are amazing, Abigail. I knew you had the strength to make me a good wife. Combined with your other charms, it makes you much, much too valuable to let go. Walters, cut his shirt open. Let me see if I'm right about something."

Walter's did his job none too carefully. The point of his big Bowie knife nicked Cam's throat. Cam felt the blood bead and run in a thin stream, but his eyes stayed on Tanner, where the real danger lay.

Abby grabbed Tanner's arm. "Stop this. Leave the poor man alone."

Brushing her aside, Tanner strolled over to Cam. He smudged a finger across the ridge of scar on his belly. "Hello, Garrett."

"What's gotten into you, Franklin? That's Mr. Friederich."

"The charade is over, Abigail," Tanner snapped. "Cameron and I became acquainted over a knife, what, eleven, twelve years ago?"

"Thirteen." Cam managed to keep his voice calm. "Thirteen years next month, as a matter of fact."

"I should have done a better job. At least now I understand why you always stayed in the background. Karl Friederich's your uncle, of course, and the real Willem would be your cousin. An excellent disguise."

"How did you figure it out?" Cam asked.

"Eleanor remarked how long it had been since she'd heard a Swiss-German accent. Her comment made me think of your mother. I recalled she'd sent you off to her brother after our little run-in, and then I remembered he lived in St. Louis. The rest just fell into place." A muscle twitched at the corner of Tanner's jaw. "Poor Eleanor is truly a hazard to any secret. The funny thing is, she still doesn't realize who you are, even though you held her prisoner just a few short weeks ago. Remarkable. Where are the papers?"

"What papers?"

Domingo's vicious kick took Cam's legs out from under him. In seconds the man found the contract in the calf of Cam's boot. He handed it to Tanner.

Standing directly in front of Cam, Tanner tore the contract to shreds. "I already destroyed the other copies. That will be the end of Friederich and Sons' interest in this ranch. I imagine Abigail's bank balance came almost as much of a shock to you as it did to me. I doubt I'd have even seen her again if you'd known."

"You wouldn't have."

"What are you talking about?" Abby asked.

Tanner's lips thinned, and he jerked a thumb over his shoulder. "You two, out."

"Mr. Tanner," Walters began, "I don't think—"

"Out. Domingo, you stay outside the door." The two hands left, and Tanner turned back to Abby. "I was talking about your trust fund, my dear."

Abby looked confused. "The one my mother left?"

"Be logical, Abigail. I would hardly spend thirty thousand to get you back only to gain ten. I'm talking about the one your dear grandfather arranged."

"Grandfather hates me. I haven't even seen him in years."

"Since your mother's tragic accident. I know. It seems old Abner, however much he blames you, still sees it as his duty to provide you with a sizable income, which will certainly be enough to pay off my debts and make the Fidelity the biggest ranching operation in Colorado. Of course, he also wanted to protect you from opportunists like Mr. Garrett and myself, so he didn't bother to tell anyone but his lawyers, including your father and, apparently, you."

"Then how did you find out?"

"Let's just say there's a Lucius Beebe in most large firms. They pair off when the occasion arises and bits of useful information spread." With an impatient shrug Tanner stopped. "Enough of this."

"If money's all you want—"

"It's not. I don't know what gave you that idea." Tanner circled her, like a wolf around an injured doe. He stopped behind her, pulling her back against his chest, his large hand spread flat across her waist. "So, were you going for a midnight stroll with your lover, my dear?"

"He's not my lover."

"So sweet, so false. You're quite an actress, Abigail. Tomorrow—today, that is—you can try out your talents on our guests at our wedding reception."

"I'm not marrying you." She struggled against his restraint, but he held her easily.

"I wonder if you'll show as much spirit in bed. The next few weeks will be such a delight," Tanner murmured against Abby's neck, his voice mocking. Lacing his fingers into her hair, he forced her head back. His lips and tongue moved over the soft skin of her throat in a lewd kiss that sent a shudder down her spine.

Cam lunged against the ropes that held him to the post. "Leave her out of this, Tanner! It's between you and me."

"You're the one who put Abigail in it!" Tanner roared. Eyes glittering like steel, he dragged Abby onto her knees at Cam's feet, raging down at her. "I would have cherished you, done everything in my power to keep you happy, but he had to turn you into his slut. It's true, isn't it, Abigail? You went to his room last night. You let him spread your legs in my own house." Tanner pulled his gun, aiming it at Cam's temple. "Eleanor heard you go. Answer me!"

"Yes!" Abby screamed. "Yes. Oh, no, don't!"

With the scream of a wounded animal, Tanner side-armed Cam. The weight of the big Colt slammed into Cam's head, momentarily blinding him with pain. Tanner cursed him, "Goddamn your soul to hell!"

A second blow split Cam's ear and left him sagging against the ropes, on the edge of consciousness. He flinched away as Tanner's hand rose again, but the third blow never came.

It took Cam a moment to focus, to realize that Abby had

her arms around him, shielding him from Tanner. Sweat and blood pouring down his neck, Cam felt the change in Abby before he could see it.

"Don't be stupid, Franklin," she said, staring straight up the barrel of his pistol.

The hatred resonating in Abby's voice caught Tanner off guard. "What?"

"If you kill him, you'll never see my money."

Tanner stared at her, the raw fury in his eyes slowly banking to a low glow of greed and cunning.

Abby's voice turned soft, soothing, the voice you'd use to lull a child to sleep. "That's right, Franklin, you need him alive. You can't get to that trust without me, and if you kill Cam, you lose your hold on me. There will be no way for you to make me marry you."

Marry him. The words ripped through Cam's gut. The nightmare was happening again, and he was just as powerless as he had been at fifteen. "Abby, don't. For god's sake, don't."

"Did he ever tell you how he got that mark on his belly, Abigail?" Tanner asked, his voice low and taunting. "The little whelp tried to kill me after he found me with his mother. Not very grateful of him, considering Marthe and I were . . . negotiating the outstanding balance on the note his father had taken just before he died. If Garrett had just left us alone, he'd have kept the ranch. I'd have had his mother. Instead, I got the ranch, and his mother shipped him off and then killed herself out of shame." Tanner wiped at the corner of his mouth. "You know what I think, Abigail? He was using you to get even with me. I think he wanted to screw you because I screwed his mother."

"No!" Cam shouted, but the truth in Tanner's accusation rang in his ears.

"You thought he was in love with you, didn't you?" Tanner asked.

"It doesn't matter, because I'm in love with him. I love him even more than I hate you, and that's a lot."

The fire blazed in Tanner's eyes again. The gun trembled in his grip with his desire to kill.

Abby put her hand up slowly and pushed the barrel aside. "You should be happy about that, Franklin. It's your key to all that money. It's your power over me."

"Yes, it is, isn't it?" Tanner backed a few steps away, casually lowering the hammer on his pistol. The greedy smile that twisted his mouth made Cam wish he'd shoot, end the torment. "You're going to regret giving that power to me, Abigail, but now that we all know where we stand, we can proceed."

"I've been to better than fifty weddings in my life, and I swear, I've never seen a bride quite so nervous and pale." Ellie Nagle paused in her brushing. "Are you all right, Miss Morgan?"

"I'm fine." *You sold us out. You forced me into this devil's bargain.* "Why don't you pin my chignon, and then give me a few minutes alone before I put on my dress."

Abby stared at the hollow-eyed reflection of herself in the dresser mirror as Ellie put the finishing touches on her elaborate hairstyle. A part of her admired the woman's unexpected skill; another part wished she'd strangle on her own chattering tongue.

"Shall I pin these silk rosebuds in your hair?" Ellie asked.

"No, I—"

"I think they'd look charming," Franklin said from the doorway.

"Mr. Tanner, you know you're not supposed to be here," Ellie scolded. "It's bad luck to see the bride before the wedding."

"Indulge me in this small whim. Abigail?"

"But she's in her dressing gown."

"Go on, Mrs. Nagle." Abby waved the woman off impatiently. "You'll be right next door. Besides, it's not as if Franklin's going to do anything."

Fussing, Ellie slipped out.

"Not yet, anyway," Franklin echoed Abby's thought, a sly smile on his lips. "I think half the valley's here to help us celebrate."

"Good." The more witnesses around, the safer Cam was, at least for the time being.

"Show more enthusiasm, my dear. You put on a much better act last night. Let's see a smile."

"Go to hell. I'll smile when I have to, but I'm not going to let you pretend to yourself this is anything but what it is."

Franklin crossed the room in two strides and picked Abby up as if she were a doll. "You'll let me pretend whatever I want. Remember all that power you granted me. I intend to enjoy it, every drop of it. Domingo and I can correct any tendencies you have toward disobedience and still keep Mr. Garrett alive." He set her down abruptly, then bent and came up with a wickedly sharp knife from a scabbard in his boot. He laid the tip flat against her sleeve. "Would you like a demonstration?"

"You promised to turn Cam over to the law."

"I decided to renege on that particular portion of our arrangement. It's obvious I'm going to need him around to encourage you to fulfill your wifely duties."

"I'm not a fool, Franklin. As soon as you get your hands on the trust money, you'll kill Cam if he's still here. I won't sign any papers until Cam's in custody, until I've *seen* him safely in a cell, with somebody other than your pet sheriff on duty. You're not going to get the money without my express permission."

"Maybe, maybe not. You don't know the terms of the trust."

"But I know my grandfather, and I know the way my mother's trust is set up. She used his personal attorneys. Not everyone in the firm is like Mr. Beebe. You won't be able to break the trust without raising someone's suspicions. Married or not."

"As I said, Domingo and I can encourage you to do

it my way." The point of the knife slipped an inch and the sleeve of her wrapper gaped, sliced cleanly. Though unscratched, her arm throbbed as though it had been cut to the bone. Abby knew that once he started, the torture would never end.

"If you make so much as one more mark on either me or Cam, there is no power on this earth that will make me release that money."

Abby made the statement flatly, with no emotion of any kind. She felt the blade of Tanner's knife waver and withdraw.

"You know, I think I believe you. In the interest of a peaceful wedding day, I grant you this little victory." He slipped the knife back into his boot and tugged his pants leg down to cover the hilt. "I'll stick to the bargain then and send a man to Alamosa for the law immediately after the ceremony. If you betray me again, in any way, I'll carve his heart out right in front of you, even if I have to break him out of the state prison to do it. Now, my sweet, traitorous bride, put your dress on and come downstairs. With a smile on your face."

"I want to see Cam."

"I assumed you would. When all our guests are out front, I'll take you back for a moment. You'll see he's healthy." Franklin's lips tightened into what might pass as a smile. "Now it's up to you to keep him that way."

"Dearly beloved, we are gathered here . . ."

With its froth of cream Bruges lace and row upon row of pearls and *passementerie*, Abby's wedding gown weighed nearly thirty pounds. She'd actually weighed it at the final fitting, convinced she'd never be able to stand up through the hours of ceremony and reception. Today, it seemed like the lightest thing she had to bear.

One of Franklin's henchmen had tied a rag around Cam's head, but hadn't cleaned him up, and the entire left side of his head and face was swollen, bruised and caked with blood. Franklin had refused to let her touch him for fear her wedding gown, already dusty from the walk across the yard, would be stained.

Abby saw the damage clearly in her mind, against the somber black garb of the minister as he spoke.

But the physical damage wasn't the worst of it: What horrified her most was the agony in Cam's eyes. It was the same agony she'd seen after his nightmare, but now much, much deeper. Her bargain was making him relive every ounce of the pain.

For that, my love, I am truly sorry, but at least you're alive.

To keep him alive, she would do anything, even consummate this farce of a marriage.

"If any man can show just cause why they may not be lawfully joined together . . ."

Murder. Theft. Extortion. Perversion. General viciousness.

The crowd around the veranda stood mute. She wondered if Cam had been right about Franklin owning them all.

It didn't matter. Cam was alive.

Her bridegroom's fingers tightened around hers, his thumbnail cutting into her palm. Abby glanced up. The minister was waiting.

"I will," she said. *I will get you. I swear it.*

Franklin's bass boomed out, repeating his vows, and then it was Abby's turn.

"I, Abigail, take thee, Franklin, to my wedded husband . . ." The vows tasted rancid on her tongue. She stared at the minister's white collar as he droned the words.

"I now pronounce you man and wife. You may kiss the bride."

Dizzying amounts of food poured out of the kitchen: pies, breads, smoked venison, fresh duck, and of course, beef in every form imaginable to man. The wedding cake alone stood five layers high and filled half a table, and beer flowed like a mountain stream out of the pavilion tent.

The guests brought food as well. Everyone who came, from the merchants to the families Franklin would break next week, contributed something, even though the Fidelity larder could have fed them and twice more with no trouble.

When appetites were sated, music and games provided entertainment. The string band Franklin had hired demonstrated extraordinary flexibility, switching easily between reels and schottisches, square dances and Mexican folk tunes.

Abby didn't give a damn about any of it.

She stood next to Franklin on the porch with her plate full of food, stirring it around with a fork, smiling and chatting with whomever stopped by with congratulations and best wishes. Franklin stayed within a few feet. Abby knew he listened to every word she said, waiting for her to betray herself. She knew any slip would cost Cam his life.

"Everyone is taken with my beautiful new bride," Franklin said when a lull caught them alone. He set his plate down on a little table behind them and reached for a glass of beer, which he downed in one draw. Tiny flecks of foam clung to the corners of his mustache. "Let's really impress them. Come dance a waltz with me."

A waltz. The most intimate dance he could choose. "I can't. I'll be ill."

"No, you won't," Franklin insisted, dragging her toward the well-stomped circle of earth that served as a dance floor. "You'll enjoy yourself, just like you did in New York last year."

This was a test, Abby told herself, and if dancing with Franklin kept Cam alive, she would do it all afternoon.

After the dance they went back to the porch, and a new contingent of well-wishers swarmed up to greet them.

"I wish I could dance like that," a largish woman said. "You two look so handsome together, like you belong in a big old ballroom with crystal chandeliers."

"And you with a dance card a mile long, and all filled up," said another, wearing a plain blue linsey-woolsey dress.

"Those days are over, I'm afraid. Franklin gets all my dances now." Abby couldn't remember the women's names ten seconds later.

There were more dances, more uneaten food, and more introductions that passed without notice. Abby bore the long hours with neither pleasure nor complaint.

The Mexicans were the last to come up to pay their respects. They drifted up almost hesitantly. The women wore dresses the colors of jewels, the men white cotton shirts with rainbow-colored serapes over their shoulders.

It was clear Franklin didn't like them, but in playing the part of grandee, he had to tolerate the peons' adoration. He stepped away slightly when the women crowded closely around Abby, as though he'd be soiled by any contact with them.

"It is a beautiful gown, Señora Tanner. Was it made especially for you?"

"Yes. I have a dressmaker in New York who does wonderful work."

"You will need one here. I hope you will consider me. My name is Maria Santiago."

Jesús's wife.

The silver fork rattled on the plate in Abby's hand. With a start she trapped the errant utensil under her thumb just as Maria grabbed for the plate. A few drops of cream gravy spattered over the skirt of her gown.

"Oh, no, no, no. I am so sorry, señora. Let me take that for you." Maria snatched the plate from Abby's trembling hands and set it aside, then several women began blotting at the stains with napkins. "Come, we must clean this before it is ruined."

"What's going on?" Franklin pushed through the knot of women.

"The señora spilled on her beautiful gown. Come, come." Maria took Abby's hand and started to lead her away.

"What a minute. You can't leave the reception, Abigail. Just wipe it off."

"And let the grease ruin the fabric?" Maria looked horrified. "No, no. I know the way to clean it, but we must have something from the kitchen. I will take her before it is ruined, Señor Tanner. It will take only a moment, and then you will have your lovely bride back. *Promesa.*"

Maria tightened her grip on Abby's hand, and tugged her through the front door and down the hall past the dining room. A gray-haired woman followed. Out of the corner of her eye Abby saw Franklin motion for one of his men. Domingo separated from the crowd and headed for the back of the house.

The kitchen was still a storm of activity as the cooks prepared for the next round of eating. Maria burst through the swinging door and drew Abby past everyone and into the pantry. She fired off an order in Spanish, and the older woman disappeared.

Maria's voice dropped to a murmur that wouldn't carry beyond the open door.

"I am sorry for your dress, señora. I have been watching all afternoon to speak to you, but your husband will not let you from his side. Where is Cameron?"

"How do I know you're who you say you are?"

The woman smiled. "Rico said you are clever, clever enough at least to stay alive, yes? I sent you a green calico dress. Did it fit?"

With a nod of relief Abby sagged against a shelf bearing an earthenware crock of pickles. The movement stirred up the scent of vinegar and spice.

The other woman came back, a small lighted lamp and a canister of corn flour in her hand and a pair of clean tea towels over her shoulder. After putting the lamp on a shelf, she stationed herself by the door.

Maria grabbed the canister and dumped a quantity of the meal over the gravy stains. "That will soak up the grease. Now, where is Cameron?" She knelt and stuffed one of the tea cloths up under the stained layer of silk and began blotting.

Again Abby hesitated, this time staring at the woman with the lead-gray bun. Maria glanced up, smiling once more.

"This is Juanita Montoya. There are others here, dancing, eating. Waiting."

"Cam's in the smokehouse, the little shed in the back corner of the yard. Franklin has a man, maybe two, watching him."

"Then Tanner knows who he is?"

"Yes. Cam tried to get me out. We got caught."

Heavy boots tromped into the kitchen, sounding hollow on the plain wooden floor. Maria scrubbed vigorously at the smallest of the stains, lips pursed in silence, but the voices belonged to guests, offering to carry out the next round of pies. Their footsteps faded, and Juanita nodded.

"Why have you married Tanner?" Maria asked, still scrubbing.

Abby summarized her deal with Franklin in a few broken sentences.

When she finished, Maria looked up. "You are a very brave woman, señora. I do not know if I could let that animal touch me."

"You could for Jesús," Abby said firmly.

Maria's hands stilled and her eyes held Abby's for a moment. Then she nodded. "Yes, señora. You are right."

"Where's Rico?"

"Nearby. We will move soon. Watch me, señora. I will do this." Maria raised a hand to the ornate twist of raven braids that rode on the back of her head. She pulled a painted comb out and tucked it back in. "When I do, you must find a way to get away from Tanner—quickly."

"I haven't been to the privy all afternoon."

"Good. I can meet you there."

"Franklin will send someone after me."

"Ask for a woman to go with you, to help with your dress."

"Mrs. Nagle," Abby said. "She's the one that gave Cam away. Franklin's been using her to watch me. He'd let her go with me. He still might have someone watching from a distance."

"*Sí*. Do you think we can restrain her, the two of us?"

Abby nodded wholeheartedly. "I don't think there's a muscle in the woman's entire body."

"Good." Maria spent another moment over the stains. "That will have to do. I do not know exactly what will happen, but it will be soon. Watch. Be ready."

Chapter 18

"I see Maria didn't get the gravy out of your skirt," Franklin said at the first opportunity.

Abby brushed self-consciously at the stain. "Not completely, no. Grease can be so difficult. She told me a formula to try, but if it doesn't work, she thought it might be possible to borrow a hidden portion of the underskirt to make a replacement for this section."

"Good. I'll make arrangements for her to come around next week before the dress is put away. She'll do it at no charge, I'm sure, since it was partly her fault."

"I can't ask her to spend her good time without pay over an accident. Besides, I doubt the gown will ever be worn again."

"Nonsense. Our daughter will want it when she marries."

Heat washed Abby's skin, as much in anger and fear as in embarrassment. The idea of bearing the man children was grotesque.

"You blush charmingly, my dear, considering your history." Franklin brushed a kiss across her cheek. "I can hardly wait to discover what Garrett taught you."

"If you continue, the whole town will know he had me."

Franklin turned livid, but Abby let the double meaning stand as Mr. Evans and Mr. Beebe came up with a group of ranchers. Talk quickly turned to the sheep wars on the western slope, and she turned to look out over the company.

Abby almost laughed out loud.

Jesús was there, dancing with the same delicate, raven-haired wife who'd returned Abby to Franklin's side just moments before.

Bursting with hope, Abby furtively scanned the guests. There stood Antonio, talking to Juanita Montoya, his broad tan sombrero replaced by a smaller, black version of the hat.

Pete tipped a mug of beer under a cottonwood.

Ephram helped himself to a huge piece of cake, not twenty feet away. Two other men conversed under the tent; another stood over by the barn, rolling a cigarette as he chatted with a couple of Franklin's hands.

Abby's growing excitement rattled her. She fought to keep from staring too much, though she felt certain Franklin wouldn't recognize Cam's men even if he knew who they were. She had barely spotted them herself, even having spent weeks with them. They were cleaner than she had ever seen them: freshly bathed, hair and beards or mustaches neatly trimmed. Pete even had his long whiskers shaved off, though it didn't change his appearance as much as it did Cam's. They had dressed in their Sunday best, in clothes Abby wouldn't have suspected they even owned. To top it off, almost every man had a lady on his arm. Some looked like wives or sweethearts, some like aunts or mothers, but all looked natural next to each other.

Cam's men blended into the reception crowd in every way, drifting back and forth between table and dance floor like the Fidelity's other neighbors.

She turned back to the conversation surrounding Franklin. "I don't quite understand why it's so important to keep sheep and cows from grazing in the same pastures to begin with."

Her naive comment set the men off like skyrockets—as she'd known it would. The bloody range wars made popular reading in the yellow press back East, and feelings ran high among these ranchers. A ruddy-faced man with nearly white hair began explaining how cattle wouldn't eat off a pasture where sheep had been run.

Abby maneuvered Franklin's friends around so she could watch Maria simply by glancing past Mr. Beebe's shoulders. She continued to feed questions and ignorant comments to the men, drawing the conversation out as long as possible until, finally, Maria reached up to adjust the painted comb crowning her tresses.

Abby met her eyes and made a barely perceptible nod, then watched Maria disappear around the corner of the house.

"Pardon me, gentlemen." Abby lifted her skirts and started down the stairs, gesturing to Ellie Nagle.

Franklin pounded down the steps, slid into step beside her, his fingers biting into her arm. His voice was low, suspicious. "Where do you think you're going?"

"To ask Mrs. Nagle to accompany me to the privy. I couldn't very well announce it in front of those men, could I? And Mr. Hawkins is simply not an appropriate escort."

With a begrudging nod, Franklin turned her loose. "Ten minutes, Abigail."

"You've been away from fashionable women too long. It will take me nearly that long just to arrange my skirts."

"Fifteen."

"Fine." Abby raised her voice for those nearby to hear. "I'll hurry back, you jealous creature, don't worry. Do you mind helping me, Eleanor?"

Franklin beamed, proud of his power over her, the ass.

* * *

Tanner liked his meat smoked with piñon. The heavy, almost sweaty fragrance of the wood permeated every fiber of the shack, soaking into Cam's pores and burning his lungs.

Cam drooped on the ropes that secured him to the post, as if succumbing to his head wounds and the thick air.

The change of position gave him a fresh portion of the post, a sharper corner to wear at his bindings. He'd been working on them from the moment Domingo had tightened the rope around his wrists, even while Abby made her pact with that serpent.

Up. Pause. Down and up.

A stroke at a time, Cam wore at the hemp, shredding individual strands. He could only work when his guard wasn't watching, but at least it was something. It demanded little mentally, so he could concentrate on any other escape possibilities that presented themselves. His hands and wrists ached with the tiny, subtle movements, but by the feel of things, he'd worn through nearly half of the thickness. He had to break it soon, before someone thought to check his bindings and noticed his work.

Jake Walters, the current guard, squatted comfortably in one corner of the smokehouse, whittling a fine point onto a piece of wood with a penknife. The bone handle of his heavy Bowie knife peeped out of the scabbard that decorated his right side. His Smith & Wesson revolver hung on his left, butt forward; he must cross draw. Cam had been watching since noon and still had no idea what Walters was whittling, if anything.

"Gave yourself all this trouble over a bitch like that," Walters had taunted as he held the door open a crack for Cam's benefit during the ceremony and the first few dances. "Men like Frank Tanner and me end up winning in this world because we remember what's worthwhile about a woman, keep our hearts out of it. You, you're going to be thinking about her eyes and her pretty sweet words while Tanner's on top of her tonight, teaching her what's important between a man and his woman. Shoulda kept things straight, Garrett. Shoulda kept things straight."

Walters's words played through Cam's mind over and over, all through the long afternoon as the guitars and fiddles played in the distance: Tanner on top of Abby.

The idea nearly drove Cam crazy, skewing his thoughts to murder instead of escape. He had to bury the spasms of hatred, banking their poisonous energy for future use.

Right now he had to focus on Walters and the knives. The knives were what he needed, either one of them, and they might as well have been on the moon. Unless Walters or one of the others slipped up, Cam could only continue his slow grinding at the rope. He flexed his arms and felt the rope give a little.

Walters stabbed his whittling into the straw and rose, stretching. He reached for his canteen and slugged down a mouthful of water. "When Domingo comes on in here, I'm getting me some of that beer. Wash this stinking wood smell out of my mouth."

"It's pretty bad," Cam agreed in a croaking voice. "I could sure use some of that water."

Walters eyed him doubtfully, then shrugged. "Sure, why not? Tanner said to keep you alive in case she gave him any trouble tonight." He wiped the neck of the canteen on his sleeve and leaned over Cam, arm outstretched. "Here you go."

As the canteen touched his lips, Cam lashed upward with his foot, putting all his strength behind his kick. His square-toed boot caught Walters under the chin, and the gunman flew backward. His head clipped the wall with a sickening *thunk*. He was out cold before he hit the ground.

With a curse Cam watched the pocketknife tumble away, and land near a bale of straw, ten feet away.

One heel hooked over Walters's leg, Cam tried to drag him and his Bowie within reach. No use.

Cam hoisted himself to his feet, where he could saw at the ropes in long strokes, using his full weight. Walters began to stir.

The image of Tanner on top of Abby boiled up like steam through an engine. Powered by rage, Cam surged forward. The final strands of hemp separated and Cam tore his hands free. He quickly stripped the other ropes off and reached for the pistol.

Walters came to just as Cam touched the grip. He grabbed for Cam's hand and rolled away, jerking Cam off balance. Locked in a battle for control of the gun, they wrestled across the floor. Cam felt the hilt of the Bowie dig into his side, then Walters was beneath him again. Cam found the Bowie, ripped it from the scabbard.

Walters froze as the point of the knife touched his throat right under his jaw.

"Hand away from the gun," Cam ordered. "I could drive this clear into your brain without batting an eye."

Slowly, carefully, Walters obeyed. He lifted his hands away from Cam, spreading his arms wide across the floor in surrender. Cam replaced the knife with the gun and quickly checked Walters for other weapons. He found another knife strapped to the man's arm, a deadly looking blade not much thicker than an ice pick.

"Facedown." Cam watched Walters roll over obediently.

Gravel crunched outside as someone approached.

Without a second thought Cam lifted the gun and brought it down butt first on the back of Walters's already swollen head. The man melted into the floor, unconscious again, and Cam darted aside. He flattened himself against a wall in a shadowed corner.

A hand lifted the drop bar. Sunlight poured in, illuminating Walters's prone form on the floor.

"What the . . ." said Hawkins, hand slipping toward his pistol.

"Hold it. Shut the door." Cam stepped out of the corner, gun in hand.

With a disbelieving shake of the head, Hawkins pulled the door tight behind him.

"Now check our friend there. Make sure he's out cold."

Hawkins did as Cam said, enthusiastically pinching and twisting the skin on Walters's flaccid cheeks. Walters never flinched.

"You cold-cocked him, all right." Hawkins glanced up. A grin lit his face as he pushed Walters onto his back and began unfastening the man's gunbelt. "Damn, Cameron, I thought I was going to get to be a hero for once. Looks like you're one step ahead of me."

"Sorry about that. I wasn't sure when you'd be back."

"Let's strip him down. You'll be wanting some different clothes." Hawkins dragged a boot off Walters and went to work on the other one.

"I've got to get Abby."

"There's plenty of folks here to take care of that."

"Rico's here?"

"Ain't seen him, but most everyone else is at the party, leastwise the ones folks don't generally know ride with you. I'd guess Rico and the others are close by. At any rate, there's plenty of 'em to get Miss Morgan out okay. They coulda got you out, too, but I thought I'd have some fun."

"You're not supposed to be in on this." Cam ripped off his bloodstained shirt. "Do you want me to knock you out, too, make it look like I got the drop on you? If this all blows up, you can at least still stay in town."

"Nah. I'm tired of Callie Jones lookin' at me like I crawled out of the same stink hole as Frank Tanner. At least this way she'll know where I stand."

"It's going to be dangerous out there for you if any shooting starts. None of my men know you're on our side."

Hawkins shrugged. "At least I'll be shooting at the bad guys this time. We got about five minutes to get you out of here."

"I'm getting Abby first," Cam repeated.

Hawkins gave him a hard look. "Guess I can understand

that. You'll be wanting my clothes, then. Miss Morgan and Ellie Nagle headed for the necessary as I was coming in here. I'm supposed to be watching 'em, but I got the idea she and Maria cooked up something a little bit ago. Thought I'd give the ladies some room and see if I could help you out."

"Maria's here?"

"All the women are." Hawkins handed Cam his shirt and bent over Walters.

"What's Rico think he's doing?"

"All those men showin' up without their ladies wouldn't look natural-like. Besides, after this, they all got to hightail it anyway 'cause Tanner's going to know who's who."

Cam sighed as he stuffed the long shirttail into his borrowed pants and buttoned up the fly. "It wasn't supposed to get to this, Hawk. All the years of work were to keep this kind of thing from happening, to get Tanner without any killing."

"I doubt anybody's going to shoot unless they have to. Nobody wants a hangman's noose waitin' for them."

"Tanner's men may not give them a choice."

"Maybe I can help out on that."

Hawkins was a little smaller through the shoulders, but the fit of his clothes satisfied Cam. From a distance he'd pass for the wrangler, and Hawk was right: The clothes would let him move around easier.

Hawk looked fine in Walters's clothes, too, provided nobody looked too close.

Cam buckled Walters's gunbelt around his waist and slipped the S&W into its worn black holster.

Together, he and Hawkins tied the unconscious Walters to the same post where Cam had been. For good measure, Cam slashed every remaining article of clothing and stuffed the pieces into the smoke vent. That would keep Walters out of action in case he managed to wriggle free. He saved one strip of his own shirt for a gag and tightened it between Walters's teeth.

"Hope you're using a sweaty part," Hawkins said with a grin. "Now, if you got to be in the middle of this shebang, we'd best try to put you as close to the lady as we can. Let me see what's up."

Hawkins reached for the door, but it was jerked out of his hand. The long barrel of a rifle poked through the door, aimed right at Hawk's forehead.

Still partially hidden behind Walters and the post, Cam drew his pistol and crouched low. He recognized the stubby brown fingers gripping the gun just before he heard the familiar voice.

"Back inside, señor, before I remove the top of your skull."

"Hawk's one of us, Rico." Slipping his gun back into its holster, Cam stepped out from behind Walters. "Nice to see you. Now get inside here before someone spots you and tell me what the devil's going on."

"I can't get the ties," Abby whispered as she fumbled beneath her layers of skirts.

"Here." Maria hoisted the yards of fabric out of the way and pulled a knife out of a sheath on her calf. A couple of slices and the awkward bustle dropped away, steel springs jangling softly in Maria's hand as she caught the contraption and lowered it to the floor.

Before Abby dropped her skirts, Maria also yanked away three of Abby's four petticoats. They fell in a pile around Abby's ankles, and she kicked them away.

"Can you ride so?" Maria asked.

Abby lifted one foot onto the board seat of the privy and spread her knees to stretch the skirt. Unladylike as the maneuver looked, it told her she could straddle a horse. She nodded her head. "Fine, but you'd better trim the back."

From her awkward seat wedged in the corner of the privy, Ellie Nagle squawked against the gag in her mouth.

"Eleanor, for once in your life, be quiet," Abby suggested. Ellie shrunk into the corner.

Ellie had been even easier to overpower than Abby predicted. As soon as Maria flashed her small blade, Ellie collapsed in a sobbing heap. Abby's only concern had been to push her inside the odorous shack and stuff a hankie in her mouth before someone saw them. That accomplished, she'd helped Maria tie the woman's scrawny wrists and ankles with wide strips from Ellie's own petticoat.

Abby twisted her head to see over her shoulder as Maria gathered the dragging hem in her hand. The excess two feet of silk had allowed for a graceful drape over the oversize bustle; now it presented a hindrance.

"Such a beautiful gown," Maria mourned as she hacked at the fabric.

A brisk knock on the door made them all jump.

Abby looked quickly to Maria, but the woman shook her head. "Not yet," she mouthed, crossing herself. The knife gripped firmly in her fist, she motioned for Abby to speak.

Abby cleared her throat. "I'll be out in just a moment."

"We don't have that long," came the low response.

"*Cam.*" Abby flipped the hook latch out of the way and pushed the door open. "Oh, dear lord, your poor face."

Fortunately, no one else was near, for only Maria's warning hand on her shoulder kept Abby from throwing her arms around Cam's neck.

"It looks worse than it feels," Cam said. "Come on, let's go."

"How did you get away? Why are you wearing those clothes?"

"Later. Start walking toward the house, but when I say so, head between the barn and the tack shed, and run. Someone will be there with a couple of horses."

"What about you?"

"I'll be right behind you," Cam promised.

"Good. She is worth your trouble, this one." Maria slipped past Abby. "Now, my place is with my husband. *Vaya con Dios*. I will see you soon."

"Ready?" Cam pulled Hawkins's dark brown Stetson low over his eyes, so its shadows hid the bruises around his temple, but the dry blood streaking his cheek still showed.

"For days," Abby said fervently. "Good-bye, Mrs. Nagle."

The ranch yard seemed twice as big and three times as open as it had a few moments before. Abby spotted Franklin at the corner of the veranda, once again engaged in conversation with Evans and Beebe. His eyes lifted, searching. When he saw her in what appeared to be his wrangler's company, he visibly relaxed.

Just as Abby thought he'd surely notice the state of her gown, or of Cam's face, a man in the crowd shoved one of the fiddlers to the ground and started yelling about his playing. Friends on both sides quickly jumped in.

The music screeched to a stop. Franklin leapt off the porch and into the middle of the knot of men, calling for his hands to stop the brawl. She could see his hat among the swarm of people.

"Now," said Cam.

After four days of wanting to run and not being able to, Abby sprouted wings. Wedding dress hiked to her knees, she dodged between the buggies and wagons and pelted down the wide aisle between the buildings. She ran past the corner of the barn, straight into a man who stepped out of the building's lee.

Cam caught Abby as she bounced off, then stood there, dazed. One of the horses the man was leading whinnied and danced away.

Abby gaped. "Hawkins."

"Yes'm." He handed the reins of the second animal to Cam and went after the horse that had broken free. Abby looked from him to Cam in confusion.

"That's the man who's been watching me."

"He doesn't think much of his job," Cam said briefly as firecrackers exploded in the ranch yard.

Not firecrackers, Abby's mind registered. "That's gunfire. Something's wrong."

"Just warning shots," Cam said. "Rico's letting everyone know they'd better listen up. Hawkins here is going to take you to a friend in Del Norte. Noreen."

"Hannah's Noreen?" Abby asked.

Cam nodded. "I'll be along later."

"I've been thinking about this." Hawk walked up and held out the other set of reins. "You better go with the lady. She needs you more than Rico does."

"Those are my men. I have a responsibility to them."

Gunfire rattled the barn siding, and women began to scream. Cam and Hawkins went for their guns. In the strip of yard visible between the barn and tack shed, Abby saw people hunched over and running for cover.

"Go on. Get out of here." Hawkins shoved the reins of the extra horse into Cam's hands and darted around the back of the barn.

"Mount up," Cam said to Abby. He laced his fingers together, ready to boost her up.

Instead, Abby reached over past him and grabbed the rifle perched in the saddle scabbard.

"What do you think you're doing?" Cam demanded, straightening.

"I'm going back to help. Just like you intend to do."

The look on Cam's face told her she'd guessed correctly, but he still argued with her. "What makes you think you can kill a man?"

Ignoring both him and her own doubts, Abby levered the trigger guard down halfway. A cartridge glinted in the chamber, and she popped the lever home. "I can do at least as much as Maria and those other women."

"You stubborn . . . I won't—" Another burst of gunfire interrupted Cam's objections. A small group of Tanner's guests dashed into sight and started toward them.

Abby swung the rifle around, but Cam pushed the barrel down with one finger.

"Hold off," he warned, turning his head a shade so his bruises weren't so obvious.

"It's okay, it's one of Tanner's men," the man in the lead said to his friends as they reached Cam and Abby. He glanced back nervously. "Band of outlaws took our guns. They were about to rob us, but the cook came out of the kitchen shooting, and a couple of your men got away. Glad to see you're all right, Mrs. Tanner."

"I'm fine, thanks to this gentleman."

"Where are Domingo and the others?" Cam continued to let him think they'd found help as he looped the two sets of reins around the branches of a sturdy bush.

"They headed back that away." The man waved his hand. "We were running too fast to take much notice."

"And the robbers?"

"All over," a rotund man huffed, wiping his face with his sleeve. "Even the women are armed to the teeth. They're holding everybody corralled in that tent. Let me have that other rifle." He started for the second horse and caught a glimpse of Cam's face. "What happened to you?"

"Ran into Tanner's gun." Cam showed his pistol, and the man stopped in his tracks. Abby followed his lead, backing away slightly to have a broader field of fire. "On the ground, all of you. Facedown and arms spread."

"I'll be goddamned." The man backed away, fingers splayed.

"You, too, Harvey. Nice to see you again."

Squinting into the afternoon light, the heavy gent took a good look at Cam, but he still seemed confused.

"My men wouldn't have robbed you, by the way, any more than we ever have," Cam said. "Now get on down before I have to shoot you. I'd hate to do it, but I will to keep Abby here safe."

Mr. Harvey snorted, but he dropped to the ground, the bulk of his round belly arching his back like a turtle's shell. "You can't expect the ladies to wallow in the dirt."

"I do. They'll be safer that way."

The rest of the group followed, the men sheltering their wives as best they could. Abby split her attention between their captives and the ranch yard, where shots still rang. Cam quickly searched the men for weapons and tossed the women's handbags aside. A little derringer spilled out of one purse.

Cam picked it up and handed it to Abby, who tucked it into a convenient pouch in the remains of her polonaise.

"I don't suppose there's a chance you'd get on one of these horses now?" Cam asked her as he jammed his revolver in its holster and reached for the other rifle.

Abby shook her head. "No more than you will."

"Then you can watch this group."

"But I—"

"Someone has to keep them out of the way. If anybody you don't know comes around, shoot first and ask questions later."

Swallowing hard, Abby nodded. "What are you going to do?"

Cam quickly checked the rifle over and pumped a round into the chamber. "Whatever I have to."

"Cam . . ." Too many words crowded Abby's heart—be careful, I'm scared, I love you, come back to me. . . . None of them said enough. As Cam looked at her expectantly, she blurted, "I'll buy twenty yards of red flannel when this is over."

Eyes sparkling, Cam gave her a quick nod and a grin. He grabbed a handful of shells from the bandolier on the saddle and stuffed them into his vest pocket. "If I'm not back in ten minutes, get on one of those horses and ride out of here as fast as it will take you. Meet me at that place I mentioned a few minutes ago. Promise?"

"Promise."

Cam disappeared around the rear of the tack shed, taking the opposite direction from Hawkins.

With an inward sigh, Abby stepped around so that the oxide-red wall of the barn protected her back. She kept the rifle trained on the nearest of her band of captives, but her heart followed Cam down the row of outbuildings. Her ears strained to hear the next round of gunfire, hoping none of it flew in his direction.

"You called him Cam," the fat man said. "By golly, that was Cam Garrett. I'll be. I haven't seen him since we were kids."

"I don't understand you, Mrs. Tanner." One of the women lifted her head a few inches. Abby recognized the woman who'd been so taken with the waltz she'd danced with Franklin. "How can you go against your new husband like this, and with criminals like Cam Garrett and his men?"

Abby glanced down. "Do you live around here?"

"Of course."

"Then you are remarkably ill-informed. My so-called husband is the only real criminal in this affair, and the only thing Cam's guilty of is trying to stop him." Abby suddenly felt charged with some of the recklessness that usually possessed her only when Cam touched her. A smile crossed her lips. "Please put your head down, madam, before someone decides to use your bonnet for target practice."

The woman shrieked in dismay, but flattened out. The long pheasant feathers traced tiny figure eights in the dust above her head.

"I thought you were leaving with the señorita," Rico said as Cam ducked around the corner of the cookshed.

"Couldn't leave you in trouble. What's going on?"

"They're in the bunkhouse. Three of them, including the snake himself," Rico finished with a grimace.

"Tanner? How did he get away? He was in the middle of everybody else."

"While we were trying to get the cook, Domingo cut Pete. Not bad, but enough for him and Tanner to get away. The cook, also. They did not get far. We have the building surrounded."

Cam scrambled around the boxes Rico had upended to

provide cover and took a look at the lay of things. The bunkhouse stood about fifty yards away, its plain, white-washed clapboard stark in the late afternoon sun. Glass lay in sparkling shards on the ground where the two front windows had been punched out from the inside. Movement drew Cam's eye to the farthest window. He had an instant to register a flash of silver on black before a pistol barrel appeared and he had to retreat back behind the crates.

"He's in there, all right. I saw that hammered silver band he wears on his dress hat." Cam squeezed off a round toward the window, but Tanner withdrew unharmed into the inky interior shadows. "Who do you have around in back?"

"Antonio and Ephram. Your friend Hawkins is over there." Rico pointed toward the back of the main house. "I hope he is truly one of us. Jesús has the near end. The others watch over Tanner's men and the guests."

"A few of them almost got away. Abby's keeping an eye on them."

Another shot from inside the bunkhouse pinged off the cookshed wall, and Cam hunkered lower with his friend. Rico raised one eyebrow in question, then swung his Winchester around the boxes and fired.

"She said she had to do as much as the other women," Cam said, trying to ignore the sick worry in his belly. He took another long survey of the ranch yard. "Let's get this over with. I'll work my way across to Hawk's position. There's another window down at that end of the bunkhouse. We'll come up from behind those bushes and see if we can't get the drop on them."

"*Sí*," Rico agreed. "Except I will go with Hawkins."

Cam started to protest, but Rico cut him off with a frown. "I have waited as many years as you to get Tanner. Now I am an old man, and there is little chance we will get the rancho back, but at least I can have the pleasure of forcing Tanner to lie in the dirt with the others before we ride for Mexico. Do not rob me of this."

Reluctantly Cam agreed. "But you be careful, old friend."

"Do not worry. I wish to dance at your wedding." Rico gathered his feet under him and disappeared back the way Cam had come.

Cam gave him a few seconds to get clear, then signalled Jesús to start firing. Between the two of them, they put up enough distraction to keep the gunmen inside too busy to notice Rico weaving through the crowd of buggies and wagons. He soon reached Hawkins, and the two of them dropped out of sight behind the house.

Cam quickly reloaded and settled back to wait, periodically firing a shot to keep the men inside focused on this end of the building.

It didn't take long.

Someone shouted surrender, then a shotgun clattered into the broken glass on the ground, followed by two handguns and a knife.

Hawk poked his head around the end of the bunkhouse. "Seems the fight's gone out of 'em, boys. They don't like that old Winchester of Rico's."

His rifle held high and ready, Cam rose and stepped out from behind the crates. Jesús quickly joined him.

The door creaked open, and Domingo sauntered out looking as deadly with his hands up as most men did armed with a gun.

Jesús ran his hands over the man's body. "He is unarmed."

"Where's Tanner?" Cam demanded.

Domingo smiled but kept silent. A bulky figure stepped into the rectangle of doorway, a black Stetson with a silver band perched on stringy red hair. A grease-stained apron covered his clothes. He, too, smiled.

"Damn," Hawkins said. "That ain't him at all."

Blood thundered in Cam's head. He pushed past the cook, taking in the cluttered bunkhouse in one sweeping glance. Not a man in sight, and no place big enough for Tanner to hide. At the far end Rico broke glass out of the frame with the butt of his rifle. He pointed at the back wall. The window there stood wide open, the cheap print curtains blowing on the breeze. Cam dashed to it, and saw the tracks of heavy boots in the dust beneath.

"Tony!" Cam bellowed. "Tanner came out this way."

Ephram poked his head out of a clump of brush. "Not while we were here, boss."

"I will go around the back," Antonio said.

Maybe Tanner had never been there, but the hat on the cook's head said he had. He'd head for the barn, Cam thought. And for Abby.

"Cameron, I—" Rico began.

"Check to see if they caught him with the others. I've got to get Abby out of here."

Pulse pounding, Cam ran for the barn.

Chapter 19

The shots stopped.

Abby waited one minute, then two, and still there was silence.

Not sure whether to be relieved or more frightened, she shifted away from the shelter of the barn to peer toward the ranch yard. Voices carried through the thin haze of gun smoke and dust, the sounds too muffled to make out any words.

After an eternity she recognized Pete's voice. He sounded calm, even pleased, as he called to someone across the way. Several familiar forms passed by. Abby chewed her lip, anxious to see one in particular.

A deep premonition of danger grated through her senses an instant before she heard the muffled exclamation of one of her captives.

Abby whirled, lifting the rifle, but it was too late. A fist the size of a small ham clamped down on the barrel, wrenching it away from her before she got halfway around. Abby stumbled backward, hands stinging.

"My darling wife." Franklin bit the words off as he leaned the rifle against the barn and brought his pistol to bear on Abby.

"Who's winning this fight?" one of the men asked, raising his head.

"As of now, me," Franklin said. "You all stay here while I put a stop to this little fracas. Go on, Abigail. Let's go find your lover."

"No."

"I'm your husband now, and you will obey me. Move."

"So you can kill Cam and the others?" Watching Franklin out of the corner of her eye, Abby spoke to the group on the ground. "I didn't want to marry this man. He forced me into it."

The portly man, Mr. Harvey, looked up harshly. "How?"

"Shut up," Franklin said.

"You saw Cam's face. Franklin pistol-whipped him in front of me to make me agree to marry him."

"Is that true, Tanner?" Harvey demanded.

"He's an outlaw. He's stolen me blind, and now he's seduced my fiancée. Ruined her. I had a right to shoot him." A couple of the men nodded at Franklin's words. "I didn't, though, out of regard for Abigail. I see now I should have blown him to Hades."

"The only reason he didn't is because—"

"That's enough." Franklin stepped toward Abby, letting the pistol touch her ribs.

A leaden coldness weighted her limbs. Abby forged on before it could reach her throat. "Someone is going to know the truth. This isn't about jealousy, it's about money. He kept Cam alive to use him to force me to sign over a large trust fund, so he can finish taking over the town and everything around it. He wants this whole corner of the valley to belong to the Fidelity, and he'll hire more gunmen to drive you off if you don't go easily. Cam's on your side, he has been all along. He took me to stop Franklin."

"*Shut up*!" Franklin roared. He threw one arm around Abby's throat, dragging her back against his chest. "Must you preen over your adultery? I swear I could break your neck with my own hands, if—"

"If you didn't need my money to ruin these people," Abby croaked against the choking pressure of his arm.

"Sweet Jesus," moaned the woman with the pheasant plumes, burying her face in the dirt.

"By god, it's going to be sheer pleasure breaking you, you traitorous little bitch," Franklin said. "You and your lover."

"Then start with me."

Cam stepped around the corner of the tack shed, the large caliber Spencer aimed squarely at Tanner's head. He longed to pull the trigger, but Tanner clutched Abby so close that strands of her hair waved across his face in the breeze. Without a chance to properly sight-in the unfamiliar gun, the risk of hitting her was simply too great.

Tanner's welcoming smile chilled Cam. "I thought you'd show up sooner or later."

As Cam held his sights trained evenly on Tanner, he read everything he could of the man: how Tanner balanced back on one foot; the way his fingers toyed with the puffed shoulder of Abby's dress; the sour smell of fear that drifted off him. He could see Tanner's finger trembling within the trigger guard, and Cam's mouth went dry as sand. He blocked Abby's wide, frightened stare out of his brain before it made him do something dangerous to them both.

Tanner, only Tanner matters, Cam told himself. Get Tanner, and Abby will be fine.

"It seems we're back to the same place we were last night," Tanner said, his calm voice at odds with the beads of sweat that rolled down his forehead to collect on his eyebrows. "Let's see if you are as willing to sacrifice yourself for our darling Abigail as she was for you."

Holding his position, Cam coaxed his breathing into a slow, even rhythm, one which would let him squeeze off a shot with precision as soon as an opening was presented.

"Harvey, get these folks out of here," Cam said.

"Don't move," Tanner barked.

"Go on, Quent. He can't shoot you right now."

Quentin Harvey scrambled to his feet, then pulled his wife up, dragging her in the direction Cam indicated, toward the brush. The others hustled after him.

Tanner called after them, "The first man that comes back with help gets five hundred dollars." His attention quickly returned to Cam. "Your next suggestion, I suppose, will be to let Abigail go."

Cam nodded. "That would be a start."

"A foolish one, on my part. It's only a matter of time before one of those men comes back with help."

"Ah, but *I* am here already, señor."

Tanner's gaze flicked past Cam, and he smiled grimly.

"Padilla. I should have shot you when I had a chance."

"Your error. There are others here, as well, señor." Rico stepped forward, stopping about ten feet out to Cam's side, and tipped his head toward the far end of the barn.

"I think I'll just believe you." Tanner refused to be drawn off, and Cam didn't dare check to see who was there. He just prayed nobody took a shot until Abby was in the clear.

Tanner blew a strand of Abby's hair out of his face. "As I said, help will be coming, and I can stay here a long, long time, waiting for it. You can't shoot me. I can't shoot you."

Tanner was right, Cam thought. If he could hold on to Abby long enough, something would crack. The question was, in whose favor?

Abby's voice, quiet and contained, cut through the tense silence. "Rico, I want you to leave. Right away."

"Very wise, Abigail," Franklin said.

"Señorita?"

"Wire my father. Say, 'Tanner thief. Wants trusts.' " Tanner pulled his arm back tighter. Abby's voice faded, but she forced the last words past lips tinged with blue. " 'May murder me and others.' "

Rico looked from Abby to Cam. Cam nodded a fraction.

"As you wish." Rico backed away quickly.

Face contorted by rage, Tanner swung his pistol toward Rico. Abby slumped against his choking arm at the same instant Tanner fired. His aim was off wildly from Abby's weight dragging against him. The shot splattered into the ground to Rico's right with a spray of yellow dust. Rico dived for cover. Cam held his position, waiting.

Tanner dragged Abby toward the rear of the barn, firing off two more shots as he went. One peeled a piece of shingle off the tack shed a few inches over Cam's head. Cam dropped and rolled, and came up searching for a clear target. Tanner heaved Abigail at him, then dodged for the corner, twisting to fire at Rico once more. Rico cursed as his gun misfired.

Abigail came to her knees in a flash, the little derringer in her hand pointed straight at Tanner's heart.

A single shot echoed between the barn and tack shed. Tanner twisted and arched from the impact, then turned back to Abby and began to crumple. The pistol dangled from his nerveless fingers, waving aimlessly at the dust, then dropped away.

Three guns followed Tanner down as he crumpled.

Tanner caught himself on hands and knees. Blood-tinged spittle drooled from his mouth.

"I would have cherished you," he groaned, reaching for Abby.

"You would have owned me," she answered bitterly.

Hand balled into a fist by pain and fury, Tanner swung at Abby. She ducked the weak blow easily and scrambled away.

The effort finished Tanner. He pitched forward onto his face. His lungs collapsed with a liquid, bubbling sound, and his last breath moaned out into the dust.

Suddenly Abby was in Cam's arms, holding him with a strength that eased his mind.

"I thought he'd killed you," Cam whispered against the warmth of her temple. He tangled his fingers in her hair. The scent of lavender soap wafted up, and his chest tightened with emotion.

"I'm fine," she claimed, but she trembled like the leaves of the aspen in the grove.

"You shouldn't have had to do that, Abby. I should have been the one to shoot him."

"I didn't do it."

"But I thought—"

A slight motion drew Cam's glance past Tanner's still form, to where Antonio stood just beyond the open rear door of the barn. Holding Cam's gaze, Antonio very deliberately pumped the action of his rifle. A spent cartridge popped out, and he drove a fresh shell home.

"Now we are even, my friend," Antonio said, his face rigid and emotionless. He turned and walked away.

Rico stooped to close Tanner's eyes. "I will get something to cover him."

"No time," Cam said. "Get everyone together and finish this up the way it was supposed to go. Nobody else is to be hurt. We'll get out of here."

"Why?" Abby asked. "He's dead. It's all right now. We don't have anything to worry about."

"There's still a reward on my head, and Antonio just had to shoot your new husband in the back. It's not all right."

"But the ranch. Your ranch." Tears welled in her eyes, and she blinked them back. "All this has to have been for something."

"We'll straighten it out later." All Cam wanted was to get Abby away from here, to find some safe place before anything else could go wrong, but she pulled away. Her gaze flickered over Tanner's body. Blood soaked the back of his wedding suit, turning the black to dusky crimson. Already blue flies swarmed around his nose. She wobbled a little, and Cam gripped her arm firmly.

"Get on the horse before Harvey and the others get any ideas."

"Too late for that." Harvey stepped out from behind a bush where he'd been squatting. Rico and Pete swung around, their weapons ready, and Harvey flung his hands out from his sides. "Don't shoot, boys. No gun."

Cam waved his men off, but he held his own rifle at the ready. "What do you want, Harvey?"

"I got kind of embarrassed, hunkering down in the gully back there like some rabbit when the lady here had the guts to face Tanner down. I've been doing that too long. We all have, and that's why things got to this point. Some of the others feel the same way. They're sitting on the ones that don't agree, so you won't have to worry about the law coming in, for the time being."

Cam nodded. "Thanks. It doesn't change much, though."

"Well, now, maybe it does. Something struck me when she asked about the ranch. That's why I stood up. Before my brother died, I read a couple of years in the law trying to be a lawyer instead of a rancher. The way I see it, the lady's Tanner's widow. He didn't have any children with his first wife, so . . ."

"It may all be Abby's," Cam finished the sentence, the wheel's beginning to turn in his mind as Harvey's direction grew clear. For the first time in two days, a glimmer of hope coursed through him. Cam weighed the risks, then motioned for Pete. "Get that weasel Lucius Beebe and put him in the sitting room. Evans, too."

"Surely Franklin had a will," Abby said, but a glimmer of anticipation lit her eyes behind the shock.

"Maybe. Maybe not." Cam gave her a squeeze, reassuring himself as much as her. If Harvey was wrong, this gamble would only delay their escape, but he had to try. For his men and for himself, he had to try. "Harvey, I hope you don't mind sitting in on this. We're going to need a witness both sides can trust."

"Just let me round up my wife. Oh, and I'll need a man or two along, to bring back the dissenters."

"Then it's mine." Abby sagged a little as the full weight of the Fidelity's ownership crashed onto her shoulders.

"So it appears, Mrs. Tanner, despite the, er, unusual circumstances." Lucius Beebe rubbed his thumb across his palm as though it itched. His color, at least, had come back. The first few minutes he'd looked as though he actually expected Cam to kill him. He scooted forward onto the edge of his chair and lifted his chin higher. "To the best of my knowledge, your husband died intestate and without other heirs. There are some financial concerns, however."

As he elaborated—on problems she was certain Cam had created to begin with—Abby stared at the papers and records strewn across the leather-topped desk, the contents of Franklin's safe. Cam had taken a cold chisel and hammer to it. Between him and Hawkins, they'd been able to crack the lock and force the bolt back, though it had taken better than an hour. While they'd worked, she and Mr. Harvey had gone through Franklin's desk and found nothing.

When he'd realized the course of things, Beebe had grown obsequious. "Willem here—that is, Mr. Garrett—can advise you further," the lawyer continued, "and we at Beebe, Craig, and Beebe will, of course, do anything in our power—"

"Stop fawning, Lucius," said Cam. The lawyer's jaw snapped shut, and Abby could have sworn he shrunk three inches. "Tomorrow morning you'll wire Denver and make absolutely certain your father has no record of a will."

"If Franklin had a will, I'd know about it," Beebe asserted.

"Nonetheless, you'll send the wire. One of my men will be with you, to see that you stay sober and out of trouble until you get a reply. Meantime, we've got some explanations to make to the folks outside."

Rico headed out, and the room cleared behind him, leaving Cam and Abby alone among the remains of Franklin's records.

She rose and moved around the end of the desk and into Cam's arms with a great sense of relief. The steady rhythm of his heart melded with her own. She closed her eyes and surrendered to the peace, just for a moment.

"I want to spend the night like this," she said. "Instead I'm going to have to go out there and be the Widow Tanner."

"I'm sorry, Abby. I never asked you if you wanted this. It's not too late for you to say no."

"It was too late the minute you asked for the key to my trunk. Let's go send those people home."

With Cam close behind, Abby marched outside to the corner of the porch and stared down into the group of townspeople clustered in the yard.

She made her explanation of Franklin's death brief, then continued through the shocked silence of her audience. "So, it appears I own this ranch. I can see by your faces that some of you think I shouldn't. I don't much care what you think. The fact is, the Fidelity's mine.

"Over the next few weeks I'll be trying to set some of Franklin's *dealings* aright." A mutter of assent rolled through the group. Abby softened her tone. "I may know very little about ranching, but I do know how to be a decent neighbor, which is something my late husband disdained. I will do my best, my very best, to see that any of you he harmed receive compensation and the return of your lands. Under the circumstances, I believe it best if you all go home now. Lanterns will be supplied for those who need them. Please travel safely."

"Any of you with a ways to go are welcome to stay at my place," Quentin Harvey cut in. A few voices raised to accept his offer. He added under his voice, "This'll give me a chance to set folks straight about a few things."

"Thanks, Quentin." Cam thumped him on the back. "We'll need you in town tomorrow, to sort this mess out with the sheriff."

"I'll head in as soon as I get my stock fed. I doubt you'll have any trouble with Denham, though. He respects money too much to argue with Mrs. Tanner, here."

Abby added her thanks and watched the man lead his band out into the growing dark. When the last few buggies rolled out, she turned her attention to the Fidelity hands, who sat in a tight bunch in the dust, Cam's best men surrounding them.

"What am I supposed to do with them?" she asked.

An odd smile twisted up one corner of Cam's lips, and the gold and orange paper lanterns strung for the wedding dance reflected in his eyes. "It's your ranch. You decide."

Abby considered a moment. "Mr. Hawkins, you know these men. Are any of them worth keeping on?"

"Yes'm." Hawkins pointed at a couple of the men. "Ben, there, and J. D. That's it, ma'am."

"Thank you. Call them aside and ask if they're willing to continue on." Abby raised her voice. "The rest of you are fired. You have ten minutes to get off this property. Jesús, make certain they don't take anything that's not theirs."

"No guns, no cartridges," Cam added as his men herded the hands toward the bunkhouse. "They can come back one at a time tomorrow to get their own."

One of the men Hawkins singled out refused to work for a woman and rode off with his mates.

The other came up to Abby and offered his hand. "Name's Ben Freemont. Thanks for the job, Mrs. Tanner."

Abby gritted her teeth at the name. "Give me honest work and we'll do fine. Your first job is to see that a coffin is built for Mr. Tanner. Tonight. You can do it yourself, or find someone else, but I don't want to have to think about it."

"Yes, ma'am."

Cam waited until the man disappeared around the house, then called Maria over. He gently steered Abby toward the door and headed for the front steps. "Take her inside and get some hot tea into her."

"You're every bit in as bad a shape as I am." Abby lifted her hand toward the matted hair over his ear. "Worse. That needs to be cleaned and bandaged."

"I'll be back in a few minutes, and you can wrap me in as much linen as you like. I just want to make sure Antonio's okay."

"He is gone," Jesús said, coming up the steps.

"What?"

"I have not seen him since just after . . ." Jesús looked at Abby uncomfortably. "I thought only that he went to walk, to clear his head, but he has not returned. I just checked, and his horse is gone."

"He's not the type to run." Cam paced the length of the porch and back. "Rico!"

Rico popped around the corner. "*Sí?*"

"Where would Antonio go if he's upset?"

After a pause Rico answered. "To see his children, perhaps. At Lucia's."

"Get Hawk and have him saddle three good horses," Cam ordered. "Jesús, you and the others stay here. Keep Abby safe."

"You're not leaving me again, Cam Garrett." Abby had more to say on the subject, but the sound of galloping hooves interrupted her. A half dozen gunhands touched leather as Antonio's horse tore into the yard. A tiny, white-clad figure flung itself off and dashed toward the porch and Cam.

"Señor, señor," the boy began, and a torrent of Spanish followed.

"I want those horses. Now." Men scrambled, and Cam looked at Abby. "Don't argue, please, not now. This is Antonio's son. He says Tony started drinking, and the sheriff ran into him and arrested him on general principle.

If he hears about Tanner before we can rein him in, Tony's as good as dead."

"Nonsense. He won't just kill him."

"This is Tanner's man we're talking about, and he hates Mexicans. He'll arrange an accident or a lynching."

Pete and Hawkins lead three mounts into the yard. Cam headed for one and gave the cinch a quick check.

"You can't just break him out."

"Nope. I'm going the other way. I'll get myself thrown in along side him."

"No. No. You can't do that. If he'd kill Antonio—"

"With Rico and Pete sitting outside, nothing's too likely to happen." The horses whinnied nervously as the men mounted up. "If Denham tries anything, they'll put a stop to it."

"And just what am I supposed to do while you're busy saving Antonio?"

"Take care of his boy and get a good night's sleep, then show up first thing tomorrow with Lucius and Quent Harvey. I'm counting on you to get us both out."

"But they only did it to save me."

The sheriff laughed. "From your own husband? Come, Mrs. Tanner, you can't expect me to believe that. Unless of course you were consorting with these criminals to begin with. It was all a plot, wasn't it? You married Tanner to get his property and had these men kill him for you."

Abby sat cross-legged in the middle of Cam's bed, playing the scene over and over again in her mind. It always came out the same: Cam and Antonio behind bars while the sheriff laughed at her.

A good night's sleep—any sleep at all—eluded her, as she'd known it would from the minute Antonio's son rode in. In a show of womanly confidence neither of them felt, she and Maria had fed the boy a meal off the wedding leftovers and tucked him in bed. Abby had already been up to check him twice.

She checked a third time, then wandered downstairs. The clock in the study chimed twice as she struck a match to light the coal-oil lamp. Next to the clock hung a photograph of Franklin with his yellow dun stallion, the sun at a high angle, throwing his features into relief. He looked like a warrior, a hero.

That was the man I thought I came to marry, Abby reminded herself, lifting the photo down. *Confident, strong, bold, intelligent: all the qualities that actually belonged to the scruffy outlaw that took me hostage.*

Who now sat in the county jail.

Abby pushed back tears. Maybe if she got her mind off the problem, a better way to handle the sheriff would occur to her.

Laying the picture facedown on the nearest table, Abby turned to the mess on Franklin's desk to begin making some sense of it.

As she sorted through stacks of deeds and bills and contracts, the magnitude of what she'd taken on hit her. If she did own the Fidelity, she needed help, more help than even Cam could give her. On the back of an envelope she started her list: Wire Father and Mac. Hire a decent attorney. Sort out land titles. Find an accountant.

At least the ledgers looked to be in good order. Perfect order, in fact, like the rest of Franklin's possessions. Abby flipped the ledger shut and ran her thumbnail down the green cloth spine. The Fidelity's FT brand stood in the lower right-hand corner, burned in, just exactly the size of Hannah's scar.

Somewhere in this house she'd find a little branding iron.

Abby flung the ledger into the corner in disgust. "Damn you, Franklin. Even dead you're a bastard."

Green. She stared at the ledger she'd tossed aside, then at the stack. They were all green.

Where was the red ledger Franklin was always scribbling in?

A quick search of the desk drawers, the safe, and the bookshelves left Abby empty-handed, but with a vague sense of excitement. Convinced by its absence of the ledger's importance, she began a more careful search. An hour later she still had no red ledger.

"Where? Where did he hide it, and why?"

Abby started through the desk again, this time methodically dumping out each drawer and examining its underside. In the kneehole she thought she found a loose panel and went to work with her fingernails, but it wouldn't open.

The creak of a board in the hallway jerked her head up. Guilt rushed through her, like a child caught in her mother's face cream, before Abby remembered Franklin was dead.

"Are you all right, señora?" Maria poked her head through the crack in the door.

"I will be as soon as I find something. Help me with this. I want to check underneath."

Between the two of them they cleared the desk in a few minutes, then tilted the desk up. Abby gave it a shove and jumped back as it dumped over.

The crash echoed through the silent house, but it had the desired effect. The panel popped open, revealing a corner of brick red fabric. Abby yanked the book free. A second ledger tumbled out in back of the first.

"Maria? Señorita?" Jesús burst into the study, rifle in hand, his faded pink long johns sagging through the knees and seat. A half dozen others trotted in behind him.

They all stopped dead, staring at Abby where she sat in the middle of the wreckage, flipping through the ledger.

"I knew it," she mumbled. "I knew it."

"What has happened?" Jesús asked.

Maria whispered something and shook her head.

With a laugh Abby glanced up. "I know I look crazy, but I'm not. Look at this." She clambered up with Maria's help and pointed at a few lines. "It's Franklin's private journal. He was so precise, he kept records of everything: stolen cattle, poisoned wells, everything."

"That is wonderful, señorita! We can use it to prove what kind of man he was."

"We can use it for more than that." Abby flipped a few pages and chuckled again. "He even kept track of bribes and political graft."

A light came on in Maria's eyes. "Like what he paid to Sheriff Denham?"

"Exactly. Maria, somewhere in this mess I saw a fresh piece of paper. I'll copy what we need so we can keep this safe. Jesús, I'd like someone to hitch a buckboard and load the coffin in the back. Oh, and I'll need an escort into town. I want to be at the sheriff's office by sunrise."

The conversation with the sheriff went very much the way Abby had imagined it, until she mentioned Franklin's special ledger. At the sight of Abby's neatly detailed notes, the sheriff crumpled. Suddenly Mr. Harvey's word was good enough for him. "Yes, ma'am, Mrs. Tanner, you can drop those other charges if you want. After all, you're the Fidelity now."

Abby also made a statement about Stanton's death for the record, and after brief stops to arrange for telegrams and drop off Franklin's coffin at the church, they headed home. She expected jubilance, but the men were strangely quiet, watching her as if they expected her to break. Her excited explanation of how she found the ledger and what it contained eventually trailed off, and Jesus and Maria covered the stillness with gossip. When they got to the ranch, Abby led Cam upstairs and began cleaning his face.

"Ouch! Is this some kind of revenge?" Cam batted Abby's hand away. "That horse liniment is going to eat my hair off."

"Fine, if it grows back in blond. I don't like Willem nearly as much as Cam."

"That's a shame. He'll be here in a few days."

Abby dropped her cloth back into the porcelain washbasin and surveyed Cam's head. Thanks to hard work and plenty of hot water, the encrusted blood was nearly gone, leaving a web of half-sealed gashes across welts on his scalp. "You're lucky. It looks like you'll heal cleanly. Except for that ruffle across the top of your ear."

"What? Where?" Cam peered into the hand mirror.

"Right here." Abby touched her lips to the spot. "Actually, I'm partial to ruffles."

Cam's eyes glowed back at her in the mirror. "Show me again."

She leaned forward expectantly, and Cam shifted and met her lips with his own. She could feel his uneven breathing on her cheek as he coaxed her around the chair with tender hands and trapped her legs between his knees.

"We can't," Abby whispered, reluctantly pulling away when all she really wanted was the protective shelter of his arms.

Cam must have heard the ambivalence in her voice, for he ignored her and pulled her down on his lap. Sure fingers freed the three pearl buttons that held the high, lace-trimmed collar of her black mourning gown. "Do you realize this is the first time we've been alone since you got Antonio and me out of jail?"

"We're not alone now. This house is full of people."

"I don't hear anyone." The next few buttons gave, and Cam spread the gap and pressed a kiss to the curve of Abby's shoulder. "We nearly lost each other, several times over, and the only reason we didn't was your incredible courage and your faith in me. In us."

Abby shuddered as his lips touched her bare skin again, and then the shudder turned to a sob. She clung to Cam as tears streamed down her cheeks.

"There you go, love," he whispered, stroking her hair. "I knew they were in there. You've been holding them in too long."

"God, I hate him," she railed over the sobs. "I hate everything he did to me, to you, to everyone. I'm glad he's dead, and I hate that he could make me glad of anyone's death.

That's why I hauled his body into town, Cam, because I couldn't stand the thought of him in the ground of this ranch, fouling it forever. I hate that I have to wear his name, even for a day. I hate him. God, I hate him."

Days of terror and rage, swallowed back for survival, poured out. Abby sobbed until her eyes burned with the salt and her throat ached, until the image of Franklin Tanner drowned in a flood of bitter tears and she fell into a dreamless sleep.

Hours later, in the purple and gold light of dusk, she awoke in Cam's bed. She didn't remember him removing her dress, but it hung over the footboard, and he lay beside her, his arms a protective circle. She drifted back to sleep.

The next time Abby woke, it was full morning and she was alone. She sat up in a panic.

"Cam?"

"Right here." Cam stepped out from behind the closet door. A froth of shaving soap covered half his chin and he held a straight razor in his hand. "Maria will bring breakfast up in a little bit."

Abby groaned. Her head had that thick, cottony feeling that follows tears, but her heart, for the first time in days, felt at ease. "Does the whole ranch know I spent the night in your room?"

"Probably. Where does this sudden reluctance come from? My men have known about us for a long time."

"But their wives . . . And besides, things have changed. They're going to call me the merry widow."

"Not likely. I had Maria bring a change of clothes from your room. They're on the chair." Cam went back to his shaving. "Charlie and Digger rode in last night, just after supper."

"Oh, Cam. He's all right, then? I've been half afraid to ask. I don't think I could take anyone else being hurt."

"He's fine. The bullet missed the bone. The doctor told him to take it easy for another few days, but he heard about Tanner and convinced Digger to bring him on out here. Maria put him straight to bed. He's down the hall, when you're ready to see him." Cam reached for a sheaf of papers from the nightstand. "And then there are these. Answers to all your telegrams came in late yesterday. Beebe Senior says there's no will. Apparently Tanner thought he'd live forever. The Fidelity's yours."

The last of the cotton dissolved as Abby pored over the telegrams. "Father had our lawyers recommend a firm in Denver. He's already arranged for one of the senior partners to come. He should be here tomorrow, that is, today, if this is Monday. Mac's already left to come out, too. Papa had to arrange for his patients, but he's coming next week, and he says he'll bring a draft of my mother's trust. That will be enough to keep things running until the lawyers work things out. What's the matter?"

"Nothing." Cam swiped away the last traces of shaving cream with the towel and tossed it aside.

"I know that frown. What's wrong?"

"It's just not exactly how I had it imagined." A crooked grin gave his bruised face the look of a boy who'd been in a fistfight. "Lawyers, trust funds, accountants. Fathers and brothers, for heaven's sake. They're going to shoot me on sight."

"Papa will be too busy helping the attorneys sort out the estate to worry about you. He loves that sort of thing. He probably should have become a lawyer instead of a physician. It's definitely Mac you'll have to worry about. He's about three inches taller than you and has a good fifty pounds on you."

"Wonderful."

"He won't hurt you, however, once I explain everything. I can be very persuasive."

Cam laughed softly as he joined her on the bed and pulled her gently into his arms. "That, love, is an understatement. I saw the way you made that poor sheriff squirm. I thought he was going to wet himself. Between that ledger and your tongue, I don't think Denham will be quite the same again."

"That's the second time you've said that," Abby pointed out, smiling happily. "I thought last night I must have imagined it, but I didn't."

"What?"

"You called me 'love,' just like it was the most natural thing in the world."

"It shouldn't be. I don't have the right." A shadow of guilt passed over Cam's face, and he set Abby away a little. "What Tanner said was true. I didn't just kidnap you for the ransom. I'd planned to seduce his fiancée all along. When all this started, it didn't make any difference who she was."

"You wanted to use her—*me*—to hurt him, to give the knife an extra little twist," Abby said quietly.

Cam nodded and rose to walk to the window. He stood there staring out over the land. "I wouldn't blame you if you want me to leave. . . ."

"You won't be shed of me that easily." Abby slid out of bed and padded up behind Cam. She slipped her arms around his lean waist and pressed a gentle kiss to his spine. "I suspected you had other motives from the beginning, and I accepted that because I discovered I loved you anyway. But I'm warning you, if there's anything I find more despicable than setting out to seduce a woman for the wrong reasons, it's refusing to say aloud that you fell in love with her along the way."

"Then I'd best confess," he said softly. "I did fall in love with her, just about the time she threatened to feed me to the hogs."

"They wouldn't have had you," Abby whispered. "But I would."

Cam turned to her and wrapped his arms around her. His eyes glowed with happiness as he covered her mouth with a long, passionate kiss that sent a thrill of joy into Abby's being.

"I love you with all my heart, Abigail Macaulay Morgan Tanner, and if you'd be so kind as to tell me how I can make amends for being such a jackass, you'd have a most grateful, most humble man on your hands."

"Amends. Let me see." Abby pulled free and paced back and forth in front of Cam a few times, her finger to her lips in thought. "I know. I have this ranch. There's a lot of work to be done. I'm going to give most of it away."

"Most of it?"

"Well, there's one piece I thought I'd hang on to. You see, there's this outlaw who's been trying to get his hands on it, and I thought maybe he'd get back on the right side of the law if he had a partner. A lady partner."

"Only if she was the right sort," Cam said, grinning. "She'd have to be smart and tough, and it probably wouldn't hurt if she could ride and shoot. And play poker. She'd definitely need to play poker."

"Then I have a proposition for you."

Epilogue

November 1886

The door opened behind Abby, and a wave of light and sound washed over the veranda. She turned, and a smile lit her face as she caught the glint of neatly trimmed gold hair and recognized her new husband's lean shadow in the doorway.

"There you are," Cam said. "I wondered where you'd gone."

"It's too close in there. Too many people."

"Put this on before you catch a chill."

Abby accepted the crocheted shawl he offered and stared out at the distant peaks. "Those clouds look like more snow coming. Mac and Papa may be here a while longer."

"Delightful. I always wanted to spend my honeymoon with my wife's family in the house."

"Your family's here, too," Abby countered. "Actually, I kind of like your cousin Willem, now that I have the real Cam back."

"It's a good thing. I'd hate to have you get us mixed up, especially tonight."

"No chance of that. He uses too much macassar." Abby glanced up and caught the scampish twinkle in his eye. Her heart skipped a beat in response. "At least their rooms aren't too close to ours."

"But the lawyer's is. And the accountant's. Then there's Jesús and Maria. Ephram and Louise. Hannah and Digger. Those two are a pair, aren't they? She's even got him sleeping indoors." Cam continued ticking off their houseguests on his fingers. "And the rest of them are either downstairs on cots or out in the bunkhouse with Charlie and Hawk."

"They all had to be here so we could give them their deeds. You know that."

"The fact that they'd be staying the night escaped me when we were planning this."

The lowing of the few remaining cattle in the south pasture drifted up on the wind. Most of the stock had gone to the various people Franklin had damaged. She and Cam would buy more in the spring and start over honestly. Abby felt fiercely protective of the few that wore the new Rocking AC brand burned over Franklin's old mark. "We'd better bring them in."

"Hawk will take care of it. Stop worrying about cows. This is our wedding night." Cam brushed her hair to one side and kissed the back of her neck, then he slipped his hands under the shawl to massage her shoulders. "Are you aware, Mrs. Garrett, that between the lawyers and your family and taking Charlie to see his father, I have not had a chance to sleep next to you since the day you proposed to me?"

Abby shivered for the first time, but with anticipation, rather than cold. "I am. Hush before someone hears you."

Beneath the cover of dusk and the heavy shawl, Cam slowly slid his hands around Abby's rib cage and flicked his thumbs over nipples already erect. "Are you also aware just how much I want to rectify that situation?"

The restless heat that rushed to his touch curled around on itself and settled at the apex of her thighs. Abby sighed softly as he nipped at her shoulder.

"I suppose," she said, "that everyone will stay downstairs for a while to give us some privacy."

"Probably to give us a charivari later on."

"We don't do that in New York." They drifted toward the door, where Abby pulled away from Cam. "I'll need a few minutes."

"Don't undress, Abby. I want to do it."

"All right," she whispered.

The knowing smiles when she excused herself nearly made her head back outside, and she fled in an excited dither. Maria trailed her upstairs with a lighted lamp, to the room Cam and Abby had claimed for their own, well away from either Franklin's or the one where he had watched her sleep.

"I will help you, señora," Maria said.

"That's very kind," Abby muttered to the floor. "Have I thanked you for the dress?"

"Only as often as I have thanked you for giving our land back." Deftly Maria stripped open the tiny mother of pearl buttons and helped Abby out of the stiff powder blue satin. She then loosened Abby's corset. "Where is your night dress?"

Abby picked up her brush and pulled it through her hair. She'd left it loose for the wedding at Cam's request. "If you don't mind, I'd rather do that myself."

"As you wish." Maria hung the dress neatly in the massive cherry-wood wardrobe. "If you need anything . . ."

"No, thank you. I'm fine."

It only took Abby a moment to find what she wanted in the dresser. She quickly grabbed the garment and scooted behind the dressing screen to remove her underthings. By the time Cam's boots sounded in the room, she was ready.

"Are you coming out?" Cam asked.

"In a minute."

She stood behind the screen, listening to Cam move around the newly decorated room in the small rituals of undressing: the soft clink of his pocket watch on the marble dresser top, the squeak of his new boots as he kicked them off, and then the creak of the wardrobe door as he hung his coat.

"You were supposed to let me do your dress," he chided.

"I know. I just thought, well . . . since it's been so long, and since we've never actually . . . done something like this on a real bed before, I thought it would be nice to have at least one thing familiar."

Taking a deep breath, Abby stepped around the screen.

If she had the skill, she'd sketch him like that, she thought, his face frozen in amazement and wonder, the desire as warm in his eyes as the red flannel shirt was on her bare skin.

Cam stepped closer, so close the cloth of his trousers brushed her bare thighs. With infinite gentleness he cupped Abby's face in his hands, pressing his lips to hers in a lingering kiss.

"I love you, Mrs. Garrett," he whispered against her mouth. His gaze dropped lower, and he shifted his hands to the opening of the shirt.

"I love you, Mr. Garrett."

Cam gave a tug. White buttons flew around the room to the sound of laughter.

Author's Note

While the town of Saguache did exist in 1886—and still does—I created its residents out of the whole cloth of fiction. None of the people I knew from the San Luis Valley would have ever tolerated the likes of Franklin Tanner.

The town of Henry changed its name to Monte Vista in the spring of 1886, but railroad schedules still listed it as Henry as late as December of that year.

In the early sixties I had the good fortune to live in a pink stucco house right on the banks of the Rio Grande outside Del Norte, Colorado. The time I spent exploring the mountains with my parents and the riverbanks with my friend, Linda Smedley, created the foundations of *Hostage Heart*.

However, 1964 is not 1886, and childhood memories, while brilliant in color and rich in pattern, lack detail, so I found myself relying on those who know the area and its history to fill in the patchwork. My thanks to Suzanne Off, of the Rio Grande County Museum in Del Norte; Darryl Cox, from the Saguache District Office of the Rio Grande National Forest; Ron Jablonski and Jack Lewis, of the Regional Headquarters of the Rio Grande National Forest; and Jim Blouch, from Southern Pacific (formerly the Denver & Rio Grande Railroad).

My special appreciation to Sue Page, who helped light the forest fire, then fanned the flames with appropriate nagging.

Thanks also to Heather Jackson, my editor, for her help and patience.

Finally, I'll be forever grateful to Judith Stern, who saw the potential in a four-page rough outline and had the generosity of spirit to hold out the carrot of publication. Everyone should be so lucky.

* * *

I would welcome hearing from readers. Write to me in care of the Publicity Department, The Berkley Publishing Group, 200 Madison Avenue, New York, NY 10016.

FREE
Romance
(a $4.50 value)
Send in the Coupon Below
To get your FREE historical romance and start saving, fill out the coupon below and mail it today. As soon as we receive it we'll send you your FREE Book along with your first month's selections.